WICKED BURN

WICKED BURN

Beth Kery

BERKLEY SENSATION, NEW YORK

THE BERKLEY PUBLISHING GROUP
Published by the Penguin Group
Penguin Group (USA) Inc.
375 Hudson Street, New York, New York 10014, USA
Penguin Group (Canada), 90 Eglinton Avenue East, Suite 700, Toronto, Ontario M4P 2Y3, Canada
(a division of Pearson Penguin Canada Inc.)
Penguin Books Ltd., 80 Strand, London WC2R 0RL, England
Penguin Group Ireland, 25 St. Stephen's Green, Dublin 2, Ireland (a division of Penguin Books Ltd.)
Penguin Group (Australia), 250 Camberwell Road, Camberwell, Victoria 3124, Australia
(a division of Pearson Australia Group Pty. Ltd.)
Penguin Books India Pvt. Ltd., 11 Community Centre, Panchsheel Park, New Delhi—110 017, India
Penguin Group (NZ), 67 Apollo Drive, Rosedale, North Shore 0632, New Zealand
(a division of Pearson New Zealand Ltd.)
Penguin Books (South Africa) (Pty.) Ltd., 24 Sturdee Avenue, Rosebank, Johannesburg 2196,
South Africa

Penguin Books Ltd., Registered Offices: 80 Strand, London WC2R 0RL, England

This book is an original publication of The Berkley Publishing Group.

This is a work of fiction. Names, characters, places, and incidents either are the product of the author's imagination or are used fictitiously, and any resemblance to actual persons, living or dead, business establishments, events, or locales is entirely coincidental. The publisher does not have any control over and does not assume any responsibility for author or third-party websites or their content.

PRINTING HISTORY
Berkley Sensation trade paperback edition / December 2008

Library of Congress Cataloging-in-Publication Data

Kery, Beth.
    Wicked burn / Beth Kery.—Berkley Sensation trade pbk. ed.
        p. cm.
    ISBN 978-0-425-22437-3
    1. Apartment dwellers—Fiction.   2. Neighbors—Fiction.   I. Title.
    PS3611.E79W53   2008
813'.6—dc22
                                                            2008030846

PRINTED IN THE UNITED STATES OF AMERICA

10 9 8 7 6 5 4 3 2 1

Acknowledgments

I must thank my husband, for supporting me even during my annoying, angst-ridden moments. No one told me that taking up writing would make me occasionally act like an adolescent all over again. Thanks to Lacey and Mary W. for looking over the manuscript and giving me tips when I was banging my head against the wall. And of course I would like to express my appreciation to my agent, Laura, and editor, Leis, for their taking the chance on my writing.

ONE

The goddamned walls in his temporary apartment residence might as well be made of cardboard, Vic Savian thought as he came into full wakefulness at the low, mellow sound of a voice emanating from the hallway. He'd never actually heard the mystery woman who lived across the hall from him speak, but he recognized her immediately, nonetheless.

Weird. Just her voice made his cock stir and stiffen against the cool sheets.

He'd seen her twice now, once in Louie's—the steakhouse located in the lobby of Riverview Towers. The other time they'd been alone on the elevator together.

He'd have bet the finest stallion in his stable that she was as aware of him on that elevator ride as he was of her.

Sort of an understatement, actually, to say that Vic had been *aware* of her. He'd noticed everything about her . . . the light sprinkling of freckles on her nose, the movement of her lips when they closed and parted, the pulse at her elegant throat, the shape of her breasts beneath the conservative yet sensual silk blouse that she wore.

She was beautiful. Vic knew better than most how overused that word was when it came to women. But other descriptors— pretty, attractive, sexy—fell far short when it came to the woman across the hall.

She was luminous.

He liked women. He liked them smart, feisty, sexy, skilled, and hot. But this woman's beauty irked him. He steered clear of beautiful women. Ever since the debacle with Jenny.

His head came up off the pillow when he heard her speak again. Did her voice sound strained?

When he heard a man respond in an angry tone, he swung his legs over the side of the bed and reached for his jeans.

"Evan, I've made it very clear where I stand with you. I've never played coy. And no, I can't give you some kind of timeline as to when I might feel differently," she said before Evan had the chance to say the predictable.

What was it about getting dressed up for a black-tie affair that made a man think he was going to get laid? Niall Chandler wondered dispiritedly. God, she was an idiot. She should never have agreed to accompany him to the Chicago Metropolitan Museum of Fine Art fund-raiser tonight. As a member of the museum's board of trustees, Evan Forrester had the potential to make her job very difficult if he chose to play the part of a rejected lover.

"You're not even giving this a chance. Look, I don't have any of the details, but I'd have to be an idiot not to know that I'm supposed to treat you like fine china, given all the vague references and dirty looks your boss is always giving me, not to mention that secretary of yours. But sometimes the only way to get over something is to just take the plunge. Come on, Niall . . . jump off that pedestal of ice, sweetheart," he coaxed. "The weather down below is nice and hot."

Niall's eyes widened in disbelief not only at his knowing, almost sly tone but the fact that he put his hands on her shoulders and pushed her back, sandwiching her between the door and his body. She twisted her face away when he tried to kiss her, but he merely transferred his attentions to her neck.

"You were driving me crazy tonight in this dress," he muttered against her skin. His hands began to press and slide along her back and waist.

"Evan, stop it," Niall insisted. When he brushed aside her wrap and planted a kiss on the top of her right breast, her hand rose instinctively. He looked up when she gave him a hard, flat-palmed thump to the side of his head.

"Why . . . you little bitch, that hurt!"

Niall barely had time to register the tall shadow out of the corner of her eye before Evan cried out and winced in pain. He crashed loudly into the far wall of the hallway, then bounced forward, looking stunned and dazed. He grabbed frantically for his ear, as if to assure himself that it was still attached to his head. Niall realized that the man who stood with them in the hallway must have twisted it viciously before he threw Evan off of her.

"Get out of here," the stranger said tersely.

Niall stared up at the man in amazement. His tone had been one of annoyance and profound distaste, as if he'd just come out into the hallway and seen a dog humping her leg instead of a man pawing her body without her consent. It was especially striking, that tone, since Evan was the picture of urbane sophistication in his tuxedo and black cashmere overcoat.

Her savior, on the other hand, brought to mind comparisons to ruthless cowboy outlaws and primitive, raw sex.

Niall blinked in surprise at her turn of thought. Well, it wasn't the first time her mind had strayed that way against her will. It had done the same on the other two occasions she'd seen the man who lived across the hall from her, especially when she'd been forced to breathe his spicy male scent in the six-by-six-foot confines of an elevator.

He made her nervous, agitated . . . stirred up.

At least on the elevator he'd been wearing clothing, though. Tonight he wore nothing but a partially fastened pair of faded jeans that looked like they'd been washed and worn so many times that they'd shaped themselves perfectly to his lean hips, tight butt, and long, hard thighs.

Niall forced her eyes away from that compelling sight when she heard Evan speak.

"Who the hell are *you* to think you can tell me to leave like that?" Evan sputtered in furious disbelief. He took several rapid steps down the hallway, however, almost tripping on his own feet, when Niall's neighbor abruptly lunged toward him. The tall man never responded verbally, but Niall thought she saw Evan's answer in his rigid profile and steely gaze.

He's the guy who looks like he's ready to kick your ass from here to next week if you don't get a move on, Niall thought.

"You'd better just go, Evan," she managed shakily. "Please," she added when Evan opened his mouth like he was going to argue. He finally turned, keeping the grim, tall figure that menaced him in the corner of his eye until the last second before he headed down the hallway.

Niall exhaled unevenly when she heard the ding of the elevator door as it closed. She found it difficult to meet her neighbor's stare.

"Thank you," she said.

"You okay?"

His voice reminded her of a stark landscape of open plains domed with the vast mystery of a starlit sky.

"Sure." She laughed a little unevenly. "Feeling a bit dense, actually. I didn't see it coming."

"How about a drink?"

She shook her head. "No. I'm all right. He just caught me off guard, that's all."

"I wasn't asking if you wanted to have a drink with me in order to calm you down."

Her eyes snapped up to his. For the first time, she saw that they were a light gray, the outer rim edged by a defining black line.

A second passed . . . then several. A tiny smile pulled at his well-shaped lips, softening the hardness of his mouth infinitesimally.

Had he really just propositioned her so casually? Niall questioned herself. And was she really considering taking him up on the offer?

Something flamed to life inside of her as she met his steady stare . . . something Niall had assumed had been snuffed out of existence three years ago. His lips twitched slightly, and she realized she'd been wrong.

What she experienced at that moment wasn't anything she'd ever known in her thirty-three years of life on this planet.

"All right," she agreed softly.

He stepped back so that she could move past him toward the door of his apartment. Niall noticed that he didn't look smug at her acceptance.

Nor did he seem even vaguely surprised.

Niall smiled a moment later as she glanced around his living room while he moved about in the kitchen.

"I see we have the same decorator," she said through the little window over the counter that overlooked the kitchen. She heard the anxious tremor in her voice and admonished herself for it. Just because she had agreed to have a drink didn't mean that she was going to sleep with him—a complete stranger.

His dark brown hair fell over his brow as he bent to retrieve a bottle from a lower shelf. When he stood, her gaze brushed appreciatively across his ridged abdomen, the sweep of his wide shoulders, and the hard, defined muscles of his upper arm. Most of the men that she knew would have put on a shirt in this situation. But Niall was glad that he hadn't.

He was such a beautiful, sinuous male animal that it seemed a shame to cover his body.

He never responded to her attempt at small talk, but Niall found that his silence didn't make her feel awkward. When he handed her a glass through the window, she held it up in a brief salute and took a drink. Her sensual appreciation of the taste must have shown on her face, because he gave a small smile before he took a swallow of his own. Heat expanded in Niall's lower belly at the sight of the muscular movement of his throat.

"You approve," he stated rather than asked.

Niall blinked. Had he been reading her mind? A modicum of

common sense returned to her, however, and she realized that he'd been referring to the liquor, not his beautiful body.

"I don't drink much, but when I do, I'm a Scotch drinker. This happens to be my favorite brand," Niall said. She realized that her voice had become unintentionally husky as she stared at his mouth. His upper front tooth slightly overlapped the one next to it. She thought of what it would feel like to run her tongue over that sexy little imperfection, and then wondered how many women he encountered every day who had the exact same fantasy.

She forced her eyes away from him and transferred her gaze to the windows. It unnerved her, this strong, unprecedented physical reaction to him. She felt awkward and foolish, like a gangly teenage girl.

She took a deep, uneven breath and tried to focus on what she saw.

His apartment faced east, granting him a spectacular panoramic view of Chicago. The lights of the high-rises shimmered in the black, winding river. The Riverview Towers offered their residents every luxury and convenience: a concierge, a dry cleaner, grocery delivery, shopping, and a central location in downtown Chicago. Residents and the corporations for which they worked paid sky-high prices for the flexibility and conveniences of the apartments. But to Niall the temporary residences felt depressingly sterile. She longed for the stability of a home again.

"So what's your excuse for staying in this god-awful place?" she asked him when he came around the corner into the living room. She glanced up when he leaned his hip against the counter next to where she sat on a stool.

"I'm working in the city for a while. I sleep here Tuesday through Thursday nights and drive home on Friday."

"To the suburbs?" Niall asked as she took another sip of Scotch.

With him standing and her sitting, her eye level was at his chest. His nipples were dark brown and even more erect than she'd speculated when he was feet away from her instead of inches. She inhaled slowly, and the male scent that she recalled all too well from sharing the elevator with him filled her senses, more subtle, but nevertheless more potent, than the fumes of the Scotch.

The desire that he'd awakened in her reared its head, causing a shimmering sensation of heat to spread along her tailbone, only to surge and swell at her sex, liquefying her in a matter of seconds.

His singular gray eyes flickered down to her lap when she stirred restlessly on her stool.

"I have a farm downstate. You?"

She blinked. "Oh . . . I'm waiting for my condominium to be finished. Hopefully, I'll be out of here in a month or two, but they keep putting me off." She shrugged and gave a shaky laugh. "It could be worse. I work downtown at the Chicago Metropolitan Museum of Fine Art, so Riverview Towers are convenient. If it weren't for the fact that I feel like I live in a beige and white nightmare, things would be great," she added with a chuckle.

"What's your name?"

She paused in her mirth. "Oh, sorry. I'm Niall. Niall Chandler."

She started to put out her hand for a friendly handshake but paused in surprise when he began to laugh. "What's so funny?" she asked in amazement.

He set his drink on the counter as he stilled his mirth. "Your name. You're the most feminine thing I've ever seen in my life, and you've got a boy's name."

Niall inhaled sharply. He was usually so terse and impassive that it unsettled her to hear him compliment her—for that was undoubtedly what it had been, given the warm, husky tone of his deep voice.

Her anxiety mounted when he took her glass from her stiff hand and set it next to his on the counter.

"I'm Vic."

His hand rose to cradle her chin, lifting her face until she met his gaze. Niall's pulse throbbed madly at her throat when she saw the heat in his gray eyes as they fixed on her mouth.

"Now that we've got that out of the way . . ." His head dropped slowly. "Let's get down to the good stuff, Niall."

From the very first, Vic incinerated her. The thought of pushing him away never entered her mind, Niall realized the next day. It *should* have, logically. Not ten minutes before, she'd put a halt to Evan's attempts to get her into bed.

But this was different. Vic seduced her so effortlessly. The strength of her desire for him burned away the few remaining insubstantial shadows of rational thought.

The hand that wasn't already holding her chin came up to join its twin, holding her steady for the onslaught of his kiss. His tongue drove between her lips without preamble. He didn't seem particularly interested in mutuality at that moment. He probed deeply, sweeping his tongue everywhere, establishing dominance over her body with a stunning attack on her senses.

Niall moaned as his taste registered in her brain. Her hands clutched desperately at his back as he continued to fuck her mouth with his tongue. He tasted like premium Scotch with just a hint of mint. Her fingertips explored the sensation of smooth skin stretched tautly across dense muscle. Heat resonated off his body. Niall pressed closer, wanting to share that heat, *needing* to be thawed . . . desperate to be burned.

Her hands began to move over him greedily. He groaned, deep and savage, and tore his mouth from hers. For a tense moment, he just stared down at her. Then he lifted her in his arms. Niall held on tightly to his shoulders. A kaleidoscope of images from his apartment spun before her eyes as he quickly moved toward his bedroom, adding to her chaotic emotional state.

He tore off the wrap that she wore around her shoulders before he lowered her to his bed. The zipper of her sophisticated little black cocktail dress came down next.

"Arms up," he muttered.

She complied. He tossed aside her black dress a second later.

Niall's hips moved restlessly on the bed, instinctively trying to relieve the pressure growing at her sex when his gaze dropped over her. She wore a black bra and panty set and some thigh-high stockings. And her pearls. *As if that counted for anything,* she thought with a touch of hysteria.

Vic's expression didn't alter much, but his eyes blazed so hot as they toured her body that she felt sexually scorched.

"Take off your panties and move back on the bed."

She felt like she was in a dream as she did exactly what he'd demanded. But it was a very hot, exciting dream . . . and she hadn't the slightest desire to resist the carnal allure of it.

He covered her body with his own by the time her head hit the pillows. He palmed her thighs, spreading them to accommodate his body in the process. He immediately took possession of her mouth again. Their tongues tangled and mated wildly. His hands ran down her sides, one pausing at a small, silk-covered breast, the other sliding down her waist and cradling her hip.

He tilted her pelvis up and pressed himself to her, forcing her to feel the strength of his desire.

Niall moaned into his mouth. He felt so vibrant next to her, so alive. It was a dizzying sensation for someone who had been one of the walking dead for the past three years to suddenly awaken as if from a jolt of sexual electricity. He molded her breast in his palm gently, then roughly . . . always surely. Niall strained up, desperate for more of the sensation of him. Her hands ran over his back and shoulders, sliding and rubbing, consuming him with her touch.

Vic grunted at the feeling of her slender, curvy body pressing to him so tightly. Her skin felt like warm silk. Her nipple pressed into the center of his palm like a hard little dart, maddening him. The feeling of her hands moving anxiously over him blinded him with lust.

He rolled off her onto his left hip, ripping at the button fly of his jeans. He shoved them down his thighs with precise, rapid movements. His cock sprang free, stiff, tight, straining toward her. His eyes caressed her body. She was the color of pale honey, looking like she could tan easily if she chose, but refrained. She'd tasted so good . . . her skin, her mouth, her sweat.

He couldn't wait to eat her pussy.

He winced in agonized pleasure when he moved and his cock brushed the bare, satiny skin of her thigh. She whimpered.

She reached for him, but he stopped her by grabbing both of her wrists, then transferring both of them to one hand. The feeling of her small, cool hands on his body had enflamed him earlier. Vic didn't think he could take it right now and maintain his control. He pushed her wrists down over her head at the same time that he reached between her thighs.

He watched her face while he burrowed his fingers through damp, silky pubic hair, dipping into the warm cream of her pussy before he spread the abundant moisture between her labia, sliding and pressing against her clit.

Her back arched up off the bed. She squirmed frantically at the restraint of his binding hand.

But he only gripped her wrists and held her tighter. He played a hard, ruthless rhythm with his fingers, plucking and strumming the nerve-packed flesh until the tension in her body broke and she cried out sharply in stunned ecstasy. Two of his fingers plunged into her tight sheath. He watched her intently as her body clamped and convulsed around him.

She was ready for him so quickly. It excited him to know that she was as hungry for him at that moment as he was for her. He stretched, reaching for a condom in the drawer of his bedside table. His excitement to be inside her made him roll it on his cock in record-breaking time.

Without a word he spread her thighs and arrowed into her. Her body resisted him, but he was crazed by the sensation of her hot, narrow channel as it enclosed the thick head of his penis.

"You're tight," he grated. He held the base of his cock with one hand, working it into her clamping channel with subtle up-and-down motions while his hips provided a steady, hard pressure. She moaned, still in the aftershocks of her climax. Her slender body undulating and straining against him made him desperate. He thrust.

Hard.

He might have been half-crazed with lust, but he paused when he heard her cry out. His cock had burrowed less than half its length into her.

"Shhh, try to relax, baby," he soothed. His head dropped next to hers. He pressed hot kisses along her neck, pausing to run the elegant strand of pearls that she wore between his lips, licking at the smooth globes lightly before he nipped at her tender skin. Her lips were parted when he found them, the taste between them sweet and addictive. His cock throbbed painfully inside of her as his tongue sank into her warm cavern.

Pearls and honey.

She was driving him right over the edge. Her pussy gripped at him mercilessly.

He pushed back a smooth thigh, opening her body to him, demanding admission. His thumb found her clitoris, circling, plucking, and coaxing. She groaned into his mouth and pushed up for more pressure, seating his cock farther into her body in the process.

"That's right," he whispered gruffly next to her damp lips. "Let me in, Niall."

Niall cried out in sharp desire as he began to pulse his hips. His cock felt too large to be in her body, invading her, forcing her to make room for him . . . but indescribably good as well. His pressing thumb on her clit drove her further into a frenzy of lust. A friction began to build in her unlike anything she'd ever known. She began to push and rotate her hips around his cock, up and down, around, in and out, desperate to feed the mounting flame that grew and expanded in her sex and belly. Niall saw the way his lip curled, the way his light eyes gleamed as a result of her actions. She mewled in pleasure and increased the pressure against him, desperate with need.

She writhed and whimpered beneath him, begging him in a primitive fashion to take total possession of her. He accepted her wordless invitation. He drove his cock into her, pressing his balls tightly to her damp hilt, grunting in animal-like pleasure. When she cried out and arched her back, he secured her wrists tighter, pushing her back to the bed.

He began to thrust into her with tight, concentrated strokes.

"You've got a hot little pussy, but you're teasing me with it, aren't you, Niall?"

Niall just shook her head when he growled out the question ominously. She was too tight with mounting pleasure, too full of him . . . too close to orgasm to speak. His cock massaged her more deeply than she'd ever been touched, stimulating her with a hard, relentless pressure. He pried her body open to make way for him, but she was wild to get him back deep every time he withdrew from her, needing to have the thick, hard knob of his penis stabbing and rubbing and demanding something from her that she had only just learned she could give.

She gasped loudly when he leaned down and encircled her silk-covered nipple in the heat of his mouth. The suction that he applied made the inferno at her sex flame higher. When he bit at the tender morsel and thrust into her hard, creating a loud smack of flesh against flesh, she exploded again.

Vic grunted savagely as he felt her squeeze and convulse around his cock in orgasm. Her heat flooded around him. His eyes crossed at the sensation.

He reached up and roughly pushed down both of the thin pieces of black silk that covered her breasts. He bent and sampled one hard, pointed crest, lashing with his tongue, sucking hard, nipping and biting with his front teeth. She tasted so good—like berries, sweet cream, and musky woman. He wanted to eat her up in two ravenous bites. When he leaned up slightly, the sight of her white, thrusting breast capped by an erect, glistening pink nipple nearly sent him over the edge.

He focused on her sweat-dampened face. Her shoulder-length blonde hair was scattered across the pillow. She stared at him with desire-glazed eyes, her breath coming in choppy, shallow pants. The muscular, tight walls of her vagina tormented him. Every time he moved out of her, she pulled and sucked at his cock, demanding that he sink back into her depths before he was ready.

He pushed back first one thigh, and then the other, into her chest and began to pound into her. She shrieked in shock. It might have been in pain. It might have been in desire.

The only thing Vic knew for certain was that she had the tightest, sweetest little pussy he'd ever ridden.

"Vic! Vic?" she cried out in disbelieving ecstasy. He rocketed into her again and again, every driving downstroke pushing her body farther and farther up on the bed until her forearms were trapped between her skull and the wrought iron headboard.

Vic paused for a moment, still fully sheathed in her, and reached between their sweat-dampened bodies. His fingers spread the lips of her outer sex wide before he ground his pelvis against the nerve-packed tissues between her labia. She shimmered around him in post-orgasmic bliss. Her whole body began to tremble and shake when he surged up against her, scraping the narrow path of hair that trailed from his taut bellybutton to the thatch around his cock against her sensitive, exposed cleft and erect clit, applying a steady, relentless pressure.

When she groaned in misery, Vic knew she shook not only in post-orgasmic bliss but also in pre-orgasmic anticipation.

She opened her eyes dazedly. Vic watched her through narrowed eyelids.

"You want to come again?"

"*Yes*," she entreated.

He smiled at the stark evidence of her need. He used his forearm to push her knees down hard into her shoulders. She keened at the increased pressure from the altered angle of his cock stabbing deeply into her body. When he grabbed a round buttock and smacked her ass twice lightly, she cried out in surprise.

"Give it to me, then," he demanded harshly.

Her entire body began to shudder and shake once again in release.

Vic gave a tense bark of laughter, immensely pleased and aroused when he felt her heat rush around him.

"You liked that, baby?" he rasped as he began to pound into her quivering, hot pussy with quick, ruthless thrusts. Not that he expected her to answer. She was too busy climaxing, gushing liquid heat around him and squeezing his cock until he saw only a red haze in front of his eyes. Silk and pearls aside, Niall had liked it when he had spanked her plump little ass.

He struck their flesh together rapidly now, holding back nothing, striving madly to find relief in her farthest depths. She was immobilized against the headboard. He smacked their flesh together once more, the walls of her vagina still convulsing and pulling and taunting him.

God, she was a sweet fuck, he thought dazedly in the seconds before orgasm ripped through his flesh.

He threw his head back and roared between clenched jaws, pumping her hard and fast, shooting off what felt like gallons of his semen in a gloriously scalding climax.

Niall's eyes clenched closed at the sensation of Vic throbbing in release even as he continued to fuck her. Tears leaked onto her cheeks. The truth of the matter was that the sensation of him coming so powerfully in her body was one of the two most poignant, profoundly wonderful experiences she'd ever had in her life.

The other had been when she'd first heard the sound of her baby's cry and felt the slight, precious weight of his damp, warm body against her breast.

This had been, by far, the craziest, most impulsive thing Niall had ever done in her life. She didn't even know Vic's last name.

She couldn't regret a second of it, though. Not then. Not at that moment, when blood pounded in her veins, vibrant and hot.

She felt reborn—raw, confused, shaky . . . and utterly, completely alive.

TWO

Vic collapsed over her, his ribcage expanding and contracting wildly for air. His cock was still hard as a pike. Her muscular channel still clamped him tightly inside her. All he could think about was taking her again and repeating that hot, pounding, exhilarating ride.

But his lungs couldn't seem to catch a sufficient amount of air, momentarily stilling him.

So did the soft whimper that he heard her make in her throat.

His head came up. Their eyes met. Something in her wide-eyed stare made regret flicker through his awareness. He'd pounded her so hard. True, Vic liked his sex rigorous and hot, but because of that, he usually chose robust, experienced women who liked it that way as well.

The woman who lay beneath him, watching him with huge hazel eyes, was curved enticingly, but also slender and delicate. The smattering of freckles on her nose made her look young, bely-

WICKED BURN   19

ing her natural elegance and grace. He grimaced slightly when he glanced at her wrists, still pinned next to the headboard. He'd kept her in a ruthless hold while he plowed into her body—into that wet, tight pussy that enfolded him like a second skin even now. He'd probably bruised her.

His head lowered slowly to scan her for any damage.

Big mistake. Vic wasn't talking himself out of his singular lust, he just enflamed it by examining her. He could see the blueness of her veins beneath her small, pointed breasts. The nipples were dark pink verging on red, large for the size of her breasts, erect and distended . . .

Succulent.

He swallowed convulsively as his cock jerked in agonized pleasure in her clasping sheath.

Niall felt the surging of his penis and the tightening of his body. It echoed her own increasing tension. She also saw the unrest on his rugged face as he stared fixedly at her breasts.

"What's wrong?" she whispered.

His light gray eyes flickered to her face.

"Nothing."

Niall gasped when he rolled off her. The abrupt withdrawal of his cock from her body felt harsh and completely unnatural. Uneasiness seeped into her awareness as she studied his stark profile. She saw a muscle twitch in his lean cheek.

Was this it? she wondered in rising confusion. Was she supposed to get up and politely make an exit before awkwardness settled in? Was that how these impulsive, carnal, completely irrational trysts between two strangers typically ended?

She wouldn't know. This had been her first, Niall thought in rising disorientation.

He didn't say anything as she scooted to the end of the bed, but

she sensed his gaze on her back. She quickly readjusted her bra
and found her panties. She didn't stand and turn to face him until
she'd pulled her dress back over her head. It struck her as surreal,
how she'd been lying beneath him just minutes ago as he pried and
pounded his essence seemingly into every cell of her being, and
now they were apart, separate . . . once again what they truly were
to each other.

Complete strangers.

A lump formed in her throat when her eyes lowered across his
muscled, lean torso as he lay there in repose. His jeans were still
shoved down around his thighs. Perhaps it had been wrong to say
that he was in repose. His cock may not have been as iron-hard as
it had been when he'd hammered it into her body a while ago, but
it was still ample. It lay along his taut belly, still stretching the
latex of the condom tightly . . . still glistening with moisture.

Her mouth went completely dry. Those were her juices coating
the most shapely, beautiful cock she'd ever seen. The sight should
have made panic rise in her.

But it didn't. Desire swamped her instead, the magnitude of it
shocking her.

She opened her mouth to speak, but there was nothing she could
say that wouldn't seem ridiculous under these circumstances.

Niall turned and left the room. She fumbled as she picked up
her purse, dropping it clumsily in her haste to get out of there.
She'd made it to within three feet of his front door when he called
her name from directly behind her. She stopped dead in her tracks,
afraid to turn around.

Afraid to face him.

She made a choking sound of longing in her throat when she
felt his hands encircle her waist. He leaned down, brushing aside

her hair with his lips and nose before he pressed a hot kiss against her neck.

Vic sprang off the bed, quickly disposing of the condom in the bathroom and jerking up his jeans before he followed Niall.

He cursed himself for not just letting her go. She was trouble. A woman as beautiful as she was, a woman who seemed formed for the express purpose of making a man hunger and want—how could such a woman not be selfish? How could she not drain a man of every last bit of himself, all of his energy, his creativity . . . his self-worth?

And once you were just the shell of the man that you had been, when you could no longer give her everything that she demanded of you . . . everything she needed? She'd go elsewhere to find it. It was only natural.

A woman like her was like a bright, blinding star that consumed as fuel everything—and everyone—in its path.

He should know. He'd learned that lesson firsthand from Jenny. It had taken him four years to recover. Only recently had he begun to truly be satisfied again with his life and his writing.

And what was he doing, but setting himself in the path of another woman so beautiful that it made him ache to look at her, unable to resist her steady, magnetic pull?

He reached, snagging her even as she stretched out a hand for the front doorknob.

He closed his eyes as Niall's sweet, musky scent filled his nostrils. He spread his hands wide across her belly and hips as his lips brushed and rubbed against her silky skin. She was so small in comparison to the voluptuous women he usually favored. But

Christ, hadn't she cradled him like she'd been tailor-made for his cock?

He inhaled slowly. She smelled different from Jenny. She felt different. Niall obviously hadn't been intimate with a man for a long, long time.

That was a significant difference from Jenny. Jenny couldn't exist without a man in her bed . . . someone to constantly be holding up the figurative mirror that reflected her undeniable brilliance back to her, assuring her of its existence. Even though he'd built a career with words, Vic had failed miserably at providing her with what she needed. He couldn't say it right for her, couldn't say it fast enough. He couldn't read Jenny's enigmatic female mind and give her what she needed just when the desire occurred to her.

Yeah, Vic accepted that he was a complete and utter failure at understanding women . . . even the one that he'd wanted to comprehend most.

But no matter what Niall was or what Vic wasn't, she deserved something more from him than what he'd given her just now.

Vic didn't let himself think about why it was so important for him to prove to Niall Chandler that he could be soft as well as hard.

Niall tilted her neck to grant Vic more access to her skin. Her throat vibrated with pleasure as he kissed and nibbled with a potent mixture of patience and hunger. His hands moved over her belly, waist, and hips in a sensual caress.

She should stop this, shouldn't she? How could adding to the foolishness of her actions make things any better?

"Vic? I'm not so sure this is a good idea."

"I am," he replied in a gravelly voice. He turned her in his

arms. Her head fell back as she looked up at him. His eyes burned
like flames in his otherwise stony countenance. He looked so hard
and formidable that it took her lust-impaired brain a few seconds
to interpret what he said next.

"You haven't been with a man in a long time, have you?"

Her lower lip fell open in surprise. "I . . . Was it that ob—?"

She stopped abruptly. Her cheeks flooded with heat. She'd been
about to ask him if it had been that obvious when she realized how
stupid that would have sounded. Her body had been so stiff and
resistive to his presence that he'd probably wondered if she was a
virgin. Humiliation swamped her awareness. She noticed the way
his eyes narrowed as he looked at her face, and she glanced away
uncomfortably.

"No. No, I haven't," she finally answered throatily.

He tilted her chin so that she faced him again.

"I must have made you burn."

Niall blinked in amazement. Made her burn? God, *yes*, he'd
made her burn—like a thousand suns.

"I . . . Vic, I don't know . . ." she began awkwardly before a
choking sensation in her throat muted her. Tears flooded her eyes,
but she couldn't say why. It had been something in his tone that
did it, something that belied his stark, cold features . . . something
that sounded very much like tenderness.

"Let me make it better for you, Niall," he whispered. He
leaned down and brushed soft kisses across her cheeks and nose
before he settled on her parted lips.

Niall's eyelids fluttered closed as he used his lips and teeth to
gently nip at her mouth. His big hands spread across her ribcage
in a light, elusive embrace. The distant thought occurred to her
that he was an expert at this—at soothing anxious animals, at
mesmerizing with his deep voice and spare words, at coaxing a

creature with his magical touch until its will perfectly matched his own.

She craned up for his mouth, hungry for the remembered rich taste that she knew she'd find in his depths. They both turned slightly. Their mouths slid and fastened into a perfect fit.

Niall's bones turned to jelly. God, it had been way, *way* too long for her. She'd had no idea that her body was so primed, so needy for the pleasures that a man could give it.

She sighed at the sensation of his hands on her breasts, his fingers rubbing and pinching lightly at her sensitized nipples. Heat swept through her genitals, leaving a dull ache of longing in its wake. A sound of protest rose in her throat when his mouth left hers. Her eyes blinked open when she felt him back her against the wall of the hallway. She stared down, the image of the top of his dark head as it sank before her emblazoning itself on her memory.

When he matter-of-factly raised her dress to her waist and told her to hold it, Niall did it without hesitation. Her gripping hands shook as he slowly lowered her panties. He put his hands on her legs, spreading them until the strip of silk stretched tautly midthigh.

She whimpered when he leaned forward within an inch of her pussy and inhaled.

Vic tilted his head slightly in order to fully catch her heady scent in his nostrils. The impact of her odor affected him instantly. His cock stiffened. His mouth watered. His eyes closed in anticipation as he nuzzled the soft, damp, dark blonde curls over her swollen, tender cleft. His tongue parted her folds in a firm, questing caress.

He was distantly gratified when he heard her uneven moan and her body weight sagged slightly against the wall. His hands caught her beneath her buttocks, but most of his focused attention was on the exquisite taste of the abundant, sweet cream he found between her flushed folds. He circled and played with her nerve-packed flesh for a while, thoroughly enjoying her soft whimpers, the silky sensation of her on his tongue, and the intoxicating flavor he sought out with increasing avidity.

When he sensed her growing arousal, he stabbed at the erect kernel of flesh that nestled between her creamy lips with a stiffened tongue before he soothed her with a gliding caress . . . stabbed and soothed, plucked and glided . . .

His eyelids opened heavily and his gaze flickered up to her face when he registered her exclamation.

Oh, God.

His nostrils flared at the sight of her lividly pink cheeks. The first time he'd seen Niall, he'd sensed a sadness about her. Vic much preferred to see her large eyes darkened and glistening with stark arousal, the way they were right now. His hand left the taut curve of a peach of an ass cheek. Her lower lip trembled as he inserted two thick fingers into her wet vagina.

"Hold these apart for me," he directed as he used his other hand to part her sweet, nectar-coated labia. "That's right," he whispered as her hand lowered and her fingers replaced his own, spreading herself wide for him. He used his free hand to support her again below her ass.

For several seconds Vic just stared at her swollen, moist folds before he tilted his head and covered her. She keened as he took her clit captive in his mouth, sucking her tautly and whipping the erect tissue with his stiffened tongue.

Slippery warm juices flooded his fucking fingers. God, he needed to drink from that sweet, gushing fount.

But first he wanted to hear her scream.

He twisted his wrist, corkscrewing his fingers into her tight pussy. He sucked her clit between his teeth and bit lightly until she cried out and sagged into his hand.

His mouth nursed her through the brunt of her climax before he grabbed her hips and upper back and lowered her to the soft carpet. He tugged her panties over her feet and pushed her thighs wide until her black pumps thumped against either side of the narrow hallway.

He dived between her legs, his stiffened tongue immediately plunging into her pussy, driving deep and hard.

"*Ahahahahah,*" Niall cried out in ecstasy as her orgasm kicked up its initial strength and her throat and jaw vibrated with the potent blasts of pleasure coursing through her.

Vic drowned himself in her, loving every second of it. He could die happy with the taste of her filling his mouth and running down his throat. Her narrow channel was drenched with sweet, flavorful cream. Without thinking about what he was doing, mindless with pure lust, he ran his finger below his piercing tongue, spreading her juices along her perineum. Her honey already slicked the taut crevice of her butt cheeks and the tiny, puckered entrance of her asshole.

He heard the change in her whimpers and cries when he pushed the tip of his finger into that tight opening. For a few seconds, his lust convinced him to ignore the rising tension in her sleek body as he gently probed her. She gripped him in a smooth, hot clamp.

But he could ignore reality for only so long.

Vic's muscles clenched so rigidly it felt like they would break. He muttered a foul curse and pushed himself up into a sitting position.

"You should go."

He heard her panting breath cease abruptly at his harsh statement, but he didn't relent. He couldn't. If he so much as looked at her at that moment, he would undoubtedly live to regret it.

Niall blinked heavily when her good friend Anne Rothman spoke. She felt like she'd been living in a daze for the past week and a half. The din of the crowded restaurant blended into a lulling white background noise. The Art was one of her and Anne's favorite places to duck in for a quick bite after work. The museum was only blocks away and the Metropolitan Art Institute, where Anne was the Dean of Students, was just two buildings down from the restaurant. They'd come early tonight, so The Art bustled with the pre-theater crowd.

"I thought that salad was your favorite thing on The Art's menu," Anne managed between bites of seafood linguine. She pointed her fork at the enormous, untouched salad that sat in front of Niall. "*Eat,* girl! You look like you've lost five pounds since you came back from Tokyo, and you couldn't afford to lose one ounce." She shoved another forkful of pasta into her mouth. "You were gone for only a week. What . . . did you catch a bug or something?"

"No, of course not," Niall replied as she picked up a heavy silver salad fork and unfolded a linen napkin. "I was just really busy getting things ready for the exhibit, that's all." She referred to her job as the Curator of the Department of Nineteenth Century, Modern, and Contemporary Art. She traveled quite a bit for her job, viewing collections everywhere in the world and negotiating for pieces for the exhibitions she planned. Her trip to Tokyo had been unusual in that her main contact hadn't been with a museum, but with a wealthy industrialist who owned a vast collection of Cezanne, Picasso, and Vollard paintings.

"That was quite a coup for you to get those paintings lent for the exhibit, wasn't it?" Anne asked as she tore apart a steaming roll.

"Yes. Most of Nakamura's paintings haven't been shown publicly in almost half a century. I could have done an exhibit with his collection alone. As it is, the addition of his paintings is going to make the show in April spectacular. Mac is thrilled," she admitted, referring to her boss, Alistair McKenzie.

Both women looked up when the waiter asked them if they needed anything. Anne ordered another glass of wine, but Niall had hardly touched her first glass.

"So what's wrong, then?" Anne asked once the waiter left, threading his way through the crowd in order to get to the bar. Before Niall had the chance to answer, Anne leaned forward in the booth. "Did you go to Evergreen Park? Is that why you're so preoccupied?"

"No. I just got back from Tokyo yesterday morning. I'm just a little jet-lagged, that's all," Niall answered evasively.

"Has there been any change in his condition?"

Niall chewed her food slowly, not overly eager to start this line of conversation at the moment . . . *never* eager to do so. That was why so few of her acquaintances knew much about her past. But she'd been close with Anne since the older woman had been her advisor back when they both were at Northwestern, Niall as a graduate student and Anne as a professor.

She took a small sip of wine before she spoke.

"Have you forgotten that I'm no longer in a position to get regular updates?"

"I'm too thrilled about it to have forgotten. I just thought I recognized that expression on your face," Anne said grimly.

Niall set down her wine glass and sighed. "Apparently it's going to take a while before everyone else gets used to the fact. Ever-green Park *did* call yesterday. There's been another relapse. Dr. Fardesh decided to make another significant medication change."

Anne winced slightly. "Again? You know as well as I do, Niall, that he's got to *want* to get better." She took a drink of her ice water, trying to calm her overwhelming urge to vent her personal opinion on the matter fully. Niall had heard it before, and she didn't need to hear it again.

"I hope this doesn't change your mind about your decision," Anne said cautiously.

Niall's mouth pressed into a thin line. "No. I've made up my mind. Nothing has changed since we spoke a month ago," she finally said in a low voice.

Anne reached out and covered Niall's hand with her own. "You're doing the right thing, Niall. You'll get through this, whether you have your parents' blessing or not." Anne couldn't help but give an irritated frown at this juncture. How Niall's parents thought they were being supportive of their daughter with their actions was beyond Anne's comprehension. "I don't know how you've done it, honey. It's just not possible for someone to *exist* the way you have for these last few years."

Niall laughed softly. "Exist? Trust me, Anne, millions of people on this earth exist, and even thrive under conditions exponentially worse than you or I could ever imagine. I'm *existing* just fine, thank you."

"You're right," Anne said with her professorial stern look. "I shouldn't have said *exist*. I should have said *live*. You can't call what you've been doing since Michael's death and what Stephen pulled afterwards *living*."

Niall took a slow inhale of air to calm the effects of the unexpected blow of hearing her son's name spoken out loud. She really needed to get better at this. She wanted so much to be able to hear Michael's name, to *speak* it and be able to remember the wonderful things—the sweet baby smell of his neck that still hadn't completely dissipated at age four, the serious and thoughtful expression on his face as he drew with a crayon in one hand and held a purple popsicle to his mouth with the other, the sound of his laughter . . .

How fair was it to her little boy that her most significant memory of him was his utterly meaningless, shockingly abrupt death?

But beyond that, Anne's words hit a little too close to what she'd been thinking recently, ever since she'd blazed to vibrant life beneath the touch of a complete stranger twelve days ago, ever since she'd remembered what it meant to be alive. It was a little difficult to go back to the routine of a robot once you'd been awakened to the wonders of the flesh.

You've got a hot little pussy, but you're teasing me with it, aren't you, Niall?

Niall squeezed her eyes shut briefly to chase away the memory. A shiver ran down her spine. Even the recollection of his raspy whisper had a potent effect on her. She kept thinking it would fade, but no . . .

It seemed, in fact, that the memory of that wild, carnal tryst only grew stronger as the days passed.

Vic.

She hadn't seen him since that night. He'd told her that he left for his farm in downstate Illinois on Fridays, and it had been Thursday night when he'd . . . done what he'd done to her. She wasn't quite sure how to describe what that was, exactly. *Fucked her, consumed her, burned her to life?* Niall thought desperately.

She had left for Tokyo for a planned weeklong business trip last Sunday night and just returned yesterday. Had he tried to contact her? And if he had, exactly what would she have done?

She wasn't any closer to knowing the answer to that than she was to comprehending precisely what had happened to her that night in Vic's apartment.

Surely it was a moot point, anyway. He was the one who had practically thrown her out of his place while she'd been lying spread-eagled in his hallway.

You should go.

That was it. Nothing else. Not a touch, not a word. Not even a glance, despite the fact that his mouth and nose had glistened wetly with the juices from her pussy.

"Honey, are you okay?" Anne asked anxiously, alarmed by the two spots of brilliant color that suddenly bloomed in Niall's otherwise pale cheeks.

"I'm fine . . . really," Niall replied. She smiled at her friend reassuringly as she tried to gain a semblance of control. For a second, she'd been lost in the incredibly erotic memories—shadows of images and sensations that she'd tried to bring to life again and again with her silver bullet vibrator. The little gizmo had gotten more of a workout in the last week and a half than in the first two years that she'd owned it.

Anne must have misunderstood the dazed expression on Niall's face. "I'm sorry. I know I just stress you out more by bringing up the subject, but I worry about you."

Niall laughed abruptly.

"What?" Anne asked, surprised by the sound of Niall's laughter.

"Do you know what I would *give* sometimes to have it so that people didn't feel like they needed to say that to me?" She smiled and reassuringly grabbed Anne's hand when she saw her crest-fallen expression. "I know you're concerned about me because you care. I love you for that. But I'm fine. *Really.*" She thumped the older woman's hand teasingly on the tablecloth until she saw her smile.

"Why don't you tell me about that new dormitory the Institute is planning on Randolph Street? That's going to cost a bundle, the way the Theater District has built up in Chicago, isn't it?" Niall asked engagingly as she stabbed her salad with her fork.

Anne sighed. By this time she was very familiar with her friend's sidesteps in conversation. But she let herself be sidetracked, knowing how much Niall needed a relaxing evening.

By the time Niall had finished a cup of decaf cappuccino and Anne had polished off a creamy slice of tiramisu, both of them were much less uptight and discussing in a semiserious manner where they should take a vacation together the following year. They agreed on Italy, but Anne thought Rome and Florence would be ideal, while Niall was more in the mood for a sunny, sleepy getaway in Tuscany.

"Tuscany," Anne snorted. "We'd be much better off staying in Chicago in regard to the supply of men. Which—" She suddenly stopped and blinked twice as she stared past Niall's right shoulder. "Oh, my, get a handle on the hormones . . . speaking of *men* . . ."

Niall laughed. "I hadn't realized we were."

Anne ignored her. She took a quick drink of her ice water, as though her mouth had just gone dry.

"I'll be damned if Vic Savian himself isn't staring at the back of your head right now like he thought he just discovered the secret of the universe in your hair."

"Vic . . . Savian?" Niall asked slowly.

Anne set down her water glass and averted her eyes for a second before she glanced back surreptitiously to the bar.

"Sure, Vic Savian. The playwright?" she muttered under her breath. "The Hesse Theater—not to mention Chicago—scored a real coup by signing him on as the director and resident playwright. He's won the Pulitzer several times, not to mention dozens of other awards. But the man *hates* New York. Genuine article of the West, you know. It's a miracle he agreed to live this far east." Her expression shifted subtly, as if she'd just put two and two together. "*Oh*, and the first play they're doing is one of his. It opens next week. It's been in all the papers. One of the professors in the Theater Department has been working with an assistant of Savian's to get a program going where a few students can help out on the set, get some good experience in the trenches. Of course, he had to especially encourage the boys to apply, since the girls immediately filled up the roster. Vic Savian is one hell of a sexy beast."

That was it. The last remnant of Niall's self-control slipped away.

She twisted around in the booth and stared. Her eyes met his immediately.

He stood out at the crowded bar, or at least he did to her. He was sitting and leaning forward, but even so, his head topped everyone around him. His shoulders were broader than anyone else's, too, especially emphasized as they were by a well-cut brown blazer. The shirt that he wore underneath looked starkly white against his dark skin. Even though his posture might look relaxed to a casual observer, Niall sensed his alertness, his focused attention.

For a few seconds they just looked at each other, both of them motionless.

Then a dark-haired woman at the bar spoke to him. Vic's chin shifted to the side to catch what she said, his steady gaze on Niall fracturing slightly.

Niall turned around quickly, as if she'd been given an unexpected reprieve from the snare of his eyes.

Anne hadn't missed the charged, nonverbal exchange. "Do you *know* Vic Savian, Niall?"

Her hand shook slightly when she took a drink of water. "No. Yes. Sort of." Niall cleared her throat, realizing how stupid she sounded. Her heart pounded in her ears so loudly she wondered if a blood vessel would break.

"He actually lives across the hall from me at Riverview Towers. At least for part of the week he does," she added lamely.

Anne grinned hugely. "He *does*? Holy shit, you are one lucky woman! Ever see anything worthwhile, like him coming out in the morning to get his newspaper just wearing his boxers? And why the hell didn't you ever tell me that Vic Savian lived twenty feet away from you?"

Niall grimaced. She'd seen *plenty* worthwhile in regard to Vic. She also knew firsthand that he didn't wear boxers. In her experience, Vic didn't wear anything beneath his jeans but smooth, warm skin. She shivered slightly in nervous excitement at the same time that a wave of nausea swept through her. The man from her wild night of raw, sublime sex suddenly possessed a name and the outlines of an identity.

And she could feel his stare on her again.

"I didn't know who he was," Niall said when she realized that Anne was waiting tensely for an answer. "You said he's a playwright? That's so strange."

"Why would you say that?" Anne asked in puzzlement.

"Because he hardly talks at all," Niall muttered.

Anne looked like she was about to pursue that vague reference before she raised her eyebrows and flipped her napkin onto the table in an affected casual gesture.

"Well, he just got up from the bar, and he looks like he has every intention of coming over here. Savian obviously has *something* he wants to say to you, Niall."

THREE

Niall wondered about Anne's statement, however, when Vic approached their booth but didn't utter a word. Just when he seemed about to say something, his gaze flicked over to Anne. Niall experienced a moment of panic in the tense silence. She stared up at him, taking in his all-too-well-remembered image—the long, jean-clad thighs, the rugged, stoic facial features, those singular light gray eyes. He looked good in the casual sports jacket—he looked *very* good—but his clothing couldn't quite disguise the animal-like, sinewy grace of the man beneath them.

It felt surreal to be staring up at him in the midst of a crowded restaurant.

Niall grasped for something to say, but nothing came.

Nothing.

She blinked when he abruptly queried her in his typical laconic fashion.

"Where'd you go?"

Niall forced a smile despite a rising sense of panic. "I just got back from a business trip to Tokyo."

She thought she saw irritation flicker across his handsome face at her unintentionally stiff reply, but it was gone in an instant. A small smile shaped his lips, deepening the lines that parenthesized his mouth.

"I thought maybe you'd cleared out . . . decided the neighborhood was too dangerous or something."

Niall stared. His grin had widened just enough to display that deadly, slightly off-center front tooth. The humor and heat that flashed into his eyes left Niall speechless. She hadn't expected him to subtly tease her, so how could she have prepared herself for the potent result?

Talk about pure, distilled sexuality. If only Vic could package it, he'd be a billionaire.

She laughed nervously. "Of course not. I have to travel quite a bit with my job. I just got back yesterday."

He nodded slowly, his eyes never leaving her. She recognized the tiny, almost imperceptible movement he made with his closed mouth, a slight roll of his angular jaw while he considered her unhurriedly. Just looking at his mouth and thinking about his teeth made a dull ache of longing expand from her lower belly downward.

"Vic." A female voice broke Niall's trance. She glanced over and saw the attractive, statuesque brunette who had been speaking to him at the bar. Niall thought she seemed vaguely familiar. There was nothing indistinct about the hard look she gave Niall, however. Despite the woman's obvious irritation at her, she smiled when Vic turned.

"Our table is ready," she said brightly.

"I'll let you get back to your dinner," he said with a brief nod of apology to Anne.

"There's nothing to get back to," Anne piped up with a broad smile. "Nothing but the crumbs."

His eyes met Niall's briefly before he started to walk away. Niall tried to smile but suspected she only grimaced. He stopped abruptly after he'd taken a step.

"Would it be okay if I called you?"

Niall, Anne, and the brunette waiting for Vic all froze simultaneously.

"Yes," Niall finally croaked. Her eyes widened when he continued to stare at her.

"I don't have your number. It's not listed," he said after a silence that lasted for only a few seconds, but seemed like eons to Niall.

He'd wanted to call her? He'd *tried* to call her?

"I'll get it for you," Niall managed eventually when her shock faded.

She fumbled in her bag, finally pulling out her business card and a pen. She wrote her cell phone number on the back, pointedly avoiding the significant looks and barely repressed smug grin that Anne was giving her from across the table. "Either work or my cell is fine. I never had a line installed in the apartment. Too temporary," she stated lamely as she handed him the card.

He nodded once before he took it and followed the dark-haired woman away from their booth.

"It's okay, Niall," Anne said as she choked back laughter once he was out of hearing distance. "You can breathe now."

Anne took the first cab in the queue outside of The Art; Niall, the second. Niall adored Anne, of course, but she was all too glad to escape her friend's nearly nonstop questioning in regard to Vic

Savian. By the time Anne had gotten into the cab and waved good-bye, Niall was fairly confident the older woman knew that Vic and Niall's relationship consisted of more than occasional glimpses of one another and neighborly hellos.

Niall's proclivity to blush at the most inopportune moments ensured that.

Her cabdriver rocketed down Randolph Street at an alarming speed, but Niall didn't even notice. She was too busy picturing Vic as he looked down at her while she sat at the booth, too preoccupied with replaying his request for her phone number.

It had been wrong of her to give it to him without a shred of hesitation, just as it had been wrong of her to give him her body without a thought of refusal.

Hadn't it?

Both things had felt so right and natural that refusing him had never even occurred to her on either occasion.

Her phone started to ring at the same moment that the cab made a tight turn down Wacker Drive, making her purse slide along the backseat. Niall lunged for her bag before she'd righted herself. She swallowed heavily when she saw the 217 prefix of the caller's phone number.

Wasn't that an area code from downstate Illinois?

Surely Vic wasn't calling her *already*. He'd just walked away from their table not ten minutes ago!

"Hello?"

"Niall?"

"Yes?"

"It's Vic."

"Oh . . . hi," she said breathlessly. The cabdriver made another wild left turn down Lake Street, causing her to grip tightly at the opening of the hard plastic window that separated the driver from his passengers in order to keep her body upright. The way the guy drove, he was lucky to have a little protection from what Niall assumed were frequently irate customers.

She floundered both physically and mentally in the seconds of silence that followed.

"You headed back home?" Vic finally asked.

Niall closed her eyes and let his voice wash over her, allowing it to still her wildly chaotic emotions. She loved the sound of it. The vague thought struck her that Vic Savian was not a man who should use the phone. Phone talkers couldn't abide extensive silences, feeling the need to fill the unbearable void of nothingness. His words were as spare and lean as the man himself, calling to mind a stark, rugged landscape that was far, far from being simple.

"Yes. It's going to be an early night for me. I'm a little tired after my trip," she murmured.

"Tokyo, you said, right?"

"Yes."

Another short silence followed. This time Niall sank into it . . . embraced it instead of fighting it. Her eyes remained closed. Her whole world narrowed down to the fragile, temporary connection with a man via the means of a technology she couldn't even begin to comprehend.

Where, exactly, was he as he talked to her? In the entryway of The Art, protecting himself from the cool November wind? Or perhaps on the sidewalk with theatergoers strolling by, arm in arm?

Outside, Niall decided unequivocally. A man like Vic embraced the elements, never shunned them. She could picture him perfectly—his broad shoulders hunched slightly, his back angled to the street in an unconscious gesture of self-protection . . . not from the elements but from people's prying eyes.

What did his attractive, dark-haired companion think about Vic's absence as he talked to Niall and she sat alone at their table, waiting?

Those were all distant thoughts that had nothing to do with what she asked him next.

"Where did you grow up?"

"In a li'l pissant town called Avery, South Dakota, just outside the Black Hills. I've lived in Montana for the past fifteen years, though. Why?"

"No reason," she murmured. "I like your accent, that's all."

"I don't have an accent. You do, though."

Niall laughed softly at his matter-of-fact declaration. She could picture the small smile curving his lips perfectly. She pressed the phone tighter to her ear, thoroughly mesmerized, wanting him closer, even in this nonphysical sense.

"What accent is that, exactly?"

"The one that sounds like you grew up on the North Shore . . . Glencoe? Lake Forest?"

Her eyelids popped open. His assumption and something in the tone of his voice had stung her—although he had been entirely correct . . .

"Kenilworth, actually."

"Ummm."

The cabdriver made another wicked right into the circular drive in front of Riverview Towers. It hurt, his little grunt of acknowledgment, as if she'd suddenly confirmed something nasty about herself to him, as if growing up in an affluent neighborhood was a shameful crime.

"I should probably go. I'm home," she said huskily, realizing that the words sounded far more intimate to her ears than she'd intended.

"I'll probably be working late tomorrow but I'd like to have dinner with you afterward if you're available."

"I'm available," Niall said rapidly. She closed her eyes in mortification when she realized how that must have sounded to him. His quick bark of masculine laughter suggested that he'd liked her response, however.

"I'll give you a call around eight and tell you how things are looking on my end. Okay?"

"Okay. Have a good night."

"Night."

Niall was distracted as she walked through Riverview Towers' luxurious lobby. She didn't realize why she was so preoccupied until she reached her front door and glanced over at the entrance to Vic's apartment. Against her will, the powerful image rose in her mind's eye of what she must have looked like lying spread-eagled on his hallway floor, her dress around her waist, flushed from multiple orgasms, vibrant life surging thickly in her veins.

Guilt washed through her. She knew what rankled at her spirit. She'd told Vic that she was available.

And Niall herself couldn't decide if that was the ultimate truth or not.

A pile of things had accumulated on her desk in her absence, each one seemingly more important than the last. Niall coped with her anxiety and excitement about seeing Vic that night by throwing herself into work. By the time she returned to her office from a late afternoon meeting, she wasn't feeling any less jumpy about her date, but she did feel good about how much she'd accomplished that day.

"Any calls?" Niall asked Kendra Phillips, her administrative assistant and good friend. When she heard the eager tone of her own voice, Niall realized that she was half hoping that Vic might have called, which was ridiculous. He'd specifically told her that he wouldn't call until this evening. God, she was like a teenager with her first crush. The only difference being how wet her panties got every time she thought about Vic touching her. That aspect of her infatuation was definitely very adult.

She must not have been hiding her eagerness very well, because Kendra gave her a slightly suspicious look.

"Who were you expecting to call? Not Evan Forrester, I hope."

Niall blanched. She hadn't spoken to Evan since the night that he'd practically attacked her in the hallway . . . since the night Vic had branded her with his touch.

"God, no."

"Good, because I saw him at Toulouse during lunch," Kendra said, referring to the upscale restaurant housed within the museum. "He really likes his martini lunches, doesn't he? He cornered me and asked if you'd returned yet. I told him that I thought you'd be spending the weekend with your parents in Kenilworth."

"Nice one, thanks," Niall said.

"Mac said that Forrester was trouble from the first when it came to you, although he has to tiptoe around the issue, seeing as how Forrester is on the board," Kendra said with a grin, referring to Alistair McKenzie, the director of the museum.

Niall rolled her eyes. "If only Evan could be that subtle in return. The guy's like a Mack truck." Kendra looked concerned about that statement, so Niall quickly changed the subject.

"Any other calls?"

"Here are your messages."

Niall glanced through the pieces of paper. Rose Gonzalez's

name caught her eye. What had the State of Illinois Public Guardian been calling her for? Niall wondered. Rose had patiently explained to her that she was wholly in charge now, not Niall. She knew that Rose usually left the office by five P.M. She'd have to call her first thing in the morning.

"Your mom was one of the callers," Kendra broke through Niall's preoccupation. Her voice level dropped until it was just above a whisper. "She wanted to know if you wanted to attend church at St. Patrick's before the three of you go out to Evergreen Park this Sunday. You're supposed to call her on her cell."

Niall grimaced. How like her mother to suggest a good dose of Catholic-style guilt just when Niall was considering having a sexual fling with Vic. Alexis Chandler was damn scary sometimes, the way she could foresee events.

And Niall did *not* plan to go to Evergreen Park this weekend. That was one of her mother's well meaning, but thoroughly irritating, machinations. Niall had made it clear that the ritualistic, soul-wrenching Sunday visitations at Evergreen Park were a thing of the past.

God, it made her feel slightly nauseated even to consider challenging her mother on the issue when she knew she was only doing what she thought was right. The lament of every child since Cain and Abel, no doubt, she thought sourly.

"Thanks." Niall started to walk toward her office, but she paused, her feet moving restlessly. "You go to plays a lot, don't you, Kendra?"

"Sure, when I can get Mark to let go of his death grip on the remote control for a few hours," she teased, referring to her husband.

"Ever seen a Vic Savian play?"

"Yep. *Misfit Cowboys* and *Aidan's Fall*. Are you thinking

about seeing his new one that's opening at the Hesse Theater? I've already got tickets."

Niall plucked at her wool skirt, averting her face. "I was thinking about it. Is he any good?"

"Better than good," Kendra said resolutely. "The guy's a genius. Don't get me wrong, his stuff isn't a frolic in the park. His plays are gritty and intense, volatile, thought-provoking, but very . . . erotic, too." Kendra shook her head and laughed sheepishly. "*Tons* of restrained lust is a Savian key ingredient. It's what makes his plays so unpredictable and exciting. Hey, Niall?"

"Yes?"

"Why are you blushing?" Kendra asked with a fascinated expression on her round, earnest face.

Niall rolled her eyes and resumed walking to her office. "I am not *blushing.*"

"Sure looked like you were," she heard Kendra say thoughtfully before Niall shut the door to her office.

She glanced into an antique mirror mounted on the wall. Kendra had been right. Her cheeks were bright red. In fact, the utterly foreign thought struck Niall at that moment that she looked like a very sexy, desirable woman.

All that, merely because when Kendra had talked about Vic's plays, it had occurred to Niall that he wrote the way he made love.

Vic called her a few minutes after eight and said that he was running behind.

"Would it be all right with you if we just met downstairs at Louie's, say at around nine thirty?" he asked.

"Of course," Niall agreed as she eyed the outfit she'd laid out on the bed to wear on their date. "I'm actually relieved. I can just throw on some jeans."

"I was going to be wearing jeans whether we went to Louie's or Everest," he said under his breath, humor lacing his tone as he referred to the famous Chicago restaurant.

Niall laughed. "I'm sure Everest would be happy to have your business, jeans or no. Everest caters to the pretheater crowd, you know. It'd be a feather in their cap if you showed up in swim trunks and a T-shirt, no doubt."

"You know what I do for a living?" he asked.

"Oh . . . yes. My friend Anne—the woman I was with last night in the restaurant—told me that you're a playwright."

He laughed shortly. "Well, I know for a fact that Louie couldn't give a shit about what I'm wearing as long as my ass is covered, so let's stick with that. Besides, I hate French food."

Niall smiled. His proclamation hadn't particularly surprised her.

When she arrived at Louie's, she immediately saw Vic in a booth near the bar, chatting with Louie himself. He was wearing a fitted, dark blue, Western-style shirt that accentuated his long, lean torso and broad shoulders. The shadow of a beard darkened his jaw. Heat flooded Niall's lower belly when she recalled how his whiskers had erotically abraded her sensitive skin during their lovemaking.

Vic looked up and held her gaze as she approached, even though he continued to chat with Louie. His eyes lowered over her in leisurely appreciation before he stood as she greeted both men.

Vic caught her hand when she began to move to the opposite side of the booth from where he'd been sitting.

"Sit here."

Louie grinned broadly as he watched the exchange. He nodded his head once in obvious approval when Niall assented to

Vic's terse request and slid into the seat before he sat down next to her.

"Let me see here—a glass of chardonnay and the salmon for the lady, and a beer and a medium-rare steak for the gentleman. Am I right?" Louie asked, amusement and his rich Chicago South Side accent flavoring his tone.

"On the nose for me." Niall grinned. Her eyes widened when she realized that Vic had turned and was looking at her.

"Sounds good, Louie," Vic murmured, never taking his eyes off Niall.

"I guess neither one of us has to worry about cleaning our ovens when we've got Louie downstairs," she teased. Her breath stuck painfully in her lungs when Vic reached up and grabbed a wavy tendril of her hair between his thumb and first two fingers.

"Do you like to cook?" he asked absentmindedly as he rubbed the golden curl between his fingers.

"Yes," Niall replied. She inhaled unsteadily and caught a whiff of Vic's clean, spicy cologne. It brought back myriad sensations and images from the night in his apartment, increasing her sense of mixed anxiety and excitement. "But not here at Riverview Towers. All of my cooking utensils are packed away. I can't wait to get them all out for my new kitchen. What about you? Do you like to cook?"

"Nope. But I like to eat, which means that I do it. We usually take turns cooking whenever I'm on the farm." He studied her face before he released her hair. "You're nervous, aren't you? There's no need to be."

Laughter burst out of her throat. "Easy for you to say."

She paused when that dead-sexy grin abruptly curved his lips. Jeez, talk about an unfair advantage. A woman couldn't think straight when Vic resorted to using that weapon. The deep lines around his mouth said that despite his typical stony expression, he did his fair share of grinning. He could probably turn a woman to sex jelly at a distance of fifty feet with that smile. Never mind what it could do to you when you sat so close to him that you could breathe his rich, male scent and he casually reached behind you to stroke your shoulder with his long fingers.

"It is pretty easy for me to say. Why should you be nervous? It's not like we haven't already had sex."

Her mouth gaped open at his calm statement. Luckily, Louie chose that moment to interrupt as he set down their drinks.

"What's wrong?" Vic asked once Louie had left. He took a sip of his beer with the hand that wasn't stroking her shoulder. His touch on her was seemingly casual enough, but Niall felt like every fiber of her consciousness was focused on the tiny patch of her body where he gently molded and massaged her muscle. "You didn't forget about us having sex together, did you?"

Heat flooded her cheeks. "*Hardly*," she answered drolly, borrowing his habit of charged laconism.

His gray eyes locked on hers. He started to laugh, low and heartfelt. Niall found that she couldn't remain anxious in the presence of his deep laughter. She shook her head in mock exasperation before she started to laugh right along with him.

The magic of their combined laughter seemed to melt away her nervousness, leaving only excitement and growing desire in its wake.

Niall had a wonderful time at dinner. True, she spoke three words for every one of Vic's. He was adept at keeping her talking with just a few terse prompts. He was actually quite easy to talk to, once one got over the fact that he was not only a gorgeous hunk of man but a Pulitzer Prize–winning writer. Although he never gushed or rambled on any topic, he was surprisingly forthcoming about his work. She found herself truly relaxing as she listened to him describe in his succinct, spare language the challenges involved in getting his latest play ready for opening night. When he mentioned his leading lady's first name, Niall tapped her forehead in recognition.

"Right! Eileen Moore. She used to be on that sit-com, *Different Wavelengths*. I thought she looked familiar when I saw her last night with you at The Art."

Niall recalled the pointedly furious look the attractive actress had thrown her way and wondered once again if she and Vic were involved or if Eileen just wished they were.

"She's too talented a stage actress to have been doing that crap in Hollywood," Vic said as he set down his knife. "This is the third play of mine that she's done."

"Oh?"

His eyes flickered over to her face when he heard the tone of her voice. "Are you wondering if I've slept with her?" he asked bluntly.

For a few seconds Niall floundered for an answer. Nothing would come to her except the truth.

"Yes."

Vic considered her for a second, his angular jaw making that increasingly familiar subtle rolling motion. "Yeah, I have," he finally said.

Niall glanced down at her plate. She was embarrassed by how much his admission hurt. She clearly was losing her mind. Vic Savian had likely slept with hundreds of women before that moment and would sleep with hundreds more before his life was over. Niall was just one more name on a list of casual conquests. If she'd had to say whether or not he'd slept with Eileen Moore before he'd made his admission, she would have bet that he had. The flaming darts that the actress had thrown at Niall convinced her of that.

So why did hearing him say it out loud hurt so much?

She shook her head and laughed at her naïveté. "It's really none of my business," she said softly. "I shouldn't have asked."

Vic didn't respond because a busboy arrived to clear the table. After the busboy left, Niall asked him about his farm in downstate Illinois, desperate to change the subject.

He explained that he'd inherited the farm from his mother's brother over a year ago. Vic still couldn't figure out why in the world his uncle Manny had made a specific point of leaving him the enormous farm while Meg, Vic's sister, was designated as the beneficiary of Manny Padilla's financial estate. It wasn't that both inheritances weren't generous far beyond expectation, of course; it was just that Vic clearly wasn't a farmer. He'd thought about selling it, not having the time or interest for running a large farm since he already owned a ranch in Montana. But his sister, Meg, and her husband had said they would like to manage the extensive property.

"It's worked out okay," Vic said as he accepted the bill from a smiling Louie. "Maybe Uncle Manny knew something I didn't. I'd already been in talks with the Hesse Theater when I inherited the farm. I guess it's no secret how much I hate living in the city. They were willing to negotiate the actual amount of time that I spend in Chicago. I brought out some of my horses from my ranch in Montana. Meg and Tom live up at the big house and I live in a cottage that was built for a farmhand and his family years ago. We get along, but if we get sick of each other, we can hightail it to our respective houses and lock the doors. My contract with the Hesse is for only two years, anyway."

Niall's eyes crept up to study his face while he was focused on leaving a tip and signing his name to the bill. "Do you have other brothers or sisters besides Meg?"

"Nah, just Meg and me."

His eyes abruptly leapt to her face, catching her skittish gaze and holding tight.

"I slept with Eileen Moore years ago, Niall. It was after I went through an ugly breakup with a woman I was supposed to marry. I was dead drunk for almost six months after the fact. If you want to know the truth, Eileen probably thought of it as a series of pity fucks. I was damned *pitiful*, that's for sure," he said with a wry twist of his handsome mouth.

Niall just stared at him for a long moment. His stark honesty always took her off guard, but she was undoubtedly drawn to it. She had no doubt that he stated things the way he saw them. He either hadn't noticed or chose to ignore the fact that Eileen Moore still carried a blazing torch for him. And after having sex with Vic, Niall sincerely doubted that Eileen's motivation for sleeping with him was pity. But Niall kept that to herself.

Vic surprised her a few seconds later when he reached for the hand that she wasn't using to sip her coffee.

"I see that you were married before."

Niall froze in the action of setting her cup back on the saucer. "What?" she asked.

He lifted her hand. Before she could guess what he was about, he gripped her first two fingers in his right hand and pushed back her ring finger with the other. His thumb made tiny little circles at the tender apex, making Niall shiver with pleasure.

"I can see the outline of a ring here," he said gruffly, referring to where his thumb rubbed.

"Oh . . . yes, I was."

"How long ago did you two split?"

"Three years ago."

The sound of Niall's husky, low voice caused a burning, tingling sensation of excitement to pass from Vic's tailbone to the root of his cock. He wondered idly if he could come just from the sound of her voice alone.

Still, it had been strange that she'd said she and her husband split three years ago. The imprint on her ring finger, the paleness where the sun never shone, would have argued for something more recent. Maybe she'd worn her wedding ring for years after they'd divorced, hoping that one day they'd get back together.

That would be something he and Niall had in common. Didn't the psychotherapist that he saw for a year after he broke up with Jenny always tell him that his actions, more so than his words, were those of a man who was holding out hope for lost love?

Yeah, right.

As if Jenny would ever think of leaving Mr. Smooth Hollywood Producer for a man who would rather eat his dinner in the saddle than at a restaurant like the nauseatingly trendy one that Mr. Smooth owned—among myriad other properties and businesses—in Los Angeles.

Who fucking cared about Jenny anyway, when such a beautiful woman stared up at him with phenomenally sexy eyes?

Vic felt Niall's indrawn breath on his knuckle when he reached up and pressed a thumb to her lush lower lip. Her mouth was the same color as her nipples—a lush, dark pink that became red under the ministrations of his teeth and tongue. He'd lost count of the number of times he'd jerked off in the past twelve days while he pictured her pointed, rosy nipples trembling slightly as he'd pounded into her tight little body.

"I want you again, Niall. I have every second since you walked out my front door the other day," he admitted quietly.

Her eyes cast downward, but almost immediately leapt back up to consider him through thick eyelashes. He'd been in varying states of arousal since Niall first walked into Louie's tonight, looking fresh and sexy in a pair of jeans and high-heeled boots. But that single, shy, seductive glance made him harden into full, leaden readiness. When she started to speak, Vic transferred his hand from her mouth to the side of her neck, where he refamiliarized himself with the incredible silkiness of her skin.

"You told me to leave. You sounded so . . . hard," she whispered.

His fingers sank into the soft hair at her nape. His movements were causing the fresh, fruity scent of her shampoo to drift up to his appreciative nose.

"I told you to leave only because all I could think about doing was nailing you down on that hard floor until your ears rang. I figured you'd had enough of that back in my bed." He watched as her eyes flickered around them and realized that she was checking to make sure they weren't overheard.

"I liked it," she finally whispered.

Vic's eyes narrowed. His stroking fingers stilled. "You liked being taken hard?" His cock swelled uncomfortably behind the fly of his jeans when she just nodded her head, her eyes overtaking half her face. "You weren't a little scared, Niall?" he goaded her gently.

"No. Not of you."

"Then what?"

He saw her glance away, sensed her hesitation.

"Of myself, I guess. I've never done anything like that. It was impulsive, crazy . . ."

"Fucking great," he finished succinctly. He cradled her chin in his palm when she glanced down, forcing her to meet his gaze again.

"What do you say, Niall? Do you want to get crazy with me again?"

Her delicious lower lip fell open.

"Yes," she finally replied.

Vic just smiled and grabbed her hand, helping her out of the booth.

FOUR

"Vic!" Niall admonished a minute later when a harassed-looking man in a suit tried to hurry to get on the elevator with them and Vic blocked the entrance until the doors closed with the man on the other side of them.

Vic chuckled as he turned toward her. He reached under her armpits, lifting her slightly until her ass rested on the brass railing. He had his belly pressed tightly to hers and his considerable erection snuggled between her thighs before Niall could blink. She felt so small in his arms. So good.

"He'll get another one," he mumbled as he pressed his mouth to her neck. "This elevator is obviously being used," he muttered before he dipped his head and took her mouth.

"God, you taste good," he said a few seconds later when the doors dinged open on the seventeenth floor. "Do you know how much I wanted to do this on the night we rode the elevator together a month ago?" He nibbled and bit at her damp, upturned lips.

Niall moaned as desire uncoiled powerfully inside of her. She started when he reached back lightning quick and stopped the elevator door from closing.

"Do you, Niall?" he repeated roughly.

"I know." She wiggled her hips against him insistently until he stepped back, his jaw hanging partially open. She paused in the hallway to consider him. His gray eyes gleamed with desire. His dark brown hair had fallen forward on his forehead when he'd ravaged her mouth. "I wanted the same thing, Vic."

She unsuccessfully suppressed a smile when the elevator door started to close between them and he pushed it back violently, as though it had personally offended him by having the temerity to separate them. He reached for her hand and hauled her down the hallway.

Vic paused with his keys in the door and glanced down at her. Niall had only the impression of something sparking into his gray eyes before he reached for her. He covered her mouth with his and provided a thirsty suction at the same time that he sank between her lips, thrusting again and again, pausing to sweep her depths and rub against her tongue. When he eventually lifted his head, their breathing had escalated noticeably. He pressed his thumb into her lower lip.

"What was that for?" Niall asked dazedly. Her head spun from the taste and sensation of him.

"You had a witch's smile on your face," he said as he drew small circles on her damp lip. Niall stared at his rugged face, thoroughly hypnotized. "Come here."

She stumbled behind him as he took her hand and entered the apartment, slamming the door loudly behind him. He pulled her into the bedroom. When he dropped her hand, he immediately began to unbutton his jeans.

"You were born on the North Shore and you look pretty damn near perfect in pearls. But when I see your mouth, all I can think about is you on your knees being very unladylike," he told her.

Niall watched, spellbound, as he shoved down his jeans and a pair of white boxer briefs to his thighs. His cock jutted forward, heavy and hard, darkened and swollen with blood . . . ready to do business. He took the stiff pillar into his hand and stroked it slowly while she watched.

Niall felt warm fluid gush into her panties at the erotic image. She moaned when Vic put his hand on her shoulder and pulled her toward him. She began to willingly sink to her knees, but he abruptly stopped her. He rapidly unbuttoned her blouse.

"I want to see these while you suck me," he muttered as he ran his fingers over one of her breasts. Her nipple immediately puckered tight for him.

Vic felt her eyes on him. He paused in the process of whipping her blouse over her shoulders and met her gaze. For a second he froze at the sight of the mixed desire and confusion he saw glazing her eyes. He thought about telling her that he was so desperate at that moment because he'd thought of her time and again since he'd last touched her, recalled the musky, sweet taste of her pussy on his tongue, jacked off countless times as he replayed fucking her while she convulsed around him in orgasm.

He could have gone to bed with another woman to take the edge off. There'd been plenty of opportunities to do just that. But Vic doubted that the tension that grew in him could be alleviated by anyone else . . . at least not totally. He'd anticipated having her again until his restraint sharpened his desire to a stabbing pain.

So even though he saw uncertainty in her beautiful eyes, he chose to let the heat of the moment burn it away. She would either accept his ways or she wouldn't. He couldn't change who he was for a woman. He'd already tried that once.

Didn't work.

He tossed her blouse onto his bed and reached behind her to unfasten her ivory satin bra. His eyes remained glued to her pointed little breasts after he'd bared her. He wanted to suck on the pert beauties until the fat nipples stood red and distended above the pale, tender flesh of her breasts. The crests were already hard and pebbled with arousal. She'd melt like sugar on his tongue . . .

But his desire for Niall was so strong, so pure, that he couldn't think of anything else but finding release at that moment. Once she'd taken the edge off, *then* maybe he could think about loving her slowly.

Maybe.

"Down on your knees, baby," he ordered softly.

Niall had to use Vic's hips to steady herself as she sank before him, so dizzy had she become with desire. She didn't know why she did what he demanded without hesitation. She couldn't imagine allowing it with another man. His manner was harsh . . . crude, even.

Her vaginal muscles contracted almost painfully. Her clit burned, starved for friction when she stared at the heavy erection that bobbed just an inch before her nose. The head of his cock was fat, fleshy, and smooth, clearly defined by a quarter-inch-thick ridge from the stalk.

He was going to stretch her lips just as he had her pussy.

The realization caused a wild hunger to spread from her lower belly in every direction until it pervaded her, leaving nothing un-touched. She admitted the truth to herself before she pushed her tongue into the sensitive slit on the steely-hard knob of his penis, causing Vic to grunt sharply.

She did what he wanted because it aroused her, because she wanted to. Vic Savian pitched her into an almost unbearable level of excitement.

With that final thought she leaned forward and gave herself over completely to the sensation of him. Her tongue circled the fleshy head curiously, tracing the hard ridge beneath the full cir-cumference once. Then she stiffened her tongue and polished that smooth knob until it was shiny, coating her tongue in the flavor of him—salty, musky man. Her eyes fluttered closed rapturously as she encircled the girth of his cock with her hand and began to slowly pump the steely hard, straight flesh of the stalk. Her tongue circled, pressed, and fluttered across the head. He felt indescrib-ably good, like distilled power trapped and sheathed in the con-finement of taut skin.

She knew perfectly well she was teasing him. She sensed the tension in his lean body, heard his muted grunts. Her eyes opened and she glanced up at him furtively for confirmation—and yes. His handsome mouth pulled tight into a feral snarl. The sight made her clit pinch with excitement.

But still she teased the tiger.

Vic watched her through narrowed eyelids as her red tongue and tight, pumping hand tortured him. Her tongue was a limber tease, quick and elusive one moment, hard, stiff, and pressing the next. When she slapped at the straining head rapidly while she jacked the stalk with a loose fist, making his cock bob like a thirsty dog's tongue, he cursed violently and palmed her head.

"Suck on it, Niall, or I'm gonna spank your ass so hard you're not going to be able to sit tomorrow."

He could have sworn he saw her give him that witchy little smile before she arrowed his cock into her warm, humid depths. Her tongue pressed up on him sinuously until he was lodged securely against the hard ridge of her upper lip. She applied a steady, eye-crossing suction.

Ah, Christ, he'd been so right. Her mouth was made for sucking cock. Her mouth was made for sucking *his* cock.

His fingers sank down into her soft hair, pressing against her skull as he began to thrust between her lips, subtly at first . . . just tiny electrical pulsations. But her strong suck drew him deeper. So he gave it to her.

Yeah, he was a greedy bastard when it came to Niall.

He rocked against her more strongly, insisting she take him deep. When she did, sliding the tip of his cock into her muscular throat, Vic's eyes sprang open in ecstasy. He groaned gutturally when she slid him out sinuously until the head of his cock was trapped by tight lips, but before he could protest, she took him deep again. She repeated the process again and again until he became frantic with mounting need.

"Yeah that's right, suck me deep with that pretty mouth," he rasped mindlessly.

His eyes popped open moments later when he felt her move his cock so that she was taking him more shallowly in her mouth. He realized how forcefully he'd been thrusting his cock into her throat when he saw the tears that wet her cheeks.

Still, she was hungry and horny for him. He could tell by the way she bobbed her head over him so rapidly and hummed a tune of pure satisfaction in her throat, vibrating his cock clear to the root, making his spine tingle with excitement. She gave the meaty head a healthy slap with her tongue on each outstroke. She made such an erotic picture with her soft, wavy blonde hair framing her face, her red lips stretched wide over his girth, her bare breasts trembling delicately as she moved back and forth on him, the nipples pulled tight and hard.

When he felt her small hand caress his inner thigh and then cup a testicle, massaging him gently, Vic reached his limit. He immobilized her head with his hands and began to pump between her straining lips, deeper and deeper with each stroke.

"If you're going to tease, you're going to have to pay the price. Suck it good and hard, sweet Niall."

Tendrils of excitement rippled in Niall's lower belly, making her clit burn. Her nipples tightened painfully. Vic's raw language and actions during sex turned her on like nothing she'd ever known. Perhaps it was crude, but it also struck her as being the most honest communication she'd ever heard in her life.

He began to buck wildly into her mouth, the head of his cock massaging her throat. She gripped his ass with one hand, enthralled by the density of the large, tensing muscle as he fucked her mouth furiously. Niall knew that he wouldn't let go of her head until he shot off in her mouth.

She didn't want him to.

She loved him like this, so wild, unrestrained . . . raw. It was like having a beautiful, untamed animal allow her to ride him. Pride mixed with her arousal that she was able to pleasure him so greatly that he lost all sense of restraint.

She felt his penis swell noticeably in her mouth. He clutched her head, keeping her in place. His body shuddered violently.

"*Fuck*, that's good," he muttered almost incoherently and began to fill her mouth and throat with his creamy, musky cum.

Niall continued to suck and lick him long after the last burst of semen spilled on her tongue. His taste excited her to a fever pitch.

Vic opened his eyes. His cock was still stiff in Niall's mouth. She looked up at him with those big eyes and he smiled. He distantly recalled telling her to *suck that cock hard, little girl*. Vic had a habit of saying some pretty outrageous things when he was horny—they just sort of spilled out of his mouth—and it had occasionally gotten him into trouble with women. Jenny especially hadn't appreciated it, given the seriousness of their relationship. She'd called him a pervert on more than one occasion. Toward the end of their relationship he had refrained from speaking at all during sex.

So he was glad to see that Niall didn't seem to mind his language. She looked incredibly sexy slurping away at his cock like a starved waif who had been given a rare treat.

For a few seconds Vic seriously considered letting her bring him off all over again. But no . . . another time. He drew his partial erection out of her warm mouth, grimacing in agonized pleasure when he heard the moist popping noise his cock made when the thick rim cleared her tight lips. He put his hands on her shoulders and raised her to her feet.

"Get undressed," he muttered gruffly. But when she hastily began to unfasten her jeans, he stopped her with a hand on her jaw.

She moaned softly into his mouth when he lowered his head and gave her a slow hot, open-mouthed kiss. His fingers came up to pluck and pinch her right nipple. His other hand lightly skimmed the bare skin at her waist, causing her to shiver.

Vic forced himself to release Niall's erect nipple, determined to make love to her for once while they were both completely naked. He'd never even gotten his jeans all the way off the other day, he thought with amused self-disgust.

"Go on," Vic prodded with a grin when he lifted his head and Niall just continued to stare up at him with a dazed expression. He brushed aside a tendril of silky hair from her cheek. She was so lovely. She didn't seem to have the vaguest interest in playing the bedroom sophisticate, but she seduced him constantly with her desire-glazed eyes, her total response to his touch, and her sweet but paradoxically scorching hot smiles.

And innocent, elfin appearance or no, she'd just deep throated his cock like no woman ever had before.

Niall blinked at the sound of his amused voice. Her hands trembled in excitement as she unzipped the leather boots she'd been wearing with her jeans and peeled off her socks. Color flushed her cheeks, making him wonder if she was embarrassed about undressing in front of him. Her sexy smile when she glanced up and saw that he was already sprawled nude on the bed, his back propped against the headboard, belied self-consciousness in a big way, however.

So did the fact that she unsnapped her jeans slowly, giving him a peak of her ivory satin underwear. When she knew that she had his attention, she inserted two fingers between the, fabric and her jeans and worked them between her labia, rubbing herself sensually. His breath stuck in his lungs when she deliberately pulled aside the satin and exposed her pink, glistening folds to him. Her hips rolled against the pressure of her rubbing fingers subtly . . . sensually. He stared, recalling all too well the sensation of her plump, juicy lips against his own fingers and tongue. After a moment he peeled his eyes away and met her gaze.

His nostrils flared when he saw her little smile.

"Get your naked butt over here," he muttered darkly.

He saw the flash of anxiety that leapt into her gaze, spicing her arousal. He waited tensely while she drew her jeans and panties over her legs. She approached the bed cautiously, more than likely sensing the rising tension in him. When she drew near him, he reached up, drawing her down next to him. He grabbed her wrist. Before Niall knew what he intended, he shoved both of her fingers into his mouth. He sucked and ran his tongue between them, greedy for her sweet cream. She yelped in surprise a few seconds later when he abruptly hauled her over his lap.

"Oh!" she cried out in alarm when he spanked her bottom twice. *Smack, smack!* She struggled in his lap, but he held her down tightly with his left arm at her back. She twisted her hips desperately but he didn't mind if she made her pretty little fanny a moving target. He gave her three more brisk spankings.

"This is what you get for teasing me, Niall," he told her warmly before he popped her ass twice more. She squirmed beneath him but he took his time palming and squeezing her bottom. Her ass was like the rest of her: curvy, firm, and tight. She fit in his palm perfectly.

He removed his arm from her back and urged her up. What he'd just done had shocked Niall, but it had profoundly aroused her as well. She had tried to delete from her mind the fact that Vic had spanked her that first time while he pounded into her body . . . not to mention that she had climaxed thunderously when he did. She had never considered herself to be the type of woman who would become aroused by being spanked. But her clit throbbed and burned unbearably while she had struggled against Vic's hard body, her belly pressing tightly to his erection as he held her down and swatted her bottom at his leisure.

Guess you learn something new about yourself every day, Niall thought dazedly as Vic pulled her up until she straddled his lap. He had already torn the wrapper off a condom and was in the process of sliding it down the considerable length of his reanimated cock. Her pussy sizzled at the erotic sight, but she forced herself to frown in disapproval when Vic met her eyes. She couldn't let him get away with spanking her as he just had.

Nevertheless, when his lips curved into that naughty, sexy cowboy grin, she didn't utter a word of protest. Her body moved in synchronization with his as his left arm encircled her waist and he held up his cock.

Niall gasped when he lowered her slowly, skewering her with his steely hard flesh.

Vic's grin faded into oblivion at the sensation of her muscular, clasping vagina enfolding the first several inches of his cock. He pumped up with his hips while he held her steady for his thrust. A grunt of savage satisfaction vibrated his throat when he slipped into her tight, slippery sheath another few inches.

"Ah, Christ, you've got the sweetest little pussy," he muttered between clenched teeth. He felt her tremble in his hands. His eyes leapt to her face. He immediately paused when he saw discomfort blending with her arousal. Guilt dimmed his lust. Maybe he shouldn't be fucking her like this until she'd become more accustomed to him. When he was on top of her, he could apply a steady downward pressure at the same time that he opened her body wide with his hands.

But then he felt her vaginal muscles tightening around him, drawing him inward, and he knew he wouldn't be able to back out of her.

"Try to relax," he soothed. He sent the thumb of the hand that
cradled her between the flushed, swollen folds of her labia. He felt
her quiver and flex around his cock as he began to stimulate her
clit. Her eyes fluttered closed as he plucked and pressed against
that well-lubricated little button. His teeth clenched tight in restraint when she began to make tiny circular undulations with her
hips, stroking his cock to as much good effect as she stimulated
herself.

She put her hands on his shoulders and bucked forward slightly
with her hips, getting the indirect pressure she needed on her clit
in order to come.

"Fuck," Vic grated out as he watched Niall do a subtle, erotic
little dance on the end of his cock. When he felt her heat flood
around him and heard her sexy little whimpers, when her muscular walls began to massage him, he growled in agonized pleasure.

"Get down on that," he muttered through a snarl. He grabbed
her hips and thrust up until his aching balls pressed snugly to her
wet, delicate tissues.

She cried out sharply. Her body began to shudder more violently in orgasm. She pressed her face to his neck and whimpered
mindlessly as pleasure crashed through her.

Vic's eyes remained clamped shut. The combination of holding
her while she shuddered in climax and being buried in the epicen-
ter of it was indescribably arousing. He hung on desperately for
control as Niall trembled and milked his cock like a silken fist.
When her spasms finally waned, he took a few moments to gather
himself, feeling like the survivor of a particularly powerful storm.

Niall's eyes blinked open heavily when she felt Vic spread his
big hands along her hips, sinking his fingers into her buttocks.

"Ahhhh," she moaned uncontrollably when he began to slowly rock her up and down and around on his cock. She had dazedly wondered earlier, when he had first pierced her flesh with his cock, how she could have loved it so much that first night. He filled her to the point of unbearable tightness. But as the hard, smooth knob of his penis slowly massaged some supersensitive place deep inside of her, Niall recalled why she'd become so frantic with lust.

She remembered all too well.

"Yes . . . oh, *yes!*" she cried breathlessly. Her hips began to join in the pleasurable rhythm of their mating.

"Lean back a little," Vic ordered tensely. When she did, his eyes fixed on the hard, dark pink berries of her nipples as she moved on top of him like a sleek, sinuous cat. When she held on to his shoulders and started to wildly buck up and down on his cock, he winced at the pleasure. He spanked her bottom lightly, getting her attention.

"Hold still a minute," he ordered, his eyes flashing up to her sweat-glazed face. He willed his hips to stay still even though he was sheathed in a wet, warm pussy that was both about two sizes too small for his cock and fit him perfectly—whichever way you wanted to look at it.

Niall stared down at him, panting heavily as he secured her hip with one hand while the other trailed gently up the sensitive side of her torso. She bit her lip to restrain a loud moan. Something about the way that Vic could be so hard and relentless during lovemaking, but at the same time gave the lightest, most sensitive caresses, excited her unbearably.

"Vic," she entreated huskily as his hand swept beneath her armpit and cradled a breast from below. Niall squirmed in his lap in intense arousal when he stared at her for a few seconds. He smacked her bottom once to still her and then leaned forward—as though he had all the time in the world—and flicked her nipple with his tongue.

Niall's vagina flexed inward in excruciating arousal as she watched him lick and lave the sensitive kernel of flesh. Vic must have felt her uncontrollable inner caress because his eyes flashed up to her face. Her eyes widened at something she saw in his gaze. The next thing she knew, he'd flung his arm over her shoulder and gripped her hip and ass tightly, completely immobilizing her body on his lap.

He took a good portion of her breast into his warm mouth and began to agitate and torture the captive nipple. Niall whimpered and moaned as he lashed at the sensitive flesh with his tongue and bit her between his front teeth. She felt his cock surge and swell inside of her body at the same time that he held her nipple still with his teeth and rubbed tightly against it with his stiffened tongue.

She exploded again. Because he forced her into immobility, her orgasm had a tight, concentrated quality to it that verged on pain.

Vic growled at the sensation of liquid heat gushing around his cock. He leaned back on the pillows, dug his fingers into her ass, and began to lift her up and down on him at the same time that he pumped and withdrew in short strokes. He moved her over him in a tight, sinuous, circular rhythm, rocking her hips back and forth as he moved in and out of her, stimulating her clit. She continued to massage and suck his cock inward as she came. She was so light that he lifted her with ease before plunging her back down, serving her sleek little body to his straining cock.

Why, exactly, had he always preferred ample, voluptuous women when he might have been enjoying such a taut, fluid ride?

He'd always assumed that they'd be able to weather his rough manner in bed, and for the most part he'd been right. But Niall stood as solid proof that a woman didn't have to be nice and fleshy to like it good and hard.

When he felt himself cresting, he lifted her high off his penis and rocketed into her in four long, furious hammer strikes.

Niall's surprised scream of renewed orgasm ignited him.

He wanted to pump her tight, spasming channel as he came, but he found that he couldn't move as orgasm crashed though him. It was like his brain short-circuited from the immensity of the pleasure, temporarily paralyzing him.

He held on to Niall desperately, his face pressed to her soft breast. He shook as he poured himself deep inside of her.

They remained clasped like that for minutes, their breathing at first harsh and ragged, segueing to an agitated pant, and finally smoothing to a shared rhythmic, waving motion.

Vic nuzzled her breast, inhaling her singular scent. It felt so good to hold her like this, his sharp lust dulled for the moment to the soft ache of desire. He absorbed her fluttering heartbeat into his lips and cheeks until it slowed to a strong, steady beat. Tenderness welled up in him. The tension of reawakened arousal mixed with it, causing his cock to stir inside of her.

It dumbfounded him.

He was going to have to have her yet again. The realization made his satiated muscles stiffen slightly.

Just what the hell did he think he was doing with Niall Chandler, anyway?

FIVE

Niall felt exhausted and extremely well-satisfied, but she'd still noticed the tension that leapt suddenly into Vic's body.

"What's wrong?" she mumbled into the crevice between his shoulder and neck.

"Nothing," he grunted. He lifted her and set her down carefully on the bed next to him.

Niall sat up and shook her hair out of her sweat-dampened face. "Yes, there is," she stated after inspecting his stony expression. "What is it?"

He made that characteristic subtle rolling motion with his jaw as he studied her.

"I guess you must think I'm a grade-A asshole for not asking you this until now, but can you get pregnant?"

Niall blanched. Her gaze flew down to his cock. "Yes. Oh, my God . . . Was there something wrong with the condom?"

He winced slightly. "No, I didn't mean that. I just should be more careful about withdrawing from you afterward if you can get pregnant, that's all," he mumbled. Niall watched him, feeling perplexed. He got up and sauntered to the bathroom, reminding Niall of a wild animal, supremely confident and graceful in his natural state of nudity. When he returned a few moments later, he kissed her lightly as he came down next to her on the bed.

"Aren't you worried about catching something from me?" he asked bluntly.

Niall's cheeks burned. The answer was "no," but she felt like too much of a fool for saying it. She was like a teenage boy in the first hormonal throes of lust, wild to have sex with Vic for the lame, downright pitiful reason that if *felt so damned good* . . . and she was so hungry, so desperate to feel alive.

"Hey, it's all right," Vic said in his slow, soothing drawl when he saw how her face collapsed with emotion. His hands came up to cradle her head, his fingers furrowing into the waves of her hair. "I'm as healthy as one of my horses, I swear. Granted, that doesn't mean much to you, but if you knew me, it would. I just had a checkup two weeks ago and I got a clean bill of health. I always wear protection, Niall—without fail."

His face stiffened in concern when she just shook her head, made speechless by emotion.

"Course, I should turn you over my knee if you actually believe a line like that from a guy who screwed his neighbor the second after he knew her name."

That pierced Niall's temporary mortification. She blinked rapidly, bringing him into focus. His handsome mouth quirked ever so slightly into a grin.

"I'm kidding, Niall. I might be a moody son of a bitch when

I'm writing, and my sister and a hundred or so other people have told me that I've got a foul temper, but I don't lie. That's not one of my vices. I hate lies."

Niall burst abruptly into laughter. It felt bittersweet to have Vic encircle her in his arms and tighten his hold while emotion washed over her. Laughter continued to burble out of her throat uncontrollably. She carefully hid the tears that scattered down her cheeks.

What could she tell him? Nothing about the intense passion she had for him made any sense. She felt too embarrassed . . . too vulnerable to say out loud that she couldn't picture herself in a million years behaving in this wild, uninhibited, impulsive fashion with another man.

She had some kind of intense crush on Vic Savian.

And he would undoubtedly be the one who was mortified if she ever went into the ugly details of her life, poured out her heart, told him how it felt so heavenly to feel life coursing vibrantly in her veins again. This was supposed to be a mutually satisfying sexual relationship, not an opportunity for Niall to cry all over Vic while he played psychotherapist for her.

How desperate could she get? Niall stared sightlessly at Vic's iron bedstead, and muffled laughter came in semi-hysterical bursts past her lips. She'd been so frozen, so numb for the past few years.

Why couldn't she have been like most people and awakened from her trauma gradually instead of in the fierce, volatile explosion of desire and passion that Vic had ignited in her?

Vic stiffened when he felt a splash of wetness fall on his shoulder. For some reason he couldn't bear the sadness that he saw in Niall's eyes at times. He gently scooted her down on the pillows.

He refused to look at her face as he came down over her, not wanting to acknowledge her sadness.

There was only one way that he knew of to get rid of it, temporary though it was.

Maybe it was selfish. Who knew? Vic was the first to admit he was a savage when it came to dealing with a woman's tears. If he couldn't beat the hell out of whatever was making Niall miserable, than he'd fuck her until he saw the look of glazed ecstasy in her beautiful eyes that he much preferred.

Yeah, they were caveman tactics, but *shit* . . . he barely knew her, right? He wasn't certain that he *wanted* to know more about her. As drawn as he was to Niall, he was skittish about jumping into the dangerous, shark-infested waters of a woman's emotions.

He noticed how she furtively wiped at the tears on her cheeks but forced himself to focus on the sight of her naked body. It easily distracted him. He reached up and fondled her breasts. He lifted both and removed his hands quickly, enjoying the sight of them popping pertly back into their original position.

Enjoying it a lot.

He popped the pert little beauties several times, scraping his palms across her stiffened nipples as he released her, and growling in aroused satisfaction like a big cat playing with its prey.

"You're so firm," he muttered. He plucked and pinched her nipples. The red tips made his mouth water. Her breasts were perfectly shaped, but the unusually large, succulent nipples drove him wild.

"You liked it when I spanked you earlier, didn't you?"

Niall's lips fell open in surprise at his abrupt question. His light eyes flickered to her face and held her gaze.

"I . . . I'm not sure . . . I . . ." Niall stammered.

His stared down at her, unrelenting.

"Yes," she whispered after a few seconds.

He leaned down without any further comment and slipped a tasty, fat nipple between his lips and teeth, drawing on her. He consumed her greedily, sucking and nipping at the sensitive flesh. Niall beaded tight at his harsh treatment, which was creating an unbearable ache in her sex. He continued to play with her other breast with his hand, fondling and squeezing and pinching.

Niall moaned. Her hips lifted off the bed in an instinctive motion. His hard suction on her nipple pulled at some invisible cord deep in her vagina, making her long to have the hard length of his penis rubbing and agitating it like he did when he fucked her. He made her forget her self-consciousness and anxiety so easily, transformed her into a purely carnal creature.

How did he do it so effortlessly?

She arched her back and purred with desire. When she reached for his head and ran her fingers through his thick hair, however, he sat up slightly and grabbed her wrists. He pinned them over her head with his left hand and returned to feasting on her achy, distended nipple in the matter of a second.

Niall whimpered and cried out in increasing desire as he held her down and took his time with her, teasing, sucking, and biting gently at her breasts until he finally sat up to appreciate the results. Her nipples looked lividly red in comparison to her white breasts, like juicy, sweet strawberries topping the two mounds of creamy flesh. They felt unbearably sensitive. He'd drawn so much blood to the surface with his steady, hot suck, enflaming the nerve endings with his lashing tongue and pinching fingers.

He turned to her sensitive flanks next, biting, scraping, and licking hotly along the tender skin from just a few inches below her armpit to her waist. She gasped in pleasure. Her skin roughened against his tongue. He eventually let go of her wrists so that he could run his lips over her stomach, exploring her slowly, eventually dipping the tip of his tongue into her bellybutton. She inhaled sharply when he traced a warm, damp trail from the indentation to just above her pubic hair.

Niall gasped in the throes of a sharp arousal that quickly accelerated to an agony. She threaded her fingers into his thick hair, then pressed her fingertips to his neck. She couldn't get enough of his texture or the fierce heat that always seemed to resonate from his body. She spread her thighs wide . . . inviting him . . . *begging* him to put her out of her misery.

But as she was rapidly discovering, Vic went strictly by his timetable when it came to making love.

She made a startled sound of protest when he shifted off her suddenly and she was deprived of his elemental heat. He stood and grabbed his discarded jeans off the floor, roughly whipping the supple leather belt through the loops. Niall's eyes widened when he came back on the bed with the strap held in his hand.

"Grab one of the posts on the headboard."

"W . . . Why?" she asked, her eyes wide with anxiety.

"I'm going to tie you up. I want you completely at my mercy."

He was curious as to how she would respond. Although he'd just spoken the truth, it wasn't the only reason he was going to tie Niall up. The fact was that her small hands on his body, her hungry, sensitive touch, drove him nuts. He'd been enjoying himself nibbling and licking and kissing her beautiful body. He couldn't wait to get on with the feast of the rest of her tasty, silky skin, not to mention his juicy, luscious dessert—Niall's pussy. But twenty seconds of her fingernails scraping his scalp, of her sensitive fingertips skimming along his neck, and her palms molding the muscles of his shoulders had turned Vic's cock into a stiff, straining spear, thoroughly eager to be sheathed in her tight pussy all over again.

Vic would be the first to say he liked the idea of tying her up. He liked it a lot. But he demanded it now for his own control as much as for hers.

Niall wondered in rising anxiety if it really was possible for one's heart to stop altogether, because that sure was what it seemed like when Vic calmly told her that he wanted to tie her up.

I want you completely at my mercy.

She'd never done anything like that before in bed, although she had admittedly fantasized about it dozens of times over the past week and a half. Maybe it was because of the way Vic had held her wrists so securely that first time while he'd played her clit expertly, forcing her body to experience shattering pleasure before he fucked her pussy like it was his to do with as he pleased.

Niall had to bite her lip to refrain from moaning out loud at the impact of that forbidden thought.

Her eyes lowered to the brown strap that was bunched in his hand and immediately flickered over to his jutting penis. She longed for the sensation beneath her fingertips of the swollen veins that ran under the taut, smooth skin. She hungered for the feeling of the tapered, thick cap in her throat . . .

Heat flushed her sex and face.

He would give her his touch. He would eventually give her his tasty cock if she agreed to what he wanted. She swallowed convulsively and reached for the bedpost.

She might as well grimace and bear it.

Her eyes stayed fixed on his cock when he lunged forward on the bed. It bobbed less than a foot away from her face, teasing her.

When she felt him twist his belt around her wrists several times, however, pulling them comfortably but still tightly to the bed-posts, she pulled her gaze off the arousing sight of his cock.

"Oh!" she murmured in surprise when instead of buckling the supple leather, he tied it into a taut knot with sure hands and bunching biceps that seemed to shout loud and clear that Vic knew *exactly* what he was doing. Was that because of his background with horses or because he was used to tying a woman up in bed? Niall fought rising anxiety. She had vaguely imagined that her re-straint would be more for show than anything if she could merely use her fingers to unfasten the buckle in a panic situation.

But as she ran her fingers clumsily over the impossibly tight knot and jerked down with her wrists, Niall was forced to admit that she really *was* at Vic's mercy.

Her eyes flickered up to his face. He was kneeling over her, six feet and several inches of lean, hard man. Her gaze skimmed across his powerful thighs dusted with black hair and lingered on his penis. Had it grown and stiffened in the last few seconds since he'd tied her up? It looked ruddy, ready . . . and, in truth, down-right intimidating from this angle.

Vic resisted a powerful urge to touch himself when he saw the whites of Niall's large eyes as she stared at him. He had another urge, a darker one, to straddle her chest and give her one hell of a face fucking. She looked incredibly lovely lying there—his little captive—sexy, aroused, and just a bit anxious about what was going to happen next . . .

"Niall," he said. He waited until she stared into his face.

"Do you trust me?"

Niall looked into his piercing gray eyes. Something seemed to

pass between them, something beyond a mutual message of profound, distilled lust. She nodded quickly.

The shadow of a smile pulled at Vic's thin, well-shaped lips.

"Good," he murmured. "Now spread your thighs nice and
wide."

His nostrils flared like a feral animal's when she complied and
he saw firsthand just how flexible Niall was. He realized he'd never
had her open her shapely thighs wide for him, so he'd never known
until now just how good she was at doing it. His cock throbbed
greedily at the sight of her naked, spread-eagled, and tied to his
bed. He couldn't wait to get between those silky thighs.

But first . . .

He knelt over her and filled his hands with her breasts. With
her hands tied over her head and her back arched slightly, they
were begging Vic to pay them their due. The fleshy, milky cones
and the fat red nipples really did something to him, Vic thought,
distantly amused at his sharp excitement. He shifted his hips,
stroking his cock along the satiny skin of her belly while he played
with her breasts to his heart's content, molding them in his palms,
bouncing them, pinching the nipples.

"Damn, these are the prettiest tits I've ever seen."

His eyes leapt to her face when he heard her groan. Her cheeks
were stained bright red. Her eyes shone with lust. Sweat glistened
on her upper lip and forehead. She panted shallowly through parted,
lush lips. He laughed shortly, thoroughly in approval of her obvious
arousal, before he moved between her thighs.

He felt her eyes on him as he ran his hands down her thighs
and palmed a slender calf. Her skin flowed like warm silk next to
his lips when he bent and brushed them against the inside of one
knee. He began to make his way up her thighs, taking his time,
stroking her contours, kissing and nibbling at her honey-colored

skin. He could smell her musk perfuming the air as he made his way closer to her pussy. The fact that she began to tremble and vibrate in his hands and make desperate, sexy little whimpers in her throat made him press a smile to her inner thigh.

He could easily become addicted to this woman.

He finally hovered above her pussy, shaking with desire at the anticipation of eating her again. His hands came up to cradle her restless hips, keeping her still for his attack. He flicked his tongue over her swollen labia quickly, gently. Even with such a darting caress he came away drenched with her cream.

When Vic's brain registered that intoxicant, he lost it.

Niall felt like she was about to shatter into a million pieces. She couldn't take the tension anymore. She couldn't take being stretched on the rack of Vic's singular brand of torture. She'd never been so focused on anything in her life as she was on Vic's hands and mouth over the past several minutes. He'd taken away the possibility of fragmenting her attention from his sensual onslaught by tying her up. There was no way she could reciprocate . . . she could only take what he gave her.

Take . . . and anticipate what she would have to endure next. Take and receive.

Oh, *God*, did she receive. Her entire body had become an exquisite receptor of sensory stimuli.

Niall felt herself rise over the crest of orgasm as she watched Vic's tongue flick ever so lightly against the sensitive folds of her outer sex. She tried to raise her hips to press herself against that elusive, teasing tongue, but he held her steady. A plea rose in her throat, but before she had a chance to release it, he abruptly plunged his stiffened tongue between her sensitive labia and licked everywhere, agitating her clit, lashing it, sucking the nerve-packed flesh without mercy.

She screamed as orgasm crashed violently into her. Her back arched off the bed. Her wrists pulled at her restraints, but she couldn't escape Vic's mouth. He continued to eat her, moving his jaws in a relentless rhythm, sucking her clit between his teeth, nipping, biting . . . abusing her delicate tissues.

And God, she loved it.

She writhed in an agony of pure ecstasy. The first climax that broke over her was almost too sharp to bear, but her tension level and his ruthless treatment of her hypersensitive tissues had her crashing in orgasm again almost before the spasms had waned from her previous climax.

After she'd quieted as much as she possibly could when Vic continued to slurp and suck at her, she whimpered for him to stop. She couldn't take this anymore. Never in a million years would she have guessed that someone could make her *feel* so damn much.

Vic dimly heard her calling out to him. When he saw the desperation on Niall's face, he forced himself to pull his tongue from between her luscious, swollen lips. He wouldn't allow her to talk him out of plunging his tongue into her pussy several times, though, high and hard. He held her gaze while he did it. He loved how wide her eyes got as she watched his tongue fuck her almost as much as he did the flavor of her honeyed musk. She tasted so damn good that he wanted to keep it up, but his protesting cock wouldn't let him.

He slapped her inner thigh lightly as he loomed over her.

"Spread your legs wide again," he rasped. He grunted in appreciation when she opened her golden thighs so wide she was pretty damn near doing a split for him. Her pussy looked red and wet . . . like an invitation to his wildest fantasies. His eyes kept returning to the luscious sight while he rolled on another condom.

He knelt in front of her and lifted her up over his knees, hold- ing her hips with one hand while the other arrowed his cock into that welcoming little tunnel. Their shouts entwined as pleasure jolted through both of them when he flexed his hips and plunged his length into her.

Vic's gaze was on her when Niall opened her eyes after she'd absorbed the shock of his cock pushing into her body. His mouth twisted.

"Is that what you wanted, honey?" he taunted softly as he be- gan to thrust in and out, keeping her thighs spread wide in the air. His pelvis smacked loudly and rapidly against her completely spread pussy and thighs. As exposed as she was, she felt like he stimulated every inch of her sensitive flesh . . . the defined, hard knob of his cock massaging the sweet spot deep in her body, his heavy balls slapping against moist, sensitive skin, his pelvis crash- ing against her tender lips and clit.

"God, yes," she whispered breathlessly, barely able to speak as he pummeled her.

Vic's eyes glowed with manic lust. He abruptly pushed her legs back, making her scream as he fixed her feet beneath the horizon- tal wrought-iron post of the bedstead.

"Keep 'em there," he ordered before he rose over her, support- ing his body on the bedstead. He pounded into her. The angle of the position that he forced her to take was as uncompromising as it was wickedly arousing. She couldn't have maintained it for long,

as hard as Vic drove into her, but Niall could tell by the fierce,
wild expression on his face that his orgasm loomed.

"Fuck *yeeaaahhh!*" he grated out as he hammered into her one
last time. He clenched his eyes shut and groaned in agonized pleasure.

Niall felt a genuine level of discomfort as she felt him swell inside her vagina. But by the time she felt him throb in climax within
her, the angle making the sensation of him coming even more potent than ever before, her lust overcame her pain. She pressed against
him tighter, tilting her hips up rhythmically to get the pressure she
needed.

And she was exploding right there with him.

"Ah, baby, *that's so good,*" he muttered. He pumped her hard
throughout his orgasm. Finally, his upper body sagged against the
bedstead as exhaustion overcame him.

Niall blinked her eyes open and took in the expression on his
face. She released her feet. "Untie me, Vic," she whispered. "I want
to touch you."

"Sorry," he grunted sheepishly.

"Where are you going?" Niall asked in stunned disbelief when
he suddenly got off her and stood.

"Hold your horses. I'll be right back," he assured her. He came
back a few seconds later, carrying a large pair of scissors.

"Vic, what the hell . . . ?"

"Calm down," he muttered with a grin. "It's the only way I'm
gonna get you loose. I tied off a tight fucker."

She gasped when he matter-of-factly cut his belt in half, free-
ing her wrists and making the buckle clank loudly as it fell on the
iron bed.

"Your belt is ruined," she murmured huskily. She held out her arms for him. He tossed aside the scissors and clambered onto the bed.

"You think I care? That was a damn better use for a piece of leather than holding up my pants any time," he said through a widening grin that he pressed repeatedly to her neck. She chuckled softly and lifted her hands to touch the smooth skin over his solid shoulder muscles. She closed her eyes and inhaled the sublimity of the sensation. A satisfied lethargy pervaded her. Because he let her indulge so infrequently in touching his beautiful body at her leisure, she appreciated doing it exponentially.

She sighed deeply.

Vic raised his head at the sound. She watched him through the narrow slit of eyelids that grew heavier by the second. She registered that he smiled . . . not wide, but enough for her to see his crooked front tooth.

And then she succumbed to a deep, profound sleep.

It should have been you, Niall. It should have been you!

The sharp, staccato cracking noise of gunshots followed by a muffled cry of terror—

Niall started into hyperalertness, knowing immediately that the sound of distress had been her own. She experienced this too frequently to think otherwise. Instinct told her that she lay alone in Vic's bed. A beam of light glowed through a crack in the bedroom door. She rose and fumbled for her shirt and panties on the floor.

She noted her perspiration-glazed face when she looked into the mirror in Vic's bathroom. This, too, came as no surprise. The nights that she didn't awaken with her heart pounding in fear and her body drenched in sweat were becoming less frequent.

Still, good nights were the exception, not the rule.

She wet a washcloth with cool water and used the soap at the sink to repair the aftereffects of her nightmare and several rounds of phenomenal sex.

It was nice to think of their lovemaking while her body still tried to recover from the bad dream. Her hand slowed as she washed her thighs. The slight soreness and tingling sensation at her breasts and sex strangely satisfied her instead of striking her as unpleasant.

A few moments later she padded barefoot into Vic's living room. She paused next to the end of the couch when she saw him. She studied him while he worked, completely unaware of her presence.

He wore only a pair of black sweats tied low on his lean hips. His dark brown hair fell on his forehead as he leaned over in deep concentration. What looked like a typed manuscript lay in his lap. Other pieces of paper and tablets were scattered on the coffee table in front of him. He occasionally wrote on the pages with quick, almost angry movements of his pencil or turned a page briskly.

His glasses intrigued her. How could such a big, masculine man who looked like he would thrive in the brisk outdoors doing hard manual labor look so natural wearing glasses while he worked at his art with total focus?

A strange, unwelcome feeling overcame her. At that moment Vic Savian seemed so vast to her. She'd come to know only the tiniest part of him . . . the outer limits of the universe of his character.

Niall didn't think that she'd moved or made a sound, but suddenly his chin shifted and his eyes pinned her. A feeling overcame her that took her a moment to recognize.

Shyness? She laughed at herself for that. Why would that feeling overwhelm her at *this* moment and not when he'd tied her to his bed and had his way with her as he had earlier?

"I'm sorry, I saw the light. I didn't mean to bother you," she said in a hushed voice that paid tribute to the early morning hour.

"Come here," Vic said after a moment of silence.

Niall came around to sit on the sofa. She'd just seen something in his usually impassive expression that amazed her.

"You're nervous, aren't you? About the opening of your play next week?" she asked as she sat and folded her legs beneath her.

He yanked off his glasses and pressed his fingers into his clenched eyelids. Niall could almost feel the burn he must be experiencing. Had he slept at all?

"I always get nervous, but this fucking monster is gonna flop hard enough to give me whiplash. Forget about the damage it might do to the unsuspecting public," he muttered after a few seconds.

He glanced up sharply when Niall chuckled.

"What's so funny?" he asked sourly.

Niall refused to be cowed by his scowl. She'd been around artists since her undergraduate days, which meant she had plenty of exposure to the artistic temperament. "I just had this image of you madly flipping switches at a control panel behind the eyes of some kind of raging Godzilla monster. I have a feeling the citizens of Chicago will survive, Vic."

He stared coldly at her a few seconds before he exhaled, the taut muscles of his abdomen relaxing slightly. "Not so sure I will, though."

"You always have before."

"That's debatable," he replied sullenly. His expression shifted as if he'd heard himself and hadn't cared for the sound. He wore a small, sheepish grin by the time his gaze met hers. She returned the smile.

"What's your play called?" she asked softly.

His eyes flickered over her bare legs. He reached for the knitted throw folded across the back of the couch. "Lie back," he directed. When she did, he picked up the manuscript in his lap, replacing it with her feet. "*Alias X,*" he finally replied. "Do you want to see it? We're having a run-through tomorrow night," he said while he tucked the blanket around her.

"Are you worried I'll get trampled by the fleeing crowd on opening night?" she murmured.

He palmed one of her thighs through the blanket. "You've got good legs. You'll likely get out alive." He smiled at her muffled snort of laughter. "You're better off seeing it tomorrow night. No one likes to be around me on opening night. No one. Not even my mother."

"Hmmm," she hummed contentedly from inside her warm knit cocoon. "Godzilla's night to rampage, huh?"

He gave her a glance of dark amusement before he briskly picked up the manuscript. Niall sensed he was finished chatting, but it didn't feel like a dismissal. She found herself getting sleepy at the sound of his scratching pencil and the lulling sensations of his movements vibrating down into her feet.

"It's gonna be great," she muttered sleepily, more to herself than to him.

This time she slept without dreams.

SIX

Vic put two extra scoopfuls of coffee into the filter before he switched on the pot the next morning and headed toward the bathroom. He needed the extra caffeine. Niall's sleeping form on the couch drew his gaze. His pace slowed and then stalled for a few seconds as he examined her. Her hair spread across a pillow and partially covered her face. The morning sunlight shimmered in the golden strands, almost making them seem alive. She looked so small huddled beneath the knit blanket. He could easily imagine how good it would feel having her soft, warm body mold against his as she slowly awakened to his touch. The fantasy was potent enough to make his cock lurch almost painfully against his sweatpants.

He forced himself to move away from her. He smiled as he turned on the shower in the bathroom. Niall hadn't moved a millimeter since she'd fallen asleep last night. She must have been exhausted. Not too surprising after the great sex they'd had, Vic thought with a trace of smugness. He'd slept solidly himself for three and a half hours afterward—a small miracle, given Vic's typical incessant restlessness in the weeks before an opening.

By the time he exited the bathroom door in a billow of steam ten minutes later, he felt fantastic—strong and full of purpose. As he poured himself a cup of coffee, he glanced up distractedly at the sound of someone pounding loudly on a door out in the hallway.

"Niall? Honey? Wake up!" a woman called.

Vic catiously set his cup on the counter and moved out into the hall of his apartment, ear cocked to catch the voices.

"Why didn't she ever give us a key in case of an emergency?" the woman asked impatiently.

"She was supposed to have lived here for only two months. There wasn't any need," a man responded in a clipped voice. Another round of loud knocking ensued. Vic stepped back into the living room and gently brushed aside the hair from Niall's face.

"*Niall.* Wake up, baby," he ordered.

His mouth pressed into a hard line when she moved restlessly and then settled back into deep sleep. The people in the hall conversed in a tense tone before they started another round of door hammering that made his jaw clench in irritation.

"She's not in there."

Vic registered the amazed expressions on the couple's faces when they turned around a moment later at his harsh proclamation.

Niall's parents, he thought immediately when he saw the woman's face. It was like looking into a magic mirror to see how Niall would look in twenty-odd years. If that was the case, Niall was one hell of a lucky woman. The woman who stood in front of him was a knockout—more polished than Niall, less approachable, diamond-hard . . . completely flawless. Vic found himself staring at her nose, not realizing until later that he searched for what he missed—the adorable imperfection of Niall's freckles. Her eyes— not hazel like her daughter's, but instead a startling shade of azure—flickered over his body. Vic forced his expression into neutrality.

Great. Stellar first impression. He wore only a towel.

"How do you know Niall isn't in there?" the tall, distinguished-looking man barked sharply. "Did you hear her leave this morning?"

"No. She hasn't left for work yet."

The man glanced back uneasily at Niall's front door. "But you said—"

"I'm right here, Dad." Vic turned at the sound of Niall's low, sleep-roughened voice. Sunlight flooded her from behind, making the exposed skin of her legs and face look ethereally pale.

Vic didn't need to look at Niall's parents in the tense seconds that followed to know that they were doing the equivalent of manually lifting their lower lips off the hallway carpet. Niall's face, on the other hand, looked like it had been carved from marble.

"Is it an emergency?" Niall asked, dread lacing her tone.

Her father recovered first from his shock at seeing his daughter half-dressed in the company of a nearly naked man. "*Yes*, Niall. It is."

Vic tensed unconsciously at Niall's father's tone of voice. Something in it seemed to imply that Niall was somehow responsible for whatever the emergency was. Vic didn't take too kindly to that insinuation, especially when he saw that whatever tiny remnant of color Niall possessed in her cheeks had faded completely.

She ducked her head as she turned. "I'll just get my things," she murmured.

Vic glanced back at the hostile-looking couple before he let the door close heavily with them on the other side of it. Trying to make "nice-nice" with Niall's parents at that moment would have been a big mistake.

"I'm sorry," Niall said a few seconds later when she came out of his bedroom. She paused as she hastily zipped her leather boot. "I don't think I'll be able to make your play tonight."

"Don't worry about it," Vic said from the doorway of the kitchen.

She gave him a harried look of apology before she started for the door.

"Niall," he said, garnering her attention before her hand reached the knob. He waited until her big eyes met his. "I'll call you later this afternoon," he added pointedly.

Her gaze shifted away from his. "*Don't*. I mean . . . it's not necessary. I . . . I have to go."

Vic stood there after she left, listening. No more voices from the hallway, just the sound of Niall's keys rattling in the hostile silence.

Niall glanced up when her father approached her in the waiting room of Covenant General Hospital. They'd done nothing but sit and wait since arriving four hours ago.

She accepted the cup of coffee that Niall Chandler Sr. handed her. *Niall* was a family name, passed on for seven generations of Chandler men. Since Niall and Alexis Chandler hadn't supplied the required male, their baby girl had been the recipient of that particular family honor.

The original Niall Chandler had made a lasting name for himself almost two hundred years ago by building a financial empire for his descendants through several activities, the milder of which was usury and the more stringent of which would be called extortion and loan-sharking in this day and age. Niall had mixed feelings about reverting to her maiden name a year ago. She'd wanted a fresh start, but the name Chandler was associated with almost as much emotional baggage as her married name.

Almost.

For well over a century now the Chandlers had been squeaky clean in regard to their business activities. Still, the taint lingered sufficiently that Niall's father didn't take too kindly to his daughter's tongue-in-cheek references to their august ancestor's checkered past.

"You and Mom should go home," Niall told her father quietly.

"Don't be ridiculous," Alexis Chandler said briskly. Her erect carriage hadn't wilted in the slightest during the interminable wait. Alexis worked out for two hours every day at her health club. Her ramrod-straight posture came from a lifetime of riding horses. She rode rain or shine, every day without fail.

Niall knew firsthand just how strong her mother was, both mentally and physically. Niall herself practiced a fairly rigorous yoga routine, but she nowhere near approximated the magnitude of her mother's fitness and energy level. During the crisis three years ago—at the frenzied heights of Matthew Manning's trial—Alexis had been as staunch and solid as a marble pillar while Niall's world crumbled around her to ashes.

Her mother removed the lid from the coffee cup and blew on the steaming liquid delicately. "We wouldn't dream of leaving when a family member is in a crisis, Niall. You know that."

"There's nothing we can do here, Mom, least of all give comfort," Niall said wearily. She'd sat like this in waiting rooms too many times not to feel the sense of suffocating helplessness press upon her. This was all part and parcel of the chaos of Stephen's life, something that Niall knew all too intimately.

Her mother and father didn't know the half of it.

"They said there was no permanent damage done," Niall continued. "I was considering going myself."

Alexis's hand froze in the act of replacing the lid on her coffee.
Her expression was rigid with disbelief when she met Niall's gaze.
"How can you say that? Would you really feel right about walking
out of this hospital? Is it because that woman—What's her name?
Menendez?—just got here?"

Niall set her coffee cup on her knee to make it less obvious that
she trembled. When would this get easier? Would it ever?

"Her name is Rose Gonzalez. She's Stephen's legal guardian
now, Mom . . . not me," Niall added pointedly. "I'm sorry that
they contacted you this morning from Evergreen Park. You were
the follow-up contact from before . . . from before Rose became his
legal guardian. They must not have changed their records yet."

"Just because you gave up the right to make his legal decisions
for him doesn't mean that you're not Stephen's wife, Niall," Alexis
said, her eyes glittering like a pair of cut and polished blue to-
pazes.

Niall swallowed convulsively, keenly aware that her father
listened closely to the conversation. She took a deep, fortifying
breath.

"I won't be that for long, either," she reminded them both, even
though it was her mother's hurt, furious gaze that she met steadily
while she spoke.

"Then it's no wonder Stephen tried to commit suicide again,"
Alexis said before she stood and crossed the waiting room. The
full cup of coffee landed with a dull thump in the trash can.

She'll apologize for it when she calms down, Niall assured herself repeatedly as she returned to the waiting room after a stroll
around the hospital grounds. She'd told Rose Gonzalez that she

would wait to speak with her before she left, but Niall didn't think
she could wait alone in that room another second after her parents' cold departure.

Her mother's verbal stab had hurt for many reasons, the least
of which being that what she said wasn't true. Stephen had not in
fact tried to commit suicide.

Not this time.

On this particular occasion Stephen had attempted to strangle
a fellow patient at the Evergreen Park Mental Hospital and then
viciously attacked the two employees who tried to restrain him.
He had suffered a dislocated collarbone and several severe contu-
sions in the altercation, which is why he'd been transferred in a
heavy state of sedation to Covenant General. Although suicidal
behavior was the symptom that Niall's parents chose to focus
upon almost exclusively, her husband had just as frequently become aggressive and even homicidal in the past several years.

Niall possessed firsthand knowledge of both of those particular symptoms of her husband's psychosis.

In all fairness to her parents, Niall hadn't always been forthcoming about Stephen's past episodes of violence toward her. It
was painful enough to learn the language of mental illness and to
speak of suicide openly. But Niall doubted that many people ever
became comfortable talking about how their spouse had once
nearly strangled them in a drunken, psychotic rage and had threatened to do something similar countless times since then.

Rose Gonzalez's kind, open countenance was the first thing
that Niall saw when she returned to the waiting room. The Illinois
State Guardian always looked polished and professional in her
grooming and dress. But her round face, wide forehead, colorful
clothing, and plump waistline always made Niall think of a cozy
kitchen and savory smells from a bubbling pot on the stove.

Nevertheless, she was more than a little surprised when Rose
gave her a searching look before she stood and hugged her tightly.
Such an act of caring and generosity from a person Niall had
known for less than six months made her eyes burn with repressed
emotion.

"Sit down, Niall," Rose encouraged. She watched Niall closely
as she followed her instructions and then sat down next to her. "I
was going to ask how you're holding up, but I think I've already
got my answer."

Niall shook her head impatiently, irritated by the rogue tears
that escaped her eyes. "I've been doing well, actually, until this
latest incident."

"I was a little surprised to see you and your parents here at the
hospital," Rose admitted gently.

Niall explained about Evergreen Park's mistake with the emergency contact information.

"Your mother and father still think it was a wrong decision for
you to give up guardianship of Stephen?" Rose more stated than
asked.

Niall nodded as she swiped the back of her hand over wet cheek.
"Thank you," Niall murmured when Rose reached into her large,
bright pink bag and withdrew a tissue. "They could accept the
guardianship part, I think. It's the fact that I filed for a divorce
that's really bothering them. A male heir has always been important
in the Chandler family. When I married Stephen, my parents got the
son they'd always wanted. They were pretty disappointed when I
decided to study art instead of get my MBA and go into the family
business. But then Stephen came along and they were thrilled. He
worked for my father at Chandler Financial . . . not directly, of
course. Stephen had his own department but . : ." Niall shrugged,
not sure where she was going with her rambling. "Besides, I was

brought up Catholic. They feel like I'm abandoning Stephen because he's broken or something."

Rose sighed. "If only it were that simple. Stephen's condition has been an anomaly in regard to traditional psychiatric understanding. His first symptoms occurred after a terrific stressor, of course, but his age of onset was too late to be a classic schizophrenia. He hasn't responded to medications for a psychotic type of depression, either. He goes through periods of remission but, well . . . you know how he is then," Rose said sadly.

Listless, lifeless . . . vacant, Niall thought automatically. She couldn't say what had pained her most over the years—Stephen's manic, agitated, often violent psychotic episodes, or the long periods where he sat and stared out the window without uttering a word, refusing to eat or attend to his most basic grooming and hygiene needs, completely immune to her presence. When he ranted at her it was awful, but at least in doing so he acknowledged her existence.

Against her will the image arose behind Niall's eyelids of the way her parents looked this morning in the hallway as she stood at the door beside a potently virile, nearly nude Vic. They had remained icily silent about the whole incident, but even a second of considering what they must be thinking of her made Niall cringe internally. Some part of her struggle and mortification must have shown on her face, because Rose put her arm around Niall's shoulders in a gesture of compassion.

"Niall, thousands of family members of severely mentally ill people have to make similar decisions, and very few of them have suffered the awful extenuating circumstances you have. Didn't the counselor you saw tell you that there's no right or wrong to your decision? It's you who has to be at peace with it. Not your parents. Not your friends. Not me. Not even Stephen. *You*, Niall."

"Stephen suffered as well."

Rose nodded briskly in agreement. "He did. I can only imagine what he must have suffered . . . what he still suffers." She studied Niall with kind, dark eyes. "He's responded in the only way he knows how. I can't say for sure that I wouldn't have drunk myself into a psychotic oblivion and decided to stay there if forced to face the same circumstances the two of you have. But here's the thing, Niall . . ." Rose added more gently, "You *can* say that. You *do* know. You chose to continue with your life even when it meant you had to carry on alone."

Niall just shook her head, made speechless by the emotion that gripped painfully at her throat. Why did it always hurt so much when someone said something like that to her? Was it some sort of deficit on her part that she hadn't crumbled under the stress and grief as Stephen had? Did that mean that she'd cared less for their son than Stephen had, *loved* Michael less?

No. *No*, now she wasn't being fair to herself, just as she hadn't been fair to herself by stretching out this tragedy for so much longer than need be. Niall wondered if there would be a day in the rest of her life that the thought of her precious little boy's senseless murder wouldn't cause such an acute stab of pain that she was left literally breathless.

Tears streamed silently down her face. Rose had only meant to be reassuring and kind by her words. Niall's lingering doubts about her decisions were the party at fault here.

The tears came from another source, as well. Niall kept so much locked fast in her heart. She had for so long now. Maybe it was foolishness, maybe it was fear . . . maybe it was nothing more than stubborn pride that made her suffer in silence.

Whatever the reason that she kept so much locked up within

her, Niall was also starved to talk to someone . . . someone who knew at least *something* about the circumstances of why her husband—once a funny, intelligent man—currently lay down the hospital hallway, restrained, sedated, almost all evidence of his humanity and vibrancy squeezed out of him by the ruthless fist of grief. Niall longed to connect with someone who had more than just a verbal description of what her husband had become . . . of what Niall had lost.

The clinical psychologist that Evergreen Park had referred Niall to had been kind and attentive, but he'd never really broken through to her. Niall had felt like he was a well-meaning scientist studying a dolphin through a pane of glass. He'd *wanted* to reach her. But the unavoidable difference in their histories had seemed to make contact between Niall and the psychologist as difficult as communication between members of two separate species.

"*Oh . . . dear,*" Rose said brokenly when she noted Niall's expression. "I didn't mean to make you cry, honey." She reached into her pink bag and brought out a wad of tissues.

Niall blinked in bleary-eyed surprise when Rose stuffed half the tissues in her hand and used the rest to mop the tears that had fallen on her own ample cheeks.

"Sorry," Rose offered with a sheepish grin. "Not very professional of me."

Niall gave a choked laugh that freed her trapped voice. "Maybe not. But human. And I mean that as a very big compliment. It can't be easy for you to remain so emotionally available." Niall reached out and covered Rose's hand with her own. She held up the tissues meaningfully. "Thank you, Rose."

She was glad to see by Rose's wide, warm smile that the woman knew she was grateful for much, much more than the tissues.

When Niall had composed herself sufficiently both women stood and dumped their respective wads of tissues in the garbage can.

"Niall, there's something important I wanted you to know, especially now. I tried to call you last week about it," Rose said as they picked up their coats.

"I'm sorry. I was in Tokyo all week on a business trip. I just got your message at work late yesterday afternoon."

Rose nodded in understanding. "I figured it was something like that. You're usually so prompt about returning my calls."

"What is it?" Niall asked anxiously when Rose didn't speak for a second, but just bent to retrieve her purse.

Rose patted her arm reassuringly. "I just wanted to inform you of something. In light of the circumstances, I wish I had gotten hold of you sooner but . . . well, it couldn't be helped. I was calling you to tell you that I'd received official notice from the state of your impending divorce," Rose continued. "Now, I have a long-standing principle as a legal guardian that I follow in these situations. If I judge—given psychiatrists' and other mental health professionals' feedback—that the person who is under my guardianship is mentally stable enough to hear information like this, I provide it to them in person. People like Stephen aren't children. They're adults with clear legal rights. As part of my duty I have to decide if the harm to my client or to others outweighs his right to at least hear the truth about critical legal decisions that impact them. I've told you from the very beginning—haven't I, Niall?—that I'm Stephen's advocate."

"Yes, of course," Niall agreed quickly, not in the least offended by the slightly stern edge that came into Rose's voice. She wasn't sure she could have given guardianship to anyone who didn't get the militant gleam in her eye that Rose did when she discussed the rights of mentally ill individuals. "I would have told Stephen myself if I hadn't thought it was possible he would destabilize. You know how he can get around me sometimes."

It should have been you, Niall.

She shut her eyes reflexively, trying to banish the automatic thought. Another one, equally unwelcome, abruptly rushed to take its place.

"Wait . . . are you saying this because you told him about the divorce?" Niall asked in shrill panic. "Is that why he attacked that man at the hospital?"

"No," Rose said firmly. Her hand rose to Niall's elbow reassuringly. "I'm bringing this up because I thought you might have this kind of reaction if you thought about it in the future and I wasn't here to tell you otherwise." Rose made sure she had Niall's full attention before she continued. "I *haven't* told Stephen about you filing for divorce. All of my reports from Dr. Fardesh and the staff at Evergreen Park argued against the wisdom of that."

"Then why did you call me?"

"Because it was my duty to tell you my philosophy on the matter—that if Stephen was deemed sufficiently stable, I would at least inform him of the fact that he was about to undergo a legal divorce from his wife and ask him if he would like to state his opinion on the manner. Not that it would change the outcome of things. But he is a human being, after all. You would rather I make attempts at acknowledging Stephen's human rights instead of just signing the divorce papers at work between responding to an e-mail and taking a bathroom break, wouldn't you?"

"Of course!" Niall responded desperately. "Just tell me again that this recent relapse wasn't related to you telling him about the divorce."

"*No*," Rose repeated passionately. She glanced over when a

male nurse at the nursing station cleared his throat loudly, subtly informing them that they needed to calm down. "The reports from Dr. Fardesh have been far from encouraging that kind of communication. Then Stephen had this recent relapse—"

". . . which had nothing to do with—"

"No! *Dios*, believe me, girl!" Rose insisted, earning another frown from the male nurse for her loud volume. She toned it down a notch as she continued. "I had already decided that it wouldn't be in Stephen's best interests to have any more possible stressors placed upon him. Then he had this latest relapse . . ." Rose paused and shook her head dispiritedly.

"I should probably also tell you that after this particular incident of violence I've agreed, at Dr. Fardesh's urging, to give consent for Stephen to be given a new medication."

"Another one?" Niall asked dully.

"We have to keep trying. I've held off on consenting to this medication because it has a dangerous side effect. A small percentage of patients experience a drastic drop in their white blood cell count when taking it." She saw Niall's worried expression. "Evergreen Park will monitor Stephen's blood closely for that *very* rare side effect, Niall. It's not as if he's out in the community and might miss regular blood draws. And who knows? This is an older drug, but it has had amazing results for people with severe psychosis.

"Stephen's most recent relapse aside," Rose said, "in my capacity as his legal guardian I felt it was important to tell you that if Stephen should stabilize while your divorce is still ongoing—which we both know is highly unlikely, given that it will probably finalize in the next few months—that I *might* consider telling him what is occurring that legally concerns him. *Might*, Niall. And even if that should happen the chance of it actually affecting your divorce proceedings is a million to one."

"And this is definitely what you called to tell me last week, right?"

"*Yes*," Rose repeated with an amused laugh of frustration. She knew perfectly well from her experience with clients' families that they needed to be frequently reassured that they were not somehow directly responsible for their family member's mental illness or the sole cause of a relapse.

"I told you before that given the circumstances, it was a shame I hadn't spoken with you first. But Stephen's latest relapse had nothing to do with your filing for divorce, Niall. Absolutely nothing. Understood?"

She waited until Niall nodded.

"Good," Rose said. She put her hand on Niall's elbow. "Now let's get out of this place. I shouldn't say it, considering what I do for a living, but I really can't stand hospitals."

Niall gave an exhausted bark of laughter. "God, I couldn't agree more."

SEVEN

The brisk wind coming off Lake Michigan and whipping down the tunnels of the high-rises couldn't prevent Vic from walking back to Riverview Towers from the theater that Saturday afternoon. The run-through on Thursday night only served to highlight myriad problems and concerns that needed to be taken care of posthaste before opening night next Friday. Vic couldn't justify returning to the farm for the long weekend, as he usually did.

That was it. Lack of fresh air and rigorous exercise on the back of one of his horses were responsible for his extra edgy mood for the past two days. Sure, Vic would have been a bear no matter the circumstances, given the fact that he had an opening in six days and that not only was it his own play but his first production as director of the Hesse Theater.

Although, his tension level *might* have something to do with the fact that Niall Chandler had specifically told him not to call her. Or that she'd looked so pale and fragile as she'd said it that it had made him irrationally want to wrap her in his arms and forbid her to go anywhere near her own parents.

None of your business or your concern, he told himself as he walked down the street. Still, his mind kept churning as if it had been set on automatic by somebody other than him.

Maybe his touchy mood and near inability to sleep at night related to the fact that he was hornier than hell for a woman who slept less than fifty feet away from him, the only thing separating them being a few thin walls and—more crucially—Niall's choice.

He knew she was over there. He'd come home late on Thursday following the dress rehearsal and meetings with his staff. But as he'd stood outside in the hallway debating whether or not he should knock on her door, the light that he could barely see at the bottom of her doorway suddenly blinked out.

He'd grimly turned away, recognizing a dismissal when he saw it.

Vic nodded in greeting to the doorman at Riverview Towers and put out his hand to push through the revolving doors. He stopped abruptly when he caught a glimpse in the distance of a solitary figure and pale gold hair blowing in the wind.

He hesitated for a few seconds. Something about her bent head and the way her shoulders hunched forward slightly as she braced against the chilly November wind decided him.

He'd intended to confront Niall immediately when he saw her walking alone, but instead he found himself following her at a distance of half a block or so. Something about her posture intrigued him, seeming both vulnerable and fragile and aloof and closed off at once.

She wore a pair of black sweat pants with wide legs, a pink shirt that fit over her hips snugly, and a short, black hooded sweatshirt. She bent slightly forward as she walked, her hands in her pocket. The tight shirt unerringly highlighted the feminine sashay of her hips and the beguiling outline of her ass. Vic's gaze glued to the sight for several minutes, and he experienced a pleasant, warm tingling at his sex even at this distance from her.

When she progressed farther down Lake Street into Chicago's wholesale food and warehouse district, Vic frowned. Where the hell was she going? This area was iffy at best on a weekday, despite the fact that it was one of the latest frontiers for urban development. But on a Saturday the warehouse district practically became a ghost town. Niall shouldn't be walking alone in this deserted, run down area of the city. Maybe she had a health club tucked into one of these warehouses, Vic reasoned as he picked up his pace to keep up with her.

She suddenly jogged across a small side street, not even bothering to look for cars because the area was so still and quiet. Vic wondered as he followed her why the seedy convenience store on the corner was even open, since it probably made all of its business from the warehouse workers who filled the area Monday through Friday.

Niall stopped at the entrance to a five-story brick building, which—given the stickers on the new panes of glass in the windows and the unfinished sidewalk out front—appeared to be not only empty, but still under construction. When he saw her draw some keys out of her pocket and unlock a service entrance door, Vic sprinted across the street in order to catch her in time.

"Don't they call this trespassing?" he asked at the same time that he just prevented the heavy door from separating him from Niall. The whites of her big eyes showed clearly when she wheeled around to face him. *Good*, at least she recognized that a degree of caution was warranted when she went wandering alone in vacant buildings in deserted parts of the city.

"Vic!" she exclaimed, clearly shocked to see him.

"What are you doing?" he demanded. He allowed the door to slam closed behind him. They stood in a concrete stairwell lit with fluorescent lights.

"I . . . my new condo is in this building. The project manager gave me a key so that I could stop by on the weekend, when the construction workers aren't here, and see the progress they made during the week."

Vic nodded toward the stairs, indicating she should lead the way. He noticed the hesitation and bemusement on her expressive face but he countered it with a sure stride as he came toward her. In a matter of seconds he followed her up the stairs, appreciating the view of her swaying ass even more up close than he had from a distance.

"This area is pretty dodgy for a woman to be living in by herself, isn't it?" Vic asked when they exited the stairwell on the fifth floor and Niall led him down an unfinished hallway. He chose to ignore the irritated glance that she tossed over her shoulder. Women tended to hate it when a guy said things like that, but hell . . . it was a real concern, wasn't it? Any asshole could have stopped that door from closing just as Vic had a few moments ago, and had Niall at his mercy in the vacant building.

"The warehouse district has the lowest crime rate in the entire city," she stated as she inserted her key into one of the doors.

"Not surprising, seeing as how it has the same population as Mars," he responded mildly.

She pressed her lips together and pushed open the door. "The neighborhood looks a little rough, but that doesn't mean that drug dealers and gangbangers are hiding around every corner. Real estate in the West Loop is an excellent investment, given the number of people who want to live downtown these days and the limited supply of property and residences."

She paused to face him just inside the doorway. He liked the fire flashing in her eyes in response to his smugness.

Christ . . . Niall's eyes. Distilled soul fire. Two and a half days, and he'd forgotten just how explosive an impact they had on him.

He forced himself to look away and examine the space where they stood, sure that if he kept staring at Niall, he'd have her flat on her back on the dusty, unfinished wood floor in two seconds flat.

"Sounds like you've done some research into the matter," he conceded as he walked around slowly, examining the space. The interior wasn't finished, of course, and the floor was cluttered with lumber, sheets of drywall, and crates of various building supplies. But what he saw, he liked. Eleven-foot ceilings and plenty of windows. The far wall opened onto an enormous outdoor terrace. It would be a bitch to heat in a Chicago winter, but the east-facing view of the skyline was completely unhindered by a single obstacle.

"It's going to be entirely open on this level?" he asked.

"Yes, except for the powder room and closets," Niall replied from behind him, her voice warming at what obviously was a favorite topic. "It's a soft loft design. I've got twelve hundred feet downstairs and another thousand upstairs for the bedrooms." She raised an elegantly arched eyebrow at him in a subtle challenge when he turned to face her. "That's another reason why buying into this 'dodgy' neighborhood was such a good idea. I never could have have afforded all of this wide-open living space if I bought a place in the Loop."

Vic just smiled and headed up the stairs. "If you think this is wide-open space, then you should visit my ranch in Montana or my farm downstate."

"Is that an invitation?"

When he heard the tone of her low, husky voice Vic gave up all pretense of being the friendly neighbor. He spun around on the stairs, hands on the railing, and leaned down over her upturned face.

"Was *that*?" he countered.

He watched as his innuendo registered in her consciousness and sexual awareness followed quickly on its heels. The tip of her tongue traced her lower lip in an anxious gesture, making him tighten with lust. The fact that she wanted him was just as obvious as ever, although not nearly as blatant as the stiff ridge of his cock as it pressed against the suddenly constraining fly of his jeans.

"Why did you tell me not to call you the other day?"

Her lips fell open in surprise at the harshness of his question. "I just didn't want you to worry about me. Not that you would or anything," she backpedaled quickly.

"What happened? Why were your parents so upset?"

"A . . . a family member had been hospitalized."

Vic straightened from his predatory stance when he noticed her pallor. "Is she . . . *he*"—Vic paused, eyebrows raised until Niall nodded at his second guess—"going to be okay?"

"Yes."

"Are you sure that was all that was wrong, Niall?"

"Isn't it enough?" she asked. For a few seconds she just stared at him silently.

"Why don't you show me the wide-open space of your bedrooms?" Vic suggested eventually. He held out his hand to her. A measure of relief swept through him when the solemn expression on her face disappeared and she laughed.

"There isn't much to see," she teased as she moved past him down the hallway.

Vic smiled, his eyes lowering to the sexy sway of the shapeliest little ass he'd ever seen. He begged to differ. In his opinion, there were *plenty* of prime views around here. His cock surged uncomfortably when he thought about spanking that butt several days ago.

Niall proudly gave him the tour of her condo. He listened silently while she enthusiastically detailed what the finishes would look like in each room. Vic was glad to see that the construction so far looked like quality work. So many of the firms that put up condos in downtown Chicago utilized cheap materials and shoddy labor and got away with it easily because of the high demand in the market.

Niall exclaimed in surprised pleasure when they entered the master suite a few minutes later and she saw that the walls had been freshly painted and carpeting installed.

"Give me your keys for a few minutes," Vic requested once they'd examined the half-finished, luxurious master bath.

"What for?"

"You'll see. Just give them to me and I'll be right back."

He grinned when she gave him a suspicious look and the keys at the same time. On the way back a few minutes later he peered into the main entryway of her building, gratified to see a doorman's security desk in what promised to be a luxurious lobby. At least she had some protection, although he still wished she'd picked a place that was just a little more populated. Funny, he admitted with grim amusement, coming from a guy who preferred to travel miles before he ever saw another human face.

When he returned a few minutes later, carrying a paper bag, Niall was still in the master bedroom, sitting in the middle of the floor, a dreamy look glazing her pretty face. He sat down next to her on the soft carpeting without a word and drew a bottle from the bag.

"Where'd you get that?" she asked, clearly amused.

"I beat up the gangbanger who was trying to steal it from the wino on the corner." He laughed outright when he saw her eyes narrow in irritation. "I bought it from that store across the street, what'd ya think? It's not our favorite brand, but it'll do."

Niall laughed. "Vic, it's four o'clock in the afternoon."

"So? How else were we going to make a toast?" he challenged as he poured some of the Scotch into the paper cups he'd also purchased. He handed her one of them and held up his own. "To your new home, Niall. I hope it gives you all the wide-open space you need."

The sparkle in her hazel eyes made him unreasonably happy.

"So you like it? The condo?" she asked huskily after she'd taken a healthy swallow of the Scotch. It was one of the many paradoxes about Niall that fascinated him. She looked so damn feminine and petite, and yet she took a belt of hard liquor with an uninhibited sensual relish that made Vic stiff as a board. He'd known the second he'd seen her take a drink of Scotch on that first night that he had to have her. The only thing that had changed in two weeks was that his desire had become even stronger.

"I like it," he said simply before he tilted back his own cup, his eyes never leaving Niall's luminous face.

She lowered her cup slowly. "How did the play go the other night? Any monster problems?"

He shrugged. "Nothing of Godzilla proportions. More like lizard-sized. Unfortunately, there was an infestation of the little bastards."

She chuckled warmly. "Isn't that always the way with lizards?"

He held her gaze, doing nothing to shield his desire. She glanced away after a tense silence.

"I'm sorry that I missed it. I've been thinking about . . . it . . .
wondering how it went."

"All you had to do was knock on my door and ask," he chided
softly.

Her cheeks colored. "I thought you might be too busy with the
play and all."

"Really."

She blinked in surprise at his open sarcasm. Her mouth opened
as if she were about to argue, but instead she took another belt of
Scotch from her paper cup. Vic got the distinct impression this one
was for courage.

"No, not really. I was avoiding you."

Vic didn't respond, instinctively giving her the space that her
anxiety warranted. He took another drink, watching her over his
paper cup as she struggled with her discomfort. When the unwelcome thought struck him that Niall Chandler might be considering
the best way to tell him to get lost, he tilted the cup until the re-
mainder of the Scotch flowed in a burning river down his throat.

"Vic, we . . . things . . . things between us really started off . . ."

"With a bang?" Vic finished for her dryly when she paused.

Her mouth hung open. "Yes," she agreed after a moment, nodding her head in a matter-of-fact, earnest manner that he found
adorable. "With a bang. I don't really date that much. I haven't in
years, I mean. And then . . . what happened that night happened . . .
that night *you* happened." She rolled her eyes and took another
drink. "I'm sorry. I'm not sure I know how to put this."

"You think I'm coming on too strong," Vic supplied.

She tilted her head uncertainly. "Not just you. I am, too. I don't
know what to make of it."

"You think we should back off, take it a little slower?" he

prompted. Her eyes flashed warmly, as if she was relieved that he'd found the right words for her.

"Don't you think that would be for the best?" she asked.

"No."

Her lower lip trembled. "*No?*" she repeated incredulously after several seconds.

Vic crumpled the flimsy paper cup and tossed it on top of the bag. She wasn't going to like this, but—"*No.* I want you too much to take you in stingy little servings. Maybe you'll think that's greedy of me, but I'm not the kind of guy who takes what he wants in half measures." He met her gaze. "That's not who I am, Niall."

Her mouth rounded in a silent, amazed "Oh." His muscles tensed as he resisted an overwhelming urge to scoot across the floor and send his tongue deep between the lush, round target of her lips.

Shit. Who was he kidding? Could he really ever turn away the smallest morsel she offered him? Not likely. But if he could talk her into the wisdom of fucking each other's brains out every time the opportunity arose, then maybe he could purge her from his system once and for all. It made him uncomfortable, this wanting another human being so much.

There was no way that he could maintain the sharp, near-to-bursting level of lust that he had for Niall for very long. His need for her was singularly intense, primitive . . . feral. Surely it wouldn't survive for long after the initial volatile explosions that they created when they crashed together. Once their need for each other cooled, *then* they'd slow things down. Not now, though.

Uh-uh. No way.

"Want to know something else?" he challenged abruptly in a

hard tone. "I don't think that's who you are, either. I've been to bed with you. You're not the kind of woman who likes things watered down. Just the opposite, in fact. You said you wanted wide-open spaces, Niall. So how come when it comes to what's happening between us you want to hide in some confining little corner?"

Vic paused, surprised to hear the anger in his voice. Niall's suggestion that they cool things down had really pissed him off. Nothing was going to keep him from her, certainly not Niall's half-assed attempts at doing so. She wanted him as much as he wanted her. Every time she met his gaze, the desire that he read in her beautiful eyes almost undid him.

So why did she fight the inevitable?

He removed the soggy cup from her grip before he held out his hand for her.

"Time for the rest of the house christening," he informed her gruffly.

You said you wanted wide-open spaces, Niall. So how come when it comes to what's happening between us you want to hide in some confining little corner?

Vic's words swirled madly around Niall's brain. Was he right? Since she'd met him, she'd been completely bowled over by him. His touch had brought her back to the realms of the living. Had what happened with Stephen the other day—the reawakening of her guilt—made her want to retreat back into the shadows?

Stephen lived in the world of his delusional madness, unable to withstand the pain of reality. Did some part of her think that she deserved a twisted half-life as well? Did she somehow need to prove to herself that she suffered just as greatly after the murder of their son as Stephen had?

I did suffer. God, I still do . . . I always will. How could it be otherwise? a voice in her head cried out an anguished reminder.

Niall's gaze lowered from Vic's steady, fiery eyes to his outstretched hand. Forsaking Vic would be a clear, measurable indication of her torment—a tangible sacrifice to the seemingly depthless hole of her grief after the meaningless murder of her beautiful four-year-old boy.

But God, hadn't she suffered enough?

In her moment of indecision Rose Gonzalez's voice rose in her awareness. *It's you who has to be at peace with this. Not your parents. Not your friends. Not me. Not even Stephen. You, Niall.*

Instead of just taking Vic's hand, Niall rose from her sitting position and knelt before him. Because of their disparity in height their faces were at the same level. She reached up slowly and touched his lean cheek, mesmerized by the way that leashed desire made his light eyes glow.

Her touch seemingly snapped his taut restraint. He pulled her toward him roughly, lifting her until she sat in his lap facing him. He bent and fastened his mouth to hers unerringly, their fit striking her once again as being divinely engineered.

Niall closed her eyes as the incredibly potent essence of Vic once again pervaded her, mingled with her own chemistry, and took her from a slow simmer to a torrid boil in a matter of seconds. Her hands cradled his jaw as her tongue tangled wildly with his. She sank into that kiss just as she submersed herself in the carnal, sensual world that he created for them with such stunning ease.

She was so involved in that erotic, tasty kiss that she didn't realize Vic had unzipped her jacket and found the bottom of her shirt until she felt his hand on the sensitive skin of her belly and ribs. He found a satin-covered breast and palmed it roughly before he turned to lightly rolling her nipple between his thumb and fore-finger.

She moaned and arched her back. The instinctive movement caused the sensitive tips of her breasts to crush into his chest and her pussy to press firmly into the stiff ridge beneath the fly of his jeans. She rocked against him, desperate for the steady pressure that his hard body provided her in calming her throbbing nerve endings.

Vic groaned and covered her hips and ass with his hands. He added the pressure of his strong arms, pushing and pressing her against him rhythmically. Their kiss grew wild and hungry, fu-eled as it was by the sinuous, friction-building movements of their bodies.

Niall cried out in protest a moment later when leaned away from her. Although they were fully clothed, she would have been shud-dering in orgasm in a half a minute if Vic had kept her fully sub-merged in that heady kiss. God, the man knew how to use his mouth. She craned toward him as he moved away slightly, but he restrained her by spreading his hand in her hair and tugging gently.

He studied her as he touched her with feather-light fingertips. "Your cheeks get so pink when you're turned on. I know it's not an original thing to say, but you're very beautiful, Niall."

Niall swallowed heavily. Maybe the words weren't singular, but the way Vic looked at her with such hot, soulful eyes when he said them certainly was. He gave his small, sexy smile as he lightly touched her damp lower lip.

Did he know that smile made her his willing slave?

He lowered his head and kissed her mouth softly, teasing her, making her hunger for more. "Stand up and take off all your clothes while I watch," he muttered next to her lips when she strained up to try and get more of him.

It wasn't the Scotch that made Niall dizzy as she tried to stand. His hold on her hips tightened to steady her as she rose. He leaned back on his hands and stared up at her without speaking while she shrugged out of her jacket. Her fingers slid below the waistband of her sweatpants.

"Take off your shirt and bra first."

Niall smiled and shook her head, but she did what he asked. "Enjoying yourself?" she teased when she removed her bra and dropped it on top of her other clothing on the floor.

"I am, actually. Thanks for asking."

His eyes adhered to her exposed breasts. The room was chilly but Niall knew perfectly well that wasn't the reason her nipples pulled into tight, sensitive darts.

"Play with them. Pinch your nipples."

Niall started at the unexpected request. The idea of touching herself while he watched struck her as extremely intimate.

Not to mention unbearably exciting, Niall acknowledged as liquid heat flooded her pussy.

"You just have to make a production out of everything, don't you?" she asked huskily as her hands rose. He made that subtle rolling motion of his jaw that drove her lust-crazy.

"I'm a guy. The visuals excite me."

Niall wasn't a guy, but the sight of him watching her made her sizzle with sexual tension. She skimmed her fingertips along the curve of her lower breasts. Funny, she'd never realized how soft the skin was. Is that what Vic thought when he touched her? Her excitement grew when she lifted her breasts in her palms, feeling how taut and firm the flesh was. For a moment she kept the flesh cradled in her hands, as if in offering to the beautiful, sexy man who watched her actions with such an erotically intense focus. When she pinched her erect nipples lightly both of them groaned in tandem. She thought she'd just been touching herself for Vic, but the stimulation of her own flesh felt good.

It felt very good.

Her thighs clamped tightly together as she continued to play with herself more eagerly. Her gaze lowered to the obvious bulge in Vic's jeans. The memory of his heavy erection on her tongue, the sensation of the thick rim beneath the head slipping between her tight lips made her pinch her nipples tight. She tugged on them, loving the sensation almost as much as the hot flash of lust that blazed into Vic's eyes.

She recalled how he'd played with her while she was tied to the bed the other day. She cupped both breasts in her hands and lifted them before she released them, letting the firm flesh bounce back into place. She did that only three times, firmly pinching her nipples in the interim, before Vic jerked forward.

"Enough," he said tensely. "Take off the rest of your clothes and come here."

He tapped the carpeting in front of him.

Niall hurried. She couldn't wait to get down on that floor with him. She knelt in front of him, naked and breathless.

"You chilly?" he asked, his eyes running over her stiff nipples and the pebbled skin of her arms.

"Not really," Niall answered. In fact, she wouldn't have been surprised if steam rose from her throat when she opened her mouth to speak, she was so hot at her core.

Her internal temperature notched up several more degrees when Vic stood and tore at the button fly of his jeans. He shoved them down around his thighs and her eyes lowered.

She licked her lower lip hungrily at the sight of his cock jutting from his body.

He dropped to his knees, sank back on his feet, and grabbed her to him in one quick, fluid motion that surprised Niall. Within the matter of a second the dense, tapered head of his cock brushed against her cheek.

Vic's hand spread on the back of her head.

"It turned me on so much watching you that I'm about to explode. You're going to finish what you started, but I'm afraid you're going to have to give me some relief first. It won't take much, trust me. Suck, Niall." His characteristically raspy voice sounded a little desperate.

But Niall was already sliding the fat, delineated head of Vic's cock—that same delicious cap that she'd been fantasizing about for weeks now—between her tightly pursed lips. She slapped at it warmly with her tongue when it was inserted in her mouth. Vic's grunts of pleasure escalated her excitement. She pushed down on him, loving the feeling of the thick pillar of his shaft stretching her lips and sliding heavily across her tongue.

She alternated between taking him deep and slow and bobbing her head over him from mid staff to just below the head fast and forcefully. When her lust for the delicious, fat knob of his cock overcame her, she tightly fisted and pumped the slick shaft while she explored it. She fluttered her tongue over the thick rim, then pushed her tightened lips over it repeatedly, memorizing the sensation.

The rising tension in Vic's muscles caused heat to flood her tissues. She pictured in her mind what it would be like if he lost control because of her teasing and held her down on the soft carpeting, impaling her with the long, stiff spear of flesh that pulsed between her lips. She nibbled at the smooth skin on the head, scraping her teeth along the skin delicately, taunting him with her power over him.

Vic growled like an animal and gripped his fingers in her hair, applying a steady downward pressure. "Dammit, when I said suck, I meant *suck*."

He pushed her down over him. He flexed his hips at the same time that he controlled the movement of her mouth with his hand on her head. Her throat muscles relaxed with each successive stroke of his cock in her narrow channel, becoming more accustomed to the harsh treatment. Eventually he just held her steady and pumped into her with frantic upward bucking motions of his hips.

"Ah, *fuck*, that's good," he grunted as his seed began to pour into her throat. "Take it all. Every drop of it," he insisted between clenched teeth as he held her immobile on his spasming cock.

Niall swallowed madly but still struggled to keep up with the sheer volume of cum that he shot. Her mouth and throat flooded with his salty, musky, singular taste. He choked her, overwhelmed her, drowned her with the essence of him.

And she gloried in it. She wanted more.

By the time he gently raised her off his sated penis, Niall's clit burned, needy for friction. It amazed her how much sucking Vic's cock stimulated her. She loved to make herself the wide-open pasture in which he ran free and wild.

"*Now* I might be able to watch you finish with some measure of calm," Vic muttered drolly.

Her eyes raced up to meet his. "Watch me?" she rasped. Vic's cock plunging into her throat repeatedly had made her usually husky voice even more rough.

Vic palmed the side of her head and leaned down to plant a hot, quick kiss on her lips.

He nodded. "I want to watch you like before," he explained patiently as he encouraged her to lie on the floor. Niall just stared up at him, confused. His gray eyes met hers. "I want you to masturbate."

"Why?" she asked in stark disbelief.

His low, rumbling laugh made her shiver. So did his fingertips skimming along her thigh. "Yeah it's pretty hard to figure out why a guy would want to watch a gorgeous woman touch herself until she exploded."

Niall just stared, speechless as he matter-of-factly scooted her body until her knees were on either side of his hips. Before she could guess what he was about, he reached between her thighs and pushed two fingers into her pussy. Niall yelped and then whimpered as he thrust into her hard for several strokes. She pushed her hips desperately against the pressure. Vic's forceful finger penetration—not to mention his grunt of appreciation when he discovered just how wet she was—had Niall right on the edge of climax.

But then Vic abruptly withdrew with a slurping sound. Niall panted shallowly as she watched him shove his fingers into his mouth, sucking them clean while he watched her. He grabbed her hand and placed it at the juncture of her thighs.

"Go on, Niall," he prodded when he slid his fingers out of his mouth, having swallowed all of her cream. "I'm waiting."

Niall thought about telling him that he was going to keep waiting, but she wasn't a fool. It wasn't really as hard as she might have imagined, to suddenly do something publicly that had always been private. Besides, Vic had gotten her so worked up.

She really needed this.

Her forefinger slid between the swollen, damp folds of her labia. Her clit was bathed in a sticky pool of her juices. Vic made her hotter than she'd ever been in her life. He must, for her to be acting in this impulsive, uncharacteristic . . . downright *wanton* manner. Her hips began to circle and pulse against the pressure of her hand. She massaged the nerve-packed flesh until the heels of her feet sizzled in sympathy with her burning clit.

"Spread your thighs wider," she heard Vic demand through the haze of her cresting arousal.

She complied, opening herself to his gaze fully . . . exposing herself . . . holding nothing back from him.

"Do you ever use toys when you masturbate?"

That did make her pause. Was there nothing he would allow her to keep secret when it came to sex? She realized that his gaze had switched to her face and that he was waiting for an answer.

"Sometimes." *More than I ever have in my life since I met you,* she added to herself.

"What do you use?"

She bit her lip in hesitation, but her pussy didn't seem to mind the intimate conversation at all. In fact, her clit ached so acutely that she had to stroke it as she answered him.

"I have a little silver bullet vibrator."

"Is that all?"

"*Yes,*" she replied testily.

His lips twitched at her irritation before his eyes focused again on her busy hand between her thighs.

Niall moaned at the impact of his penetrating gaze. It felt like a tangible touch, sending her flame higher. Her other hand came down and dipped into the snug tunnel of her pussy. She moaned and bucked her hips against the added pressure for just a moment before she withdrew. She spread the lubrication on her fingertips across her nipple, sliding and pinching at the sensitive crest, rolling it tightly between her fingertips at the same rate that she bucked her hips against her hand.

She heard Vic curse. Her half-closed eyelids widened when she took in his rigid features and the gleam of excitement in his light eyes as he watched her pleasure herself.

That look sent her over the edge. She whimpered in tense anticipation and then cried out sharply as she fell over the edge of orgasm. Her climax escalated to a nearly unbearable pitch when Vic plunged his fingers deep into her vagina. Instead of thrusting them out of her, he kept them there, rubbing and vibrating her while she screamed in pleasure and her juices gushed around him.

When her eyelids eventually flickered open, she saw that he leaned over her, his fingers still inside her pussy . . . that naughty little grin on his face.

"You're one hell of a sexy woman."

"You *better* not be making fun of me, Vic," she admonished between pants for air.

She smiled when his deep laugh rolled through her awareness, making her nipples tighten even in her post-orgasmic state.

"If I were any more fucking serious, I probably would have had a heart attack just now." He leaned over and sealed his lips to hers.

"Show me where you're going to put your bed," he muttered when he raised his head after a kiss that had left Niall humming with arousal all over again. "I'm gonna fuck you there, and I want you to remember it when you lie in bed at night if I'm not around."

Niall swallowed convulsively as she stared up at him. *Yeah*, she'd remember all right.

She'd remember well.

EIGHT

Vic stood and helped her to her feet. She still seemed dazed from her orgasm—cheeks flushed a rosy pink, eyelids weighted, breath coming in uneven puffs across her red, swollen lips. He'd felt her muscular vaginal walls tightening and flexing around his fingers. She'd given herself a nice blast, that much was for certain.

He couldn't wait to be buried in her the next time she blew.

The image of her stroking her clit so rapidly while she tugged on her nipple and whimpered in pleasure would probably be replayed across the screen of the back of his eyelids during autoerotic moments until he was an old, dried up man. That memory would provide him with some much-needed juice, that's for sure, Vic thought wryly as he hastily removed his clothing.

"Where?" he asked tautly when he'd kicked his jeans off his feet and dug in the pocket for his wallet, extracting a condom.

Her big eyes flickered over his naked body, lingering on his erection as he slid the latex over it. *That's for you, baby.* He had to stop himself from saying it out loud when she stared at him so hungrily. *That's what you get for having such a tight, sleek little body and a sweeter, hotter response to me than I could have conjured up in my wildest fantasies.*

Niall transferred her gaze to the north side of the bedroom and nodded.

"Go and bend over with your hands up against the wall."

He watched her as she followed his orders. He loved the subtle, feminine sashay of her hips as she walked and the beguiling sway of her round ass. She peered around her shoulder when she'd positioned herself against the wall and he approached her from behind. Her eyes looked enormous as she watched him take his erect cock in his hand.

"Spread your thighs some," he said as he held back a firm ass cheek and rubbed the tip of his cock into her wet, tender cleft. He grunted when he found her juicy opening. He leaned over her and encircled her waist, raising her feet slightly off the floor in his hunger to get inside of her.

Fuck. He had a good eleven inches on her in the height department. The angle was all wrong. He could make it work, but Vic wanted to concentrate on the incredible feeling of being inside Niall, not the awkward positioning of their bodies.

"Don't move," he growled as he placed her toes back on the floor.

"Vic?" Niall asked in amazement when he abruptly stalked out of the room. She looked thoroughly confused when he returned a few seconds later, carrying an empty crate from downstairs. He tossed it in the middle of the space where her bed would be.

"Change of set plans," he said as he tossed his shirt on the plywood plank. "Stand on that, Niall."

"Vic . . ." she began when he grabbed her hand and helped her onto the fabric covered crate. He dealt with her uncertainty by leaning forward and lustily kissing her. His hands found their way to her firm breasts without conscious thought, massaging and shaping them in his palms. "There. Isn't that better?" he asked a few seconds later against her lips. "You're almost as tall as me now." He rubbed his lips hungrily against her small grin. His cock batted against her belly.

"See what you do to me, baby?" he cajoled.

"It's only fair," she murmured in that husky voice he loved. She leaned forward and nipped at his lips with her small front teeth. "I want you to know that you're the only person that I would ever stand up on this crate for like a circus elephant."

"More like a circus pixie," he muttered as he nibbled her neck.

"There's no such thing."

He just grinned.

"You're going to fuck me while I'm standing up here, aren't you?" she asked in a voice thick with both lust and amusement.

"Now you get the idea." He kissed her sweet mouth once more. "Turn around and bend over."

He smiled in pure anticipation when she did, parting her thighs, grabbing her ankles, and arching her back into a position that screamed "fuck me good and hard."

His hand spread across her hip and ass cheek, parting her for his penis. Their angle was perfect now for a nice, taut ride. He guided himself to her drenched, clinging sheath, his lungs burning because he forgot to draw air in his excitement. He finally inhaled with a hissing noise when he pushed the plum-sized head of his cock into her and he was surrounded by her heat.

She moaned shakily. His hands rose to her hips, gliding across the silky skin of her ass, soothing her.

He bucked his hips slowly at first. The wet, sucking sound that the rim of his penis made every time he drew it almost out of her made him want to skewer her tight little pussy in one stroke. But he restrained, enjoying the sensation too much, liking the way the erotic slurping sounds mixed with Niall's whimpers and purrs.

"You're so tight," he muttered roughly as he pushed himself another inch into her clinging flesh and began to rock in and out of her. "I don't think I'd ever get it in you if you didn't get so wet for me."

Niall moaned and tensed her thighs, forcing his cock another inch into her heat. He laughed and spanked her ass once.

"Hold on, little filly. I'm enjoying the slow pace and the scenery," he teased, never taking his eyes from her shapely, pale ass and the first several inches of his cock sliding in and out of her body.

"The scenery will be just as good at a nice hard sprint," Niall told him in a frustrated tone.

"It'll be better," he corrected. "But for right now, you just hold still."

He wished there was a mirror so that he could see her face while he held her hips steady and slowly burrowed his cock into her tight channel. He alternated a good, hard pump that pushed his cock further into her sublime heat with several quick, shallow thrusts that merely stroked the portion of his penis that had already been submerged.

It continued like that for more than a minute, the only sounds resonating in the empty room being the sucking sound of his cock moving in her tight, wet channel, his grunts of pleasure, and Niall's sexy, sharp cries. Twice when she tried to push back and increase the pace he gave her rump a brisk slap, making his cock leap inside her tight sheath in agonized pleasure. By the time he pressed to her damp hilt and molded her ass cheeks up with his hands, giving his aching balls some much-needed pressure, Niall shook beneath him.

"Shhh, baby," he soothed as he reached around her. One hand pinched the bottom of her swollen, tender labia together. With the other he played her clit briskly in the juicy pocket of flesh he'd formed.

His cock jerked viciously inside her muscular channel when she came. He'd never wanted to move so much in his life, never wanted to fuck until he found the mindless nirvana of sexual bliss that he knew Niall could give him.

But she was so sweet. Every time he exploded in her he almost immediately wished he was back at it, riding her sweet little pussy hard and fast. His desire to draw out the pleasure just barely outweighed his need to succumb to it, adding a sharp spice to his already potent lust.

Bent over as she was, he couldn't resist the lure of her pink, puckered asshole. He slid his thumb along her slick perineum, accumulating some of the juices that had gathered there. He grabbed her hip, holding her steady while he pierced that tiny opening. Niall still panted and moaned in the aftershocks of her orgasm, but when he penetrated her asshole, she stilled beneath him and caught her breath.

"What's wrong, baby?" he rasped. Her pussy rippled and squeezed at his cock, making it throb and swell uncomfortably in her tight confines. Still, he drew on the last vestiges of his control and kept his hips immobile. "You're not used to ass play, are you?" he asked, remembering how she'd reacted similarly even when he put just the tip of his finger into her snug little hole several weeks ago. Currently he'd pushed his entire thumb into a channel that already would have been tight without the added pressure of his near-to-bursting cock in her vagina pressing in on it.

She just shook her head. His lips formed into a snarl when she tightened around his thumb and cock at once.

"You've got such a hot little hole. You're going to give it to me some day. Aren't you, Niall?" he asked her in a lust-thick tone as he began to pulse in and out of her asshole at the same time that he rocked his cock a mere two inches back and forth in her pussy. Her gasp of pleasure echoed his peaking excitement. Her sleek vagina pulled on his cock with each outstroke like a sucking little mouth, making the thrust back into her exponentially more rewarding.

Christ, he'd never get enough of her pussy. *You're never going to get enough of her, period*, a voice in his head taunted him.

"Answer me!" he said as desire clawed at him painfully, demanding its due.

"*Yes*," she answered in a desperate, choked voice. "Everything I have is yours, Vic."

He snarled in crazed lust. He grabbed both hips and began to pound into her. A growl of pure animalistic pleasure rose from his throat as he pumped her from tip to balls again and again, striking their flesh together in a fierce tempo. A continual wailing sound exuded from Niall's throat, surging louder every time he smacked his pelvis against her ass. His arm muscles bunched tight, keeping her in place for his ramming cock.

The friction was taut, perfect . . . too fucking good to last for long.

When Niall screamed in release and her muscular walls began to convulse around him, he shifted his hand below one ass cheek and lifted. His subsequent slam into her giving flesh struck deeper than any of its predecessors.

His jaw vibrated as he roared and his body shuddered in the throes of a violent storm of pleasure.

Niall loved the feeling of Vic leaning down over her and holding her body to his while they both fought mightily to be the first to inhale the air that surrounded them. Eventually, however, her legs began to tremble slightly from Vic's added weight and her own body's desperate attempts to find balance after orgasm had shattered her equilibrium repeatedly.

Vic must have noticed her quivering, because he suddenly hugged her to him and brought her back with him as he collapsed to the floor. They laughed breathlessly as they fell in a heap of sweaty, intermingled limbs. When Niall tried to move off his big, long body, he used his hands to keep her in place.

"Let me go," Niall insisted, laughing as she squirmed on top of him.

"You're keeping me warm up there."

She snorted. "I wasn't put on this earth for the purpose of keeping you warm."

He brushed his grin along the skin of her neck, making her shiver. "Maybe not, but I'm beginning to think you might have been put here for the express purpose of making me hotter than hell."

Niall twisted around abruptly at the tone of his voice. His dark hair was adorably mussed. His light eyes sparkled with amusement. He looked younger than usual, less intense . . . wonderful.

Wonderful? Niall turned around and forced her body to relax along his length despite the tension that had just leapt into her muscles. She stared at the newly painted ceiling but saw nothing.

When she'd had that seemingly random thought just now, she hadn't meant it in the everyday sense of the word. Not like *I'm having a wonderful day today* or *The weather's been wonderful, let's go for a stroll*. No, she'd meant it in the truest sense of the word—awesome, marvelous . . . astonishing.

Anxiety warred with amazement for her full attention. She'd never had this reaction to a man before, not even in the full, flush excitement of meeting and dating Stephen.

She blinked and forced her dazed vision to clear. Did a woman who carried so much emotional baggage really have the right to be harboring such feelings?

Or worse . . . what if it was because of her emotional and psychological stress that she was having such a powerful reaction to Vic in the first place? That was certainly possible, wasn't it? Being with Vic might be the equivalent of a drinking or gambling compulsion . . . a shot of adrenaline and euphoria to an otherwise lifeless existence.

The charging train of her anxiety was derailed by the sensation of Vic hugging her more tightly to him with his encircling arms at the same time that he wrapped her up with his long legs until she was encapsulated in a divine cocoon of male muscle and vibrant heat.

"You're so little."

Her eyes fluttered closed at the feeling of his rumbling voice vibrating into her neck. "I'm five foot four." She'd meant to sound defiant, but was too sexually sated and mentally confused to sound anything but dazed.

The smug sound in his throat made Niall think she'd just confirmed what he'd said.

"That's average for a woman," she insisted petulantly.

"Ummm."

That was all. Nothing else.

"I can't wait to see one of your plays," she informed the ceiling.

"Why's that?"

"Most actors *talk* on the stage, don't they? With you as their creator, I'm wondering what your characters are going to *do* up there. Emote with stares?"

For a few seconds she'd thought she'd offended him. Then he hugged her even tighter in his warm, safe embrace. "You forgot method grunting."

Laughter erupted from her throat. "Right. Brando would have been the perfect actor for one of your plays."

"You're right. He would have."

She continued to laugh, knowing that he shared in her mirth even though she couldn't hear or see it.

"Are you going to stand me up again if I ask you to opening night?" he asked, making her laughter quiet and then still.

"I thought not even your mother could stand to be around you on opening night."

"She can't," he said absentmindedly as he ran a hand along her flank, making her skin pebble. "But she never misses an opening anyway. She loves the champagne. She usually talks about the spread at the buffet for the opening night party until even the worst gossips at the Avery Bingo Club duck around the corner when they see her coming."

Niall chuckled. She felt like her body melted like candle wax into his heat. "She still lives in Avery?"

"Yep."

"What about your father?"

"Wouldn't know. He took off when I was four."

He must have sensed her unnatural stillness.

"It's hard to miss what you never really knew. My mom always had more than enough energy to be both mother and father to Meg and me. She took it pretty hard when my dad ran off. Meg and I went to stay with my uncle on the farm here in Illinois for a while. But she got over it and ended up being sassier than ever."

"Don't you wish she lived closer?"

He sighed, making Niall's body rise and fall with his own. "Both Meg and I have tried to convince her to move closer to us, but she's got all of her clubs and her friends in Avery. She's too busy and too ornery to be thinking about moving in with one of her kids."

"I can't wait to meet her," Niall said as she smiled at the ceiling. She liked the sound of Vic's mother.

"My sister, Meg, will be here for opening night, too."

Niall moaned in appreciation when Vic ran the hand that had been tracing her sensitive side up over a thrusting breast. Her thighs pressed tightly together when he pinched her nipple between his thumb and forefinger, then soothed her with his rough fingertips. "The three of us together should be able to survive your opening night wrath, don't you think?" she asked breathlessly.

"The three of you together could probably survive the apocalypse," he commented dryly. "Niall?"

"Yes?" she asked, her voice sounding husky with rising sexual tension when she felt him stir and harden against her sensitive flesh.

"Turn around. I don't think the house christening is finished quite yet."

Vic started into wakefulness, surprised to see the gray light of dawn peeking around the blinds in his bedroom. It gratified him that he'd slept for a good majority of the night. The reason for his profound sleep was enfolded snugly in his arms.

He'd never really had to convince Niall with words to sleep in his bed that night. After they'd finally left her new condominium, exhausted and completely happy from their multiple rounds of phenomenal lovemaking, they'd ducked into a Thai restaurant for dinner. Vic had guessed from Niall's heavy eyelids after she'd drunk a glass of wine and devoured almost her entire portion of chicken pad thai that she wouldn't be long for the waking world. So he'd suggested they watch a DVD together at his place, and sure enough, within forty-five minutes he had an armful of soft, warm, sleeping woman.

He nuzzled the hair at her nape and inhaled her scent. Maybe it was the dampness he found at her neck, or maybe it had been the sensation of the tremors that periodically shook her body that had awakened him in the first place. Or perhaps the primitive part of his brain recognized the scent that mixed with the residual fresh, floral scent of Niall's perfume.

It was the smell of fear.

His fingers skimmed along her neck and back. Sweat soaked through her shirt. She moaned in her sleep. The sound pained Vic on some deep, indefinable level.

"Niall. Wake up. Wake up, baby," he murmured as he stroked her sides and pressed his lips against a flushed cheek. She whimpered, the noise reminding him of a trapped animal, both mournful and panicked at once.

He couldn't stand it.

"*Niall.*"

She jumped in his arms.

"Vic?"

"You were dreaming," he muttered close to her ear. He continued to rub her body from her thigh to her ribs, attempting to soothe her. She moved restlessly in his arms and finally sat up. For a few seconds she just sat on the edge of his bed as her breathing slowed, her face shadowed by the dim light and her huddled posture. Neither of them spoke when she finally rose and went to the bathroom.

She returned to the bedside a minute later. "I'm sorry for waking you," she said in her low, smoky voice that seemed perfectly suited to the muted, gray light of dawn.

"I slept better last night than I have in weeks. You've got nothing to apologize for," Vic told her when she perched on the edge of his bed. He wanted to reach out and pull her back into his arms. He wanted to keep her safe from whatever plagued her dreams. But something in her tense posture made him wary about touching her.

"Maybe I should just go," she whispered.

"Don't."

He saw her head fall forward, sensed her uncertainty . . . her vulnerability.

"I'm all sweaty."

"So we'll take a shower in a little bit," Vic stated with more ease than he actually felt. His jaw clenched when she still didn't move. This dawn encounter with Niall struck him as heavy . . . even threatening, although why that should be, he couldn't say. The eerie mist of dreams must be clinging to him as well.

"I'm leaving for Manhattan later today," he heard her whisper.

"You told me you're not taking off until four o'clock. There's plenty of time. Niall?"

"Yes."

"Come here," he said softly.

It was only after she'd slid back into bed and was fast asleep in his arms that he finally exhaled the burning air in his lungs.

NINE

Three nights later Niall followed the hostess at The Art, still breathless from her sprint from the museum. She'd landed late at O'Hare and gone straight to her office at the museum without dropping off her suitcase, so that she could make an important conference call. The call had gone frustratingly long. She hated to be late for the dinner that she'd planned with Vic, knowing how little time he had, given his frantic schedule during these last few days before opening night. She knew he could get away for only a limited time tonight for dinner, so she regretted not being able to spend every second of it with him.

She'd missed seeing him these last few days—more than she cared to dwell upon. She'd been busy in meetings with a curator at the Metropolitan Museum, but she'd always been all too glad to receive Vic's phone calls in the evenings. The fact that he'd hardly said anything during those phone calls only endeared him more to her. She felt more connected to Vic in the silence than she did with most people after an extended heart-to-heart chat.

In fact, something about the fragile connection of those phone calls between Chicago and New York seemed to signal a shift in her relationship with Vic. Or maybe the change had begun last Sunday morning, when she'd awakened from her typical nightmare and allowed Vic to soothe her instead of withdrawing into her typical solitude.

She doubted the wisdom of deepening the relationship with Vic. If what was between them became more serious, she'd have to tell him about Stephen. She'd have to tell him about Michael. She'd experienced a powerful urge to do just that the other day on the stairs of her new condominium. Vic had guessed that there was some story behind the "emergency" that her parents had come to retrieve her for last week. He wasn't stupid.

But Niall was so used to vigilantly keeping her life private. It was a difficult habit to break.

And there was always the chance that he would judge her—judge her as her parents had, judge her as Stephen had . . .

It should have been you, Niall.

No. She didn't want to dwell on that now. Right now she wanted to think about Vic, about how wonderful it would be to see him again. Had it really only been three days since she'd lain in his arms as the light of dawn broke around the shades in his bedroom?

Something in her chest seemed to lurch when the hostess led her to the private booth where Vic sat. He stood. As usual he showed not the least bit of self-consciousness about eating her up with his eyes. Every time she saw him after a brief absence she was struck anew by his rugged, elemental male beauty. He looked movie-star handsome in a pair of khakis that fit his lean hips to perfection, a casual green and ivory button-down shirt with a white T-shirt beneath it. She recognized his well-worn brown bomber jacket hanging on the coat hook attached to the deep booth.

Her eyes swept the length of him hungrily and lingered for a moment on his brown leather belt. She must have made some kind of face, because when she met Vic's stare, the humor and heat in his gaze made the apologies for being late for their dinner date melt on her tongue.

Her silly smile faded almost as quickly when Vic leaned down and covered it with his mouth. His kiss resulted in even worse breathlessness than her sprint had caused, not to mention a slow, hot burn in her pussy that Niall had never experienced in such a public place before. His tongue swept her depths thoroughly, just as it did that first time he'd kissed her. After he'd seemingly been temporarily sated by her taste, he tilted his head, held her chin steady with his fingers, and slowed to a tender, hot slide.

That kiss kept Niall right at the boiling point, much as the previous one had turned her up to full power as easily as if he'd flipped on a switch.

"You're the only woman I know who could look like springtime wearing black," Vic murmured several knee-weakening seconds later. A shiver went down her spine at the sensation of his warm breath next to her ear.

She smiled and turned her head, nuzzling his cheek with her nose. Her heart beat erratically in her chest. It felt indescribably good to be in his arms again . . . to inhale his singular scent.

"I see that you got a new belt."

"There's plenty more where that came from," he murmured through a grin before he bent his head and tasted her lips again.

The hostess cleared her throat. "I'll just set these menus down here."

Niall started in embarrassment, realizing that the woman had been witness to her and Vic's entire exchange. How easily he made her forget herself. But Vic would have none of her embarrassment. He tilted her chin up to meet his mouth for another hot, possessive kiss. Only after he'd had a sufficient taste of her and the unacknowledged hostess was long gone did he finally release her from his arms.

They were back around her soon enough once he slid into the booth after her. She saw that he'd already ordered her a glass of wine.

"I'm sorry for being late. I never even got a chance to drop off my suitcase before I went to the museum. How much time do we have before you have to be back at the theater?" she queried anxiously.

"I have to meet with my lighting designer in an hour."

"Oh . . . so soon," she murmured regretfully. She blinked after a moment when she realized that she'd been staring hungrily at his mouth. "How is everything going with the play?"

He shrugged. "It's going."

She smiled as she took a sip of wine. Vic's fingers stroked her nape slowly, the seemingly casual touch setting off a series of fireworks along her sensitive nerves. He abruptly removed the clip that held her hair, allowing it to fall around her shoulders.

"Did you get everything done in New York that you intended?" he asked gruffly.

Niall's eyes fluttered closed in sublime satisfaction at the sensation of his long fingers massaging her scalp. "Yes."

"Did you miss me?"

Her eyelids opened and she met his hot, steady stare.

"You know I did."

His mouth tilted into a crooked grin. His first two fingers caressed the front of her throat softly before they twisted in her strand of pearls, forcing her closer to his face.

"Do you wear these pearls just to drive me nuts?"

Niall laughed softly. "No. I sincerely doubt that most men would say that pearls were a supersexy accessory."

"Most men are idiots, then," he muttered as he nuzzled her ear and then lightly bit at the tender flesh. Niall felt her pussy flood with moisture when his lips closed around the pearl studs in her earlobes and his warm tongue flicked against the gem and her flesh.

"I can't wait until opening night," he muttered a few seconds later.

"Why?" Niall asked breathlessly. Her entire consciousness focused with unbearable intensity on every subtle movement Vic's mouth made on her ear and neck.

"Because after all this shit with the play is said and done, I'm gonna show you just how sexy your pearls really are."

"Do we have to wait that long?" she shocked herself by asking.

Vic exhaled slowly. Much to her regret he removed his mouth from where it was nuzzling to such breathtaking effect along the back of her neck.

"Yes," he replied with just a tinge of irritation flattening his handsome mouth. "I've got a million things I need to do. If the next few nights are anything like the last two, I won't even get back to the apartment until three or four in the morning."

Niall brushed his lean cheek lightly with her fingertips. "You're going to make yourself sick if you keep up that pace, Vic."

"Just a few more nights of it. Opening night is the peak of the frenzy. It'll be downhill from there. And after that, you're all mine, Niall." He leaned forward and planted a quick, hard kiss on her mouth. When he raised his head his expression was thoughtful.

"You never did tell me how you got a boy's name."

"The name Niall has been passed on to a male in the Chandler family for generations. Since my parents only had me, I was the lucky recipient."

His eyelids narrowed slightly. "It suits you somehow. Is your father named Niall?"

She nodded.

"Guess I didn't make a great first impression on them the other day."

Niall flushed and glanced away. "That wasn't your fault. They're not usually that brusque. I think it just shocked them to see . . . us . . ." She waved her hand around in front of her. "You know."

"They don't think that their grown daughter has a right to her private life, including having sex," he finished flatly.

"No, that's not what I meant."

Even though she kept her eyes averted, she could feel his penetrating stare on her. Her discomfort only grew when she realized that this would be the perfect opportunity to tell him about Stephen. But should she even assume that would be what Vic wanted? Just because he was sexually attracted to her didn't mean that he wanted to share something so intimate.

The waiter approached, and Niall's moment for self-disclosure passed. She told herself her ambivalence about talking to Vic about herself had absolutely *nothing* to do with a fear that he might condemn her.

During dinner Niall tried her best to keep her attention on the topic of conversation instead of thinking about her burgeoning relationship with Vic. But it was difficult to remain focused when she was so aware of the man that the side of her body pressed and brushed against so intimately. The movement of his neck when he swallowed beguiled her, the sensation of his fingers casually stroking her neck distracted her, the sight of his muscular, hair-sprinkled forearms just plain turned her on.

"My mother and Meg are going to be here on Friday afternoon," Vic said as the waiter cleared the remains of their dinner.

"You're going to be busy at the theater, aren't you?" Niall asked. When he nodded, she added, "I'd love to take them out to dinner before the play. Would you extend the invitation?"

"Sure," Vic muttered. Niall colored when she realized that he studied her intently while he spoke, and that the message in his eyes nowhere near matched their casual verbal exchange.

"We have some delicious dessert offerings for you this evening. May I tell you about our specials?" the enthusiastic waiter asked.

"What we'd like is some privacy."

At first the waiter looked a little nonplussed at Vic's bluntness but he recovered swiftly, merely nodding and offering a slightly offended "of course" before he walked away.

"Subtle, Vic," Niall murmured in amusement.

"He's the one who's being thick. Any fool could see that what I'm interested in isn't on the dessert menu."

Niall's gasp of surprise when he covered her mouth with his own segued to a low moan of arousal in a matter of seconds. She didn't think of protesting when his fingers lowered from her neck inside her blouse, where he lightly caressed her breast. Her nipples beaded tight beneath his plucking fingertips. She arched her back, pressing her flesh into his palm. How was it that he always knew precisely when to be soft with her and when to be hard? His gentle, stroking fingers made her burn with a desire for more of his magical touch.

When he suddenly seemed intent on granting her wish, however, Niall was shocked.

"Vic what are you doing?" she whispered against his lips when he slipped his big hand beneath her skirt and skimmed his fingertips across her thigh.

"You're wearing a garter belt?" he asked incredulously.

"Yes," she muttered when he slid his forefinger beneath the elastic of the garter and trailed it up to the bottom of her panties.

"You are *such* a good girl," he muttered with a naughty grin.

Niall's eyes widened in stark disbelief and arousal when he pressed two fingers against her labia and moved rhythmically. She glanced around the restaurant nervously. They were fairly secluded in the deep booth. She couldn't see anyone directly, but she definitely heard the muted sound of voices and clinking dinnerware in the distance.

"Vic, people will see," she whispered.

His answer to that consisted of fluffing out the tablecloth until it covered her lap and to keep right on doing what he was doing. Niall's face pinched tight with lust when he began to pulse his long fingers vertically as well, working the hard ridge of his forefinger between her swollen lips until he directly stimulated her clit.

"Your panties are wet," he whispered as he nuzzled her ear. "Much too wet to have gotten that way just now. Were you getting turned on while we ate dinner?"

"Yes," Niall admitted. She turned her head and tried to get to his lips, but he backed up slightly, eluding her. She gave a shaky cry when his fingers pushed aside the triangle of silk that covered her seeping sex. He growled in satisfaction as he stroked her clit with eye-crossing precision.

"You always get so wet for me," he murmured warmly into her ear. "Spread your thighs, baby."

"Vic . . ." she protested weakly. It felt so good . . . but they were in a restaurant for God's sake.

"Shhh," he soothed as he pressed several hot kisses against her neck. "You wouldn't be so cruel as to make me wait two more nights before I feel you shake in my arms, would you? Open your thighs and lean back just a tad . . . That's it," he praised when she allowed him to tilt her upper body back, granting him better access to her pussy.

Niall gasped in pleasure when he plunged his last two fingers
into her pussy while he continued to stimulate her clit with a firm,
ruthless pressure.

"You're turning red. Always a good sign," he murmured as he
brushed his lips over her flaming cheeks. Niall just stared up
blindly at a place where the wall met the ceiling as he finger-fucked
her forcefully at the same time that he pressed and glided against
her clit. She clenched her eyes shut in the sweetest of agonies when
the wet, slurping sounds of his fingers moving in her abundant
juices reached her ears.

"Oh," she whispered in a choked voice after a minute, "it burns."

"Just let it happen," he ordered quietly.

She couldn't refuse him. She bit her lip to still her cries a moment later as she came.

When she'd quieted and opened her eyes dazedly, Vic matter-of-
factly scooted her hips forward on the seat of the booth. He leaned
her against his arm before he reached back under the tablecloth
and pushed his first and second finger into her pussy. The new angle allowed him to penetrate her deeply. He sealed off her cry with
his mouth on her lips. Niall moaned in arousal and bemusement as
he kissed the living daylights out of her at the same time that he
plunged into her pussy with a hard, relentless rhythm.

When he finally raised his head a second later, she was—much
to her shock—well on her way to a second orgasm. She moaned in
disappointment when he withdrew his fingers before she could
reach it.

His eyes gleamed with arousal as he held her stare and quickly
dipped his fingers into his mouth. She almost climaxed from the vi-
sual stimulation of his lean cheeks hollowing and his muscular
throat contracting as he sucked and swallowed her juices. He always
seemed so genuinely hungry for her taste . . . so ruthless about get-

ting it. When he withdrew his fingers, he covered her gaping mouth with a hard, quick kiss.

"That was what I wanted for dessert," he told her gruffly. "Sit up now, baby."

Niall struggled into an upright position at Vic's abrupt command. The waiter appeared not two seconds later, carrying the bill. He waited with a stiff expression on his face while Vic took out his wallet and threw a credit card into the leather folder.

Thank God, she thought dazedly. Vic must have heard or seen the waiter approaching. She'd been too mindless with excitement to have noticed much of anything but her approaching orgasm.

Was there nothing she wouldn't do for this man, Niall wondered with a mixture of awe and unease as she studied his starkly beautiful profile.

When Niall heard the brisk knock at her front door, she studied her appearance in the bathroom mirror anxiously. Not bad, she guessed. She'd never attended an opening night at the theater and she had forgotten to ask Vic what kind of attire was appropriate. She couldn't imagine Vic showing up in anything too formal. That just wasn't his style. In the end, she'd settled for a creamy silk blouse, a chocolate brown skirt, and her favorite buttery soft leather boots that hugged her calves tightly.

Beneath it she wore a sexy bra, panty, and garter belt ensemble. That part of her attire was for later . . . with Vic. The thought made her stomach flutter with excitement as she headed toward the front door.

She smiled warmly when she let in the two women standing in the hallway. They were both tall and striking, and wore identical broad grins on their faces.

"Well, let's not stand on ceremony," the younger of the two said as she stepped forward and gave Niall a hug. "I'm Meg Sandoval, and this is my mother, Ellen. And you're Niall, of course. Any woman who can make my little brother smile on an opening night deserves a hug, don't you think, Mom?"

"Absolutely," Ellen Savian stated matter-of-factly. "She'd deserve one anyway, for taking us out to dinner."

Vic had inherited both his mother's eyes and her direct manner, Niall realized as Ellen studied her closely and unabashedly for a moment.

"Well, my goodness, you're pretty! Isn't she pretty, Meg?"

"Mom," Meg scolded, "you'll embarrass her. You'll have to excuse us, Niall. We're just a couple of country bumpkins."

Niall laughed at that as she led them down the hallway. "You hardly look like *bumpkins* to me. Won't you come in and have a drink before we go to dinner?"

Certainly Vic's mother and sister were refreshingly blunt and honest, but what Niall had said about them hardly seeming like bumpkins was the absolute truth. Their height, handsome figures, and striking features afforded them a natural elegance that most women would have killed to possess.

Niall genuinely enjoyed getting to know Meg and Ellen during dinner. She discovered that Meg was the high school principal in a small town near Vic's farm and that she loved art. She was, in fact, a member of the Chicago Metropolitan Museum and had attended three of Niall's special exhibitions in the past. She was thrilled when Niall offered to give her and Ellen a private tour of the museum the following day.

Ellen Savian charmed Niall with her combination of keen intelligence and unapologetic small town ways. She refused to be embarrassed by her curiosity on any topic, and that included asking

Niall point-blank what she thought about her son, and telling the waiter at dinner that she hadn't yet had her full requirement of calcium today, and could he please bring her a tall glass of whole milk to drink along with her wine.

"And a cup of ice, too, if you don't mind," Ellen had added before the waiter walked away. "Meg always tells me you're supposed to drink red wine at room temperature, but hot wine is about as appetizing as cold pizza, if you ask me," she told Niall with a confidential nod of her head.

"Have you ever been inside the Hesse?" Meg asked Niall after dinner when they entered the crowded theater lobby.

"No, I haven't," Niall said as she glanced in admiration at the handsomely renovated historic building. "They just reopened it last year, didn't they?"

Meg nodded. "Vic gave Tim and me the nickel tour the last time we visited him," she said, referring to her husband. "Do you want me to show you and Niall around, Mom, or would you rather wait for Vic to do it?"

"Oh, you do it," Ellen said with an impatient wave of her hand. "We won't see Vic until the curtain opens, and he'll be too distracted to be any good to us during intermission."

They were descending the elegant, winding staircase following Meg's tour when Meg paused abruptly on a step.

"Well I'll be—"

Niall's eyes flickered down the stairs to find the source of Meg's sudden discomposure. Her gaze landed on one of the most famous faces in Hollywood.

"Meg! Oh, Ellen . . . you're here, too! How wonderful to see you both."

"Jenny." Meg acknowledged the stunning woman with a nod as she neared.

"What are you doing here, Jenny?"

Jennifer Atwood's full, sensual lips widened into a smile at Ellen's blunt question even though Niall got the distinct impression that she was fighting the urge to frown. Niall had never seen a movie star up close before, and was amazed to see that Jennifer Atwood was impossibly more gorgeous in real life than she was on the big screen. What interested her more by far, however, was Jennifer's connection to Vic's family.

"I don't think you two have met my wonderful husband, Max Blake. Max, meet Meg Sandoval and Ellen Savian," Jenny said as she swept her hand toward a man who looked perfectly prepared to join Jennifer on the glossy cover of a magazine. "Max is a producer. I've told him about Vic's wonderful work. Max thinks Vic's plays would adapt marvelously to the big screen."

Ellen snorted, but Meg took a more diplomatic approach. "It's a pleasure to meet you, Max," she said as she shook his hand. "I have to tell you that I sincerely doubt Vic will be interested in doing a screenplay. I would have thought you knew that, Jenny," Meg challenged gently.

Jenny chuckled as though recalling the adorable, ornery antics of an old pet. "So Vic is still playing the rebel against Hollywood? God, you'd think he was an old hippy the way he rebels against anything that even hints of the 'establishment.' "

Max seemed to notice Meg's stiff, offended expression even if Jenny chose not to. "To each his own, I say," he said with a dashing grin. "I can't tell you the number of times a day I fantasize about thumbing my nose at the *establishment* and escaping to the country like Savian did."

Ellen's stare at Max Blake was frankly disbelieving. Clearly she couldn't picture the man who stood in front of her with the perfectly tailored cashmere blazer and the artfully tousled curls doing

much of anything in Avery, South Dakota, but become irate because he kept losing his cell phone coverage.

Meg, on the other hand, just seemed vaguely amused when her
eyes met Niall's. "Niall, I apologize for not introducing you earlier. Jennifer, Max, meet Niall Chandler."

When Niall saw Jenny's eyes lower over her in cool appraisal,
she intuitively understood that she and Vic had once been lovers.

"It's a pleasure to meet you," Niall said. "I've always admired
your work."

"Have you?"

Jenny's smile looked warm, but wasn't her tone a little conde-
scending, as if it was considered in poor taste for Niall to mention
her celebrity status? Maybe it was just Niall's insecurities that
made it seem that way. It was difficult to stand next to a divine
creature like Jennifer Atwood and think of her having shared Vic's
bed and maintain her normal confidence. Niall scoured her memory, trying to recall if there had ever been any mention of the famous actress dating a certain sexy, reclusive, talented playwright,
but she came up short. Niall had never been one to follow the entertainment industry too closely.

Jenny's beauty fascinated her, Niall had to admit. She was almost as tall as Meg and Ellen. Her figure was slender and willowy,
perfectly suited to the sophisticated black designer pant suit that
she wore with a white silk camisole beneath it. Her breasts filled
out the front of her jacket amply without subtracting from the lean,
graceful lines of her body. Her dark hair was styled like a 1940s
Hollywood film goddess, parted on the side and falling loose and
sleekly curled below her shoulders. The eyes that studied Niall
speculatively were a striking shade of light brown and amber.

"Well, I suppose we better take our seats," Jenny said after
Niall and Max had exchanged a handshake. "Please tell Vic we'll

be there to celebrate his opening at the party at Mina's afterward. Max went to school with someone who's a patron of the Hesse, so he scored us an invite."

"Just what Vic needs tonight," Meg muttered under her breath as she watched Max lead Jenny down the stairs.

"Hmmph," Ellen grunted sourly. Her sharp, light gray eyes looked suspicious as they followed the stunning actress across the theater lobby. "Vic needs her like he needs a daily dose of arsenic."

From the little that Niall had seen of Jennifer Atwood, she had to agree wholeheartedly.

Still, Meg's frank expression of worry bothered her. Would the situation warrant concern if what was between Jenny and Vic was a thing of the past?

And was arsenic by any chance addictive in addition to being deadly?

Niall supposed a mother did indeed know best when Vic slid into the empty seat next to her just seconds before the curtain rose. His thick hair stood up haphazardly, as if he'd been raking his fingers through it. He looked harried and rumpled and utterly gorgeous in a well-cut blazer, brown dress pants, and an off-white chambray shirt. His collar was unbuttoned, and Niall spied his pulse beating rapidly at his throat.

He gave Meg a dry glance when she leaned forward and gave him a big sister stare of dark amusement. Ellen just gave him a brisk wave before she turned her full attention to the stage.

"Sorry I'm late," he whispered as he picked up Niall's hand and gave her a quick, warm kiss on the back of it.

"It's okay," she assured him softly as she squeezed him back in shared excitement. He met her eyes briefly and gave a small grin before he hunched his big body down in the seat, spread his long legs as far as the confining space allowed, and turned his total focus to the production.

Niall turned her attention to the events on the stage as well, but her heart went out to the man next to her. He seemed so tense, so anticipatory. She couldn't imagine what it would be like to put so much of yourself into a creative endeavor and then sit by and watch as months . . . maybe even years . . . of hard work unfolded before your eyes. She was always nervous and proud of the exhibits she planned at the museum, of course. But this was different.

This was like watching an aspect of Vic's soul brightly illuminated on a public stage.

No wonder he got so worked up, Niall thought in awe at the culmination of the first act. She'd been held spellbound by the scenes between Sissy, the character played by Eileen Moore, and David, who was being played by an actor Niall had frequently seen in supporting roles in films. The dialogue crackled with wit. The sexual tension between the two characters was so taut as to be nearly tangible. But aggression and anger also laced almost every interaction between them, creating a potent, fascinating brew of love, lust, and rage that seemed ready to explode on the stage at any given moment.

It soon became very clear to Niall that the title of the play, *Alias X*, referred to the identities that people took on in order to shape themselves to their lover's desires. The X referred not only to an artificial, nameless existence but also to the mysterious, sometimes beautiful, often ugly, unknown depths to which human beings could sink if they sacrificed what was genuine for the sake of another's love.

Niall felt a little dazed by the intermission. She was glad that

Vic took her hand and led her into the noisy lobby, because she needed the guidance.

"Can I get you anything?" he asked solicitously when he turned to face her. "I don't think they sell Scotch at the concession stand, but I've got a bottle in my office. Just happens to be your brand, too."

"I don't need anything."

She wondered if her heart was in her eyes, because he started to say something and then abruptly paused as he looked down at her.

"What?" he drawled.

"The play is amazing, Vic," she said softly. But she meant that *he* was. And Niall thought he probably knew it when a slow grin curved his lips. Did he have any notion of how beautiful he looked at that moment . . . how happy?

She had assumed that he would go and have some terse exchange with one of the technicians or the stage manager during the intermission, but instead he spent the short break with them. Niall was only vaguely aware of Ellen and Meg approaching, and then the steady line of well-wishers who followed to offer Vic congratulations that were entirely too enthusiastic to be feigned. Not that Niall would have guessed otherwise. The electric intellectual vitality of the play had transferred to the audience. It was obvious in the expressions of the people who approached Vic, but also in the energy level of the lobby as people engaged in lively conversations about what they'd seen thus far.

Most of Niall's attention centered on Vic, however, as he patiently listened while a newspaper critic gushed or made that subtle rolling motion with his jaw as a Hesse board member raved. He glanced up once and gave Niall a quick wink when a particularly garrulous city council member walked away glowing, not seeming to notice or care that Vic had barely uttered two syllables during their entire exchange.

"Guess what they say about Chicago being called the Windy City because of its politicians is true," he murmured into her ear before he kissed it.

Pride for him swelled in Niall's breast, mixing with a host of the other emotions that had been ignited by his soulful, volatile play. He introduced her to everyone who approached. He put his arm around her while Ellen detailed every item that she'd ordered at the restaurant.

"Vic, there's something—" Meg began, but just then the lights dimmed, signaling that the intermission was over. Niall got the distinct impression from the concerned expression on Meg's face that she'd been about to tell him that Jennifer Atwood was attending his play.

When Eileen Moore came onto the stage a minute later, Niall suddenly recalled what Vic had said about sleeping with her after he'd suffered a serious breakup with a woman he'd planned to marry. Her unease deepened. Had Vic been engaged to Jennifer Atwood? And more important . . . was he still in love with her?

TEN

The second portion of *Alias X* held the audience even more spellbound than the first. Niall had never seen a production that was so carnal, so volatile, and yet so intellectually thought-provoking at the same time.

During the second half she began to better understand Vic's use of symbolism in his minimalist set design. She recalled what he'd said when they made love in her new condominium. *I'm a guy. I like the visuals.* Niall didn't know if it was because he was a male or not, but as a scholar in the arts, she recognized the genius behind his vision for set design.

Vic planned to meet Niall, Meg, and Ellen at the opening night party after he took care of some business at the theater. They paused outside his office after he'd given them the backstage tour of the Hesse to which Meg hadn't had access.

"You know the opening night party is going to be at Mina's?" he asked Niall.

Niall smiled at the dry edge to his tone and nodded. She knew of the place. It was a posh restaurant with a clublike atmosphere that overlooked Michigan Avenue. Vic caught her grin and smiled back. Just like that, Niall knew that someone else had made the opening night party plans and Vic was resigned to spending his special night at such a trendy, fashionable venue.

She saw something else in that quick flash of his eyes as he smiled at her, though. He looked forward to tonight—to them making love after almost a week's abstinence. And Niall was more than ready for it, too, especially given the near to bursting feeling she had in her chest cavity every time she glanced at Vic or touched him after watching his amazing play.

Vic abruptly grasped her hand. "We'll just be a second," he muttered to Ellen and Meg before he dragged Niall back into his office and slammed the door behind him.

"Vic, what—"

But he cut her off as he swept down and began to devour her with his mouth. He bent over her, drinking from her thirstily before he grunted impatiently. Niall felt him strengthen his hold on her and her feet rose off the ground. Her hands gripped desperately at his shoulders, instinctively recognizing she might be swept into uncharted, tumultuous territories by the magnitude of their combined desire.

By the time Vic slid her body erotically down the length of his lean body and set her boots back down on the ground, both of them were out of breath. Niall thought she would overheat at her core when he spread his hand over her breast and massaged and shaped it to his palm.

"You're spending the night at my place tonight," he stated firmly.

Niall moaned softly in pleasure at his touch and nodded.

"Don't plan on getting any actual sleep, though."

Niall laughed throatily and pressed her belly against his iron-hard erection. "Sleep wasn't on my agenda, I promise you."

He stared down at her for a few seconds, his features rigid. "I guess we should go get this over with," he said regretfully.

"You should try to enjoy yourself. You deserve to celebrate. You've done a phenomenal job."

He sighed and parted from her with a look of regret. "Niall?" he said as she turned toward the door.

"Yes?"

"Did you really like it?" he asked, a grin tilting his lips, as though he found it amusing that he wanted her reassurance.

"I thought it was incredible," she said feelingly.

"It wasn't exactly pretty."

"Pretty?" Niall repeated slowly. "No . . . I don't suppose it was. But it was very human. And there were parts of it that were"—she paused, searching for the right words—"astonishingly beautiful," she finished softly.

His brushed his thumb tenderly across her cheek before he kissed her once more.

Ellen and Meg didn't bat an eyelash when Niall and Vic returned to the corridor looking flushed, mussed, and entirely pleased with themselves. Ellen just patted her son's cheek fondly as they said their temporary farewells.

"Got no reason to be grouchy tonight, do you, boy? You got yourself a winner there," she stated baldly. She'd glanced over at Niall, who was encircled in Vic's arm, and winked mischievously. "The play wasn't half bad, either."

Vic looked down at Niall. "My mom always does pick the winners," he said in a low rumble. Then he kissed her unashamedly as Meg and Ellen looked on with identical smirks on their faces.

Niall walked out of the theater a minute later and breathed deeply of the refreshing, cool air. "The city looks beautiful tonight, doesn't it?" she asked, genuinely amazed at the surreal uniformity of the midnight blue sky, the sharp, crisp outlines of the buildings against it, how vibrant and colorful the lights from the high-rises were.

Meg laughed softly and took her arm as they headed to get a cab. "Oh, honey, you're in it deep, aren't you?" she murmured fondly. She laughed when Niall gave her a look of puzzlement.

When they arrived at the private room at Mina's, Niall was a little surprised at how crowded it already was. She realized that she knew several people there. Many patrons of the theater were also sponsors for the museum. She was glad that she didn't have to depend entirely upon contacts that Meg and Ellen had made through Vic's earlier productions in order to socialize, and could introduce them to some interesting people as well. The overall atmosphere of the party was buoyant and energetic, just as it should have been on the night that symbolized the pinnacle of achievement for a company that knew they had a hit on their hands.

The three of them were chatting with an eclectic group consisting of Caesar Ramirez, Vic's lighting designer; Marcus Alvion, a CEO for MarketTech, a Chicago-based company that supported the Hesse and who also sat on the fund-raising committee for Niall's museum; and Mya Shore, a friendly, outgoing young woman who was an entertainment writer for the *Chicago Tribune*, when Eileen Moore joined them.

Eileen greeted Ellen and Meg with a kiss. She regarded Niall curiously as Meg formally introduced them, but without any of the rancor that she'd shown that evening at The Art. Perhaps she had no time for animosity, as aglow as she was with the evening's success.

And she deserved it, Niall acknowledged. Her performance had been electrifying, and she told Eileen as much. She and the actress were in the process of feeling each other out, deciding whether or not they liked each other, when Vic entered the room. He received such loud, resounding applause from the partygoers that the regular diners in Mina's restaurant must have thought a bomb exploded. He grinned slowly, waved, ducked his head, and turned aside to speak to the man who accompanied him into the room. Niall knew instinctively that while he appreciated the crowd's sentiment, it couldn't be over quickly enough for him.

She also noticed that Eileen clapped louder than anyone else in their group, and that the expression on her face as she stared at Vic bordered on idolatry.

Eileen stiffened even more than Niall did when Jennifer Atwood suddenly appeared out of the crowd and touched Vic's elbow. Even from her distance across the crowded room Niall saw the marked change that overcame Vic's countenance as he looked down at her. Jennifer went up on her tiptoes to kiss his cheek.

"*That bitch*," Eileen hissed softly as her clapping slowed to a stop. "She's got nerve coming here on Vic's special night after what she did to him."

"What did she do to him?" Niall asked, not at all sure she really wanted to know.

"Fucked him up good," Eileen muttered under her breath before she took a long draw on her martini. Her eyes never moved from the sight of Vic staring down at Jennifer Atwood's beautiful face.

"He's never told you about her?" Eileen asked bitterly, although she was careful to keep her voice low enough so that only Niall heard her.

Niall's lips pressed together tightly. If Eileen had asked the question condescendingly, in a way that implied Niall couldn't possibly mean anything to Vic if he'd never revealed his secrets to her, than Niall probably would have tried to turn the subject. But she hadn't. Instead, she'd asked like she was totally preoccupied by the situation. Eileen obviously cared deeply about Vic and didn't want to see him hurt again.

The fact that Jennifer still had the power to wound Vic was becoming uncomfortably obvious to Niall.

"No," Niall admitted finally. "He hasn't mentioned her to me."

Eileen finally ripped her eyes away when Jennifer brushed Vic's arm with her hand in a lingering caress and turned back into the crowd. "He was supposed to marry her, you know. But she was never happy with him, always scolding him for not living up to his *potential*, harassing him to move to Los Angeles and compete with the big boys like her slick-ass husband, complaining that his provincialism was bringing her career, as much as his own, to a halt," Eileen said before she took another long drink, nearly emptying her glass.

Eileen gave a harsh bark of laughter after a few seconds. "I swear she tore him apart from the inside out. Vic wanted to please her, but he never could, you know? It got to the point where he just tuned her out, ignored her. That's the worst sort of punishment for a woman like Jennifer," Eileen murmured in that magnificent, deep voice that she used to such stirring effect on the stage.

"So she got back at him by jumping in the sack with ol' Max over there, staging things just right so that Vic found them going at it full force."

Niall flinched at the harshness of Eileen's statement. She hated to think of Vic being subjected to something so painful. *She tore him apart from the inside out.* From the look that she'd seen on

Vic's face just now Niall had no problem wholeheartedly believing the accuracy of that statement.

All the effervescence and joy Niall had felt earlier that evening seemed to be dissipating as quickly as the bubbles in her untouched champagne.

"But Jennifer ended up being the butt of her nasty tricks," Eileen continued. "She thought she'd whip Vic into a frenzy of jealousy and rage with her little plot, believed that he'd be even more desperate to keep her at all costs. But instead Vic dropped her faster than a stranger's germ-ridden snot rag." Eileen laughed softly, genuinely seeming to enjoy the memory. "She tried to get back in his good graces for months afterward, but the only thing she got from Vic was silence and ice. Finally she gave up and married ol' Max a year later. I don't think Vic has given her the opportunity to speak more than two words to him since then."

"Until tonight," Niall said softly.

"Yeah. Until tonight," Eileen agreed with wary speculation.

Both women's gazes flickered across the crowded room until they found Vic. His head stood above everyone else's, so he wasn't too difficult to spot. He was conversing in earnest with a bald man Niall didn't recognize. His typical impassive expression was once again in place, so Niall couldn't guess at his emotional state.

She cleared her throat with difficulty. "You seem to know an awful lot about the whole situation with Vic and Jennifer, Eileen."

"I should. What do you think I was acting out on that stage up there tonight?" she asked with a bitter laugh.

Annoyance flickered across Vic's awareness as he pretended to listen to a half-drunk Chicago socialite who had legs up to her armpits. He'd been trying to send Niall a "save me" signal for the past ten minutes now, but for some reason her gaze always seemed to bounce in the opposite direction whenever it got near him.

And where had all the luminescence that had been shining in her face earlier gone? Granted, he studied her from across a crowded room, but she suddenly seemed distant . . . drained.

Maybe she hated this type of affair almost as much as he did.

When he saw Niall make her way across the room an interminable few minutes later, he muttered a gruff "excuse me" during the socialite's mid-ramble, barely noticing her shocked, offended expression as he walked away without a backward glance.

"Shit," he muttered under his breath a few seconds later when he caught a glimpse of Niall's golden hair before the ladies' room door shut with her on the other side of it.

"I think the boys' bathroom is over there."

Vic stiffened before he turned to face Jenny.

"I'm waiting for my date."

"That blonde girl? Niall, wasn't it?"

Vic didn't respond, knowing that Jenny knew precisely to whom he referred. Besides, she was baiting him by calling Niall a girl.

He'd been so shocked by her sudden appearance earlier that he hadn't been clear on what he'd been feeling since then. He suspected that Jenny's presence *must* be having a profound effect on him on some unconscious level.

How could it not?

But in all honesty the only thing Vic had been focused on since he'd arrived at Mina's was being with Niall. It seemed like every goddamned person in the room had adhered to him at some point, making it impossible for him to merely cross a span of fifty feet and claim her. He saw that she was always conversing with someone, including his mother, his sister, and a middle-aged, powerfully built man who looked like he was considering taking a bite out of her as she looked up at him with her huge, sexy eyes. His friend Caesar—who went through women like Vic did number-two pencils when he was on an editing spree—had a glazed-eyed, goofy look on his face as he vied for Niall's attention. Best forget what Caesar looked like he was about to do when Niall laughed at one of his dumb-ass jokes if Vic wanted to maintain their friendship.

It never occurred to him to question the fact that he didn't have a clue as to what Jenny had been doing for the last hour in the crowded room.

"May I have a word with you in private?" Jenny asked, her omnipresent hand settling on his lower arm.

"I can't right now." Her perfume found its way to his nostrils. Just the hint of it used to drive him wild with lust.

"Just a minute of your time, Vic? Didn't what we had together warrant at least that?" Jenny asked in a trembling voice that struck Vic at that moment as totally genuine.

He answered her honestly. "I don't owe you a damn thing, Jenny." He glanced back at the closed ladies' room door. "But it's no sweat off my back if you want to talk to me for a minute."

Much to his surprise, he realized that what he said was true. Why shouldn't he listen to what she had to say? She was a human being, after all. He no longer felt the nauseating, blinding rage that he'd suffered in various degrees since he'd found her in his bed bouncing up and down on Max Blake's cock.

That image—not to mention the cumulative effect of the hundreds of cruel, petty things Jennifer and he used to do to spite each other—had clawed at his insides for years like a vicious animal demanding release. But in that singular moment when he'd caught Jenny in bed with Max, Vic had been enlightened. He'd realized that he'd become an addict whose sole purpose consisted of getting his next fix. His entire world had narrowed down to the positive reinforcement he received from stoking Jenny's insatiable fires. In the end, he hadn't cared if he did it by igniting her desire or her fury.

It wasn't a pretty thing to learn about oneself. He guessed that's what he'd meant when he asked Niall what she thought about the play earlier.

Jenny tilted her head back toward an empty corridor. "Come here," she coaxed softly.

Vic hesitated for a second as his gaze fixed on the rear view of Jenny's phenomenal body.

What the hell? he finally thought as he followed her. Better to face the truth about how he felt about her than to always be running from it.

Niall felt a little better when she left the ladies' room. She'd splashed some cool water on her face in an attempt to revive herself and then reapplied her makeup. When she'd inspected herself in the mirror a moment later, she realized how pale she looked. She dug in her purse for some lipstick to add some color to her washed-out palette, becoming unreasonably irritated when she realized she'd left if in her coat pocket.

"Get a grip on it," she whispered to her reflection a few seconds later. She took a deep breath and exhaled.

Eileen Moore might be wrong about Vic's feelings for Jennifer Atwood. Art often imitated life, certainly, but it also varied from it greatly. Besides, *Alias X* reflected a certain time in Vic's life, like a snapshot in a photo album. That didn't necessarily mean that Vic was still wildly, passionately in love with Jennifer.

Did it?

Were ties of the soul—even twisted ones—so easily severed?

Niall threw her comb back into her purse with a frown. She wasn't going to come to any earth-shattering revelations about Vic's love life by staring at herself in the mirror. *She* was the one he'd asked to his play tonight, *not* Jennifer Atwood.

Niall turned the corner that led to the coat check, planning to get her lipstick from her pocket before she went and found Vic.

She found him all right.

She came up short and stared at the sight in front of her. Vic leaned back against the wood paneling of the narrow corridor, his head bent downward while Jennifer Atwood craned up, their bodies sealed together as tightly as their mouths.

Niall didn't think she'd made a noise, but she must have. Because suddenly Vic's gray eyes were on her, the impact of them striking her like a blast of sleety, frigid wind.

She turned and fled.

"Niall," Vic called out sharply as he straightened, knocking Jenny slightly off balance in her stiletto heels.

"Vic, hold on, please! I'm sorry. I didn't mean for that to happen . . ." Jenny said breathlessly as she put a restraining hand on his shoulder.

"Yeah, you did," Vic said distractedly as he moved past her. "And maybe I did, too."

Jennifer stared after him, her jaw hanging open as he strode away from her.

Vic cursed for the second time tonight when he saw the back of Niall's shiny hair and the flash of a fast-moving, leather-covered calf before she disappeared behind yet another door . . . this time the elevator's.

Dammit, why did it always seem like Niall was just slipping through his grasping fingertips?

He paused outside the lobby doors a minute later after waiting for another elevator, searching in both directions for Niall. She was nowhere in sight. His mouth pulled into a grim line as he started west at a jog, figuring she'd instinctively head toward home.

Niall didn't even register that she was shivering like mad until she finally hailed a cab on Rush Street and came to a halt in her frantic escape. Damn. She'd left her coat behind. The temperature hovered right at the freezing mark, and all she wore was a silk blouse and a skirt.

Going back into Mina's at that moment—returning to that corridor where she'd seen Vic kissing Jennifer—was not even a remote option, however. At least she wouldn't have to worry about seeing Ellen and Meg to their hotel, Niall thought with a twinge of guilt. Vic's mother and sister were literally staying across the street from the building where Mina's was located.

"*Niall.*"

She looked around, astounded to see Vic jogging down the street toward her. She opened the door of the cab that had just neatly pulled up to the curb, and clambered inside. Vic's hand caught the door when she tried to slam it shut forcefully. From the sound of his terse curse, her action had hurt him.

Good. It couldn't come anywhere near the pain that had sliced through Niall when she saw his dark head bent over Jennifer Atwood's face as he kissed her.

"Scoot over, Niall."

"*No!* This is my cab," she countered, realizing that she sounded like a petulant child.

"*Move . . . over,*" Vic demanded through a clenched jaw.

Niall just stared up at him for a few seconds. How dare he act like *he* was mad at her? For some reason all those nasty verbal duals that Sissy and David engaged in during *Alias X* rose to her mind. Niall abruptly slid across the seat and stared forward, unseeing.

She was no Sissy *or* Jennifer. She would *not* sit here and bicker with and bait Vic like a trashy slut. If that was the kind of thing he got off on, he was going to be sorely disappointed, Niall promised herself.

She was the one who was mistaken, however, if she thought Vic was going to try and start a fight with her. He remained as icily silent during the cab ride to Riverview Towers as she did. He didn't, in fact, speak until the elevator doors closed behind them and he'd pushed the button for the seventeenth floor.

"I'm sorry you had to see that."

Niall met his gaze for the first time since he'd glared down at her before she'd slammed the door on his hand. She couldn't read his rigid expression as he stood several feet away from her and pinned her with his stare.

"I'm sorry I saw it, too. But maybe it's for the best," she replied as evenly as possible. She exhaled abruptly and stared up at the ceiling, shaking her head. "You don't have to apologize, Vic. It's not as if you owe me anything."

"No?" he drawled.

She shook her head again, still avoiding his gaze.

"Just like you don't owe me anything—right, Niall? A satisfying fuck if the convenient opportunity should arise. That's what we owe each other, right?"

Fury rose in her, despite the fact that she'd vowed to herself that she wouldn't let him push her buttons. "What's that supposed to mean?" she demanded as the elevator door opened with a ding.

His hand went up to hold it in place automatically, but he didn't really seem aware of his actions as he leaned forward and answered her. "It means that you've got a lot of nerve accusing me of not being interested in having a relationship with you when you're just as elusive and secretive about your past—even more so—than I am about mine. You just saw my ugly little secrets paraded in front of your eyes on a stage tonight. I didn't have to invite you to see that, but I did. How much more honest do you think I can be with you?"

"So I'm just supposed to shrug my shoulders at the fact that I just saw you kissing another woman, a woman everybody—including your mother and sister—believes you're crazy in love with?"

"A woman that I *was* crazy in love with!" Vic countered, his eyes flashing fiercely.

Both of them jumped when an alarm suddenly started blaring because Vic had held the elevator door open for too long. Vic blinked as if the sound had roused him out of a dream. Niall found herself meeting his eyes again, curious as to what he would say next . . . hungry for it.

"We'd better get off," he said quietly, disappointing her. Their gazes remained locked for the next few seconds as she moved toward him cautiously, as if afraid on some primitive level that she would glom on to him like he was a powerful magnet and she was a flimsy filament of iron that was helpless to take voluntary action in his vicinity.

She made it down the hallway without submitting to as much as a glance. She paused when she reached their front doors and looked back at him, feeling shaken and unsure.

"I kissed her because I wanted to, Niall. I kissed her because I had to *know*. Do you understand?"

Niall's lips fell open. It wasn't the explanation that she'd expected. But it was the one she needed.

"And?" she asked, her voice wavering with anxiety.

Vic shrugged, his singular eyes never leaving her face. "I'm here with you, aren't I?"

ELEVEN

For a few tense seconds, Vic didn't know what Niall was going to do. He was surprised when she suddenly launched herself at him.

Nice . . . having her small, compact little body collide with his, having her hands reach up hungrily to hold his head and pull him down to her. He groaned in pleasure at the impact of her feverish kiss and her taste pervading his senses.

Better than nice.

He'd always liked the fit of a tall woman against his body. But he had to admit that Niall's taut curves filled his palm just right. So what if he had to bend his knees and lift her against him so that he could feel the soft heat between her thighs pressed against his cock? Her entire weight in his arms only made him exponentially more aroused. He spread both hands across her ass and she automatically encircled him with her legs. God, he needed to get inside of her. Anywhere . . . anyhow.

Just as long as it was *soon*.

He grunted as he tried to move toward his apartment, but misjudged and backed into his door with a bang. Niall didn't even seem to notice the jarring sensation, continuing to rub and suck at his tongue, turning kissing into what felt like the main event of making love instead of the first step. He dimly realized that he should set her down and at least get her into his apartment, but her sweet mouth blinded him with lust.

Moans vibrated both of their throats when he tightened his hold on her ass and began to move her in a tight, circular motion against his straining erection. After thirty seconds of that torture, Vic couldn't take any more. He sealed their kiss, gasping desperately when she continued to tempt him by plucking at his lips, cheeks, and neck with her red, swollen lips.

"Dammit, Niall," he muttered almost angrily before he set her down, hissing as her pussy dragged against his aching cock.

"I want you so much, Vic," she whispered, staring up at him with a wide-eyed expression that conveyed both innocent awe and pure carnal lust.

He'd never forget the way Niall looked at that moment.

"Good, because you're going to get me, baby," he assured her grimly while he fumbled in his pocket for his keys. His erection made his pants way too constraining for comfortable movement.

He pulled her hastily through the opened door, only to push her against the other side of it once it was closed. He spread his thighs and bent his knees, his mouth fastening on her neck and feasting on her fragrant skin before she'd even fully regained her balance. She moaned, the sound vibrating into his pressing lips and somehow even sending a buzz to his throbbing cock. He tasted her skin with the tip of his tongue, dancing it across the dewy surface thirstily. When he encountered her pearls, he rolled them between his lips, liking the feeling of their smooth, hard surface.

"Vic, what are you doing?" she murmured a few seconds later.

"Taking off your pearls."

"I can see that. Why?"

"I warned you that you drive me nuts when you wear these things," he said as he held the now unclasped necklace in his hand. "Now you're going to have to pay the price."

He watched as her eyes darkened with excitement. The tip of her tongue darted out over her lush lower lip, making Vic even more determined. He began to rapidly unbutton her blouse.

"Take off your skirt," he demanded once he'd tossed aside her blouse.

He just stared at her for several long, cock-throbbing moments after she'd dropped her skirt on top of her blouse. The peach colored silk panties covered about as much of her trim little bush as the triangles of silk that covered her small, thrusting breasts. She wore a matching garter belt that highlighted the shape of her thighs as well as the healthy glow of her honey-colored skin. Her stomach was smooth and flat. He knew from experience that he could span her waist with his hands. He loved the way her hips swelled into a taut, feminine curve, promising a welcome harbor for his cock despite her petite proportions.

"You make my mouth water, baby." His jaw clenched when he glanced up and saw that witch's smile on her lips.

"Push your bra down beneath your nipples."

He watched as she did what he asked. Her little breasts thrust proudly from the plane of her chest, easily keeping the cups below the tender flesh. The sight of her fat, dark pink nipples poking out of the silk made his cock surge like a snake at the strike. He instinctively reached up to stroke himself as he stepped toward Niall, desperate to sooth the beast within. He spread his thighs, bringing himself down closer to Niall's level, and leaned down.

"Hmmmm," he groaned in primitive satisfaction after slipping a plump nipple into his mouth and beginning to suck greedily. Niall writhed against him, trying to increase the pressure of his body against her. In order to fix her into place while he feasted on her breasts, he grabbed her wrists and pushed them against the door above her head. The sounds of her moans and whimpers spiced the boiling brew of his arousal.

He suckled on her until his cock felt like it was going to burst. When he leaned back, keeping Niall's wrists pinned over her head, and inspected the results of his endeavors, he couldn't unfasten his pants quickly enough. He shoved them down around his thighs along with his boxer briefs. His cock felt tight and ponderous when he fisted it. It surged in his hand when he noticed Niall's large hazel eyes fixed on it.

He released her wrists. When she met his gaze he merely glanced downward . . . that was all. And sweet, sexy Niall sank to her knees for him.

"Wait," he rasped when her hand encircled his shaft. "I want you to use only your mouth. Put both of your hands behind your head."

His nostrils flared in feral arousal when she followed his instructions and her erect, swollen nipples poked out from her bra even more prominently in her new position. The silence had weight as they both watched while he wrapped her pearl necklace around his cock just below mid-staff, pulling it tight at the side. A desperate little moan leaked past Niall's lips when he moved his hand, rolling the hard, cool globes back and forth on his erection.

His hand rose, cradling Niall's head at the back, below where her fingers laced together. "Suck down to the pearls, baby. Wherever I put them, I want your lips kissing them. Do you understand?"

The combination of the stimulation from the rolling pearls and her huge, sexy eyes looking up at him almost made the instructions unnecessary. He was going to have to start blindfolding her when she gave him head.

"Niall?" he prompted when she didn't answer immediately.

She nodded quickly.

He rolled her pearls down to the ridge beneath the head of his cock.

"Open," he ordered tensely. He gripped her hair in his hands, holding her steady, wanting to penetrate her instead of having her enfold him. Her lips immediately closed around him in a tight hold. He grunted in primal pleasure at the sensation of the tip of his cock sliding along her warm tongue. She began to flutter her tongue everywhere on the head while he stroked himself with the pearls.

Shit. He wasn't going to be able to take much of this. But while he could, he was going to squeeze out every last bit of the pleasure.

He pulled the pearls back several inches on his cock. Without waiting for her to come to him he flexed his ass, sliding his cock into Niall's warm mouth until her widely spread lips bumped against the pearls. He'd let her take the initiative once the pearls were rolling on the back half of his cock. But right now she could easily manage a face fuck.

"That's a good girl," he muttered thickly. "Hold still while I fuck your pretty mouth." She stared up at him while he pumped between her lips. As usual the sight drove him a little crazy. His grip on her pearls tightened slightly and the pace of his moving hand increased. After a moment of plunging between her lips he stilled inside her mouth and beat at his cock with the gems. Niall moaned shakily as the pearls gently slapped against her lips. He could tell by the expression in her eyes that she liked it almost as much as he did.

He rolled the pearls back to mid-staff and waited. She dipped her head forward, pushing him to the back of her mouth. Her lips tapped against the pearls after she'd pulsed him in and out between her lips three times. Vic kept still and watched her for a minute while she slid back and forth on his cock. She looked so beautiful with her cheeks hollowed out as she applied a healthy suck. Her eyes shone with lust as she gazed up at him.

"Come on back, baby," he whispered hoarsely a minute later as he rolled her pearls to the back half of his cock. He took a step back with his right thigh so that he could stroke himself with the pearls unhindered, without bumping into his thigh. He both saw and felt the moment when the tip of his cock slipped into Niall's muscular throat, stimulating her gag reflex. She flinched at the contraction of her throat, but then he saw her breathe deeply through her nose, calming herself.

"Yeah, that's it," he praised as she accustomed herself to his presence and began to move up and down on him in a sleek, rapid rhythm. Since she couldn't easily balance herself without the help of her hands, he gripped his fingers tightly in her hair, making sure that as her movements became more strenuous, she didn't fall forward on him and choke herself.

He couldn't take much more of this exquisite torture. His cock felt like it was going to burst through the stretched, tight skin that covered it. A burning sensation began to grow at the base of his spine, warning him that orgasm hovered close. He rolled the pearls back to within an inch of his balls. Sweat coated his abdomen and neck. His breath came harsh and ragged as he watched Niall struggle to take him deeper.

"Shhh," he murmured, rubbing her head to soothe her when she made a choking noise and her eyes filled with tears. The expression in her gaze told him that she was determined, however. That, along with the lust glazing her eyes, made Vic's muscles clench tight with unbearable tension.

"Ahhhh . . . fuck, that's good," he grated out between rigid jaws several seconds later when she took him down her throat in one sinuous stroke. Her lips tapped against the pearls. She purred in satisfaction, vibrating into his flesh before she slid him out of her muscular channel.

It was too much. Vic backed out of her, sliding his entire length between the tight clamp of her lips, gasping loudly at the exquisite sensation.

"Open wide," he demanded.

He placed the fat head of his cock on her tongue and rolled the pearls down to the sensitive area just below the thick rim. His arm moved rapidly as he jacked himself with the creamy, hard globes. He groaned gutturally as his cum jetted onto Niall's red tongue.

In retrospect, he was glad that he didn't shatter the strand that held Niall's pearls at that moment, because he pumped himself so forcefully with them while he came. His cock jerked viciously despite his tight hold, spraying his semen into Niall's mouth and onto her widely spread lips, providing ample lubrication for the rolling pearls.

He gasped wildly for air as he fell forward, catching himself on the door with an outstretched hand. His face tightened in pleasure when Niall closed her lips around him and slid his cock into her mouth, fluttering her tongue over the hypersensitive flesh, causing small post-orgasmic detonations to go off in his shuddering body.

"Jesus Fucking Christ, that felt good," he muttered incoherently as he met Niall's gaze.

When he felt her lips tighten around him in a smile, he straightened and reached for her.

"Come here, little witch," he whispered gruffly.

A soft whimper of loss vibrated Niall's throat when Vic pulled his still ample sex from her hungry mouth. She couldn't get over how much it aroused her to suck on his cock. Oral sex had certainly been a part of her and Stephen's repertoire for making love, but those experiences didn't begin to compare to the mindless excitement she felt when she took Vic's cock into her mouth. It drove her into a literal sexual frenzy to know that she gave him so much pleasure.

Ripples of excitement spread from her belly down to her sex, resulting in a friction-demanding burn at her clit when she registered the gleam in Vic's eye.

She was next.

Just thinking about what Vic could do to her with his mouth made her vagina tighten almost painfully. Despite her body's wild excitement and requirement for oxygen, her breath stuck in her lungs when Vic pushed her against the door and started to lower over her. He paused at her breasts, sucking a nipple between his teeth and biting down enough to gently scrape the sensitive flesh, making Niall cry out at the agony of the intense pleasure.

When he finally knelt before her, his dark head hovering just inches away from her silk-clad sex, Niall pushed at his head, frantic with anticipation. He didn't immediately put his mouth on her, however. Instead, he reached up and pinched the silk of her panties until a half-inch-wide bunch of cloth pressed tightly between her swollen labia, down across the sensitive tissues near the opening of her pussy, even stimulating her asshole.

He looked up at her with blazing eyes as he began to lightly jerk the taut cloth against her. Niall moaned shakily at the sensation. Her clit burned. The soles of her feet sizzled in sympathy. He altered his movements slightly to include a horizontal motion as well as a vertical one, working the cloth of her panties between her lips, tugging it up and down on her erect clit. Through her weighted eyelids she saw him mouth a curse when the wet, squishy sounds of the fabric moving in her juices reached both of their ears at once.

The hand that still had her pearls laced between his fingers separated her labia.

He covered her with his mouth, sucking on her sensitive tissues and her soaked panties at once, flexing his jaw, seemingly dying of thirst for the taste of her cream. He must have sensed that she teetered right on the edge of orgasm, because he went straight for the kill. His tongue laved her clit warmly and then stabbed at it repeatedly. When her knees weakened he squeezed the lower curve of her ass into his palm, fixing her in place, forcing her to take every last tremor of pleasure that he gave her.

Niall blasted into another realm. She could think of no better way to describe what happened to her. When she came to partial awareness, she realized that the back of her head thudded against the door in the same tempo that shocks of orgasm convulsed her body. The sensation felt so overwhelming that she desperately sank her fingers into Vic's thick hair and tried to pull him away from her pussy. But he only glanced up at her with a white-hot expression of furious lust, released her sex lips, stilled her tugging hand at the wrist, and continued to lick and suck at her clit relentlessly. He must have known that she would survive the powerful explosions, because they did eventually wane.

Still, while Niall experienced the most potent of those blasts, she wouldn't have made the bet that survival was inevitable.

His voice brought her back to herself, as did his lips pressing warmly to her thighs.

"You're so sweet, baby. Nobody comes like you," he muttered roughly between kisses. "Nobody."

Niall watched him through slitted eyelids. He moved his face between her spread thighs, soothing and igniting her flesh. His gray eyes met hers, his gaze striking her as both demanding and comforting at once.

"Are you all right?" he whispered next to her thigh before he nipped at the skin lightly.

"Yes," Niall whispered shakily. Her vagina squeezed tight, desperate for something to fill it when he smiled.

"Good. Because I'm going to make you come again with these."

"*No,*" Niall whispered anxiously when he held up her pearls. She wasn't sure she could take another orgasm like that. His eyes gleamed with arousal and mischief.

"Why not? Don't you like it when I make you burn?"

"Yes, but . . ."

She paused, her mouth hanging open when he reached up with both hands and ripped her panties apart as if they were made of tissue paper.

"Vic!"

"It's okay," he assured her, a naughty grin showing off his dead sexy off-center front tooth. "I'll buy you more. Pretty little peach ones . . ." He leaned forward and kissed her damp, flushed folds. Niall groaned. "Silk." He tilted his head and sent his tongue between her labia in a quick, teasing, wet swipe against her clit. "Pixie-sized," he continued as he nuzzled her swollen lips with his nose, breathing her deeply at the same time.

"Small, not pix—oh, Vic . . . ah, *God,* that feels good." She pressed her hand to the back of his head as he jabbed his tongue several times rapidly between her labia. "More!"

But instead of giving her what she begged for, he leaned back and once again separated her sex lips, exposing her red, glistening clit. Niall shuddered in anticipation when he lifted her pearls. A whimper slipped past her lips when he laced the hard, cool little globes between her labia. He pinched the sensitive folds together tightly.

His eyes met hers when he pulled up on the pearls. Niall jerked like a puppet at the end of a string.

"Shhhh," Vic soothed, watching her face as though he saw something fascinating there. The pearls rolled with a hard pressure against her clit. He pulled on the bottom end, making her gasp in pleasure on the downward slide. He began to pull her prized gems back and forth gently, agitating her clit until it burned. Her hips began to bob up and down in order to increase the divine pressure.

He laughed softly. "Your pearls aren't so prim and proper now. You like this, don't you?"

Niall's eyes closed as the intensity of the burn magnified.

"Answer me."

"*Yes,*" Niall whispered. Her hips jerked uncontrollably against the pearls that he put to such wicked use. An unbearably excited tingling sensation spread from the nerve-packed flesh that Vic abused and agitated to such stunning effect up her spine and down to the burning soles of her feet.

Vic smiled as he leaned forward and inhaled her pussy scent. Niall gritted her teeth in agonized pleasure as he increased the pace of the sliding pearls. He lapped lightly with his tongue at her sex lips. "Hmmm . . . those pearls are getting a nice seasoning."

Niall whimpered as her hips bucked wildly. She'd never felt so helpless, so at the mercy of her desire. It was like her entire body consisted of one exposed, raw nerve.

He stabbed his stiffened tongue between her folds as he continued to roll the pearls against her clit. Niall cried out sharply at the indescribable sensation. She held his head in a white-knuckled grip. Just when her muscles went rigid in the rictus of orgasm she felt him push one of his fingers into her ass. He penetrated her fully, and rubbed at the same time the first blast of climax ripped through her.

Niall almost choked on her pleasure as she came, completely helpless as a violent orgasm shook and shuddered through her body.

"That's my girl," she heard Vic murmuring hoarsely a minute later. She realized dazedly that he was carrying her to his bedroom. She just lay on the end of his bed in a post-orgasmic stupor as she watched him hastily remove his clothes. He moved with a quick, frantic quality that she couldn't quite comprehend in her spent state. The heavy pillar of his cock jutted out before him, stiff and tight and beautiful as he rolled on a condom.

Her vagina contracted hungrily and Niall suddenly understood his desperation fully.

Vic looked a little intimidating as he came down over her, a grim expression on his handsome face. Her eyes widened when he grabbed her wrists and fixed them above her head with one hand. She saw him stare at her nipples as they poked up when her back arched slightly off the bed. She still wore her bra, even though the cloth remained below her breasts, pushing the flesh and reddened nipples up into a lewd display.

"What are you going to get for teasing me with those pearls?" Vic asked with a dangerous glint in his eyes.

Niall licked her lower lip as her eyes lowered to Vic's enormous erection where it bobbed between their bodies.

"F . . . fucked?" she asked with a combination of anxiety and excitement.

His eyes smoldered. He moved up, bumping the wide head of his cock against her wet, tender tissues. "Your little pussy is gonna be fucked *hard*," he corrected softly. His hips flexed, pressing his penis into her entry. "Open your legs wide, baby. I want *in*."

Niall spread her thighs along the cool, soft bedspread. She moaned as Vic pulsed his cock against her narrow channel, demanding she accept him. She gasped at the sensation of the thick rim beneath the head slipping into her body, rubbing and agitating the nerve-packed flesh. God, that defined, fat knob of his cock was going to kill her someday with pleasure.

Vic demanded so much of her . . . he forced her to *feel* so much.

He rocked her, prying his steely length into her farther and farther with each pass. Niall tightened beneath him, arching her back, grinding her hips, greedy for more pressure. He held her tightly to the bed, limiting her movement, however, as his cock slowly pierced her body. She saw him grit his teeth tightly in enforced restraint.

He abruptly lifted her leg and smacked her ass. "Quit squirming," he barked.

Niall whimpered in arousal. Her ass muscles flexed, pushing his cock farther into her body.

Vic's face went rigid. He fell down over her, his muscles flexing tightly as he held himself off her. He thrust his hips hard, seating his cock in her to the hilt of his balls.

Niall cried out at the abrupt impact. Her cries amplified when he began to draw out of her and plunge back into her with a brisk smack of striking flesh.

"Is that what you wanted, baby?" he asked harshly, his light eyes glowing silver in the dim light.

Niall's lips fell open, but no speech came. The nerves of her body were too busy firing messages madly: pleasure, pain, burning, pressure, stretching, *feeling*. She couldn't form words in the midst of such overwhelming sensations. She stared at him as he crashed into her again and again, riding her hard, giving her exactly what she wanted.

She moved her hips against him synchronously, increasing the strength of his ruthless strokes. The bed began to quake and rattle loudly against the wall in sympathy with their fierce mating. The hard knob of his cock rubbed and pressed deep within her, exciting her to a frenzied pitch.

Niall called out in wild dismay a second later when she thrust her hips up but Vic wasn't there to meet her.

"Put your pretty ass back down on that bed," Vic muttered tautly.

Niall complied immediately, willing to do anything to get him back deep inside of her. Instead of granting her wish, however, he grabbed his cock at the base and pushed the slick, steely head between her folds, rubbing and agitating her clit until she shuddered once again in orgasm.

"Oh, *yeah*," she heard him shout a moment later, as if from a distance, as he plunged his cock back into her climaxing pussy and rode her while she came. The bed pitched stormily for several moments before he pressed his cock almost unbearably deep inside her.

Niall cried out in wonder at the sensation of him throbbing inside of her in orgasm. It seemed as if every muscle in his beautiful, sweat-glistening body strained to the breaking point.

He fell over her, gasping wildly for air. It took even longer than usual for their clamoring bodies to return to equilibrium. At some point she whispered softly to him and he released her wrists. She loved the feeling of his weight pressing into her, marveled at the sensation of his hard, delineated muscles and smooth skin beneath her worshipping hands.

Eventually, his head rose and he nuzzled her ear softly.

"Guess I proved you wrong," he mumbled tiredly.

Niall stilled in her caressing motions. "About what, precisely?"

"Pearls really are a supersexy accessory."

"You could turn a pair of dirty socks into a supersexy accessory, Vic Savian," she scolded as she pressed a kiss to his damp neck. When he didn't say anything for a moment, she leaned back and examined him.

"Tell me you're not thinking about *how*."

Deep laughter rumbled forth from his chest before he lowered his head and smacked her lips with a kiss.

"It just sounded like an interesting challenge, that's all," he teased. He nipped at her lips until she opened for him once again.

Vic's eyes snapped open at the sound of a whimper of distress in Niall's throat. He'd spooned her body protectively while they slept, but now she trembled within his hold.

He tensed at the jarring knowledge that what frightened her came from within . . . and that he was powerless to stop it.

"Niall. Wake up."

He shook her upper arm gently, willing her to rise out of her nightmare. The small, mournful cry that leaked past her lips made his teeth clench in anguish. He shifted her gently onto her back so that he could see her face. Just as he'd suspected, it gleamed with perspiration.

"Niall!"

Her eyes sprang wide. Vic saw terror in their depths. God damn it, who or what had the power to make her look so afraid?

"You were dreaming, baby," he whispered, willing her into the present moment. He saw her throat convulse as she swallowed. When she started to sit up, he moved aside the arm that had been covering her, fighting his urge to hold her tight against him until her almost tangible fear passed.

It was almost a precise repeat of what had occurred last Sunday,

Vic realized as Niall sat on the edge of the bed for several moments, neck bent, finally rising to go to the bathroom. He stared at the ceiling, listening to the muted sounds of Niall's movement and the water running. When she came out of the bathroom a minute later, she moved so quietly that Vic wondered if she thought he was sleeping again.

Or if she merely hoped he was.

Even a week ago he might have gone along with the program and pretended that he was sleeping. But not tonight.

Once she'd settled back in bed and lay on her side with her back to him, he spoke.

"Why do you have those nightmares, Niall?"

Was it just his imagination, or did her body stiffen?

"Niall?" he repeated, trying to keep the alarm out of his voice when she didn't respond.

She turned onto her back slowly and sighed.

"I'm sorry for waking you. Maybe I shouldn't sleep over."

His head came off the pillow. Her response infuriated him.

"I didn't bring it up because I was worried about losing some sleep."

"I know that," she said quickly.

"Well, then?" he challenged.

He saw her lips part like she wanted to speak. But only silence ensued. His helpless fury faded when he realized how tense she was . . . how brittle. His arms abruptly encircled her, rolling her body into him. She felt so small pressed next to him, so precious. She still trembled. He realized with a pang of guilt that she was crying softly.

He cupped her head in his palm before he made soothing motions along her hair. "I'm sorry," he muttered. "I shouldn't have snapped at you like that."

She just shook her head rapidly. Vic got the impression that something choked her ruthlessly, making speech impossible. When he realized that her own emotions were the culprit, his sense of powerlessness amplified.

He did the only thing he could do, and held her while she cried. Eventually she fell into an exhausted sleep with her head on his chest. Vic remained awake for the rest of the night, like a sentinel standing guard.

Maybe on some stupid, irrational level he believed he could protect Niall from her dreams.

TWELVE

Niall could hear the sound of a Salvation Army bell ringer in the distance along with the muted sound of carols being blared out of speakers at the German Christmas village erected every year in Daley Plaza. The city seemed to bustle with energy and purpose all around her, echoing her own sense of happiness and vibrancy. She smiled. The real reason that she was so happy felt like a precious, wonderful secret that was practically bursting to break free from her chest.

Niall was in love.

"What are you grinning like that for?" she heard Vic ask from beside her before he pressed a kiss on her neck just above her scarf.

Niall spun around and feasted on the sight of him. They stood together under the marquee of the Hesse Theater. She'd walked over after work and had been waiting for him so that they could do some Christmas shopping on State Street before they went to dinner.

Niall wondered how much her secret was broadcast loud and

clear in her eyes when she saw Vic's mouth curve as he looked down at her. Something inside of her belly did a flip-flop. She doubted that the sight of Vic's sculpted lips tilting into a slow, sexy grin would ever leave her unaffected.

"I have a secret," she told him with a significant look.

One dark eyebrow rose speculatively before he leaned down and kissed her on the lips. "Does it have to do with my Christmas present?" he teased. "I hope you remembered that I want only sex toys."

"I'm sure that Meg, Tim, and your mother would be fascinated to see you take those out of your stocking," Niall murmured contentedly as Vic brushed his lips across her nose and cheeks.

She'd been invited by Vic to spend Christmas at his farm downstate this coming weekend. She brimmed over with excitement at the prospect of seeing his home for the first time. She hadn't seen Vic's mother since the day after Vic's opening five weeks ago, when Niall had given them a tour of the museum.

Meg had visited several times in the interim, however. She and Vic's sister had gone to lunch twice when Meg came up to Chicago for a principals' conference. Once Anne Rothman had joined them, and she and Meg had hit it off just as well as Meg and Niall had. Anne and Meg were the same age and discovered that they'd attended the University of Illinois in the same years and had some acquaintances in common. Niall had also met Tim, Meg's husband, when the couple came to Chicago in order to do some Christmas shopping, and took Vic and Niall to dinner.

"If I were you, I'd give it to me in private," Vic teased before he kissed her mouth.

"Your Christmas present isn't my secret," she replied with a mock superior look.

"Hmmm," Vic murmured. "Better tell me what it is. I can see that you're dying to."

"It's snowing," she said softly.

Vic raised his head and inspected her with his penetrating stare. "That wasn't the secret."

Niall grinned as she reached for his hand and pulled him along next to her. "No. But let's go enjoy it anyway."

It did something to Vic to see the blissful expression on Niall's face when they left the restaurant on State Street later that evening, carrying several shopping bags. Maybe it was the fact that he suspected his own countenance reflected some of those same feelings.

Or maybe it was just that he did a mental macho strut at the knowledge that Niall was so happy. He knew for a fact that her nightmares had decreased in frequency over the past month, because they spent a good majority of their nights in each other's arms. He rarely saw that gut-twisting expression of sadness in her eyes anymore.

Of course, she'd never revealed to him *why* she looked so sad or had such frightening dreams. But why should that matter, really, if her nightmares became a thing of the past?

Vic truly believed that was a possibility when Niall paused outside the restaurant and turned her face up to the falling snow. The smile that curved her lips struck him as sublime. A streetlight shone down on her but the electric glow was nothing in comparison to her radiant luminosity.

He stepped toward her. Her lips felt warm and soft beneath the cool snowflakes.

"Would it be all right with you if we walked home?" she asked breathlessly when he finally raised his head, all evidence of ice long ago melted to vapor between their pressing, plucking lips.

Vic nodded. The snow fell heavy and silent, muting the sounds of the city as they made their way down Washington Street. Neither of them spoke for several blocks, enjoying each other's company and the rare beauty of the night.

Vic felt so calm and content that the unexpected sound of a car backfiring loudly while they stood at the streetlight on Franklin really jarred him. By the time he'd finished blinking, he'd already realized what the noise was and turned to make a joke about it to Niall. His words stilled on his tongue when he took in the rigid pallor of Niall's face.

"Niall?" he asked sharply.

She didn't speak. Vic saw that the pupils of her eyes had dilated in fear as she stared down the street in the direction of the backfiring car.

"Niall!" he repeated.

She started, and dropped the shopping bag in her right hand. The silk scarf that she'd bought for her mother spilled out of it, making a crimson slash along the snow-covered pavement.

"It was a *car* backfiring," Vic said more harshly than he intended as he squeezed Niall's upper arm. The wild, cornered expression made a primitive alarm blare in his brain. He said her name again, this time more softly, a note of entreaty lacing through his tone.

She stared up at him in complete, utter nonrecognition.

Vic took one look at her and hailed a passing cab. He bent and picked up the bag and its contents before he herded Niall into the backseat.

By the time Vic unlocked his apartment door at the Riverview Towers, Niall had mostly recovered. Still, she didn't protest when Vic guided her into the living room and gently pushed her onto the couch before he went to the kitchen and began rattling around in the cabinets.

"Thank you," she muttered hoarsely when he handed her a glass of Scotch half a minute later. She shivered. The liquor tore like fire down her throat, thawing not only her profound chill but also the numbness that suffused her. She noticed that the liquor trembled in the glass. It mortified her that she couldn't seem to stop shaking, especially when she felt Vic's steady gaze on her.

She set the glass down abruptly on the coffee table. Her ears buzzed strangely in the ensuing silence.

"Why don't you tell me about it," Vic finally said quietly.

Niall inhaled deeply and stared out at the glittering skyline.

"I'm sorry," she whispered.

Vic shifted toward her on the couch. "Sorry for what, exactly? Are you apologizing for the fact that that a car backfiring on the street sent you into a state of shock? Because surely you know there's no reason to apologize for that." His fingers curved around her chin, tilting her face toward him. "Or are you apologizing for the fact that you don't trust me enough to tell me what's hurting you? Is that why you're saying you're sorry, Niall?"

Her lips fell open. The words caught in her throat, causing a choking sensation.

"I *want* to tell you about it," she said brokenly.

His eyes narrowed. "But?"

She cursed the tears that spilled down her cheeks. Dammit, why did they leave her body so easily when the words wouldn't? Niall thought bitterly. She saw Vic's expression shift when he saw her tears. She wiped at them with the back of her hand and stood jerkily. The last thing she wanted at that moment was his pity. His compassion, yes.

Although there was no guarantee that was what his reaction would be, was there?

She sensed him approaching her from behind where she stood at the windows overlooking the city.

"I know that something bad must have happened to you . . . something that causes those nightmares you have . . . something that makes you sad and scared. I see it in your eyes."

She swallowed heavily. His voice sounded so kind and gentle. She wanted to unburden herself so much that it felt like an ache in her chest. To have Vic hold her, comfort her—love her as much as she loved him, despite everything—seemed like a beautiful, elusive dream.

If only she didn't feel like she would lose every ounce of her control once she started talking. If only she was one hundred percent sure he wouldn't judge her.

It should have been you, Niall.

A spasm wracked her chest and throat when she felt his long fingers gently caressing her neck, soothing her. She wondered if she wasn't even more shocked than Vic appeared to be when she abruptly moved away from him.

"I . . . want to talk to you about this, Vic. I just can't right now," she said in a rush. She wasn't looking at him but could easily imagine his rugged features pulling tight with concern and frustration.

"All right," she heard Vic say after a long pause. "I'm not going to push you about it, baby."

Niall just nodded her head. She stilled in the process of picking up one of her shopping bags.

"What the hell are you doing?" Vic asked sharply.

Niall could barely get some saliva down her throat in order to speak, she was so choked with emotion. "I . . . I think I better go."

That galvanized Vic into action. He was beside her immediately. "*No*, Niall. You shouldn't be alone. If you don't want to talk
right now, fine, but . . ."

Niall just shook her head rapidly as she pointedly avoided Vic's
stare. Her misery threatened to explode out of her at any moment.
The feeling frightened her.

"I have to go," she mumbled. When she felt Vic's hand on her
arm restraining her, she threw him off forcefully as the fingers of
panic closed around her throat.

In the end she left the shopping bags and her coat behind,
blindly grabbing at her purse before she made a hasty retreat from
Vic's apartment.

Niall left a message on Rose Gonzalez's voice mail and shuffled to the next message that Kendra had just given her from Anne
Rothman. The first thing she'd done once the pieces of paper were
in her hand was check to see if Vic's name was among them.

It hadn't been. But then again, she hadn't really expected it to
be. Not after she'd thrown him off her and raced out of his apartment last night.

She'd spent the morning in meetings. She could only be thank-
ful that the nature of the meetings didn't require her to participate
much, as exhausted and listless as she felt after her sleepless night.
Considering how she felt, she was half hoping that Anne wouldn't
answer her phone when Niall returned her call. But she did, of
course.

"Hey! I'm glad you got back so soon. Are you free for lunch?
Guess who I'm meeting at the the Walnut Room?" Anne asked.

"I don't know, Anne. I'm really busy . . ."

"Well, you have to eat, and it's just across the street, for goodness sake. Besides, it's the holidays. When else are you supposed to take long lunches that possibly include two . . . or even three . . . glasses of wine? Besides it's practically a family occasion. That's the surprise—I'm meeting with Meg Sandoval! She told me to call and invite you. It's sort of a last-minute thing on her part. Remember how we talked the last time we all had dinner about one of my graduate students possibly going downstate to teach an art history class to gifted kids? Well, her school board just approved the money for it, and it looks like the Institute is going to approve more than just the funds to pay a graduate student. It looks good for us to offer programs in rural areas. Besides, it's good P.R. for the Institute. Anyway, you can hear more about it at lunch."

Niall's eyes burned when she clenched them shut.

"I don't think I can, Anne. I'm really swamped. Please tell Meg hello, though. Tell her . . ." Niall swallowed hard. Of *course* she would still be going to Vic's farm for Christmas. To think otherwise just because of what had occurred last night was pure catastrophic thinking on her part. She really needed to shake herself out of this pervasive gloom. "Tell her how much I'm looking forward to seeing her, Tim, and Ellen for Christmas."

Anne wheedled and scolded and then became duly concerned when that didn't work. She hung up without a further fuss only when Niall pacified her by agreeing to have dinner with her at The Art the night before she left with Vic for his farm.

"Bring that gorgeous hunk of a cowboy playwright with you, if you can," Anne encouraged slyly. "Oh . . . I better go. I'm going to be late for Meg."

Vic paused in front of Niall's front door when he arrived home that night at seven P.M. He'd stopped attending every performance of *Alias X* several weeks ago, although he was still in his office, backstage, or with a member of the technical crew more often than not for at least three nights out of the week.

The show ran smoother than a pricey piece of software on a premium hard drive. The reviews continued to be excellent, and his company usually performed to a full house. He'd started to long for the wide-open space of the farm instead of obsessing about the play, so he figured things must be going pretty well. After Christmas he planned to return to his regular schedule of spending only two or three nights in the city.

At least he had hoped to do that, if he could talk Niall into spending a good portion of her weekends with him on the farm.

Vic couldn't believe that just last night he had been feeling so content, like nothing could interfere with the smooth roll of his world. How quickly that had all crumbled to ash when he'd turned and seen Niall's face last night.

It had been like all those nights he'd awakened her from her dreams. Except that last night she'd been fully awake and he'd looked straight down into her wide eyes . . . right into the heart of her nightmare.

It made him feel like a shit to know that he'd caught a hint of her suffering early on, before they'd become more involved, and that he'd made a point of not seeing it. Now that he was ready to acknowledge everything about Niall, however—including her painful past—she was shutting him out.

He didn't know what the hell to make of that fact. The only thing he knew for sure was that he was tired of it. At some point during the past five weeks, he had decided that he wanted *in*. Not just in Niall's body, but in her mind . . . in her life.

Seeing Jenny on the opening night of *Alias X* had allowed him to resoundingly finish a scenario in his mind that had long been in need of a final act. He'd thought he'd accomplished that by refusing to see or speak with Jenny, but that particular coping mechanism had just served to make her bigger and bolder in his mind than she had ever deserved.

Opening night of *Alias X* had taught him something valuable—Niall had as much in common with Jenny as a butterfly did with a viper.

His face stiffened at the thought, and he knocked loudly on Niall's front door. His little butterfly was being buffeted by some turbulent winds, and Vic was determined that she tell him what was going on, so that he could offer her some insulation against them.

She answered almost immediately. His eyes flickered over her in concern. She still wore her clothes from work, a narrow black skirt, black pumps, and an emerald green silk blouse. His gaze lingered for a moment on her elegant, pearl-entwined neck. He couldn't quite fathom how Niall always managed to convey a sense of timeless, classic beauty and at the same time seem so earthy . . . so utterly touchable. Despite how lovely she looked to him at that moment he noticed the paleness of her cheeks. Her lips trembled slightly as she smiled. Vic stilled an overwhelming, and increasingly familiar, urge to enfold her in his arms and shield her. From what, precisely, he couldn't say.

Neither could she, and therein lay the problem.

"Hi," she greeted him huskily before she moved back in the doorway. "Come in."

Vic didn't speak as she closed the door and led him into the living room.

"Can I get you something to drink?" she asked brightly when he sat on the couch.

Vic scowled. "I didn't come over here for a social visit, Niall."

He called himself a foul son of a bitch when he saw her smile fade.

"Shit. Just . . . come here, baby," he muttered as he reached for her. She felt so good wrapped in his arms. He pressed her head beneath his chin and inhaled the familiar light, fruity scent from her shining hair. His eyes closed tightly for a few seconds as he absorbed her into him.

"Are you okay?" he asked gruffly when he finally loosened his hold and she straightened enough to look up at him. Her large eyes shone with tears and something else . . . something that radiated from within.

"Yes," she whispered. "I'm so glad you're here. I'm so sorry about last night."

Vic winced slightly. "Why do you keep apologizing, Niall? Just—"

She held up her hand. "I know," she said softly. "Just tell you why I get so jumpy sometimes. The thing is, Vic, it's not all that simple for me . . . or that easy."

Her head fell forward as she inhaled as if for courage. Vic felt an inexplicable weight press on his chest and a tightness in his throat as he watched her struggle with her emotions. He grabbed her hand and squeezed it for reassurance.

A knock resounded down the hallway from the front door.

Niall's eyes widened in surprise.

"I wonder who that is," she murmured as she stood. "Meg, maybe? She was in town to have lunch with Anne . . . but surely security would have called first."

"*Mom,*" Vic heard her exclaim in surprise a second later.

"I had to come, honey. Something amazing has happened."

Vic stood as Niall returned to the living room with Alexis Chandler at her heels.

"Oh . . ." Alexis started when she saw him. Her beautiful face stiffened. "I didn't realize you had company."

"Mom, this is Vic Savian. Vic, I'd like you to meet my mother, Alexis Chandler. I never got the chance to introduce you two before . . ."

Niall paused shakily. Something indefinable passed across Alexis Chandler's face as she looked at him that reminded Vic of a cloud quickly moving across the sunlight. But it was gone in a millisecond and her icy, impenetrable expression was back in place.

"Mr. Savian," Alexis said with a cool nod. "I'm afraid I need to speak with my daughter privately."

"Mom . . ." Niall interrupted, obviously uncomfortable with her mother's brusque dismissal.

"It's okay, Niall," Vic said quietly. He crossed his arms under his chest and met Alexis Chandler's stare calmly. He didn't want to make things difficult for Niall, but he didn't care for her mother's bitchy attitude, nor did he appreciate the way her presence made Niall's face rigid with anxiety. He wasn't going to throw Niall to the sharks so easily this time.

"Your mother hasn't been caught up on things. She just doesn't realize that whatever she needs to say, she can say in front of me."

Alexis's eyebrows rose slightly in surprise at his challenge. Her glittering blue eyes moved over him rapidly, as though she was taking his measure.

"Is that true, Niall?" Alexis asked. Vic cringed inwardly when he saw Niall's face. It looked like it'd been bleached. Even her lips were tinged with white. He opened his mouth to apologize then and there for his cockiness. It obviously wasn't helping Niall any—

"If it's true that you want this man to hear about what's

happened with Stephen, then I'll respect your wishes," Alexis Chandler continued.

"Who's Stephen?" Vic asked.

Alexis Chandler laughed shortly. "Niall's husband, of course."

Vic squinted at the woman who stood just feet away from him, as though he couldn't quite bring her into focus.

"Niall's husband," he repeated flatly. He glanced over at Niall, a grin of disbelief starting to curve his lips.

His smile was aborted when he met Niall's eyes.

"I was . . . I was going to tell you . . ." she whispered.

He felt as if he hadn't quite heard her because of the strange noise in his ears like rapidly rushing air. "You were going to tell me *what*?"

He saw her throat convulse with difficulty as she swallowed. "About Stephen," she tried to continue in a choked voice.

"He's been very ill," Alexis stated bluntly. "That's why I came by tonight. I got a call from Evergreen Park just an hour ago. Get your things quickly, Niall." Alexis's brilliant smile at her daughter pierced the daze of Vic's shock. "It's nothing less than a miracle. Your husband has recovered, darling. And he's asking for you."

Vic put up both his hands at once before he pointed at Alexis Chandler. "Can you be quiet for a second, please?" He focused on Niall. "What the hell is she talking about?" he demanded. Surely Alexis Chandler was batty or something. Niall couldn't be married.

She would have told him. He *knew* she would have. That wasn't something you just forgot to mention when you were in a relationship with someone.

Unless you were purposefully trying to keep it secret, of course . . .

He noticed that Niall seemed to be searching his face for answers just as desperately as he sought them in hers.

"You *can't* be married," Vic declared in a harsh voice.

Niall's expression sagged. Her posture wilted, as well. She lowered her gaze from his. The gesture was silent, of course, but Vic felt like a door had just been resoundingly slammed shut in his face.

"I am," she said blankly. "Let me get my purse and coat, Mom, and I'll be ready to go see Stephen."

THIRTEEN

Niall stared at the fake Christmas tree in the large, airy day room. A Christmas tree that was still up during the third week of January was always a bit depressing, but combined with the fact that this particular one was in a mental institution, the sight turned downright gloomy. All of the ornaments were made of paper, of course, no sharp edges that could be put to a harmful use. Niall actually recognized some of the ornaments from the two previous Christmases that she'd sat in this room . . . and that only added to her sense of gloom.

The day room might have been more aptly a day arena, as wide open and large as it was. Evergreen Park had been built in the 1970s, during the height of a period of psychiatric optimism. Niall thought that the original impetus behind building facilities like Evergreen Park had probably been good. But the promise of medical "cures" for such virulent conditions as schizophrenia and manic depression had fallen somewhat short of their expected glorious apex. Government funding for such facilities waned as more and more of the mentally ill were farmed out to less expensive nursing and group homes. Niall doubted that anything in the décor of the day room at Evergreen Park had been altered one bit since the 1970s, except for perhaps the new coats of paint that were likely mandated by the health code.

She sat up straighter when she heard the buzz of the electronic lock on the door that led to the patients' residential wing. A young male attendant entered the room, followed by Stephen. Despite Stephen's vast improvements over the past four weeks, it pained Niall to see him shuffle after the younger man like an obedient dog. One thing that had not improved with Stephen's new medication regimen was his appetite. His clothing hung loosely on his gaunt, stooped frame.

"Good morning, Eli," Niall greeted the attendant as they approached her. "Good morning, Stephen. How are you feeling today?"

"Okay," Stephen mumbled.

"He just got a haircut," Eli said with a smile. "Looking pretty spiffy."

"It looks nice, Stephen," Niall agreed.

As usual, Stephen didn't meet her eyes but stared at the floor. He grimaced as he ran his hand over his burr haircut. The color of it—a rich, golden brown—had once nearly perfectly matched Michael's hue. Niall saw that a good deal of gray was mixed with the brown now.

Eli laughed at his ward's distasteful expression over his haircut. "So I guess Rose told you that Stephen wanted to talk to you, right?" Eli asked brightly.

Niall nodded.

"Okay. I'll give you two some privacy, then. I'll just be over on

the other side of the day room," he told Niall, giving her a significant look. Dr. Fardesh had taken Stephen off his one-to-one status,
whereby an attendant was required to be in close proximity to him
twenty-four hours a day due to possible suicide attempts or violence toward others. Nevertheless, Stephen was still very vulnerable to stressors of any kind, easily becoming anxious and erratic in
his behavior if his daily routine was altered in the slightest.

Since he began to have periods of lucidity just before Christmas,
Niall had made a point of visiting him at least once a week, often
several times. She'd spoken with Rose Gonzalez and Dr. Fardesh at
length about whether it would actually be helpful for her to come,
determined to do what was right under these circumstances and
not just whatever her parents determined was appropriate. The
only reason she'd agreed to come at all was because Dr. Fardesh
said that Stephen had begun to mention not only Niall's name but
Michael's, both during his brief sessions with Dr. Fardesh and with
his art therapist.

"I get the impression that Stephen is trying to work through
something, Niall," Dr. Fardesh had explained last week. "This medication regime we have him on is no cure, of course, but it might be
giving him some psychological resources to try and cope, at least
minimally, with his past. He's been drawing pictures of Michael
during his art therapy sessions. A few days ago he asked me how old
Michael would have been today if he had lived. As you know, that
sort of acknowledgment of Michael—let alone his death—has been
unprecedented for Stephen since he's been under my care."

Niall had been flabbergasted by the news. To her knowledge,
Michael's name hadn't passed Stephen's lips since their four-year-old
son's funeral. It was soon afterward that her husband began to
drink heavily and that his behavior became increasingly erratic,
agitated, and eventually violent. By the time Matthew Manning's

trial came around, Stephen had declined both physically and psychologically to such a degree that Niall had no choice but to hospitalize him.

He hadn't been out of a hospital or psychiatric facility for a single day since then.

"Is there anything I can do to help?" Niall had asked Dr. Fardesh.

"Just continue to do what you have been doing: listen and offer him support. You know that Rose told him about the divorce proceedings?"

Niall nodded. She'd been glad to hear from Rose Gonzalez that she had indeed ended up informing Stephen back in December about their divorce, after he'd shown several weeks of stability. The fact that Stephen hadn't relapsed when he heard the news, but continued to have an unprecedented period of relative lucidity and stable functioning, had heartened Niall.

"He's handled that news very well," Dr. Fardesh mused. "When he does bring up your name, it's always associated with Michael. What he's trying to work through definitely relates to Michael's murder. He occasionally mentions the name *Marchant* or the *Marchant account*. Does that mean anything to you?"

Niall's brow crinkled as she searched her memories but came up empty-handed. The name sounded vaguely familiar, but . . .

"No . . . I don't think I know that name."

Dr. Fardesh shrugged. "Well, whatever the name means to Stephen, he becomes quite agitated whenever he brings it up."

"And he brings it up in association with Michael?" Niall asked, puzzled.

Dr. Fardesh had nodded. "Don't be too concerned with it. It will either come out or it won't. These things take time for an individual like Stephen to process."

Stephen typically never said much to Niall when she'd come to visit over the last month. He still quickly became restless and agitated in her presence, although never to the point of violence. But he did recognize her and call her by her name. He'd even recognized Alexis on that initial visit back in December, and Niall Chandler Sr. on subsequent visits. That had created some disproportionate expectations from Niall's parents, who seemed convinced that Stephen would be back behind his desk at Chandler Financial someday soon, barking out orders and making brilliant business decisions under pressure.

Her parents continued to cling to these unrealistic expectations despite Dr. Fardesh and Rose Gonzalez's warnings as to the monumental unlikelihood of them. Stephen needed supervision and assistance in order to maintain his most basic hygiene, continued to shy away from all strangers, and typically spoke approximately fifty words per day cumulatively to Dr. Fardesh and the various other employees at Evergreen Park to whom he was accustomed. If someone didn't put a tray of food directly in front of him and encourage him repeatedly to eat, Niall had little doubt that Stephen would eventually starve if left to his own devices.

Niall had taken to just ignoring her parents when they rattled on about Stephen's miraculous improvements. She was still furious with her mother for what she'd done in front of Vic back in December. But Niall had been so overwhelmed by her own feelings of guilt, grief, and hopelessness when it came to Stephen that she hadn't yet confronted Alexis about her underhanded, passive aggressive behavior on that day.

And she hadn't seen Vic since he'd cast one last incredulous, furious glance at Niall before he walked out of her apartment for the last time.

Better not to think about that now. It pained her excruciatingly to think of losing Vic when she'd just found him. And she needed all of her psychological resources to deal with what occurred now, here in the present. She could focus on only one step at a time. She had Stephen to consider, as well as the increasing stress and work associated with the upcoming exhibit at the museum. In addition she'd received notice that she could officially close on her condominium in three weeks, and thus had all the planning associated with that endeavor filling up her days.

Vic had tried to contact her back in December after that ugly incident with Alexis, but Niall hadn't returned his calls. Maybe he'd believed that her refusal to speak to him signaled guilt—or even disinterest—because the phone calls had stopped. Just as she'd done earlier that fall, she carefully avoided seeing him. She'd begun to wonder if he was even spending any time in his apartment since Christmas, because she rarely heard his door opening or closing at night or in the morning.

And she'd listened so carefully for any sounds indicating his presence. As she lay in bed at night, alone and miserable, that's practically all she did.

Whenever she considered what she should do about Vic, a sort of emotional paralysis overcame her. All she could do was focus on *now*, on *this* step of her life. If she thought too far into the future, she was afraid she would miss a step and spill down a steep, treacherous, emotional staircase.

"It was movie night last night, wasn't it?" Niall asked Stephen when he sat awkwardly on the couch across from her. She noticed that he glanced over to Eli in the attached solarium. Niall knew that what Rose said was true—Stephen was a grown man, not a child. Nevertheless, that was what he reminded her of presently as he affirmed to himself that Eli, a familiar, comfortable presence, hadn't wandered too far away from him.

"Yeah," he mumbled as he picked at his pant leg nervously.

"Anything good?" Niall prompted warmly.

"Clint Eastwood."

Niall remained seated when Stephen stood and began to pace restlessly in front of the couch. She sensed his rising tension.

"Rose called and told me that you said you wanted to speak with me about something," Niall said evenly. She started when Stephen suddenly struck his thigh hard with a closed fist. His movements became jerkier as his pacing quickened.

"Stephen, everything is okay." Her voice automatically shifted to the calm, even cadence that she knew from experience often soothed Stephen. Her heart began throbbing loudly in her ears. Just as frequently her efforts at calming him hadn't worked. She knew intellectually that this time was different. Stephen had made some significant improvements. Hadn't he? Still, it was hard to assure her body of that when it had experienced a mortal threat from him on several occasions. Niall's eyes skittered anxiously to where Eli sat reading a magazine in the atrium.

Stephen began to mumble in a manic, pressured fashion as he paced. The hairs on the back of Niall's neck prickled as they stood on end.

". . . Had to make that meeting . . . Richard Marchant insisted it had to be me . . . wouldn't accept Marietta doing it . . ."

"Marietta?" Niall asked in rising confusion. Marietta had been Stephen's top manager at Chandler Financial years back. It struck Niall as bizarre to hear him say her name suddenly.

". . . You acted all pissed off that day . . . know we agreed that I would take Michael to preschool on Mondays . . . but I had to be at that Marchant meeting . . . and what was your job compared to mine? Huh? I was the one who made all the money . . . Why should I have to worry about taking the kid to school?"

Niall jumped when Stephen violently struck his thigh again as he paced.

"Stephen? Don't . . . You'll hurt yourself. Stephen . . . *please* . . ." Niall attempted to break through his increasing agitation, but he paid her no heed. Out of the corner of her eye, she saw Eli putting down his magazine and standing.

In all of the terror and shock that had followed Matthew Manning opening fire on a group of children, parents, and teachers that day, killing three adults and four children, Niall had completely forgotten that she and Stephen had argued over who would take Michael to preschool that morning.

"It *should* have been you who took Michael to school!" Stephen shouted suddenly, several drops of saliva shooting forcefully from his mouth.

Niall's heart pounded horribly in her chest.

"It *was* me, Stephen," she said shakily. "I don't know what you mean . . . It *was* me who took Michael to school that day."

Stephen stopped abruptly in his pacing and whirled around. His face looked like a horrific mask, twisted and rigid. Only his eyes seemed real as they peered through to the outside world, making Niall think of a wild, dangerous, trapped animal.

"But it should have been *me*!" Stephen shouted suddenly, his tone a mixture of horror and regret. "If *I* had been there, maybe . . . maybe . . ."

Niall shook her head as tears coursed down her cheeks. She'd had no idea that he suffered from so much guilt. She'd always assumed that when he ranted at her, shouting "it should have been you," that in his confusion and madness, he expressed an anguished wish that Niall had been the one to be murdered instead of their son.

"*No*, Stephen . . . you couldn't have stopped it," she whispered. "What Matthew Manning did made no sense. No one could have predicted it. Your being there wouldn't have changed things—"

"Stephen?" Eli queried as he approached from the side, careful not to make any abrupt movements. Several other attendants entered the day room from the locked unit, moving rapidly toward Stephen. Niall realized distantly that Eli must have activated some kind of alarm. "Why don't we go back to your room for a while, bud?"

Niall didn't even blink when Stephen lunged at her violently. It was as if some primitive part of her being had been expecting it. He'd been in touch with his guilt ever so briefly, and it had been too painful for him.

The defense of madness needed to be erected once again.

"*It should have been you, Niall!*" he snarled.

And in that moment Niall knew that she hadn't been wrong in thinking that Stephen had a primitive wish that she was dead instead of their son. It was just that his wish was more complicated than she'd assumed. In truth, every time he told her that it should have been her, what he really meant was "It should have been me." Should have been him who took Michael to preschool that day . . . should have been him who died instead of an innocent four-year-old boy. But his misguided guilt was so intense that in order to survive psychologically, he needed to project it onto her.

He required the insulation of his madness.

Eli stopped Stephen's violent pitch toward her by grabbing him from behind, immobilizing his arms at his sides. Stephen's glittering, manic eyes remained glued to Niall as he bent his knees and tried to throw Eli off him, making them both lose balance and fall heavily to the floor. He struggled like a wild animal as the other attendants rushed to assist Eli, who was taking the brunt of Stephen's desperate attempts to come to terms with his own guilt.

"*Go*, Ms. Chandler. Your presence is making it worse," one of the older attendants barked at her before he turned his attention to trying to restrain Stephen's flailing right leg.

Niall stood and walked stiffly to the visitors' exit for the day room. A nurse with a concerned expression on her face buzzed her through the thick metal door. Niall heard Stephen's voice behind her already becoming hoarse from his repeated, harsh rants.

"*It should have been you!*"

The security door shut behind her for the last time, and there was only silence.

FOURTEEN

Niall looked up from where she knelt on the floor of her office when she heard the knock.

"Come in!"

She smiled when she saw her boss, Alistair McKenzie.

"Don't pack up too much," he said with mock alarm as he glanced around her office, as if reassuring himself that all the major furnishings were still in place. "You'll make me think you're never returning from your sabbatical!"

"You're not going to get rid of me that easy," she said as she put the lid on a box that contained some materials that she'd collected from her files for her summertime teaching endeavor. It still amazed her a little to think that it had been over a half year ago when she'd sat in this very office and heard Anne Rothman first mention the prospect of teaching a class to high school students downstate. At the time Niall didn't have the vaguest hint that she would end up being the teacher that the Institute hired for the job.

But that just went to show you how much could change in a half a year.

She stood and waved in invitation to one of the chairs in front of her desk. She sat in her chair and leaned forward, studying her boss with abrupt intensity. "I hope nothing is amiss with the Nakamura paintings. I saw to the packaging myself . . ."

"No, no, nothing like that, Niall," Mac said as he gave a dismissive wave. "They're wrapped up, snug as a bug and ready for shipment, just as the rest of the exhibit is. You really outdid yourself on this one."

Niall smiled, warmed as usual by his praise and the twinkle in his brown eyes. Mac had always been supportive of her, but in the six years that Niall had been at the museum, their relationship had grown into a connection that more resembled a father-daughter one than that of employee-employer.

"I have to admit I was proud of it," Niall conceded as she sat back in her chair and exhaled. "I only wish that Nakamura would have allowed me to have the paintings for longer . . . at least until the end of the summer."

Mac shrugged elegantly. "We were fortunate to have them for as long as we did. It was a stunning show, Niall. Everyone is saying so. Besides, if the exhibit went on that long, you wouldn't be able to take your sabbatical, would you?"

"No, I suppose not," Niall agreed. Something about the pause in conversation that followed told Niall that Mac had something he wanted to say but was having trouble finding the appropriate opening. She waited while he resituated himself in his chair.

"You know, I was wondering—when was the last time you actually taught?" he asked.

"I haven't officially since I was a graduate student, but you know that I give lectures here in the museum regularly about our collection."

"It's going to be quite different for you, teaching high school students, isn't it?"

She smiled. "Yes, but I'm feeling up for the challenge." She paused, experiencing a rush of gratitude when she recognized the truth of her words.

It might have taken her half a year of soul searching to get this way but Niall *was*, indeed, up for the challenge. And that meant a hell of a lot more than teaching art history to a group of high school students during their summer break. It meant reclaiming her life.

It meant going after Vic Savian—whether he liked it or not.

"Actually, Meg Sandoval says that they're quite a talented, gifted group of kids," Niall told Mac. "I'm sure it won't be that different than teaching nineteen- and twenty-year-old undergraduates."

Mac smoothed his pant leg distractedly. Her boss always dressed impeccably. "Yes, I suppose you're right."

Niall shook her head and laughed. "Mac, why don't you just say what's on your mind?"

His gaze met hers abruptly. "Can't put anything past you, can I, Niall? It's just that Kendra and I were concerned about you at the beginning of the year. All of that stuff with Stephen had to be enormously stressful for you. And of course"—his eyes flickered over her face cautiously—"I know that January has always been difficult for you anyway, seeing as how it's the anniversary of Michael's death."

Niall tensed, more out of habit than anything else. When she realized that the mention of her son's death didn't strike her with the painful, resounding blow that it used to, she exhaled slowly. Her gaze settled softly on the tri-fold of pictures that she always kept on her desk—Michael in the blue knit cap and blanket that he'd been wearing when the nurse first brought him to her from the nursery; Michael grinning from ear to ear, holding a green dinosaur clutched in one hand on his third birthday; Michael with his light brown hair carefully combed and a much more sober, sweet smile as he stood by their front door at the house in Barrington before his first day of nursery school.

"It's been three and a half years now since Matthew Manning shot Michael," she said quietly. She thought Mac might have been as shocked as she was that she'd mentioned not only her son but his murderer's name out loud. "It's hard to believe that much time has passed. In many ways, it still feels like it was yesterday. And then my divorce was finalized in February," she added softly. "So I guess you're worried that I'm running off to the country for the summer in order to bury my head in the sand—or the fertile soil, more appropriately. You're wondering if my taking this sabbatical is a good thing for me or if I'm running scared."

Mac looked like he was going to deny it, but then he raised a hand. "Yes. I suppose that is what Kendra and I have been wondering. I've approved your sabbatical, Niall. I'm not changing my mind as your boss. But as a friend I'm worried about the abruptness of your decision, the . . . unexpected nature of it . . ."

Niall felt a pang of remorse when she fully recognized Mac's concern. He and Kendra had obviously noticed that she was unusually preoccupied and tense since Christmas of last year. They'd assumed that it related to Stephen's partial recovery, the finalizing of her divorce, and the anniversary of Michael's murder. And they wouldn't have been entirely wrong in their assumptions.

But they didn't know that the primary reason for her emotional unrest related to the fact that the man that she'd so recently come to realize that she loved had disappeared from her life. Nor did they know that Niall, immobilized by a fog of uncertainty and guilt, had just let Vic go without a word of protest or explanation.

Maybe she'd deserved Vic's scorn at that fateful moment when Alexis had blurted out the truth about her marriage. Niall wasn't sure about that. The only thing that she knew for sure was that over the past few months her fog had lifted. It had taken her three and a half years to get here, but she'd arrived, nonetheless, at a state of acceptance.

She knew she'd grieve over Michael for the rest of her life. Her little boy's senseless death—not to mention the fact that Niall had been there and witnessed it herself—had left a jagged, deep wound that had been extremely difficult to heal. Niall suspected that the psychic scar would pain her intermittently for her whole life. The subsequent loss of Stephen to madness had only exacerbated her grief.

But what had happened with Stephen back in January had helped her to understand the machinations of her husband's insanity . . . and with understanding came healing.

She considered telling Mac about her lonely journey, but she refrained. For some reason, the first person she wanted to talk to about what she'd kept locked away for so long was Vic. Not that there was any guarantee that he would listen . . . but she owed it to both of them to try.

She leaned forward, elbows on her desk, and caught Mac's eye.

"I want you listen very carefully. I can't *wait* to go downstate to teach those kids art history. It will be a challenge to work with teenagers, but a refreshing one, I think. And I'm going to be boarding at Meg's farmhouse. I can't tell you how much I'm looking forward to breathing the clean air, taking long walks . . . looking into the sky at night and actually being able to see the stars."

Mac relaxed a little in his chair when he saw her enthusiasm.

"You're fired up about the whole thing, aren't you?" he asked with a laugh.

Niall sighed. "You have no idea."

Once again, Mac hesitated. "And . . . and your decision has nothing to do with . . . what's going to happen in late June?"

Niall's eyes flickered up to Mac's in surprise. "How did you know about that, Mac?"

"I read a blurb in the *Tribune* that Manning's execution had been rescheduled."

Niall exhaled slowly during the silence that ensued.

"It's been postponed twice now since they made him the exception for the moratorium on executions in Illinois. Chances are it won't happen."

"So your leaving town this summer has nothing to do with—"

"No," Niall said abruptly, shaking her head. But even as she answered so surely, she wondered if some unconscious part of her brain hadn't nudged her to plan events so that she could escape the horror that just seemed never to go away . . . if she secretly wished to be near Vic on the fateful day of Matthew Manning's execution.

She was so nervous and excited about leaving for Vic's farm tomorrow that she practically hadn't slept in a week. She also was scared witless that Vic would be so furious about Meg and Niall's little conspiracy that he'd shut her out as efficiently as he had Jennifer Atwood when he'd discovered her betrayal.

Meg still didn't know all the details of Niall's past, but Niall had told her about her son's death, not revealing exactly how he'd died. She'd also told Meg about Stephen's condition, her divorce, and how Vic had found out in such a shocking fashion that Niall had still been married during their affair.

Meg had been nothing but kind and sympathetic. But she was also baldly honest and had told Niall that every time she talked to her brother about Niall, he went cold as a frigid Chicago winter wind. Vic had never actually forbidden Meg to speak about Niall in front of him. But Meg explained to Niall just a few weeks ago that she got the impression he'd done *just* that, given the fact that he turned and walked away every time Meg tried to plead Niall's case.

Niall had felt awful about that, of course. She didn't want to cause any arguments between Meg and Vic. And she doubted that she was sowing much fraternal accord by showing up on Vic's farm to live for two months when he knew nothing about it, either. But Meg and Anne had been so convincing. And Vic's sister had implied that she was worried about Vic's state of mental health, as well.

Niall had prepared herself to weather Vic's initial storm of fury at her unexpected presence on his farm.

She *had* to do this. She just had to. When she considered the fact that she hadn't seen Vic's face or looked into his magnificent, soulful gray eyes now for over six months, it caused a sharp, nearly debilitating pain to go through her. Not to mention the fact that the last time he'd been staring at her, it had been with an expression of stark disbelief, as if he had been watching her face morph into a stranger's right before his very eyes.

But no, she wouldn't dwell on that now. If she did, she'd sink back into that morass of hopelessness and despair that had overwhelmed her when she spent last Christmas alone in her depressing beige and white Riverview apartment. Maybe she'd deserved his anger back then, but she hadn't deserved to lose him forever. Which is precisely what she'd almost let happen due to her own guilt.

But that was all over now, Niall vowed to herself as she lifted the box from the floor. She glanced back at her office, poignantly aware that she was about to embark on a new chapter in her life. Satisfaction surged through her when she turned the lock on the door and shut it with a brisk bang.

She was going after Vic. If fate had determined that he wasn't meant to be hers, at least Niall would know that it wasn't because her grief and guilt had kept her from trying.

FIFTEEN

A determined glint shone in Missy Shane's green eyes as she tossed her tray on the bar. The man she studied so intently didn't look up at the loud noise. She frowned and began to fill her own draft orders. Alex, the owner and bartender of the El Paso Lounge, must be in the back getting another keg. The El Paso would close in two hours, which meant it would be reaching its peak of Saturday night rowdiness any minute now.

Not that you could have guessed that by looking at the silent, morose man sitting at the bar. His dark, shaggy hair was in desperate need of a cut, although Missy had to admit that the wildness of it was dead sexy. The unruly waves fell forward on his forehead and brushed his lean cheeks and collar, casting him further into shadow. His elbows rested on the bar and his broad shoulders hunched forward as though he protected a bone from all potential comers.

Missy grinned slightly at her mental comparison of Vic Savian to a big dog. She was going to do her damndest tonight to get her hands on that bone. Ellie Sheerer, another waitress at the El Paso who had been lucky enough to get in Vic's pants one chilly night last April, had informed Missy with relish that the beast's bone was worth any sacrifice to taste. Her nose wrinkled distastefully at the thought of buxom, boisterous Ellie getting the privilege of sucking off Vic Savian's big, delicious cock in the parking lot of the El Paso when he'd never so much as glanced twice at Missy.

Missy was Halver County's Corn Queen for two years running, after all. Sure, it was ten years ago that she'd won those titles, but Missy was every bit as tight and voluptuous at twenty-nine as she had been at nineteen. She might not have tits as big as Ellie's but she'd been told by quite a few of her lovers that she gave head every bit as fine as her rival did, although she didn't have the experience that Ellie's thirty-eight years granted her.

Besides, Vic Savian had been so drunk on the night that he'd allowed Ellie to climb into his pickup truck with him he'd probably thought Ellie was Missy. Yeah, maybe that was it. They both had reddish hair and wore identical waitress uniforms. If that was the case, then Missy couldn't wait to prove to Vic that he'd gotten the wrong woman to steam up the windows of his cab back in April.

All Ellie or Alex had been able to tell her about Vic Savian was that he'd inherited that enormous spread that used to belong to Manny Padilla out on the west side of town, and that he was a writer or something. She hoped he wrote scary books like her favorite author, Dean Koontz. She wouldn't be a bit surprised, as dark, mysterious, and a little dangerous as he seemed. He didn't come into the El Paso Lounge very often—or anywhere in town that Missy had been able to identify—so she needed to make everything out of the opportunity that she could.

"Let me put a nice head on that beer for you," she offered suggestively.

She blinked in surprise when he raised his shaggy head slowly. He made a subtle rolling gesture with his lean jaw as he inspected her. She'd never looked directly into his eyes before, so she hadn't been prepared for their impact. Holy shit. Missy had seen how many beers he'd put away tonight as he sat there silent—and nearly as motionless—as a stone. So it shocked her more than a little to see how startlingly alert and penetrating his light gray eyes were.

His gaze lowered over her body unhurriedly. Was it wishful thinking, or did those phenomenal eyes linger for a second on her nipples, which had just obligingly pulled tight beneath her uniform? He slowly pushed his empty glass across the bar as he continued to watch her.

Missy tried to hide the triumph in her smile. She was going to get a taste of elusive Vic Savian tonight, she just knew it.

And she was determined to be the first woman in El Paso, Illinois, to see the inside of his bedroom instead of just the view of the floor mat of his truck as she leaned over to suck the tall, stiff pillar of his tasty cock.

"Wait."

Missy paused and looked over her shoulder seductively, her hand poised over the tap.

"Give me a Scotch."

Missy stared for a second, amazed at the effect his hoarse voice had on her body, like a pair of knuckles running seductively down her spine. It sounded so raspy that she wondered when he'd actually last spoken out loud to another human being. Jeez, this guy must be a real loner.

But she'd never seen a sexier hermit in her life. Maybe he was shy. Good thing Missy knew how to bring a man out of his shell. She licked her lower lip in a gesture of anticipation at the same time that she gave him a knowing wink.

"Anything you want is yours for the taking, cowboy," she promised him huskily. She turned and cocked her hip, gifting him with the sight of her ample, round ass as she took her time locating the most premium brand of Scotch that Alex owned.

Of course it was necessary for her to bend over deeply to find just the right bottle.

Vic looked his fill at the sight of the reasonably attractive redhead waving her more than reasonably attractive ass in the air for his benefit. He wondered if he could have set a drink on the shelf of the upper curve of her generous, taut buttocks. His cock stirred listlessly in his jeans, like a bear awaking from a winter slumber, sticking its head up and taking a sniff.

Only to fall back to sleep again almost immediately.

The damn thing had practically been hibernating since . . .

"Make it a double," he ordered tersely. The waitress straightened after studying the bottles in front of her for so long that Vic was beginning to suspect that she'd gotten her back stuck in that position, or else had some kind of reading disability.

"You like Scotch, huh?" she asked through curving lips as she poured his drink in front of him a few seconds later.

Vic shrugged.

"I can't say I've ever tried this brand myself." She cast her gaze in both directions. Alex was nowhere to be seen. "Mind if I join you?"

"Be my guest."

The sight of her seductive green eyes widening in alarm when she took a sip of the Scotch would have made Vic smile once.

Damn. Why had he asked for Scotch? He'd never be able watch a woman drink it again without thinking of Niall. His lips flattened into a grim line. He pried them open to take a healthy slug of the liquor.

Hadn't he expressly forbidden himself to think about that woman?

"God, I don't know how you drink it so easy like that!"

"You either like the burn or you don't, Missy."

Her catlike eyes flashed. "You know my name?"

Vic shrugged. "Sort of hard to sit here for two hours straight and not pick up a thing or two."

"Well, I'll tell you something, cowboy." She leaned forward, thrusting out her breasts conspicuously. "I don't know if I like Scotch, but I *like* the burn."

Vic's lips curved slightly as his eyes moved over her face. Nice mouth. Although that caboose she sported might be worth a thorough investigation.

Now *that's* more like it, Vic thought with vague satisfaction. He'd reacted quite differently to the fact that Niall was an unfaithful liar than he had to Jenny's betrayal. After Jenny he'd fallen into bed with practically any reasonably attractive woman who would overlook the fact that he was stone drunk.

His intoxication tonight, however, was the exception, not the rule, since he'd been kicked in the gut and ass at once with the knowledge that Niall was married. His interest in sex had dropped off drastically since last December. Technically speaking, his libido was as active as ever; it was his interest in actually spending the time and effort necessary to take a woman to bed that was lacking. A few dimly recalled blow jobs in his truck cab outside of a bar in the wee hours of morning and bringing off the woman with his hand in thanks were the sum total of his pitiful sex life for the past six months.

"You know lots of woman fight the burn," Vic told Missy as he gazed at his Scotch and rolled the amber liquid around in the glass.

"Not me," Missy assured him.

"Here's to the burn, then," he murmured, holding her stare as he drank. Missy licked her lower lip sensually before she took another sip of the Scotch, this time doing a much better job at hiding her grimace. She leaned forward until their faces were only inches apart.

"I'm going to set your bed on fire, Vic Savian."

He gave a full-fledged smile as the first wave of euphoria from the Scotch hit his brain. "Is that right?" he drawled.

She colored pinker than the liberally applied blusher on her cheeks. He caught a whiff of her scent—cheap perfume, sweet sweat, and stale smoke. He jerked back slightly and took another drink of Scotch to cover his instinctual reaction. If he drank enough, it wouldn't matter what she looked or smelled like. The only thing that was of significance was the scalding orgasm that he had deep inside her body, that nirvanic moment of pleasure when all memories were swept blessedly clean.

"Yeah, that's right, big boy," Missy assured him with gleaming eyes. "I get out of here at two thirty. You just sit tight till then, ya hear?"

Vic didn't respond as she grabbed her tray and left the bar with one last coy glance. The pleasant haze of the beer and Scotch he'd consumed, combined with the promise of a blissful forgetfulness between Missy-the-waitress's long, strong thighs, had him feeling better than he had in months.

Six months, to be exact.

His euphoria was short-lived, however. It popped like a fragile bubble when he saw who walked into the El Paso between two young toughs who looked like they'd either just gotten off the back of a Harley or wanted everyone to think they had.

"Vic!"

The whites of Donny Farrell's eyes showed up clearly behind a thick fringe of obscuring brown hair when Vic approached their booth.

"What're you doing here?" Vic demanded tersely. The kid that Meg had insisted he hire on as a stable boy six months ago appeared to be at a loss for words. The long-haired, barrel-chested, goateed idiot sitting next to Donny was having no such problem with speech, however.

"What's your problem? Who are you to question him about what he does? His fucking long-lost dad?"

"Shut up, Banger," Donny muttered under his breath.

"No, I'm not his dad. Who're you? One of his classmates in the tenth grade?" Vic countered levelly.

Banger's chest expanded so far in indignation that Vic wondered if he was going to squeeze Donny's skinny body right out of the booth.

"Why you son-of-a—"

"Come on, Donny. I'm taking you home," Vic stated, calmly cutting off Banger's tirade.

"Go on," Banger's scruffy companion taunted when Donny stood, the kid's expression mixing defiance and uncertainty in equal measure. "I told Banger you were too much of a pussy to hang out with the big boys."

"You're the pussy, Chooch," Donny muttered with a bitter weariness that was heartbreaking to see in one so young. "At least that's what I hear from Banger. That's what he calls you behind your back all the time."

"Fuck you, man!" Chooch told Banger furiously, switching the target for his aggression without a quiver of his eyelids. Banger was in the process of sizing up Vic, deciding whether or not he could take him. The majority of his bravado melted out of him by the time he met Vic's steady stare.

Vic's gaze moved over Banger in a rapid, disparaging once-over. He was at least in his mid twenties if not early thirties—old enough to know that he shouldn't be dragging fifteen-year-old kids into bars with him. But Vic knew that Donny had a multitude of older brothers—a few of whom were out of prison at the moment. The badass that he studied presently shared no physical similarity to Donny—fortunately for Donny—so Vic figured he must be one of his older brothers' partners in crime.

Alex had returned to the bar and must have noticed the tempers flaring over at the booth.

"Banger, I don't want any trouble from you tonight, ya hear? Sheriff Madigan is in the back of the bar and you're already on his shit list!" Alex shouted.

Alex's threat to sic Danny Madigan on him seemed to completely flatten an already deflating Banger. Vic couldn't say he blamed the jerk. Madigan might be a small-town boy, but he was also a six-foot-two-inch, heavily muscled ex-Marine who not only had the power of the law behind him, but could turn Banger into packaged ground meat in a matter of minutes. Still, Vic suspected there was some other reason Banger chose not to tango with Vic when Sheriff Madigan was on the premises—something Vic hoped didn't have to do with drugs or guns or some other illegal activity.

"Your ass is grass, man!" Banger told Vic with a glare he might have learned in a therapeutic acting class at Joliet Penitentiary.

Vic gave Donny a bland look. He knew the kid interpreted his expression accurately when Donny's lips curved in shared amusement.

"Banger, you're a moron," Donny said before he turned. "Let's go, Vic."

"See ya, boys," Vic said, his mouth curving at Banger's infuriated expression at his emphasis on the word *boys*.

"Hey, wait."

Vic paused in the process of holding open the El Paso Lounge's front door for Donny.

"What about our date?" Missy Shane asked shrilly.

Vic tried to ignore the smirk he saw on Donny's face from the corner of his eye. "Maybe another time," he muttered before he ducked his head and followed Donny out the front door. Vic took a long draw of the fresh, brisk air, clearing his head.

"You had a date with Missy Shane and you blew her off?" Donny asked, his voice breaking slightly in incredulity. "Shit, you're nuts, man. Missy's *hot*."

"Wasn't exactly a date," Vic muttered under his breath.

"Then you're even *more* nuts."

"Yeah? Well, you're too young to be talking about non-dates and hanging out in bars," Vic accused sourly as they started walking to his truck.

"You're just changing the subject."

Vic frowned. The kid was too sharp for his own good. Meg's bright idea to have Vic offer Donny a job in the stables had to do with the fact that she saw a lot of promise in the kid and couldn't stand to see him ending up in juvie or worse. Vic had seen Donny's drawings and had to agree. Besides, Vic was extremely picky about the people who took care of his horses, and Donny was a natural.

"You're a smart kid," Vic muttered as they walked through the parking lot. "Way too smart to be letting those assholes talk you into making drug exchanges for them or doing some other equally stupid thing. They'll tell you how you won't get in trouble for it because of your age, but they're lying. They don't give a shit about you. Am I right?"

Donny flipped the dark fringe of hair out of his eyes. "About me being smart? I left with you, didn't I?"

Vic opened his mouth to press the subject but bit off his words. Hell, what'd he'd said in the bar was true. He *wasn't* the kid's dad.

Donny had gotten across his point, just as Vic had.

"You got your permit with you?" Vic asked tersely as he dug in his jeans for his keys. He knew from experience around the farm that the kid was a good driver. Vic was helping him log enough hours with an adult driver so that he could get his license.

"Yeah."

"You been drinking?" Vic pressed. He'd already surmised that the answer was no from Donny's behavior, but the kid did have a history, after all. That was one of the reasons Meg had implored Vic to hire him to work in the stables. Meg knew that Donny needed some kind of constant in the chaotic, dysfunctional world provided by his flighty mother, a houseful of reprobate older brothers, and a father who had said sayonara before Donny had cut his first tooth.

"Nah, I don't drink anymore," Donny answered with a vaguely insulted expression.

Vic tossed the keys at him. "Well, I have been, so you're driving. Anybody gonna miss you if you sleep out in the stables tonight?" he queried as he climbed into the passenger seat of his truck and slammed the door. Donny often spent two or three nights a week after he finished work in the cozy little bedroom out in the stables and then went to school with Meg in the morning. Vic regretted asking the question so flippantly, however, when

Donny didn't answer immediately as he busied himself adjusting the driver's seat and his mirrors for their five-inch difference in height. The kid was growing faster than a stalk of corn in the fertile Illinois soil. He very well might surpass six feet by the end of the summer.

"Nobody'll miss me," Donny finally answered flatly as he turned the ignition and the truck hummed to life.

They were both comfortable in the silence that followed as Donny drove down the rural roads to get to the farm. Vic was busy regretting his chance to finally get back in the swing of things in regard to sex. He figured that Donny was too appreciative of the fact that Vic wasn't preaching at him for being in a bar at one A.M. when he was only fifteen years old to push his luck by trying to start a conversation.

Vic was so preoccupied in his dark thoughts and self-recriminations for not ordering every last thing that Missy Shane had been offering on the menu tonight that at first he didn't comprehend what Donny meant when he pulled up in the gravel driveway next to Vic's cottage.

"Who's visiting Tim and Meg?"

"Huh?" Vic asked distractedly.

Donny nodded his head at the sedan in the headlights. "Shit, it's a Benz. License plates are NFC 87987. Know who that is? Vic?" Donny added after several seconds when he realized Vic hadn't answered.

Vic blinked several times as he stared at the relatively mundane image of the familiar car as if it were a spaceship that had just landed on the driveway in front of them.

"Yeah. I know whose it is," Vic eventually said. "See you at breakfast, Donny."

"Night," Donny said, a look of confusion on his face as he
watched the tall figure of his boss stalk up to the main house with
a brisk, purposeful stride and tense posture that looked entirely out
of place, considering Vic's former mellow mood.

Whoever the driver of that car was, Donny decided he was glad
it wasn't him.

For the first few seconds after Niall awoke, she didn't know
where the hell she was. Then she saw the painting of the farm on
the wall. Meg had uncharacteristically blushed when she'd told
Niall that she'd painted it herself in a burst of creativity last summer.

"I know it's not any good," Meg had said, chuckling at Niall's
protests to the contrary. "Good enough for the guest bedroom, if
not over the mantel, anyway. This time of year on the farm really
gets the creative juices flowing, you'll see," Meg had assured her as
she'd showed her around her airy, spacious bedroom suite.

Who had just turned on the light? Niall wondered presently.
She groggily pushed her hair out of her eyes and sat up on her elbow. Her lips fell apart in shock when she realized that Vic stared
at her from the opened doorway, his finger still hovering near the
light switch.

For several tense moments neither of them spoke. Niall soaked
up the image of him. As thirsty for it as she had been, she felt that
she could have just sponged up his image for hours and still had
room to absorb more.

Her gaze moved hungrily over his long, jean-clad legs. He'd always worn low-riding jeans that set off his taut abdomen and lean
hips. Niall thought that now they hung a little loose on his tall

frame, as though he'd lost some weight. A blue and white button-down shirt hung open to reveal a plain, white T-shirt that highlighted his deepened tan as well as the long, taut taper of his torso as it sloped from his waist to his broad shoulders. She'd never seen his hair so long or his jaw so much in need of a shave.

He looked a little wild standing there in the doorway. For those few tense seconds Niall wasn't quite sure what he was going to do or say. When he did eventually speak, he cut to the chase with his typical terseness.

"What're you doing in my house?"

Niall scraped her hair back from her face and sat up in bed. She instinctively pulled the covers up around her breasts, feeling vulnerable with Vic's eyes boring into her like fiery nails. His gaze flickered over her body at her abrupt movement, causing her skin to prickle in heightened awareness.

"I thought it was Meg's house," she mumbled lamely.

"You're visiting Meg?" Vic more stated than asked. His hand lowered from the light switch and he took an aggressive step into the room.

Niall took a deep, fortifying breath. She'd expected a hostile reaction from Vic, but she hadn't pictured it taking place while she was half-asleep and wearing nothing but a thin nightgown while he towered over her in barely restrained fury. She began to seriously doubt her wisdom in concocting this plan with Meg. Encountering Vic in that moment brought to mind unexpectedly awakening to find oneself in the eye of a powerful storm. She perfectly imagined him scooping her up out of her cozy bed and tossing her out on the gravel driveway along with her car keys and suitcase.

"In a manner of speaking," she replied, glad to hear that her voice didn't tremble. "I'm boarding here on the farm for the next several months."

Vic's jaw hung open. "You're boarding here on the farm for the next several months," he repeated with acid sarcasm.

"I believe that's what I just said, yes. I'm the teacher the Institute hired to teach the art history class at the high school. Maybe Meg told you about it."

"*You're* the teacher they hired to teach—"

"Vic, you're not going to repeat everything I say, are you?" Niall interrupted. His eyes flashed, and Niall knew she'd poured fuel on the fire.

"You don't want me to repeat myself? Fine. Here's something you haven't heard, although if you had a few working brain cells, you certainly should have seen it coming. You're *not* staying on this farm."

"Why not?"

She saw him blink in surprise.

"Because I said so, that's why!" he roared.

Niall took a deep breath in an attempt to quiet her racing heart. Her nervousness had nothing in common with the anxiety she associated with Stephen's agitation and subsequent violence, but it felt extremely potent nonetheless. Vic never gave her the chance to respond, however. Instead he turned and left the room, slamming the door behind him so hard that Meg's painting rattled on the wall. Niall just sat there with her eyes closed tightly and listened to the charged, terse exchange between Vic and Meg in the hallway a few seconds later, followed by the sound of Vic stomping down the stairs, his fury apparent in every strike of his boots on the hard wood.

She looked up wearily a moment later when someone tapped softly at her bedroom door.

"Come in." She blinked in surprise when she saw the amused expression on Meg's face.

"I thought that went pretty well, don't you?" Meg asked through a grin.

"Oh, yeah, just great," Niall agreed dryly. "At least he didn't pick me up and throw me out in the driveway." Her eyebrows furrowed in puzzlement when she saw that Meg's grin only grew wider. "Meg, it's not funny! We shouldn't have done this. We should have at least warned him first or something—"

Meg scoffed. "He can handle it. Trust me, my little brother needs some stirring up. His morose act was really starting to bug the shit out of me."

"He doesn't want me here."

Meg shook her dark curls in admonishment. "Honey, you knew he wasn't going to welcome you with open arms. You're not giving up *that* easy, are you? It was a sure bet he was going to act like a bear when he found out what we planned."

Niall sighed. "I just hadn't imagined him being quite so—"

"Pissed off?" Meg asked cheerfully. "Yeah, Vic's a real ass when he gets mad. Don't worry, though, he never gets violent. At least not with women, children, or animals," Meg added as if in afterthought. "If you're an inanimate object or a bully with balls, better watch out though."

"Right. With a woman he just goes ice cold and shuts her out," Niall murmured.

Meg reached for the light switch. Niall strongly suspected she was getting a perverse satisfaction from stirring up her brother's temper, much like a mischievous child poking a branch in a hornet's nest just for the thrill of being ornery.

"*That* was hardly ice-cold, Niall. Which is all the more reason to say that Vic's reaction to you being on the farm was a *good* thing. Go to sleep, honey. Breakfast is served bright and early on the farm."

She flipped out the light, plunging the room into an absolute blackness that was completely foreign to Niall.

Vic tripped on something on the way to the bathroom just before dawn. After he'd picked up the offending boot and launched it against the wall in a fit of ineffective rage, he felt like a fool.

He hadn't slept all night. His head throbbed either from a hangover or from grinding his teeth together for so many hours—or most likely both. The image of Niall staring at him with those huge hazel eyes and looking all mussed and soft from sleep seemed to have been permanently etched behind his eyelids. It had been an unexpected, infuriating sight.

He'd rather not think about the fact that it had been a thoroughly appealing one as well.

There was no way that woman was staying on this farm another night. He didn't want to pull rank with Meg, but this was *his* property, God damn it. He had a right to say who stayed on it, didn't he?

He finished his business in the bathroom and scowled at his reflection in the mirror over the sink. He looked like some kind of wild mountain man. A strong urge to shave and make himself presentable overwhelmed him.

"Fuck that," he muttered before he dried his hands with one swipe and stalked out of the bathroom.

Why does Niall want to be here after half a year of giving me the silent treatment? he fumed as he plopped onto his bed with a loud protest from the springs. Was her husband sick again and she required a warm body in her bed? Or maybe her presence here didn't have anything to do with him at all . . .

Why'd she want to fuck with his head this way?

She'd made it clear after her mother revealed the fact that she was married that she couldn't offer Vic a viable explanation for her dishonesty. He'd tried to contact her afterward, positive there must be some logic behind Niall's incomprehensible behavior even if he couldn't conjure it up in his own stunned brain. But when she'd carefully avoided him, Vic had finally been forced to accept the fact that Niall felt too guilty to face him.

He couldn't imagine any other reason for the shattered expression on Niall's face that evening in her apartment when her mother had let the bomb drop that Niall had a sick husband. What other reason could there be besides guilt to explain how she'd avoided him after the fact as if he possessed a virulent form of the plague? Even with all that, he'd still been enough of a sucker to be shocked to see moving men in the hallway between his and Niall's apartments back in February. He'd stood there like an idiot at Niall's open door, thinking he'd finally have the opportunity to confront her about what had happened between them when a sandy-haired young man passed by carrying a box.

"Hi! Are you one of my new neighbors?" he'd called out cheerfully.

"Who're you?"

He started at Vic's terseness before he laughed good-naturedly. "I'm the guy who's moving into this apartment. Pete Sheppard." He shifted the box in his arms and stuck out his hand in greeting.

Vic just stared blankly at this stranger, this interloper that was moving into Niall's apartment. He imagined that he smelled Niall's fresh, feminine scent emanating from the open door. The sensation almost made him blind with fury. Even through his turmoil and anger in the previous month he'd never imagined her slinking away like a thief in the night, without saying a word to him.

It felt like he'd been kicked in the gut by a steel-toed boot all over again. But somehow this time seemed even worse than that evening in December.

That was when the truth hit home. There was a good chance he would never see Niall Chandler again. Niall really *was* too guilty to face him. And why shouldn't she feel ashamed of herself, damn it? Hadn't she been fucking his brains out while her husband lay sick in a hospital bed? Then her husband had miraculously improved and Niall proceeded to ignore Vic's existence, as if he was a much regretted, drunken one-night stand.

Obviously what had occurred between them had been some kind of emotional backfire for her. It had certainly been an explosive affair from the first. Vic just hadn't imagined where the impetus had come from on Niall's part.

Now he knew. Niall must have been feeling lonely and bereft while her husband was so ill. That must have been the origin of her nightmares. She was beautiful, vibrant . . . passionate. Like Jenny, she just needed a man in her bed to affirm all of those things, and Vic had been a ready convenience.

Vic grimaced and flipped onto his other side. Well, he was certainly glad to have helped Niall out in a tight spot. Fucking her had been great.

So great, in fact, that she'd subsequently ruined his sex life.

"You're as much to blame for that as her," Vic accused himself bitterly. He expressly directed himself not to in his thoughts, but his gaze still traitorously shifted over to the shut door of his closet. The Christmas gifts that he'd never given to Niall were in there, tossed far back into the darkest reaches. Somehow, the thought of what lay wrapped up in that furiously crumpled sack and the image of Niall looking so soft and sexy in bed last night rose up in his mind like the first two integers in an equation.

His cock jerked and tightened as if it'd just been yanked by a string, like his abrupt hard-on was just as obvious a result of adding those two thoughts together as one plus one equals two.

Shit. Well at least there couldn't be any doubt that his lack of a sex life had anything to do with equipment damage, he thought sourly. Not that he appreciated the fact that Niall was the one who almost instantly turned his cock into a steel pike.

"That damn sack is going into the lake later," he vowed to himself.

When he realized that he was talking to himself, he sprang out of the bed. What he needed was a big breakfast, a long ride on his favorite horse, Traveler, a few good hours writing at the computer . . . and maybe a trip back to the El Paso later. Today was Saturday. Chances were that Missy would be working again tonight, he reminded himself as he turned the shower nozzle to a frigid setting.

Vic wouldn't allow himself to dwell on the biggest question mark that kept bobbing annoyingly around his brain.

Just what the hell did Niall hope to accomplish by showing up on his farm?

Was she still interested in him, or was he just an unfortunate detail that she had to endure because of another agenda? Was she here just to take up where they'd left off? Because if she thought he was going to be her stand-in for her husband again, she definitely had another think coming. Vic despised liars and he didn't do married women.

And he damned Niall for making him break that code without his knowledge.

Why hadn't he just let Niall walk out the fucking door on that first night?

SIXTEEN

Andy, one of their full-time farmhands, Meg, Tim, Donny, and Niall all froze when Vic swung open the back screen door that led directly to the kitchen. He glowered at each one of them in turn, although he made a point of not making eye contact with Niall. Tim paused with a butter knife poised over some toast, Meg scowled from where she stood with a spatula in her hand by the stove, and Donny gawked at him from where he sat at the big kitchen table next to Niall.

"Well, good morning, sunshine," Meg deadpanned.

He threw her an "I'll deal with you later" look before he let the door slam shut behind him. He'd forgotten the kid was here. It didn't seem right to make a scene in front of him. Donny had enough of that crap at home.

"Morning, Vic," Tim greeted his brother-in-law extra cheer-fully, perhaps compensating for Vic's surly mood. Donny and Andy added their greetings, but Niall was silent. He saw from the corner of his eye, as he poured himself a cup of coffee, that Donny sat next to her and one of his sketch pads lay on the table between them.

"Where's Tony?" Vic asked Tim as he took a sip of hot coffee, referring to Tim's other full-time employee. The property that he'd inherited included thirty-six hundred acres of workable farmland. Tim needed several full- and part-time employees to help him run it during the planting season.

"His four-year-old is sick," Andy answered.

"And his wife is in Pennsylvania visiting her folks," Tim added as he set a plate of buttered toast on the table.

"You'll need some help getting those soybeans in the ground, then," Vic said stonily as he sat down at the end of the table farthest from Niall. He often helped on the farm, enjoying the manual labor and the feeling of accomplishment that accompanied it, even if he didn't want to make farming his official profession. In fact, he liked to find excuses to work on his farm. He felt a real connection with the rich, black soil, a feeling just as powerful as what he felt for the stark, barren landscape of Montana where he owned a ranch. Maybe his Uncle Manny really knew what he was doing by leaving Vic his land.

"I'll do Tony's share while he's out," Vic muttered.

"We'll get them planted one way or another," Tim assured him.

"I thought you were going to get some writing done today," Meg added as she brought plates of scrambled eggs and bacon to Andy and Vic.

Vic just shrugged and picked up his fork. He could feel Niall's gaze on him like a light current of electricity buzzing just beneath his skin. He looked up abruptly, meeting her stare. She glanced away immediately, likely put off by the message of blazing irritation in his eyes. She carefully drew back a page of the sketch pad and returned her attention to Donny's drawings.

"These are really good," Vic heard her say quietly to Donny. "You have considerable natural talent, Donny."

Donny blushed beneath his tan. "It's just comic book stuff. It's not like they're art or anything."

Vic gritted his teeth in annoyance when he saw the kid's expression when he looked at Niall's face, like he'd entered the house half-asleep as usual, ready for a ho-hum day, and suddenly found himself sitting next to Cameron Diaz for breakfast.

Not that he could necessarily blame Donny. Niall looked as fresh and pretty as a daisy, wearing a short-sleeved white cotton blouse with her golden hair falling in shiny waves to an inch above her shoulders. He'd rarely seen her dressed so casually. Vic remembered how soft her hair felt between his fingers all too well, just as he recalled the way her skin flowed like silk beneath his hands. Her complexion glowed with health . . . and perhaps an awareness of his anger at her uninvited presence on the farm. With the light sprinkling of freckles on her nose and her lack of makeup or jewelry, she looked about twenty years old. Vic's frown deepened when he noticed that not only Donny stared at her with a slack-jawed expression of awe but that Andy kept throwing calf-eyed glances at her as well.

When Vic realized he was staring just like every other male at the table, his frown deepened and he transferred his attention to eating his breakfast. Still, he couldn't shut out the impact of Niall's low, husky voice, much as he wished he could.

"What would make you think it's not art?" she asked Donny seriously. "There are some very fine artists in the ranks of cartoonists. Look at the power you've managed to convey here"—she brushed her fingertip across the page—"the inherent movement, the forward-surging energy in his body. That's some very fine artwork. And your writing for the story line is very good, as well. What's your character's name?"

Donny glanced up between his too-long bangs to see if anybody was listening, flushing slightly with embarrassment. Vic turned his eyes back to his plate.

"Stealth Judge," Donny mumbled almost unintelligibly.

"Thank you, Meg," Niall said warmly when Meg handed her a plate of scrambled eggs. "Let's close your book, Donny. I don't want to get anything on your artwork. You know, we did an exhibit at the museum a few years back of Marvel comics. I don't suppose you came to it?" Niall asked as she reached for a piece of toast.

Donny shook his shaggy head. "Nah, I've never been to Chicago." He sat up straighter in his chair. "You actually showed stuff about comics in a museum?"

Niall laughed, the sound making Vic cock his head slightly, as if trying to catch it fully in his ear. When he realized what he was doing, he determinedly shoveled the rest of his eggs in his mouth in one bite and pushed back his chair. Niall glanced up uncertainly at the loud scraping of his chair.

"Art isn't as stuffy and boring as you're making it out to be, Donny," she assured the boy as soon as she recovered. "Art reflects life, so that means it can be just about anything. It's the power and message of the reflection that make it art. I brought the book that we published for the Marvel exhibit. I'll show it to you later. It was amazing. I got to meet Stan Lee."

Vic looked over his shoulder from where he was standing at the sink with his plate in time to see Donny's jaw drop a mile.

"You met *Stan Lee*?" he croaked in disbelief.

Niall nodded, her hazel eyes gleaming with excitement. "He was really nice. Did you know that his real name is Stanley Martin Lieber and . . ."

"He changed his name to Stan Lee by splitting his first name in half?" Donny finished for her breathlessly. Meg threw Tim and Vic an amused look before she handed Donny a plate. Donny distractedly accepted it before he turned back to Niall. "Who's your favorite Marvel character?"

"The Silver Surfer, hands down. He's so mysterious."

Vic was a little surprised when Niall answered so quickly, but he supposed that there were lots of things he hadn't known about her. *Like that she was married for instance,* he thought as he opened the dishwasher door with a bang.

Donny stared at Niall like he was witnessing a miracle. "You like the Silver Surfer? He's my favorite, too. By far . . ." The boy's words trailed off as he continued to gape at Niall.

"Beginning to reconsider taking Niall's class this summer, Donny?" Meg chuckled as she sat down with her own plate.

"Yeah, maybe it would be cool," Donny said slowly. "But only if Vic said I could . . . with work and all."

Vic paused in the action of putting his plate in the dishwasher when the room went silent. With a quick sweep of his eyes, he took in Meg's triumphant grin, Donny's hopeful look, and Niall's wary expression. His gaze lingered on Niall as he slowly straightened. Fury rose in him like steam scalding his throat when he recognized the subtle trap.

"You know that the agreement from the very beginning was that school always comes first," Vic finally managed to get out. What else could he say?

"Yeah, but this is just an extracurricular class. And it's only for art," Donny waffled.

"What'd ya mean *only* for art?"

Donny looked a little taken aback. "Nothing . . . I mean . . ."

"Art always put bread on my table," Vic told Donny in a more restrained voice. He stood and slammed the dishwasher door shut. "Take the class. It'll do you good and keep you outta trouble, besides. I'll meet you two out in the barn," he told his brother-in-law and Andy stiffly before he walked out the door.

Niall glanced uncertainly at Meg before she followed Vic a few seconds later.

"Niall, let it go for now . . ." she heard Meg say warningly, but she plunged out the screen door and onto the back porch anyway. Dawn made the eastern sky a vibrant landscape of pale gold and pink. The air felt cool and pleasant on her skin as she raced down the painted wood stairs. The luminescent promise of the June morning, combined with the soft, calm breeze, seemed to stand in direct contrast with Vic's tense posture and angry, gravel-scattering footsteps.

"Vic, wait," she called out once she'd jogged up several feet behind him. She had to force herself not to take several steps backward when he spun around to face her. His handsome face was livid with fury. She lost whatever composure she possessed at the sight.

"I . . . I . . . don't want you to think . . ." She stumbled over her words anxiously. "I didn't plan for that to happen just now . . . with Donny, I mean."

"And I should believe you . . . *why*, exactly?" Vic asked with brutal sarcasm.

Niall's cheeks flushed hot at his reference to her past dishonesty. "I'm telling the truth, Vic. I had no way of knowing about the boy. I couldn't have planned that. I *wouldn't* have," she added under her breath.

He stepped closer. She inhaled the familiar scent of his skin mixing with the spicy, clean smell of his soap. Longing swamped her awareness, the feeling so overwhelmingly powerful that it made her eyes burn. She saw his nostrils flare slightly, as though he'd caught her scent as well. That, combined with the anger that almost seemed to roll off his big body like waves of heat, caused her heart to beat wildly in her chest.

"I wouldn't put anything past you and Meg at this point," he stated in a low growl. Niall started when he encircled her upper arm with his hand and pulled her closer. "What the hell are you up to? Why did you come here?"

Niall tried to inhale slowly to calm herself. It wasn't an easy thing to do while she looked up into his stormy gray eyes. Her gaze lingered for a moment on his mouth . . . on that slightly crooked, sinfully sexy front tooth.

"I came because I was ready, Vic."

"What's that supposed to mean?"

She raised her jaw stubbornly, stung by his relentless contempt. "It means that I wasn't ready before, and now I am," she replied. She saw the subtle change that her answer wrought on his rigid features.

The screen door slammed shut behind her, signaling Tim and Andy's exit from the house. Vic blinked at the sound before he leaned closer to her face, his thigh brushing her own, his eyes spearing into her.

"I don't care what the fuck you're ready for, Niall. You may have finagled your way into Meg's life, but you better stay clear of mine. Understood?" he asked in an ominous, quiet tone before he shook her arm slightly for emphasis.

"It's you who doesn't understand, Vic."

"Is that right?" he asked with an ugly twist of his shapely mouth. Tim's and Andy's footsteps crunched on the gravel thirty feet behind them. "Well, I'm real happy in my ignorance."

"You don't look very happy," she countered softly.

She felt the tension leap into his muscles, saw the flash of potent anger in his light eyes. For a second Niall thought he looked furious enough to strangle her. Instead, he released her and stepped back abruptly, as if he'd suddenly realized he was holding an intimate conversation with a poisonous snake.

"I don't care what you think I look like. Just stay away from me," he ordered before he turned and headed toward the path that led to the barn.

Niall felt her determination flagging in the face of Vic's harsh dismissal. She'd known rationally that he was going to be angered by her presence on the farm. But logic couldn't have prepared her for the impact of his boiling fury. As she and Meg spent a relaxing morning puttering around Meg's garden and then preparing lunch together, Meg assured her on several occasions that Vic's temper at her being there was a good signal, not a bad one.

Meg hadn't stood in the face of Vic's rage, however. Niall was far from confident that Vic would ever give her the opportunity even to voice her explanation for her actions last fall, let alone that he would listen with a compassionate ear to her apology.

But her sole mission on coming to the farm hadn't just been to reclaim Vic. She looked forward to teaching the art history class this summer, no matter what the circumstances. Being exposed to Donny's raw talent and having him agree to take the class made her even more excited to teach this summer. She spent an hour that morning finalizing her lesson plans and organizing the materials she planned to use for her first week.

Vic refused to eat the lunch that she and Meg had prepared when the men returned from the fields. Instead, he barked at Donny from the driveway that he was taking him home and that they'd grab lunch in El Paso. Donny looked slightly disgruntled by the change of plans but rallied quickly enough.

"Uh . . . I guess I'll see you . . . uh . . . at school then," he said awkwardly to Niall after he'd grabbed his sketchbook off the table and shuffled toward the back door.

Niall noticed the look of longing the teenager gave the platter of fried chicken she'd just placed on the table. "I'm glad you'll be there, Donny. Here. Take a piece with you," she offered, handing him a napkin and nodding at the plate. He'd come from the stables about ten minutes ago and had already asked at least five times how long it was until they'd eat.

"I'll get you registered, Donny. You just make sure you show up on Monday *on time*," Meg added for emphasis before the boy bolted out the screen door with a napkin-wrapped drumstick in one hand and his sketchbook in the other.

Niall watched as he talked animatedly to Vic through bites of chicken as they walked to Vic's truck. Vic's head tilted slightly as he listened, his manner reminding her poignantly of the silent, stoic man with whom she'd fallen in love.

"They seem like they're really close," Niall said wistfully.

Meg glanced around from the counter. "They are. Eerily so. You'd never guess that they first met only half a year ago," she said with a small laugh. "Vic thinks that I suggested he hire Donny on solely for the boy's sake. Donny had been ditching school back in November, and then he got caught by the police with beer and pot in his car several weeks later. He was headed down a path that was bound to end up with him bunking with one of his brothers at the county jail—or worse, in Pontiac or Joliet Prison. Donny deserves better. You see how bright he is. I have to admit I've grown really fond of the kid. I've gotten to know him pretty well. I *should* have, considering how much time he spent in my office his freshman and sophomore years," Meg joked as she placed the bowl of potato salad on the table.

"But I asked Vic to hire him on to help out in the stables as much for Vic as for Donny. Vic was so withdrawn after Christmas. I thought he needed something to pull him out of himself," Meg continued. She glanced out the door thoughtfully as Vic backed his truck skillfully out the long drive. "And you know, I think I did a pretty good job of things. Donny needed a strong male role model, and Vic needed . . ."

Niall looked over at Meg sharply when she paused.

"He needed someone to need him," Meg finished softly.

Niall's heart felt like it skipped a beat. Had Vic's depression originated from the fact that he'd fallen in love with her, just as Niall had with him? Or was his melancholy more based on the fact that he'd cautiously allowed someone else into his life after Jenny, only to believe that Niall had betrayed him just as callously? The expression on Meg's face made Niall cringe inwardly with guilt.

"I'm sorry I hurt him, Meg," she said softly. "No matter what happens between Vic and me, I want you to know that I appreciate you giving me this chance."

Meg's faraway look faded as she focused on Niall. "I like you, Niall. Mom and I were so bummed when you canceled your visit at Christmas, and you know how thrilled I am about having you here now. But I'm mostly doing this for Vic . . . and the kids at school, of course. Don't think I don't know that El Paso High is very lucky to get someone of your caliber as an instructor," she added as an aside before she sighed. "I know Vic's a stubborn ass at times, but I love him."

"I do, too," Niall said quietly.

"And it's a good thing," Meg stated with a wry grin as Tim and Andy came up the steps. "Because it looks like my little brother is bound and determined to prove that he couldn't care less about you, Niall."

The first three weeks of Niall's stay on the farm passed much more smoothly than she would have ever expected or perhaps hoped for, given that the easy going was mostly because Vic almost completely ignored her presence. His avoidance of her was compounded by the fact that he spent several days a week in Chicago, overseeing his play and running the Hesse Theater. She sometimes wondered if she would have had a better chance of running into Vic on a Chicago street than she would on his farm. At least the Hesse would be closed during July, and the chances were that he would spend less time in the city.

She hoped anyway, if his determination to stay away from her didn't make the city seem more and more tempting to him. Maybe he and Eileen Moore were busy sharing dinners together at The Art after performances of *Alias X*, as well as Vic's bed at the Riverview Towers—

Just the thought acted like a poison to Niall's system, making nausea sweep through her like a wave.

June—perhaps one of the most changeable months in central Illinois—segued from a crisp, refreshing spring to a humid, sweltering summer with amazing rapidity. She enjoyed her class and found her twelve students a joy to teach. The class was held three days a week for two-hour sessions, however, so she found herself having a lot of time on her hands. She and Meg grew closer as they took on several projects on the farm—expanding Meg's already extensive garden, refinishing the farmhouse's enormous antique front porch swing, or taking shopping trips to Bloomington for bulk food items or art supplies. They also took long walks on the horse paths that cut through the large property, meandering by a wooded area and a small lake in addition to the vast acreage of the fields. Sometimes they'd see Tim or one of the men in the distance on a tractor, and they'd wave.

Niall felt invigorated by country living. She'd always been an early riser, finding early morning to be the best time to do her yoga routine. Lately she'd shifted her time for her workout to the evening, since she was often busy helping with the breakfast the men ate before they left for the fields. She enjoyed her solitary workout in the empty, spacious living room that Meg had decorated, like the rest of the farmhouse, in the arts and craft style. Last Monday night she'd sensed eyes on her while she was collapsed on the floor in a stretch, only to look up and see Vic. He seemed unbelievably tall from her position right next to the floor, the top of his head coming within less than a foot from the entry archway. The sight of him struck her as compelling . . . even impressive . . . in its unexpectedness.

Their gazes met and held. Niall eventually sat up slowly and struggled for something to say. But before she could, his eyes flickered over her. His nostrils flared. Desire bloomed in her lower belly and spread, making her sex ache with a dull throbbing pain when she realized her legs were completely spread while she faced him. She knew how much she hungered for him, but in that moment the magnitude of her primitive need felt overwhelming in its intensity.

His eyes skated back up to her face.

Niall wondered what she wouldn't have given at that moment

to have Vic kiss her once again, touch her, thrust his cock deep inside her to apply friction to that elemental ache. The last time they made love seemed like a distant, longed-for memory that she grasped at so frequently nowadays that it had started to take on the quality of a dream.

He seemed to hesitate for several seconds, as if he wanted to say something . . . as if he wanted to *do* something. But then he'd inhaled sharply and turned away.

And even that poignant, brief encounter had become nothing but a memory.

Niall began to cook more and more frequently for the family and farmhands once she had convinced Meg that she actually enjoyed it and wasn't just being polite. She'd always been a good cook, and missed it sorely while she'd lived in Riverview Towers. She couldn't help but be flattered by Tim, Andy, and Tony's eager faces and exuberant praise over her cooking, or the fact that Donny planned his visits and work schedule in the stables to coincide with the meals that she prepared.

The few times that Vic did put in an appearance at the large oak table in the farmhouse kitchen, he remained silent while everyone else gushed about her homemade biscuits and sausage gravy, her marinated roast chicken and potatoes, or some other dish. But Niall couldn't help but take some satisfaction from the fact that Vic always ate everything on his plate and, more often than not, fought Tim or Andy or Meg for seconds. She was glad when Meg or Tim questioned him about how things were going at the theater or about his writing, because she felt too self-conscious about doing it when everyone sitting at the table knew that Vic disapproved of her presence there.

She felt like a thief, stealing glances at Vic covertly on those occasions. It heartened her to see that although his hair was still shaggy he at least wasn't quite as thin as he had been when she first arrived. He was shaving again. The tan that he acquired so easily from riding or working on the farm made him even more magnetically attractive.

Niall found herself staring at his bare forearms while he ate, thinking they were a relatively safe target for her covetous glances. She'd never have guessed before she met Vic that a man's bare, muscular arms or big, capable-looking hands could be so sexy. For Niall, however, Vic's forearms and hands rivaled the sight of his long, hard thighs or his tight ass in his well-worn jeans. Well—they took a close second.

And beggars couldn't be choosers.

Once he'd caught her staring and abruptly paused in the motion of cutting his pork chop. She'd looked up guiltily to find him gazing directly at her. His bronzed skin made his light eyes even more compelling in their impact. Niall froze in her chair like a small animal that had just come into the sight of a predator. She couldn't read the inexplicable expression in Vic's eyes in that moment. By the time he made his characteristic rolling motion with his jaw and glanced down, Niall was left breathless with confusion and longing.

He'd left the kitchen early that night, surprising Meg when he turned down a serving of her homemade strawberry shortcake.

Niall watched a few seconds later through the window over the sink as Vic backed out of the driveway. She'd tried not to think of where he might be going, but she was about as successful at that as she was at torturing herself by imagining what he was doing with Eileen Moore on those nights when he stayed in Chicago.

About two weeks after Niall's arrival, Donny had innocently forced Vic to acknowledge her while they were eating dinner. It was a sunny, comfortably warm summer evening. The fact that it

was a Friday night and that Vic was home from Chicago gave a
festive air to dinner that night. Niall had spent a good part of the
afternoon, after she'd returned from class, cleaning the enormous
barbecue in the backyard, which Meg admitted hadn't been used
once since they'd moved into the farmhouse. When Niall'd finally
cleaned the monstrous iron contraption to her satisfaction, she'd
put it to good use by preparing some juicy steaks, corn on the cob,
and baked potatoes on it. They were in the midst of enjoying their
summertime feast when Donny suddenly sprung his unexpected
question to Niall.

"Want me to teach you how to ride this summer, Ms. Chandler?"

Niall glanced up in surprise, noticing how Vic's angular jaw
paused in the motion of chewing his steak.

"Uh . . . I don't know about that, Donny," she equivocated
with a nervous laugh. The idea of riding one of those beautiful
animals fast and free undoubtedly appealed to her. But that was
like saying that the thought of flying in a plane sounded exciting
and wonderful when one was scared stiff of takeoff. It didn't matter how great step two seemed if one was terrified of step one.

"Don't you think she could learn on Velvet . . . or maybe Aster?"
Donny asked Vic pointedly.

Niall waited in growing discomfort as Vic took his time chewing and swallowing. When he finally transferred his gaze to her, it
made her feel hot and flustered.

"You've never ridden before, have you?"

She shook her head slowly. He'd asked her if she'd ever ridden
once while they were dating in Chicago last year and Niall had
told him that she hadn't, then neatly changed the subject.

"I was enrolled for riding lessons when I was seven. On the day
that I showed up, the horse they had picked out for me bolted as

the instructor was helping me mount. I sort of . . . refused to go back after that, much to my mother's dismay," Niall added under her breath.

In fact, Alexis had been at her wits' end trying to understand how her daughter had been so terrified by the rearing horse. She couldn't comprehend Niall's solemn and eventually fierce refusals to return to her lessons. Alexis had been an accomplished equestrian from an early age, and it was beyond her how her own flesh and blood could abhor what she so loved.

"What do you think, Vic?" Donny prompted when Vic just looked down at his plate and speared a piece of steak with his fork.

"It doesn't matter how much you want her to do it. She's got to want to do it herself," Vic stated laconically before he ate the meat.

"But those horses are gentle! Aster wouldn't . . ."

"Aster *would* . . . if someone made her nervous enough," Vic told Donny with a pointed glance from beneath his lowered brow. "I haven't got a horse in my stables that doesn't have some spirit. None of them are appropriate for a gun-shy first timer . . . except maybe for Traveler," he added under his breath.

"*Traveler?*" Meg sputtered. "You've got to be kidding. You can't be thinking of putting little Niall up on that mammoth!"

Vic set his fork down with a clanking sound. "I didn't say that I was thinking of doing anything."

Niall shifted in her chair uncomfortably in the tension that followed. Vic must have realized that everyone had paused in their eating and glanced at him, because he slowly inhaled and picked up his fork again.

"I just meant that Traveler is the best trained of the lot. He'd hold steady with a freight train barreling at him."

"If you were on his back telling him to," Donny conceded after a thoughtful moment. "But only until the last second before impact. He'd never let Vic get hurt," the boy added as an aside to Niall.

Niall had caught a glimpse of Vic on Traveler on several occasions, and she had to agree. She'd never seen a man and a beast look so natural and graceful together. She smiled at Donny warmly. They'd been forming a close friendship, and Niall got the impression that the teenager wanted to share something that he knew about and enjoyed with her, just as she'd begun to do by opening up the world of art to him.

"I appreciate you thinking about me, Donny. I do," she said. "But as much as I have to admit there is a certain appeal to the idea, I somehow don't think God meant for me ever to get on the back of a horse."

She felt Vic's eyes on her as Donny opened his mouth to protest. "But I think you'd get along great with Velvet. Maybe if—"

"Donny, just let it go," Vic muttered with exasperation. There was just enough of an edge in his voice to silence Donny for the time being.

The following Friday Vic never showed up at the farm. Niall tried to tell herself that it didn't matter—which was ridiculous, because it *clearly* did. A panic rose in her chest every time she considered that her stay on the farm was nearly half over and Vic still hadn't spoken a dozen words to her since her second day there. And she had a sinking suspicion that he was spending time in another woman's bed. What if he continued to shut her out, as he'd done to Jennifer Atwood so successfully? Was it past time for her to start accepting that their affair was a finished chapter, at least in Vic's opinion?

Meg said it was too hot to cook, so Tim invited Niall and her to an Italian restaurant in El Paso that Friday evening. It had been the hottest day of the summer so far, and the evening didn't appear to be cooling things off much. Niall came downstairs at their agreed-upon time for departure, and met Tim and Meg in the kitchen.

"What?" she asked Meg, her eyes widening in slight alarm when Meg unsuccessfully suppressed laughter at her appearance and Tim's blue eyes sparkled with amusement.

"We're not going to the The Ritz, Niall. It's a little mom-and-pop place in El Paso," Meg chuckled.

"Well, that's what I thought," Niall replied, looking perplexed.

"You're wearing a dress, high heels, and pearls!" Meg supplied the obvious since Niall didn't seem to see it.

She looked down, confused that her clothing would be the source for Tim and Meg's amusement. "I'm wearing a cotton sundress and a pair of sandals. It's scorching outside."

"What about your hair?" Tim teased as he made some swirling motions around his head to signify her upswept hairdo. Meg snorted at his masculine fumbling.

"Oh, for heaven's sake . . . there. Are you happy?" she asked with mock disgust as she pulled out the single clip that held up her hair and tossed it into her purse. It was one of the most informal of hairstyles, as Meg very well knew! Only a man would think it was fancy because it was up on her head. "A sundress is just as casual as a pair of jeans," she reminded Meg as they headed out the back door. "And I only wore the pearls because . . ."

She stopped abruptly mid-sentence. Niall hadn't worn her pearls since coming to the farm. But maybe her melancholy over missing Vic made her reach for them tonight. He'd always told her how much he liked it when she wore her pearls. And of course there had been that one time . . .

The charged memory of Vic looking up at her with hot eyes and a slow smile as he held up her pearls swamped her awareness.

Good. Because I'm going to make you come again with these.

She closed her eyes tightly. A strange, trembling sensation began to vibrate in her chest. It took her a moment to recognize it as the first stages of panic.

What was she going to do if she couldn't get Vic back?

"Niall, are you okay?" Meg asked, her grin wavering.

"We were only kidding," Tim assured her quickly. "You'd put us hicks to shame if you were wearing a burlap sack."

Niall opened her eyes slowly and realized that they'd paused on the gravel driveway. "Of course I'm all right," she said a little too quickly. "Come on, I'll drive," she offered, knowing she needed something to focus on besides Vic Savian or his glaring absence from her life.

After dinner she caught a glimpse of why Vic hadn't immediately returned to the farm that night.

It was knowledge she could, quite frankly, have done without.

The three of them strolled to the car following their dinner, all of them seemingly content and relaxed, coming from the air-conditioned restaurant with good meals in their bellies.

What Niall saw when they approached her car was enough to practically force the pasta that had been resting so peacefully in her stomach onto the pavement. Tim paused when he saw how still and pale she'd gone when she reached the driver's door. He looked at the parking lot adjacent to the restaurant, where Niall stared fixedly.

"Come on, Niall. I'll drive," Tim said softly as he took the car keys from her suddenly numb fingers.

She startled from the trance that held her while she watched Vic kissing a redheaded woman in the parking lot of a place called the El Paso Lounge. The woman's arms snaked up around his neck. She gripped his too-long hair in a greedy gesture before she ran her fingers through its length. The manner in which Vic leaned over the woman and held their bodies so close made the act look like one of consumption as much as an embrace.

SEVENTEEN

Right before Tim opened the back door, Vic lifted his head from his feeding frenzy on the redhead's mouth. The next thing Niall knew, Tim was pushing her into the backseat. Niall stared unseeingly at the driver's headrest in front of her as Tim yanked her seat belt over her and fastened it. After they were on the road for thirty seconds, Meg twisted around to look at her from the front seat.

"Niall?"

"Hmmm? Oh, yeah, fine . . ." She trailed off dazedly.

Meg cast a doubtful glance at Tim, but then an irritated expression came over her handsome features. Niall was in a state of shock at that moment, but that was nothing to what she experienced when Meg next spoke.

"I thought you came down here to get Vic back!"

"I *did*."

"Well, when are you going to start doing it?" Meg asked with obvious frustration.

"Honey . . ." Tim began in a conciliatory manner, only to stop when his wife gave him a blazing look that reminded Niall of Vic.

"She's been here a *month*, Tim. And she folds up into defensive mode whenever Vic is around." Meg transferred her attention to a stunned Niall in the backseat. "Vic is a virile man, Niall. He has needs—"

"Oh, and I don't?" Niall challenged, her anger breaking through her shock.

Meg gave an exaggerated shrug. "I don't know. Do you? I haven't seen any evidence of it."

"Well, they're not the kind of needs I discuss in an open forum," Niall defended herself hotly. She blinked as she realized that was exactly what she was doing.

Meg sank back into her seat and sighed regretfully. Niall wondered if she was thinking it had been a big mistake to invite Niall to the farm.

"I'm sorry, Niall," she muttered after a moment. "I just can't stand to sit by and watch while you two make such a mess of things."

Niall felt her eyes begin to sting. It was like salt being poured on a wound to hear a good friend say such a thing right after she'd seen the man she loved in the act of practically having sex with another woman if it weren't for the flimsy barrier of their clothing. Now Meg was telling her it was all *her* fault that Vic Savian was mauling some strange woman in a sleazy bar's parking lot because *she* wasn't seeing to his sexual needs!

As if she could when he wouldn't come within ten feet of her.

"Let me out, Tim," Niall demanded abruptly. "I'll walk the rest of the way home."

"No, you won't," both Tim and Meg said at once.

"*Yes*, I will. It's my car." She clicked off her seat belt, forcing Tim to slow and finally stop at the side of the rural road.

"Niall, I'm sorry," Meg apologized rapidly as Niall clambered to open the door. "It's just that—"

"It's okay," Niall said. "I just need to get out right now."

She averted her eyes from Meg's distressed expression and Tim's concerned one before she slammed the door and started walking down the blacktop road. What she'd said was true. She felt like she was going to have a panic attack if she remained in the confined space of her car. Images of Vic pressed so tightly against that woman played in graphic, haunting detail in her mind's eye. Volatile emotions bubbled like a wicked brew in her chest—fury, jealousy, anguish . . . desire.

Yes, desire.

It made her nauseous to realize it, but sexual arousal had simmered in her lower belly, hot and tingling, when she'd seen Vic in such a blatantly erotic tableau. Memories and sensations of what it had felt like to have him make love to her with his characteristic intensity and passion had smacked into her awareness with the equivalent of a physical blow.

And Meg had accused her of not having any needs. What a joke.

After Tim and Meg had passed out of sight, Niall stopped on the side of the road and let out a sob of pure misery. She didn't know how long she stood like that, bawling her eyes out with only thousands and thousands of foot-high corn stalks as her witness, but it was twilight by the time she started walking down the road again. Unfortunately, her cry had done her no good. The graphic memory of Vic kissing that woman kept her right in the center of her emotional storm.

It took her a minute to realize that the low heels of her sandals were sinking slightly into the heated blacktop. She hissed a furious curse when she lifted a foot and saw that the tarlike substance stuck to her shoes. She'd never get the damn stuff off!

When she heard a car coming down the road behind her, she moved off to the side. The gravel at the periphery of the road adhered to her sticky sandals. Tears of sheer frustration slipped down her flushed cheeks.

It took her a few seconds to realize that the vehicle had slowed and stopped next to her. She glanced to her right warily. Vic was staring down at her from the cab of his dark blue pickup truck.

"What're you doing?" he asked in equal parts irritation and puzzlement.

Niall gritted her teeth as she swiped at her wet cheeks. Great, this was just *great*. "Leave me alone. I'm taking a walk."

He grunted incredulously. "It's ninety degrees plus, and it's getting dark. You're wearing high heels."

"*So?*" Niall asked furiously. Why the hell did everyone have to keep mentioning her shoes? She paused to try and pry off the widening patch of gummy gravel on her left heel with her right toe. The clod came off her heel and stuck on her other sandal. She kicked her foot in mounting irritation.

"Get in the truck. I'll take you back to the farm."

"*No,*" Niall stated emphatically, refusing to look at him as he stared down at her.

"Get in the *goddamned truck,* Niall," Vic growled when she sprinted forward several steps, trying to ignore the fact that it felt like she was walking through glue.

Without pause she suddenly did an about-face and circled around the back of Vic's truck. What the hell? Why should she care if Vic saw her at her emotional worst? He was the one who was responsible for it, after all.

Her tears cooled when they came into contact with the frigid interior of Vic's air-conditioned cab. Before she shut the door, she sat sideways in her seat and removed her ruined sandals. She glared at him after she resoundingly slammed her door shut, glad to see that he looked as angry as she was. Her rage required an outlet and a calm, reasonable man wouldn't have supplied it.

"Where's your girlfriend?" she asked sourly as she jerked her seat belt with unnecessary force.

Vic leaned forward, his forearms on the wheel, and studied her. His face looked dark and ominous in the shadows of the truck, reminding Niall of a storm that was about to break.

"I don't owe you any explanations."

"Then what are you doing here?" she demanded hotly. Tears continued to course down her face, but she could have given a good goddamn at this point. "Why aren't you carrying on with your parking lot romance?"

He grabbed the steering wheel tightly, as if he needed something to squeeze besides what he really wanted between his hands—her throat.

"Why aren't you with your husband?" he countered, his gray eyes flashing.

"My *ex*-husband is in the Evergreen Park Mental Hospital, where he has been for nearly three and half years!" she shouted.

His head flew back several inches, as though she'd just slapped him. "Your *ex*-husband?" he repeated.

Niall swiped at her soaking cheeks in rising agitation. "Yeah, that's right."

"Why'd your mom say he was your husband back in December, then?"

Niall stared at him as she exhaled slowly. "Because Stephen still was my husband back in December, Vic. Technically speaking, that is."

His eyes narrowed as though he were trying to focus on some place in her spirit to see if she was lying or not. He must have decided her depths were too dark to even attempt to read, because he abruptly put the truck into Drive and pulled onto the road.

"Obviously the technicalities don't mean anything to you. But they mean a hell of a lot to me," he said coldly as he stared straight ahead and drove.

"You have no right to judge me," Niall stated through a throat choked with emotion.

She gasped when he braked so hard that her seat belt locked and her head flung forward, spilling her hair in her face. He turned toward her, muscles coiled like a big cat about to pounce.

"I have *every* right to judge you. You lied to me. Don't you think most guys would want to know that the woman they were in a relationship with just happened to be married?" he thundered.

"Is that what you thought, Vic? That we were in a relationship?"

For several tense seconds neither of them took a breath. Niall could tell by the expression on his face that Vic hadn't liked her question at all. She took advantage of his temporary discomposure.

Her eyes scoured his face, entreating him to respond from some place other than anger. Surely if he was this furious at her, it meant that he wasn't completely immune to her. Didn't it?

"Because the thing of it is," she continued shakily, "neither one of us really ever spoke of it last year. I thought maybe for you it was just about the sex."

"Who said it wasn't?" he asked, his lips curling contemptuously.

"I thought *you* were," Niall said quietly, refusing to let him escape her gaze. "Just now. Why else would you feel so hurt that I'd betrayed your trust?"

Her words seemed to reverberate around the cab, causing the

already potent tension between them to increase exponentially. Vic's face looked rigid with anger. Niall made a startled sound of surprise when he abruptly flipped the car back into Drive and stomped on the accelerator. She wasn't sure what to make of his almost frightening intensity as they sped down the road in silence.

Gravel popped loudly beneath the wheels of the truck when he made a tight turn into the long drive to the farm. It continued to fly frenziedly as they raced up to the spot right in front of Vic's cottage. He switched off the ignition and got out of the truck so fast that Niall was stunned.

She just stared at him wide-eyed when he flung open the passenger door a second later.

"Come on," he ordered tersely. "If you need reminding of what was between us for a brief, nearly forgettable relationship of convenience last year, I'll be happy to remind you. I've got nothing better to do tonight since you ruined my date. Why are you looking at me like that?" he queried viciously as he leaned over her and unsnapped her belt. He grabbed her hand and pulled until Niall practically fell out of the cab. She hit the hard, ungiving weight of his body with a gentle thud. "This is what you showed up uninvited on my farm for this summer, isn't it, Niall?"

She winced at the impact of his words. Maybe Vic thought the flash of pain related to the fact that he'd just pulled her onto the gravel when she wasn't wearing shoes. He glanced down at her bare feet before he cursed under his breath. In one rapid, sinuous movement he swept her into his arms and slammed the truck door.

Vic charged into the cottage like a bull on the rampage. He never remembered being so worked up in his life. Even the time when he'd caught Jenny fucking Max Blake didn't compare to this. He felt like the cap on the geyser of his emotion was about to pop off and the resulting gush was going to be explosive.

Fuck if he cared, he thought as he threaded Niall's body through the narrow entrance of his front door before he shut it with a bang. Let it explode. He was sick of holding it in. Sick of watching from a distance while Niall pranced around his home wreaking havoc on his peace of mind, being forced to observe the way sunlight reflected on the golden waves of her hair when she returned from her morning walk, or being held captive at the dinner table while her big eyes ran over him hungrily with the same effect as a flickering tongue. Did she think he was superhuman, that he actually could endure the torture of walking away when her long legs were spread as wide as they could go, the way they had been that one damnable evening in the living room, maddening him with the memory of what it had been like to be between those thighs with his cock buried in her while Niall made those sexy whimpers in her throat—

That excruciating ordeal was over, Vic thought as he set Niall's ass down on his kitchen counter and spun her until she faced him. He ignored her stunned expression as he roughly raised her dress and parted her slender legs, wedging his hips between them. One hand spread on the outside of her thigh, refamiliarizing itself with the exquisite sensation of her silky skin. He pushed forward on her lower back until her opened pussy perched just off the counter. His mouth found her neck, where he lightly licked her pearls and then scraped his teeth against her tender skin.

She quaked in his arms.

His throbbing erection pressed into her warmth at the same moment that he sank his head to find the longed-for nectar of her mouth. He grunted in satisfaction when his tongue dipped into her honeyed cavern, striking thirstily again and again. Niall moaned shakily into his mouth. Her hands came up to clutch tightly at his shoulders. She began to rub her tongue sinuously against his, making his lust swell into a frothing fury.

He had thought their first joining—and many times since then—had been maddened. But Vic knew right then and there that he'd never known what a sexual frenzy was until that moment. Consequently his actions, if not forgivable, weren't too surprising when Niall suddenly twisted her head and pushed back on his shoulders. He palmed her delicate jaw and turned her back so that he had access to her mouth again, patently refusing her denial of him.

"*No, Vic,*" she whispered hoarsely, her fragrant breath flowing across his seeking lips. "Not like this. I wanted to explain to you—"

"I don't want your explanations," he said as he tilted his head and plucked at her juicy, lush lower lip. God, she tasted good. "I want to fuck you. And that's *all* I want from you, Niall." He ran his free hand from her waist up to her cloth-covered breast. He palmed the small, firm mound and squeezed as he watched Niall's upturned face. His cock surged against his jeans like a caged animal furious to be free when a tiny whimper escaped her throat and her big eyes darkened with arousal.

"You want it, too. Don't fight me." He held her gaze as he lowered his hand to her hips and slid his fingers beneath her panties. He thought he might die if he didn't get his fingers into her drenched, tight slit, with his cock soon to follow. She didn't protest. In fact, Vic was pretty sure she didn't breathe as he lifted her weight with an arm around her waist so that he could work the silk fabric beneath her bottom. When he touched a round ass cheek, he paused for a second, his nostrils flaring. She stared up at him as he caressed and then squeezed that taut package of flesh.

That was how they were posed—him lifting her slightly off his kitchen counter with Niall's sweet little ass in his palm, the heat from her core resonating out to his fingers, beguiling him, when the sound of the screen door opening and loud knocking pierced his thick lust.

"Ignore it," he ordered as he swept her panties below her bottom to her thighs, but the pounding on the door continued even more loudly after a pause. He saw Niall's throat convulse as she swallowed.

"Vic, maybe you should . . ." Her voice faded uncertainly.

He closed his eyes briefly in a fairly useless attempt to get hold of himself.

"*Fuck*," he muttered forcefully between clenched teeth. He panted like he'd just run a sprint. He almost cursed again, this time at Niall, when he backed away from her and she immediately hopped off the counter. She fumbled with her panties at the same time that her eyes skittered warily to his front door. Vic turned away abruptly when he caught the sight of pale blue panties and dark golden pubic hair before her dress fell into place.

He launched himself at the door.

"*What do you want?*" he asked Meg after he'd jerked open the front door several inches and saw who dared to get in his way when he'd just caught a glimpse of heaven.

"Did you pass Niall on the road? She said she wanted to walk home, so we dropped her off at the side of the road, but she should've been home by—oh, there you are! Is everything okay?" Meg asked when she glimpsed Niall behind Vic.

Vic was about to tell his sister that of course Niall was *okay*. Being horny as hell wasn't a reason for concern, was it? He frowned when he glanced quickly back at Niall, however. True, her cheeks were flushed a rosy pink, a telltale sign of her arousal that Vic recalled all too well. But those glowing cheeks shone with tears and her eyelids were puffy from prolonged crying. Despite his burning body and turbulent emotions, Vic was forced to acknowledge that Niall didn't really look all that *okay*.

"I'm all right," Niall said hoarsely through a tremulous smile.

Meg glanced pointedly at Vic and Niall. "Well, I just wanted to check on you. I'll go on up to the—"

"I'll come up to the house with you," Niall said swiftly. Her glance at Vic was far more uncertain. "Maybe . . . maybe we can finish talking tomorrow, Vic?"

It took him a few seconds to realize that Niall was trying to get past him and that he was blocking the way as if determined to keep her a prisoner.

Which he might have been considering on some caveman level. Vic couldn't say for sure.

"Vic?" Niall prodded softly after she'd followed Meg out onto the front stoop and turned back, holding the screen door open with one hand. Meg had retreated to wait for her, standing next to the truck.

"Don't go," he said simply. Sweat slicked his body and his cock still felt like it would burst like a grape out of its own skin, it was so tight. If he couldn't have her, Vic had concerns for his own sanity.

Pain flickered across her features. "I have to. I want to be able to explain things, Vic. You're angry at me. It's not right for us to . . . I'm sorry," she fumbled in a whisper. "Maybe tomorrow?" she asked hopefully.

Vic examined her tear-stained face as she looked up at him. The sight pulled at him so hard it felt like something dislodged and fell with crushing impact deep inside of him. The suspicion that that nameless something was his brittle defense against Niall kicked up his tumult once again. He was just frustrated, horny,

and confused enough to make her want to suffer as much as he
was at that moment. He leaned forward and spoke in a low, cutting tone.

"The time for explanations and confessions has passed, Niall.
But if you want to finish what we started here, you know where to
find me."

He shut the door with a brisk click, wishing like hell he hadn't
looked directly in her wide eyes as he'd done it.

That night Niall awoke from a restless sleep to hear thunder
and rain lashing at the windowpane. She listened for several minutes, the sound of the thunderstorm unleashing its torrent upon
the earth somehow soothing her hurt and confusion over what
had happened with Vic.

An ear-piercing crack of thunder rattled the room, but Niall
remained completely motionless, drowning in the deep wells of
memory

Michael used to be so afraid of thunderstorms. After his fourth
birthday Stephen had become impatient at the little boy's crying in
the middle of the night and his requests to get into bed with his
parents.

"He's too old to be sleeping with us! He's too old to be behaving this way at all," Stephen had once hissed at Niall, irritated at
being awakened when he had such a full schedule at work the following day.

"He's four years old," Niall had responded incredulously. "I
can't imagine a more likely age *or* time for him to be afraid than
when he's alone during a frightening thunderstorm."

She had gone and cuddled up with Michael on his little bed on
several occasions while the storm raged outside. She had taught

him the game of counting *one-one-hundred, two-one-hundred, three-one-hundred* after the flash of lightning to the onset of thunder in order to determine whether or not the storm was receding. She'd even told him that silly story about thunder being God bowling in heaven in order to get him to back away from his terror a little. It had worked and Michael had begun to laugh during the especially loud cracks of thunder, because it meant that God had bowled a strike.

Before he'd fallen asleep one night after she'd stayed with him during a storm—Niall thought it might have been the July before his death—he'd murmured groggily, "It's only fun listenin' to God bowling when you're here, Mommy."

Niall's eyes clamped shut tightly at the poignant memory. An empty feeling welled up in her. Niall thought the origin of that familiar ache originated in her womb.

Her little boy . . . her precious little boy.

She cried softly while the storm wreaked havoc outside. Right before she fell asleep, she had the thought that it was better to cry for Michael awake than in her dreams. Mourning in her nightmares always had such a painful, panicked quality to it.

But tonight—despite everything that had happened with Vic—once she'd had her cry, Niall slept restfully, without dreams.

The sun rose the next morning on a fresh, ethereal world.

"What's got you in such a perky mood this morning?" Meg asked as they carried plates and glasses to the breakfast table. Donny walked into the kitchen as Niall was distributing plates.

"How could I not be in a good mood? It's absolutely gorgeous outside today. Hi, Donny, I didn't know you slept over last night."

Donny shrugged as he shuffled over to the refrigerator, still looking half asleep. "The cops were over at my house last night," he mumbled. "All those flashing red lights sort of make sleeping difficult."

Niall and Meg exchanged a pointed glance. "What were the cops doing there?" Niall asked.

"Busting my brother Jake for armed robbery," Donny said dully. He uncapped the milk jug and started filling glasses in a listless fashion.

"I thought Jake was in Pontiac," Meg said, referring to the prison.

"He got out last week. Guess he missed it, cuz it didn't take him long to buy a ticket back," Donny said with a mirthless grin.

"Well, *shit*," Meg muttered, shedding her principal persona in her compassion for what the boy had to endure on a regular basis.

"Yeah," Donny agreed, giving the impression that he thought Meg's description was pretty much dead-on. "Hey, Tim," he said a second later when Meg's husband came into the kitchen. "I saw Vic taking off on Traveler just now, so I guess he's not eating," Donny informed them.

Niall's heart seemed to grow heavier in her chest at Donny's casual statement. Was Vic back to ignoring her again so quickly? She took a deep, fortifying breath, determined not to be conquered by her fears and insecurities on such a glorious morning.

During breakfast Donny mentioned that he was going to be exercising some of the horses in the corral.

"Are you going to exercise Velvet?" Niall asked.

Donny nodded as he shoved a spoonful of oatmeal in his mouth.

"Well, maybe I could come out and watch—sort of meet her." She paused when she saw Donny's surprised expression. "Velvet is the one that you said maybe I could try to ride, isn't it?"

Donny swallowed rapidly. "Yeah, but I thought you were too scared to try and ride."

"Well, let's take things a step at a time," Niall said with a nervous laugh. "I'm not promising anything, but maybe if Velvet and I could get used to each other . . . Well, we'll see."

"*Awesome,*" Donny muttered before he started shoveling his oatmeal into his mouth with notably increased energy and enthusiasm.

Meg caught Niall's eye and winked. Niall's cheeks grew slightly hot at her friend's subtle acknowledgment that she knew what Niall was doing. Niall supposed it was a small enough sacrifice to make in order to lift Donny out of his gloomy mood.

Or at least she thought that until she was standing outside the corral fence later, watching Donny send Velvet through her paces. Velvet was a beautiful, sleek mare that Niall supposed was rather small and delicate when it came to the average size of horses in general.

But the soft-eyed creature had looked absolutely enormous when Donny had brought her over to the fence a moment ago. The horse's nervous prancing at being restrained when she'd just been running free a moment ago evoked an old, unnamed terror in Niall. She knew logically that she was perfectly safe, but she'd still been uncommonly relieved when Donny turned the mare's head for another turn about the corral.

She put her arms up on the highest rung of the fence and watched as Velvet took a small jump at Donny's urging. It was amazing how much she enjoyed observing the beautiful animal in action when it was at a distance versus within feet of her. She didn't want to disappoint Donny, but she was doubtful that she'd ever conquer her fear sufficiently to be able to get on a horse's back.

The storm last night had broken the hot spell. The temperature was currently in the low seventies, and the sun felt pleasant on her back and neck. She grew so comfortable and drowsy watching Donny and Velvet that she didn't notice the muted sound of a horse's hooves approaching in the grass behind her. A familiar voice called to her.

"Niall."

Niall turned around, blinking in disorientation into the bright sunlight that was partially blocked by an enormous dark shadow.

"Give me your hand."

She reached up instinctively, before conscious thought struck her brain. She rocketed through the air abruptly, as if on a jet-propelled elevator. Strong hands gripped beneath her armpits.

And the next thing she knew, she was sitting on an enormous horse between Vic's long, muscular thighs.

He chirruped softly and flicked the reins with a subtle movement of his wrist.

"Oh!" Niall muttered in amazement when Traveler turned around and headed back toward the barn. For a second she felt her world tottering off balance, but then Vic's thighs tightened around her and his left arm rose to encircle her waist, anchoring her in place. Niall heard a loud whoop in the distance and dared to turn her head slightly toward the corral. Donny was waving and laughing as he raced Velvet in their direction.

"Just relax. I've got you," Vic murmured near her ear.

A shiver of pure excitement rippled through her, mixing with her anxiety. Their bodies pressed so tightly together that she could almost feel the vibrations from his low, rumbling voice resonating from his chest to her back. It thrilled her to feel the big, powerful horse moving beneath her, but it was the male animal behind her that made her heart pound even harder than it had when Vic had first plopped her in the saddle before him.

"It feels so strange," Niall muttered as Vic slightly shifted the reins again and Traveler obligingly turned onto one of the horse paths that led out of the stables. A warm, wonderful feeling pervaded her when she heard Vic's soft laughter.

"Strange bad or strange good?"

"Strange good, I think," she replied in a hushed voice, still trying to absorb the myriad unusual sensations that barraged her.

Vic's big hand spread across her waist and belly, pushing her even more snugly into him. Niall bit her lower lip so as not to moan at the exquisite sensation of being held so tightly in his embrace.

"Don't fight the movement of the horse," he breathed close to her ear, causing goose bumps to rise on her neck. "Move with it, Niall. The horse doesn't just *carry* you, it's a joint venture. That's why they call it *riding*," he added with a chuckle that made her nipples tighten.

But despite her excitement and her desire to please Vic, her muscles were still tense and rigid from the abruptness and novelty of the experience. She gave a muffled cry of alarm when Vic encouraged the horse to increase its pace.

"Shhh," he soothed softly next to her ear. "Just focus on Traveler's rhythm. Feel it with your body."

It was Vic's body that Niall focused on almost exclusively, however, even as the landscape rolled past her vision at an alarming speed. As if Vic had read her mind, he lifted her body slightly so that her thighs partially rested on his. Niall's eyes went wide. She whimpered. The new position also placed her pussy directly on Vic's balls and the root of his penis. She was painfully aware that she didn't want to jostle and crush that sensitive part of him with her body weight. The realization forced her to match the rhythm of both the animal and the man.

"That's a girl," Vic muttered huskily. "Now you're riding."

Pride swelled in her breast even as arousal spread in her sex like a molten river flowing out to every cell in her body. It felt so good, so singularly hot to move to the primitive tempo that the horse set while Vic's hard, male body surged and settled rhythmically beneath her own. She could easily sense his tension and arousal. His cock pressed into the furrow of her ass cheeks like a stiff, straining pillar. Traveler's movements beneath them created tiny, electrical pulsations against Niall's increasingly sensitive sex. The friction built until it was nearly unbearable when Vic prompted Traveler to go even faster.

Niall moaned in agony. Sweat beaded her upper lip and chest. The world flew past her, but all she was aware of was the man who held her so tightly against him, rocking her against his steely, hot flesh until she thought she would explode.

"Vic, *please* . . ." she muttered helplessly.

"I know. We're headed back," he said in a strained tone. Niall vaguely recognized that he'd turned Traveler around and that they were approaching the stables at a rapid clip.

She existed inside a sun-gilded world of voluptuous excitement and sinuous movement. She'd never been as sexually excited in her life as she was when Traveler slowed outside the stables. Her arousal felt like some kind of biological imperative that she couldn't have denied any more than she could will herself to stop breathing.

"*Donny!*" Vic swung his leg over the back of the enormous horse and lowered himself to the ground in one swift movement that he made look as easy as walking. Niall gasped when he reached up, grabbed her by the waist, and brought her down next to him with nearly as much ease. Her eyes widened when she looked up and saw how rigid his face was . . . how greatly his light eyes glowed with lust.

She wasn't even aware that Donny ran up behind them until Vic spoke.

"See to Traveler, please," he said tersely before he grasped Niall's hand in his and pulled her toward the cottage.

Niall felt dazed as she stood in Vic's dim, cool kitchen and watched him shut the front door and lock it with a decisive flip of his wrists.

"No interruptions," he said with a pointed look when he turned to face her.

"No interruptions," Niall agreed wholeheartedly before she stepped into his arms.

EIGHTEEN

She strained up to find his mouth, groaning in immense satisfaction when he dipped his head and met her with equal hunger. The taste of his salty sweat on her tongue caused a fever to sweep through her. She gave herself wholly to the exquisite sensations that flooded her body, pressing her achy nipples into Vic's hard chest, rubbing her hips and thighs against his muscles, pulsing her pussy and belly against his cock, which strained tightly against denim. Without ever making a conscious decision to do so, she stepped back slightly and began to rip frantically at the fly of his jeans. An unbearable torment plagued her, and Niall knew only Vic's cock plunging deep inside of her would assuage that hurt.

Vic broke their kiss roughly when she shoved down his fitted, dark blue cotton boxer briefs and fisted the pillar of his penis. Tears sprinkled down her cheek at the blessed, familiar sensation of his teeming, heavy, hot flesh in her hand.

"I want you so much," she confessed shakily as she looked up at him through the shimmering window of her tears.

"*Fuck*," Vic whispered tensely beneath his breath. His fingers rose to her waistband, where he unsnapped her jeans with even greater haste than she'd unfastened his. "Hold on to me, Niall," he ordered as he bent to pull her jeans and panties down over her thighs. Niall quickly kicked off her sandals before he swept her clothing down over her ankles and off her feet one at a time.

Then Vic was lifting her into the air again . . . this time to ride him instead of his horse.

Niall gasped softly when he backed her against the wall. Her hands went up to grasp his shoulders in a white-knuckled grip. She glanced down between their bodies and watched, wide-eyed, as he arrowed his ruddy penis into her. She cried out when he thrust his hips and the fat head of his cock pushed into her body. It had been so long since he'd stretched her channel over his girth. Niall found that despite her immense desire, her unaccustomed body resisted him at first. Her legs widened and then encircled his waist tighter as she struggled to accommodate him.

Vic grunted in animal-like pleasure as she opened herself farther to him. He bucked his hips in three powerful thrusts that seated his cock completely in her body. Niall shut her eyes and bit his shoulder to still her screams at the harsh impact of having his cock filling her completely once again. It felt overwhelming. She instinctively tightened her leg muscles around him as well as her inner muscles, holding him fast inside her . . . never wanting to let go.

Vic responded to her muscular caress by giving a feral growl and proceeding to pump her with a hard, relentless rhythm. Niall screamed into his rising and falling shoulder, the sound muffled by his hard flesh. His cock rubbed and agitated her depths even as his balls and pelvis slapped and pressed against her moist, sensitive outer tissues and erect clit, making her nerve endings burn. He held her body steady with his hands beneath her ass. Niall had no choice but to completely take every driving thrust—the wall behind her, and Vic's flexing arms working her back and forth over his engorged penis, increased the pressure and friction exponentially.

He bent his head and placed his face at the juncture of her shoulder and neck before he proceeded to nail her to the wall with a brutal force and tempo. Niall lifted her face and screamed out loud as she came more explosively than she ever had in her life. A few seconds later Vic's triumphant shout mingled with her cries of pleasure. More tears scattered down her flushed cheeks at the sensation of his cock throbbing while his seed jetted powerfully into her womb.

Vic's lungs moved like a bellows as he tried to slow his out-of-control breathing. He hitched Niall higher in his arms until her bottom rested on the hard ridge of his bent forearm. He pressed himself tightly against her, sandwiching her gently between his body and the wall. Their bellies and chests expanded and contracted against one another in agitated bursts that slowly segued to a sinuous, shared rhythm.

Vic closed his eyes and nuzzled the fragrant skin at Niall's neck. He never wanted to think again. He just wanted to feel.

He just wanted to feel *this*.

When the unwelcome thought eventually did reach his lust-scorched brain that he couldn't keep Niall pressed against a hard wall forever, he backed away, fully taking her weight in his arms. She made a muffled sound of alarm near his ear at the movement.

"Shhh, I've got you. I'm taking you to the bedroom," he informed her gruffly.

He fumbled a little bit in the short distance to his bedroom—his jeans were slipping down his thighs. He made it, however, gently setting Niall on the edge of his bed. He grimaced at the agony of drawing his still rigid, quivering cock out of her body.

Christ, he thought he'd embellished how good it felt to be inside of her shrink-wrapped, hot little pussy, but his memories fell far short of reality.

He began to undress hastily, but the sight of Niall's enormous hazel eyes looking up at him with a sexy, dazed expression made him pause after he'd lifted his shirt over his head. He swallowed thickly to moisten the sudden dryness in his throat.

"Take off your blouse," he said in a tone that was harsher than he'd intended.

She blinked twice rapidly, as if she were awakening from a dream. Her gaze lowered to his cock, which was still moist from her abundant juices. She bit her lower lip as she continued to stare at him.

"Vic, what about—"

"Now isn't the time for talking, baby," he said quietly. Something in his tone made her eyes flicker up to his face. The anxiety and stark arousal that he saw in their depths turned him on as much as it always had . . . more so.

His penis surged with a sharp twang of reawakened need.

"Take off your blouse," he instructed again, firmly but gently.

At first he thought she was going to refuse. Her kiss-swollen, luscious lips opened as though she was about to protest. Her eyes met his.

Her hands shook slightly as she unbuttoned her cotton blouse. She drew it off her arms. He stared at the beautiful, sex-flushed woman who sat on his bed wearing nothing but a bra that didn't begin to hide her large, erect nipples as they pressed against the insubstantial fabric. When she laid the blouse on the bed and met his eyes again, he couldn't speak.

So he just nodded once as he stared at her silk-encased little breasts.

She reached behind her and unfastened the bra, then peeled the cups of silk from firm, fleshy fruit.

Vic didn't move for several long, tense seconds. The tiny whimper she made in her throat drew his attention to her face.

"Hold them up for me," he said.

He waited until she'd slid her hands beneath the plump, curved mounds that rose so starkly from the plane of her ribs. Then he sank to his knees in front of her and fell upon what she offered him so sweetly.

He made a feast of her fat, pink nipples, ravenously suckling first one delectable morsel and teasing it into a tight peak before he transferred to the other, giving it the same treatment, sometimes teasing her with his tongue and teeth, sometimes sucking her deep into his mouth until she cried out in pleasurable agony. He couldn't get enough of her . . . *never* would get enough of her taste or the feeling of her small body twisting and undulating in his hands as he held her steady for his mouth, or the sexy whimpers she made deep in her throat that erupted into full-throttle cries of ecstasy when he suckled her nipples good and hard.

Or maybe there was a way to immunize himself against Niall's power over him. If he took her enough times at the furious, maddened pace that his body required when it came to Niall, he'd have no choice but to eventually tire of her. Wasn't there some sort of cure for addictive behaviors that prescribed the addictive substance be taken repeatedly in large quantities? Vic dazedly lifted his head and stared at one of Niall's reddened, pointed, wet nipples.

He stood jerkily, unable to unglue his eyes from Niall's breasts. He eventually had to, however, as he flipped off his boots and shoved his jeans and underwear down his thighs in a flurry of haste.

When he was nude, he nodded toward the middle of the bed.

"On your hands and knees."

He hoped she wouldn't mind his blunt direction. His arousal was such that it was all he was capable of. But he was reminded quickly that Niall had never once protested his terse or crude language during sex. In fact, elegant, classy Niall had always become more aroused when he talked dirty to her.

He came up behind her on his knees. His hands on her hips encouraged her nonverbally to move toward the headboard. When she'd moved into the position he wanted, he halted her by holding her hips steady. He reached around her, grabbing several pillows and stacking them beneath her hips.

"Put your shoulders down on the bed and reach up and hold onto one of the posts on the headboard with both hands," he said. He watched with barely restrained excitement as she presented her sweet fanny in the air for him. His cock leapt up and batted against his lower rib cage when he saw her turn her head and glance back at him, the whites of her eyes showing.

"Don't let go until I say so," he told her with a pointed look before he parted her plump cheeks and pushed the tip of his cock into her pussy.

God, this was going to feel good, he thought with a profound feeling of grim satisfaction.

She cried out when he thrust. He held her wiggling hips steady with both hands and pushed until she sheathed the fattest, most dense and swollen portion of the stalk of his cock just past the midsection. She pressed her hips down into the pillows. At that moment, Vic didn't know if she did it in order to get friction on her clit because she was aroused, or if she tried to escape his penetration of her body.

And he didn't care.

He spanked her right cheek briskly.

"Hold your ass still," he rasped.

She whimpered as he worked his cock into her while she remained motionless, drawing out several inches only to claim another half inch with each downstroke. He growled gutturally when he finally pressed his balls to her moist tissues. Her pussy squeezed and flexed around his length, torturing him. Niall cried out in agonized pleasure when his cock jerked inside her tight sheath.

Vic's hands fell on the top of the headboard, and he began to pump her long and slow. He shut his eyes tightly when he realized that he stared fixedly at where their bodies joined and that the sight, in combination with the sublime sensation of her hot, muscular channel, was about to make him lose all remnants of restraint.

Christ, how could he have forgotten how good she felt? She was so wet from her arousal, so hot it was as if her muscular vagina was lined with heated, slippery oil. The scent of her arousal reached his nostrils, taking away the little control that he'd gained by closing his eyes. The sounds of her sexy little whimpers and cries hardly helped his cause, either.

He was going to have to fuck her morning, noon, night, and then some, to get her out of his system.

He increased his tempo and the strength of his thrusts, smacking their flesh together briskly. His bed banged into the wall with each of his forceful strokes. Niall whined plaintively, the sound driving him sexually berserk. He saw that her knuckles were white as she desperately clung to the bed, as though she were trying to hold on as a storm swirled around her, beating at her ruthlessly. She began to shift her hips in tiny little electrical counterstrokes up and down the length of his cock.

Vic gritted his teeth and swatted her bottom twice. She stilled immediately. He waited until she turned her chin over her shoulder and looked at him with one wide eye.

"I'm going to set the pace, Niall."

He knew that she'd understood his double meaning when an indefinable expression settled over her lovely, perspiration-damp features.

Good. It was best that she knew he was determined to be the one who set the parameters of their relationship. As long as it was purely sexual, Vic thought he could handle things just fine.

Just *fucking* fine, he thought wildly a few seconds later as he began to pound into her with a hard, forceful rhythm and the bed began to pitch and squeak in protest at his strenuous movements. Niall screamed at the impact. Her pussy began to convulse around him. Fluid heat gushed over his cock. The sensation was not something that a human male could endure without going temporarily mad.

He roared like a chained animal that had just chewed through its restraints. He dropped his hands next to her head and pressed his face to her neck, flexing his hips hard. Pleasure tore through him as her vagina squeezed every last drop of cum out of him. They weathered the tumult of their orgasms pressed tightly together, skin to skin.

Oh, yeah, Vic thought as he panted desperately for air a moment later. He could survive this just fucking dandy. He'd just have to be careful not to lose any vital organs in the process.

Or anything vital. Period.

Niall felt like her bones had been removed and warm mush put in their place. She gently thudded onto Vic's chest, incapable of volitional movement when he came down next to her and curved his arm beneath her, tilting her against him. Seconds passed, then minutes. Their ragged pants eventually smoothed to a matched, even rhythm.

Niall knew that Vic didn't want to talk. So for several full moments she allowed herself the sublime pleasure of lying in his strong arms, feeling his crisp chest hair on her cheek . . . breathing in his unique scent. There were plenty of times in the past few months that she'd despaired of ever experiencing those things again, after all.

But eventually the need to speak could be ignored no longer.

"Thank you for taking me with you on Traveler," she whispered into his skin. "He's a beautiful animal."

"You weren't afraid?" Vic asked in a soft rumble. Niall rubbed her cheek against the subtle vibration resounding through his chest.

"A little, at first," she admitted. She lifted her head and met his gaze. "But once I was up there, all I could think about was you."

He watched her for a few seconds. His hand rose jerkily, as though it'd been restrained where it lay on the bed and he'd suddenly broken free. Niall purred softly when he plunged his fingers into her hair and lightly massaged her scalp.

"My guess is the next time you get on a horse will be easier for you, and the time after that, easier still. You just had a block you needed to get past."

She closed her eyes, savoring the pleasure of his touch. She figured she was either a moron or a masochist for ruining such a lovely moment.

"Vic, we need to talk about this."

His hand stilled in her hair. "There's nothing to talk about, Niall. We wanted each other and we had sex. It's simple, really."

Niall placed her elbows on the bed and looked up at him. He suddenly seemed so distant.

"I want to be able to talk to you about what happened last December . . . what happened before that . . . what happened to me years ago—"

He sat up so quickly that it left Niall a little stunned. One second she'd been staring into his impassive face and narrowed eyes, and the next she was looking at his naked back as he sat at the edge of the bed.

"Why now?" he asked gruffly. He didn't turn around. "You obviously didn't think it was worthwhile to tell me anything back then."

A heaviness pressed down on her chest, constricting her lungs as Vic stood and sauntered over to where his jeans were on the floor.

"I *did* want to tell you, Vic. You have no idea how much."

He pulled his jeans up over his muscular ass and fastened the bottom buttons. "Well, it's all water under the bridge now."

Niall sat up, pulling the comforter around her as she did so. His cold, calm manner caused a tendril of panic to unfurl in her belly.

"How can you say that?"

He glanced at her, his eyes like liquid steel.

"Don't you think we'd be better off discussing the fact that we just had intercourse twice and that I didn't wear a condom?"

Niall's mouth fell open. She hadn't been expecting him to say that. She fumbled for something to say. And why in God's name did Vic have to be feet away from her while she sat in bed, naked and alone, when he asked such a distressing question.

"It . . . it should be all right," she said shakily. "It's not the right time of month for me to get pregnant. I should have my period in three or four days." Her mouth went dry with dread when she thought about him kissing that woman in the parking lot last night. Surely Vic would have worn protection with her, wouldn't he have?

He peered at her from beneath a lowered brow as he pulled his shirt down to his waist. "I've never had sex with the woman you saw me with," he said flatly, making Niall wonder if he'd read her mind. For a few seconds he just stared at her, the struggle on his handsome face obvious. "The only thing we should have to worry about is pregnancy. I'm sorry. I won't let it happen again."

"I was as much to blame as you," Niall murmured uncomfortably. "But, Vic, I want to talk to you about what—"

"*No*," he said abruptly, taking two steps toward the bathroom. "You said that you wanted to tell me back then, but you didn't, despite the fact that I wanted to be there for you. I wanted it a *hell* of a lot, Niall! Now you want to talk, but I'm no longer ready to listen."

Tears stung her eyes. He seemed about as accessible as the summit of Mount Everest to a handicapped person as he stood there looking down at her, his light eyes conveying fire and ice fused. Was it really possible that they'd just been pressed skin to skin while their sexes throbbed in tandem and his face pressed so intimately to her neck?

"So that's it?" she asked throatily. "We're just going to make love whenever the mood strikes us and ignore the fact that I hurt you last year by not being honest with you?"

"By not being honest about a particularly important fact," Vic corrected in a hard voice. "By not telling me the entire time we were fucking each other that you just happened to have a husband. Did it ever occur to you that I might have strong feelings about sleeping with a married woman? Did it ever *once* strike your self-centered brain that I might have morals when it came to that?"

Niall's face collapsed. "I'm so sorry, Vic. That's why I've wanted to explain . . ." Her voice faded. "Do you mean religious morals?" she asked uncertainly. The entire time she'd been with Vic, he'd never once struck her as being a strict adherent to organized religion.

He shook his head slowly. "I'm talking about personal principles. My father ran off with another woman when I was four years old, leaving behind his wife and two kids. My mom was blown away by his infidelity and abandonment even though she eventually got back on her feet and did an amazing job of raising Meg and me alone."

Her chest cavity felt like it had been filled with tiny pieces of gravel that scraped her lungs as she watched Vic turn to his dresser and open up a drawer. God, that look on his face before he'd turned away . . . like she'd caught the briefest glimpse of a four-year-old child's hurt and complete confusion at being abandoned by a parent for no apparent reason. Why hadn't Meg ever told her that this might be one of the reasons for his intense fury at her? The realization that he might be comparing her in his mind to his unfaithful father made her wretched.

"Not all circumstances are the same, Vic."

He shut his eyes and pressed his fingers to them. "I know that. I *know* that, Niall. But that doesn't change anything I said before." He dropped his hands and opened his eyes, meeting her gaze directly. "This is what I can offer you right now," he said with a grim hitch of his head toward the bed, leaving little doubt in Niall's mind as to what he meant. "If you can't accept that, then there's nothing else to say at the moment. If you *can* accept that, then what I said still stands. There really is nothing for us to talk about."

Niall stared blankly at Vic's six-foot-by-seven-foot bed. It was a small space, yes. But it was a space where he was agreeing to meet with her . . . where he would have to at least acknowledge her existence. If Vic truly cared for her, he would eventually have to face his feelings on this tiny little island that he'd agreed to share with her.

Wouldn't he?

Niall swallowed convulsively. "All right, then," she said softly before she rose and gathered her clothing, afraid to think about what she might have just sacrificed by making such a pact with the man she loved.

NINETEEN

Niall quickly shoved the letter she'd just received into her shorts pocket when she heard someone approaching on the gravel driveway that evening.

"The mail finally came, huh?" Meg said in a friendly fashion. They'd quickly made up last night after their tiff in the car.

"Charlie's mail truck gave out on him," Niall explained as she passed the mail to Meg.

"I'll bet he was fit to be tied," Meg murmured amusedly as she flipped through the envelopes. Charlie Travers was a local institution whose mail deliveries usually arrived like clockwork. They began to walk slowly back to the house. The crystalline day had evolved into a delicious, lazy summer evening, the sort of night that Niall associated with youth and innocent dreams and endless possibilities. Definitely not the kinds of things that went along with the letter that burned in her pocket at present like a piece of hot coal.

"How's Donny been doing in your class?" Meg asked.

"He's excelling at the class itself. He never misses, never is a minute late. He's very intelligent, but he gets really quiet sometimes . . . moody, you know? I was hoping he would make more friends," Niall mused. Her step slowed as she studied Meg's profile. "Why do you ask?"

"I saw Sheriff Madigan today in town. He said that Donny's oldest brother, Errol—the worst of the bunch—is home on parole. That's sure to make Donny a little extra moody. Just what the kid needs this week, first Jake getting arrested and now this." Meg shook her head worriedly. "The last time Errol got busted, it was for selling guns along with drugs. He was doing it out of their house."

"But surely with the police watching him so closely, and being on parole, Errol won't—"

"It's not what Errol is selling or not selling that I'm worried about most," Meg said, cutting her off. "It's the guys Errol double-crossed and cheated regularly before he got sent up to Joliet that I'm concerned about."

"He was in Joliet Prison?" Niall asked shakily. She knew the kind of prisoners they kept in Joliet. She knew all too well.

Meg nodded.

Niall inhaled slowly. "Have you told Vic?"

"He's going to drive over in a little bit and try to talk Donny into staying here tonight."

"Good," Niall responded quickly. Her eyes inevitably flickered over to Vic's cottage. It wasn't a long-term solution, but the more the boy was safe at the farm the less time he spent in the unhealthy environment of his brothers' home.

Meg sighed and scraped her fingers through her dark hair, as though trying to clear her mind of worries over which she had limited control. "Do you want to take Vic's mail out to him?"

Niall blinked, realizing Meg must have noticed where she'd

been staring, maybe even recognized the longing in her gaze. She knew that Meg was curious about what was going on with Niall and her brother, but Niall felt too vulnerable about what had happened earlier that day to chat about it.

"He's writing right now," Niall said as she began to walk slowly. "I'm sure he wouldn't want to be disturbed."

"Is that right?" Meg asked doubtfully.

"Yes," Niall said firmly. And then, in an attempt to change the subject, "Hey, do you want to go see a movie in El Paso with me right now?"

"Sure," Meg said as she studied Niall's face closely.

Niall forced a bright smile. "Good. There's a romantic comedy playing at that little theater downtown that I never got to see when it first opened."

All in all, Niall thought her idea for the movie had been inspired. Later that night, when she bade Meg good night and retired to her room, Meg hadn't had much of an opportunity to question Niall about Vic. They raced to town in order to catch the beginning of the show. Of course they'd been totally absorbed during the movie and Niall managed to keep Meg talking about the plot and the actors on the ride home. By the time she'd hugged Meg and gone upstairs to bed, she'd managed to spend a nice evening with her friend without having to discuss the potentially volatile topic of her relationship with Vic.

In the middle of the night she startled anxiously into wakefulness. She was so accustomed to awakening in such a fashion that it didn't strike her immediately that she hadn't been dreaming.

"Shhh," a deep whisper soothed, followed by a hand caressing her neck.

"Vic?" She blinked in amazement at the large shadow that sat on the edge of her bed. Her surprise at him being there never got the chance to ease before he stood and pulled back the covers. The air-conditioning felt cool on her skin, but Vic radiated heat when he slid his arms beneath her and lifted her as if she weighed as much as her pillow.

"Vic, what the—"

"I'm taking you to my bed, where you belong," he said in a low voice as he reached for the door.

It felt like heaven to hear him say that, to pretend that he meant more by it than just the purely sexual parameters in which he'd defined their relationship. She pressed her face briefly to his chest and inhaled his clean, spicy scent.

"How'd your work go?" Niall asked him huskily when they were on the gravel turnabout beneath a globe of bright stars set in a lacquered midnight blue sky. She pressed her lips to his neck lightly, skimming them across his skin between kisses. His footsteps faltered slightly at her caress, then speeded up.

"Good," he said simply.

"Was Donny okay when you picked him up?" she asked. Meg and she had offered to get him after the movie, but Vic had flatly forbidden them to go over to the Farrell farm. It had left Niall feeling chilled that the young man that she'd come to care for so much lived in a place that Vic didn't want them to go near.

Vic grunted. "Yeah."

"You worry about him, don't you?" Niall asked quietly as he paused to open the screen door of the cottage.

Vic didn't answer until he'd closed and locked the door and carried her into his bedroom. He set her on the edge of his bed and turned the bedside light to a dim setting before he sat down next to her. His dark hair had fallen forward onto his forehead. Earlier, when she and Meg had looked in on him before they'd left for the movie, he'd been wearing his glasses while he worked. Niall couldn't decide which of his personas she liked better, the handsome, intense intellectual or the man who sat before her now—the long, lean, dead sexy cowboy who had come to claim her for his bed. Maybe the fact that he was such a magical combination of both was what fascinated her so much.

And aroused her almost beyond her comprehension.

"I worry about him," Vic said simply. He reached out and began to matter-of-factly unbutton the satin pajama top she wore with a pair of matching shorts. "But there's not much I can do about it. I'm not his father."

Niall put her hand over his, stilling his actions between her breasts. Her nipples pulled tight at the nearness of his fingers. Niall tried to ignore the sensation.

"You're more of a father figure to him than he's ever known," she said softly. "You should hear how he talks about you. He worships you, Vic."

He gave a small, off-center grin. "It doesn't take much to please Donny." He tried to resume removing her top, but Niall again halted him gently. He looked up at her in slight surprise.

"You're kidding, right?" she challenged. "Donny trusts about as easily as I climb on a horse."

Vic's smile widened to show off that sexy off-center front tooth, making Niall's lower belly seem to erupt into a slow, molten, downward-moving burn. Still, she refused to be sidetracked until it was absolutely necessary.

"You got on a horse today," Vic reminded her, his light eyes sparkling.

"Only because you hauled me onto it," she admonished. "Seriously, Vic, Donny trusts you . . . maybe more than anyone. And he's very vulnerable right now."

Vic threw her a dark look. "You're not about to recommend

that I go have some kind of heart-to-heart talk with him, are you?"

"No, it's not that. He's a boy. I know how boys are. They communicate everything through actions. But maybe if you took him out riding, or you two did a project together, he would open up about . . ."

Vic smirked slightly as he deliberately removed her hand from restraining him and slid two buttons through satiny fabric before he spoke. "How would you know so much about how boys operate, Niall? You're the most girly girl I know."

"I know because I had one."

His grin faded. His light eyes flashed up to her face.

"What'd ya mean?"

Niall swallowed convulsively. Maybe because she hadn't been planning on saying it, the words came easier. "I had a little boy," she whispered. "He died three and a half years ago."

Vic's lips moved silently. His eyes narrowed as he studied her closely. When he finally spoke, his words surprised her a little. "What was his name?"

"Michael. He would be eight this September if . . ."

Her voice faded. She hadn't realized that tears spilled down her cheeks until Vic cradled her face in his hands and slid his thumbs over her skin gently, sweeping away the moisture.

"You were a mother," he stated rather than asked. He looked awestruck.

"Yes."

Much to her surprise, Vic smiled. He leaned forward and brushed his lips against hers, at first reverently, then with increasing heat.

"You know . . . I can see it perfectly, Niall," he whispered hoarsely before he gently pushed her back onto the pillows. Without saying another word he removed her satin shorts and parted her nightshirt. He studied her in the golden glow of the dim light for an eternal few seconds before his dark head lowered to her breast.

Niall gasped out loud at the pleasure of his slow, sweet suck. Her back arched off the bed.

Boys communicate through actions, she reminded herself dazedly.

She closed her eyes and listened very carefully as Vic spoke to her in his own poignant fashion.

She groaned in rising arousal and his warm, abrasive tongue lashed tenderly at her left breast, as if to soothe her for drawing on her so stringently. His big hands spread wide across her ribs and back, in an embrace that struck Niall as cherishing as well as possessive, as he held her off the bed for his hungry mouth. Her chest seemed to ache with love even as her womb drew inward with desire. She wondered if Vic really knew how much he held her heart both literally and figuratively in his hands.

Her fingers raked through his thick, unruly hair when his mouth lowered down over her ribs and belly, whispering his lips across her sensitive skin, scraping his teeth ever so lightly on her sides, dipping his tongue into her bellybutton. She cried out his name when he transferred his hands down to her hips and lifted her pussy to his mouth. His warm tongue prowled between her swollen, damp labia, sometimes a gentle tease, making her whimper with longing, other times a firm and insistent master that caused her to cry out sharply with desire at each hard lash and stab.

Niall writhed in a haze of blissful agony when he inserted two fingers into her drenched slit and twisted his wrist before he withdrew. Her hips bounced on the bed at the unexpected harsh jolt of pleasure that rocketed through her. Vic's steady suck on her clit pitched her excitement unbearably higher. When she felt his fingers withdraw from her aching vagina, along her perineum to her sensitive asshole, her lips and eyes parted wide in tense anticipation.

His tongue polished her clit until Niall was surprised it didn't burn, it sizzled with so much heat. She begged him for release between cries of bliss, without ever being conscious of forming the words. When he pushed his finger into her ass to the first knuckle, withdrew and quickly reinserted it all the way, Niall screamed helplessly in orgasm. He kept her flying around the realms of bliss for a seeming eternity by sucking on her clit relentlessly and finger-fucking her ass with increasing force while pleasure blasted through her.

When her spasms finally slowed and dissipated, Vic withdrew his finger and sat up.

"I have something for you," he muttered hoarsely as he drew his shirt over his head. His eyes glowed with banked desire as he stood and looked down at her.

"What?" Niall asked as she watched him unsnap his jeans. She was a little disappointed that he didn't lower them but instead headed to his closet. He reached so far into the back of it that Niall thought he was going to fall in before he finally straightened, holding a crumpled sack. Her brows furrowed in curiosity when he paused by his dresser and removed something that she couldn't quite see because he placed it behind his thick watch, which was turned on its side. He returned to the bedside still carrying the sack.

Niall didn't question him any more in the tense silence that followed as she watched him remove his clothing. Her arousal kicked up to a slow, steady burn once again at the sight of his muscles rippling beneath taut, tanned skin and his penis bobbing up eagerly when it was released from the constraints of a pair of snug boxer briefs. The thick, tapered head seemed to wave at her teasingly as he moved, making her mouth water. Vic reached into the bag and removed a box. He opened it and spilled the contents into his hand before he dumped the packaging onto his bedside table and knelt on the bed.

"Vic? What . . . ?" her voice trailed off in amazement when he slipped something over one foot and then the other. Before she knew it, he was pulling black elastic straps over her hips, almost as if he'd just pulled a pair of underwear on her. Niall's eyes widened as she sat up slightly and stared down at her crotch while he tightened the straps with sure hands.

Only this wasn't like any pair of underwear she'd ever seen. What looked like a yellow butterfly spread its wings over her labia, the round little body directly over her clit.

"It's a vibrator," Vic said gruffly when he saw her bemused expression. As if to prove his point, he flipped a switch on the little battery pack that Niall hadn't noticed until now. She gasped at the quick, fluttering vibrations on her most sensitive flesh. "I was going to give it to you last Christmas but . . . never got the chance."

"How's that speed?" Vic asked gruffly after a moment, as he studied her face.

"Nice," Niall mumbled, wide-eyed at the delicious sensation of the butterfly buzzing. Not as nice as Vic's skilled tongue but still . . . *very* nice, indeed.

"Good," he murmured. He spread her thighs and moved between them, the action causing her labia to part and the butterfly to flutter against her more intimately. Niall groaned as she watched Vic reach for a condom in his bedside table. After he'd rolled it on, he spread one hand over her hip and pressed down on the butterfly lightly . . . teasingly. When she tried to twist her hips at the intense sensation, he held her steady.

Niall gasped. Her facial muscles tightened.

"Vic," she moaned as she stared up at him and her pleasure mounted. She spread her hand across his rib and flicked his nipple with her fingernail.

"That's right, Niall," he whispered tensely. "Touch me."

He moved, flexing the arm that held her hip while the other held his rigid member poised at the ready. Niall moaned when he entered her. Vic flexed his hips until his cock was sheathed halfway in her body. His hands fell down next to her head as his eyes met hers.

"Touch me everywhere," he grated before he pushed his cock all the way into her.

Niall's expression broke at the abrupt pleasure of his thrusting cock combined with the subtler sensation of the butterfly vibrator on her clit. But what made the moment even more poignant was his request to for her to touch him. Vic—who typically preferred to restrain her hands while he gave her almost more pleasure than she could endure—was allowing her to touch him . . . to love him.

She did, glorying in the sensations of smooth skin gloving flexing muscles as he moved in and out of her with long, satisfying strokes just as much as she did the feeling of his cock stimulating and rubbing her deepest reaches so thoroughly. Her fingers worshipped his strong back, her palms curved around his tight, flexing ass. When she skimmed her nails along the skin at the side of his torso, it roughened beneath her fingertips. She saw his small, brown nipples stiffen noticeably. Niall leaned up and ran the tip of her tongue over one sensitive morsel. She flicked at it more insistently once she'd experienced the deliciousness of the pebbled flesh, running the sensitive tip of her tongue over it to feel each fascinating little bump. She cried out in aroused disbelief when he grabbed her hips and began to thrust into her more demandingly.

"You see why I usually have to restrain you, little butterfly?" he asked between clenched jaws, his gray eyes blazing. "If I didn't, I'd probably be coming in you within minutes every damn time."

A continuous cry of delight vibrated her throat when he began to pump her hard and fast, making the bed pitch against the wall. When Vic clenched his eyes shut and a harsh shout erupted from his throat, her arms encircled him. In the moment of his climactic crisis he was weakened. She pulled him down against her. Her heart beat madly in her chest at the sacred feeling of his lean, strong body shuddering violently in orgasm while she held him so tightly.

His breath sounded loud and ragged in her ear when he fell limply on top of her a few seconds later. Niall cherished that sensation as well. It had felt indescribably wonderful to her to have Vic allow her to love him in that way. She turned her head and nuzzled his damp neck.

His male scent—sweat, spice, and musk—drove her wild.

She became aware that with his weight pressed down on her, the butterfly's buzzing was so intense that a distinct burning sensation plagued not only her sex, but crept past her pussy to enliven the nerves in her ass. She pressed her hips restlessly against the bed to alleviate the friction growing there. The bottoms of her feet sizzled with a sympathetic ecstasy. She pressed her aching nipples into Vic's hard chest, scraping them against his crisp chest hairs.

She groaned in an agony of pleasure.

Vic's eyes blinked open at the sensation of Niall's hips twisting against him and the sound of her tortured moan. His nostrils flared at the sight of her beautiful face transformed by pure desire. A light sheen of perspiration coated her features. He leaned up and brushed his lips against the adorable freckles on her perfect nose.

"My little butterfly is dancing close to the flames," he whispered before he sandwiched her full, parted lips between his own and plucked at her languorously.

"Vic, *please*," Niall whispered. Her nipples poked into him like hard little darts. He felt her push up, pressing the vibrator against his pelvis to give her more pressure on her clit. He had the little gizmo on a fairly low setting, hoping to keep her just beneath the boiling point for as long as she could endure.

Or he could endure, for that matter.

Niall gasped in protest when he withdrew from her. Vic winced in sympathy to her plight as he stood quickly and went to dispose of the condom. His cock was still partially hard and extremely sensitive to his touch. When he came out of the bathroom, the first thing he saw was Niall pressing down with her fingers on the little yellow butterfly, her hips undulating in tight little circles against it. A sharp pain of arousal stabbed through him, causing his cock to bob up in the air.

So much for a *partial* erection.

He took three long steps to the side of the bed and flipped off the vibrator. Niall's head came up off the pillows, her red lips parted in preparation to protest. Vic just shook his head when she made eye contact with him.

"I'm the one who's going to make you come, Niall, not a piece of plastic."

She panted as she watched him come down on the bed next to her. Niall always had driven him into a frenzy of lust with the magnitude of her honest, complete responsiveness to him. But seeing her tonight, sensing both the strangeness and the sacredness of what she'd told him about having a child and losing him . . . it was doing something to Vic that he couldn't even describe. He experienced an overwhelming need to take her with him into the dark, mysterious depths of intimacy, to explore a place where they'd never gone.

He leaned over her and took total possession of her mouth. God, she was sweet. He focused solely on that delicious cavern, plundering her depths repeatedly, sipping and sucking at her plump, honeyed lips until they shaped themselves into a plea. When she tried to twist herself so that their bodies were flush, however, he held her down gently at the shoulders and transferred his attention to her neck.

"Vic, I need to come."

Her low, husky voice sent a prickly excitement down his spine, stiffening his cock even further. At the same time that he scraped his teeth lightly along the muscle at the back of her shoulder, he put his fingers on her erect nipple. He growled appreciatively at the sensation of her tightening. He pinched at her rhythmically until she began to twist again on the bed.

God, he loved Niall's writhing, tight little body.

He placed one hand on her hip to hold her in place before he sank his head and sucked on one, and then the other, large, sensitive nipple until they stood up for him, proud and distended. Toward the end he had to hold Niall to the bed as she became frantic with her arousal. Fearful that he was going to send her over the edge with nipple stimulation alone—he knew damn well that she was responsive enough for it to happen—he leaned up and reached for the bag at the side of the bed.

Perhaps she was in need of the spice of pain to keep her just below the threshold of orgasm.

He knew she was watching him as he withdrew a black, silicone butt plug along with some lubricant.

"Vic . . . ?" she asked uncertainly.

His eyes flickered to her sweat-dampened face. Never one to

beat around the bush, he said, "I'm going to open your little ass so I can fuck you there, Niall."

He saw her elegant throat convulse as she swallowed. A flash of regret went through him. He didn't know why he always sounded so hard with her. His desire for her made him edgy . . . as if, on some level, he was always worried she would refuse him when his need for her was like a sharp ache that refused to be denied.

Not particularly comfortable with that thought, he focused on applying a coat of lubricant to the mushroom-shaped cap of the plug and his first two fingers. He set the plug on the table before he turned back to her. The anxiety he saw in her eyes as she stared at the glistening black plug on the table made his heart go out to her.

He gently brushed aside a strand of hair that had fallen on her cheek as he put his hand between her spread thighs.

"There's nothing to be afraid of, baby," he soothed as he pushed his forefinger into the tight little ring of her rectum and she gasped. He kissed her parted lips lightly as he began to probe her smooth, tight channel. "I've finger-fucked you before and you liked it, right?" he reminded her silkily as he watched her expression through hooded eyelids. The sensation of her hot, clinging channel had always turned him on immeasurably, but he'd always refrained from trying to fuck her there, sensing her anxiety.

But tonight he wouldn't be denied anything when it came to Niall.

"Yes," Niall admitted softly against his mouth as he plucked at her lips.

He closed his eyes, completely focused on the sensation of pushing his second finger into her virgin tunnel and burrowing into her soft heat.

"It's going to feel so good, baby," he whispered before he kissed her again, his fingers moving in and out of her more smoothly. He opened his eyes when he felt her begin to move her hips against him in a counterrhythm. "There . . . you like that don't you?"

Niall stared at him wide-eyed and nodded.

He smiled before he twisted his torso around and reached for the plug.

"Is it . . . going to hurt?" she asked as he slid his fingers out of her and moved between her thighs.

"Maybe a little at first," he admitted huskily. He lifted her opened legs by sliding his forearm beneath her knees and pushing back, exposing her pink, muscular opening to his gaze. "But then it's gonna make you burn and you're going to explode for me."

He pressed the fat mushroom shape to her tiny opening. The sight made his cock surge uncomfortably, but it made him hesitate, too.

She looked so small in comparison to the girth of the plug. He'd bought a smaller version of the plug in deference to her size, but he had to prepare her to take him, and he was much larger than the plug in girth and length.

"Turn on the butterfly, Niall—to a higher setting," he instructed. He watched as she did what he said, and the subtle tension of arousal began to settle in her lithesome muscles once again. "Press the vibrator down against you." When she pressed her fingertips down against the yellow body of the butterfly and moaned in pleasure, he pushed the fat end of the plug into her ass.

She cried out in surprised discomfort.

"Shhh," he soothed, holding the invader in place, knowing from experience that her initial sharp blast of pain would fade quickly. He caught her eye when she quieted. "That was the worst of it, baby," he assured her. Before she could say anything else, he pushed the rest of the three-and-a-half-inch plug into her and wedged the base between her firm cheeks.

"Ahhhh!" she cried out, but Vic could tell that her exclamation had been more in surprise than pain this time. Surprise and something else, he realized as she began to pant shallowly as he released her legs. He grabbed both of her wrists and came down over her, keeping the majority of his weight off of her by resting an elbow below her shoulders.

"Okay?" he whispered as he gently took her wrists in one hand and pressed them on the pillows behind her head.

"Oh," she mumbled. "Oh, Vic, it *is* starting to burn."

He felt her shift her hips beneath him, trying to get pressure once again on the butterfly. He lifted his hips off her, though.

"You're so sexy, Niall," he praised thickly. "You're the most responsive woman I've ever known."

She moaned beneath him, her hips twisting, making herself a moving target.

"Hold your ass still. I'm going to fuck your pussy for a little bit," he told her firmly enough to break through her increasing moans and pants. He rolled onto his hip and grasped his hard cock, using the tip to push aside the elastic band of the vibrator. His teeth clenched in pleasure at the sensation of her clinging, fluid entry.

He reared up over her and thrust.

Both of them gasped in tandem.

"Christ, that's good," he muttered as he began to stroke her. The plug made her usually tight channel even smaller in circumference as it pressed at her far wall. The sensation was so damn good that he forgot his restraint for a few moments and fucked her lustily. He met her eyes as he slammed down into her, tip to balls. She dripped with wetness.

Her red lips trembled. She whimpered. He glanced down. Her nipples looked like large, pebbled red berries capping her white, thrusting breasts.

"A . . . *fuck*," Vic muttered in anguish as he ripped his cock out of the heaven of her and dived for the switch of the vibrator.

"Don't you dare come, Niall. *Not yet*," he ordered harshly.

Her eyes blinked open sluggishly. Her body rose up off the bed several inches, rigid with the need for release. Her hips danced for a moment in the air as she desperately sought relief.

"Let me come, Vic. Please . . . I can't *take* this anymore," she whispered.

His heart went out to her in her misery, but he held firm. He leaned down and licked the sweat off her upper lip, letting the taste linger on his tongue. "You're not going to come until my cock is in your ass."

"Then put it *in* there," she said so frantically that he started back slightly in surprise.

"It's going to hurt some if I do it now, Niall," he told her. "I haven't prepared you enough."

The wild expression on her beautiful face was something from a man's sweetest fantasies. "I don't care. Give it to me, please. Fuck me *now*."

He gritted his back teeth and came up on his knees. Far be it for him to refuse such a request.

Her hands remained above her head when he released her wrists and knelt between her thighs. Niall's hips rose reflexively at the sight of his beautiful, rippling torso and jutting erection. God, she felt like an animal in heat. She was offering her body to him mindlessly, desperate for release from the tight, unbearable friction that plagued her. He merely captured her hips in his big hands and rolled her over on the bed. By the way he pulled up on her hips, she could tell he wanted her to present her ass in the air for him.

She slid her knees up beneath her hips, spread her thighs, and did just that, as primitive in that moment as a horny female who instinctively readied herself to be mounted by an alpha male.

They both groaned in agony when he leaned over to his bedside drawer and rustled inside, finally pulling out a black silk scarf. He grabbed the bottle of lubrication at the same time.

"I'm going to have to tie you up, Niall," he explained quietly as he reached for one wrist and then the other, placing them at her lower back. "You're so turned on, I'm scared you'll make yourself come."

Niall whimpered into the mattress, but not in protest. Not really. She knew he was probably right. Her clit felt more swollen and achy than it ever had in her life. The plug in her ass made the nerve endings all along her sacrum tingle and burn unbearably. When she felt Vic finish a firm knot around both her wrists, she wiggled her rear in a silent plea.

She knew he'd heard her request when he gave her right ass cheek a gentle swat of reprimand. She heard the cap flip open on the lubricant. A few anxious seconds passed and then Vic was gripping the base of the plug and drawing it out of her.

"Oh!" Niall cried out in mixed pain and pleasure as her anus stretched over the fat rim. But then it popped out and she immediately wanted to be filled again.

She didn't have long to wait. Vic pushed back firmly on her right buttock. She felt the cool air on her ass and realized that he kept her newly opened tunnel spread wide. Her eyes clenched shut

tight at the feeling of him pressing the tip of his slippery cock inside the sensitive opening.

"That's right," he soothed and encouraged at once when she
held steady for him. "Press back against me, Niall. Take it."

She did as he ordered and cried out brokenly when the fat head
of his penis slid into her body. The next thing she knew, the electric buzzing started again on her clit, this time at the quickest
speed she'd experienced thus far. The pain of having Vic's cock
inside of her ass segued into a burning arousal so fast that she almost choked in shock. But then Vic held her buttocks between his
hands and sank in another two inches, and the pain ratcheted up a
notch again, preventing her orgasm.

"You can come when you take all of my cock," he informed
her hoarsely.

Niall nodded, her flushed cheek brushing the soft sheets. She
couldn't speak at that moment as the thick stalk of his penis penetrated her ass and she tottered on the edge between pain and
shattering ecstasy. The butterfly kept fluttering away at her swollen clit as Vic pushed into her even farther. She began to tremble
uncontrollably as he began to pump the first half of his cock in
and out of her.

"Ahhhh!" she cried out wildly. Her body shook with a fine
tremor as sensations pervaded her like nothing she'd ever experienced.

"Hold steady, baby," she heard Vic whisper gruffly, as if at a
distance. "Hold on . . . just let me . . ."

Niall pushed her ass against him, desperate for him to fill her
so that she could finally find the fulfillment he'd promised. She
stretched to accommodate him, but her hunger and her need to
harbor him were so great that she felt relatively little pain. When
she heard Vic curse, and his fully embedded cock jerked in such an

intimate place in her body, she dived headfirst into the dizzying depths of orgasm.

Vic told himself to shut his eyes as Niall screamed and her entire body started to ripple and shudder in climax. He'd never felt her come this powerfully. The sensation was incredible, and sufficient in and of itself to have him howling in orgasm if he let his restraint snap free. But he couldn't bring himself to do either. Instead, he tortured himself by watching the intensely erotic sight of Niall coming while his cock was buried to the hilt in her ass. Her supremely tight, muscular channel milked his cock mercilessly, as though it had a mind of its own and was desperately thirsty for the quenching fountain of his cum.

By the time her electrical convulsions waned, sweat dripped between the ridges of his abdomen muscles. Wondering if he was some kind of masochist, he reached between her thighs and thrust two fingers into her pussy.

"Fuck, yeah," he muttered almost unintelligibly. Silky liquid gushed from her warm channel, but with a quick flick of his fingers he realized that her entire exterior was drenched as well. All of her pubic hair was wet, but around her puffy labia and swollen clit she dripped with juices.

He snarled with feral arousal and pinched a luscious lip, making her ass jump with surprise. He came down over her, supporting himself with his arms on the headboard.

She howled when he started to thrust in and out of her, but Vic could tell she did so in the deepest arousal, not pain. Or at least he hoped he wasn't projecting his experience onto her, because it felt so decadently good to fuck her hot little ass that he didn't think he could have stopped himself if he tried.

He was a goner, to be sure.

It seemed as if his whole world quaked for the next moments as he rocketed into her again and again, and she met him thrust for thrust. She took him on a hedonistic fantasy ride of a lifetime, allowing him to plunge into her forcefully time and again, and sending her butt up eagerly for more every time he withdrew. Niall was so small that he'd never have guessed she'd have been able to take such a thorough, rough ride, but she did.

God, did she ever.

Sweat beaded on his belly and spilled onto Niall's glistening back and ass with each powerful crashing impact of their bodies. It got so that Vic couldn't have formulated his own name in his mind, he'd become such a primitive creature of pure, driving lust.

Still, the sound of Niall screaming, the sensation of her contracting around him as she climaxed once again pierced his awareness loud and clear. As if he'd been given some kind of long-awaited, desperately sought-for sign, he smacked his pelvis into her ass one last time, pressed her plump cheeks tightly against his balls, and roared as orgasm tore through him.

He poured himself into her endlessly, not realizing until later that every last defense that he'd erected from the first moment he'd laid eyes on Niall Chandler had just been incinerated to a fine-grained ash.

TWENTY

Half an hour later Niall came out of Vic's bathroom after having washed up. She still felt a little disoriented from their lovemaking. It had taken both of them a good twenty minutes following their scorching climaxes to find the strength to move. Neither of them had done more than grunt in exhaustion as they clung to each other like two survivors of a chaotic storm. A few minutes ago Niall had stumbled to the bathroom, but Vic still lay on his side on the bed, naked and beautiful and obviously completely sated.

Niall couldn't quite identify the strange feeling that overcame her as she studied him. Only his singular gray eyes moved as he watched her slowly cross the room toward him. For some reason Niall was reminded of the first time they'd made love, when they'd crashed into each other's universes so wholly, so brilliantly, and afterward how they had been so separate . . . so far from each other.

No, that wasn't entirely correct. In fact, Niall had never felt closer to Vic in her life. Her eyes caressed his long, lean body, loving every taut plane and hard ridge with her gaze. The heavy feeling inside of her swelled until it felt as though her chest would burst.

It was the knowledge that she didn't know how he felt about her that was making her so uncertain. Or maybe she did suspect, and that was what made her so heart sore.

Something flickered across Vic's face as he stared at her.

"Are you okay?" he rasped.

She nodded quickly.

His brow furrowed, and he sat up on his elbow.

"You're not . . . hurt or anything, are you?"

"Of course not," she mumbled. Her cheeks flushed hot when she thought about what they'd just done in that bed. It amazed her how her desire for him transformed her into a wild, carnal creature she barely recognized. It took about two seconds of Vic touching her, and she morphed into that alternate existence completely.

"Then come here," he demanded softly.

Niall stepped forward at the sound of his compelling voice, but something made her waver. What was it? What had started to plague her consciousness ever since she'd gone into the bathroom a few minutes ago? Her eyes fell on the empty bag that still lay in the bedside table, crumpled and forgotten.

But she hadn't forgotten.

She quickly stepped over to the side of the bed and bent to find her pajama shorts. She pulled them up over her legs.

"Niall? What are you doing?" Vic asked as he slowly sat up to watch her, an expression of bemusement on his face.

Niall swallowed heavily, willing the bitter taste from her mouth. "You said . . ." She cleared her throat when she realized how hoarse she sounded. "You said that you were going to give

those things to me last Christmas?" she asked as she bent and retrieved her pajama top.

Vic's chin shifted to the items on the bedside table, including
the little yellow butterfly, which she'd removed before going to the
bathroom.

"Yeah," Vic said slowly after a moment, a wary expression settling on his features.

Niall nodded quickly as she buttoned her pajama top with trembling fingers. "That's what I thought you said." Tears gathered in
her eyes so rapidly that she kept her head lowered, not wanting Vic
to see them.

That was it. That was what had been eating at her. She knew it
was stupid. She knew Vic would never understand. But she felt so
raw at that moment, so opened up, so vulnerable . . . so uncertain.

He'd bought her sex toys for Christmas.

He'd bought her sex toys during what she'd considered the
most intimate, romantic time of their burgeoning relationship.
When she thought of what she'd planned to give him for Christmas, a rush of mortification surged through her.

She'd endlessly researched online and finally found something
at an auction house that she thought was worthy of him and that
he might really cherish—a monogrammed ink pen that had once
belonged to Arthur Miller. Vic had told her before how much he
admired the American playwright.

Could there be anything that better symbolized the truth of
how Vic must really feel about her?

God, she'd made such a fool of herself coming here, intruding
on his personal space when he'd made it clear he didn't want her
there—

"What's wrong? *Niall.*"

But for once she ignored her instinctive urge to respond to Vic completely. She never even flinched as she jogged barefoot toward the farmhouse, on the gravel turnabout, several seconds later. Her inner pain utterly consumed her entire awareness.

Vic sagged into one of the tall, supple leather chairs at the elegant bar of Toulouse several days later, feeling completely defeated.

Damn it all, if Niall wasn't back to being as elusive as ever. She wasn't answering her cell phone. She wasn't at her loft in Chicago—or if she was, she didn't pick up when the doorman rang her several times at Vic's request. He'd never actually been inside Niall's personal office in the museum, but he'd met her a few times in the more public work space where her administrative assistant, Kendra Phillips, worked. He'd met Kendra on those occasions, but the vivacious blonde's desk was empty when Vic showed up that afternoon. Thinking she most likely was at lunch, he'd wandered down to the upscale restaurant housed inside the museum in order to think.

As to what the hell had happened two nights ago in his bedroom . . . Vic was still busy puzzling that one out. When he'd watched Niall come out of the bathroom, a flicker of panic had gone through him when he registered the expression on her face. Had he hurt her physically? He'd been far from gentle with her there at the end, but she'd seemed just as eager and wild for the ride as he was. The realization that he might have harmed her caused a wrenching sensation in his gut.

Then she'd asked that question about the sex toys, and his uncertainty had spiraled into confusion, which eventually progressed into a vortex of regret. What had made him pull sex toys out of the closet at *that* moment, for Christ's sake?

He'd hardly left her feeling secure with their relationship, after all.

You told her the only relationship that existed between you was a sexual one. You told her that what had happened between you before was a brief, nearly forgettable relationship of convenience, he reminded himself bitterly. *Not* a brilliant move before subjecting her to the type of sex that requires the deepest form of trust. What's more, why had he done such a thing right after she'd revealed something as intimate as the fact that she'd had a child . . . that she'd lost a child?

All in all, Vic was starting to understand all too well why Niall had fled up to her room the other night and come downstairs several minutes later, fully dressed. He'd tried to stop her, but in the end there'd been nothing he could do but watch her get in her car and pull out of the driveway—unless he bodily restrained her.

He'd tried to reach her on her cell phone several times yesterday and this morning, only to grow sick with frustration every time he heard her recorded voice repeat the same lines over and over again.

Vic had been talking with an equally concerned Meg on Sunday evening when the phone rang in the kitchen. The way that Meg glanced at him immediately when she answered gave him his first clue that Niall was on the other end of the line. He'd approached Meg and held out his hand tensely, but Meg had just shaken her head as she spoke to Niall.

When she said good-bye and hung up before Vic could grab the phone, he had stared at her in open-mouthed shock.

Damn if he'd ever be able to understand women! First Meg was pushing Niall on him when he wasn't ready, and now she was leashing him when he was straining at the bit to talk to her.

"What'd you do that for? You knew I wanted to talk to her," he'd accused incredulously.

"I know, Vic . . . but she said . . . she said she was *fine*. She . . ." Meg had swallowed and glanced away uncomfortably. "She said she didn't want to talk to you right now."

"What else did she say?" Vic had demanded after a tense silence.

"She asked me to cancel her class tomorrow." She must have noticed Vic's reaction, because she added quickly, "But she assured me that she would be back for Wednesday's class. She said she just needed a little time . . ."

But Vic had been too worried about Niall to give her time. He'd gotten into his truck before dawn had fully broken after a sleepless night and driven up to Chicago to try to find her . . . to try to make things right.

If that was possible . . .

The bartender who approached him looked wary when he noticed the scowl on Vic's face.

"Can I get you something, sir?"

"Scotch on the rocks."

He glanced around the crowded restaurant blankly. The bar was the only place that had seating. The museum was filled with tourists. Even though she worked here, it suddenly struck Vic that there wasn't a more unlikely place to locate Niall than this restaurant.

Maybe he'd try to call Niall's friend Anne Rothman. She might have a clue as to where Niall might have gone. He pulled his cell phone out of his pocket. Surely he still had Anne's number—

"Don't I know you?" a man sitting several chairs down from him at the bar asked.

Vic's gaze ran over the man. He wore a preppy pink button-down and a dark blue blazer with anchors on the gold buttons. A flicker of irritation went through him when he recognized the man's face.

"No," he stated flatly before he flipped open his cell phone, pointedly ignoring the intrusion.

The dark-haired man stood and grabbed his drink before he scooted closer down the bar. "No, I *do*. I've met you before—"

"Don't think so."

The man's puzzled transformed into recognition. "Hey, you're that jerk who ran me out of Niall Chandler's place."

Vic gave him a blazing glare of irritation that made speech unnecessary.

Evan Forrester's pique melted when he saw it. He plopped down into the chair next to Vic's.

"Ahh, I got nothing agains' you, I guess," Evan said. "Niall Chandler's the kind of woman who turns all men into raving lunatics. You'd think I'd have learned by now to avoid a woman that beautiful." He took another long draw on his martini and held up the empty glass as a signal for the bartender to get him another.

"She wouldn't have anything to do with me after that night. She's a cold one. If I'd a known about her history, I would a steered clear of her. Woman like that's gotta be a bit . . ." Evan paused and twirled his finger next to this temple. "Still, she's so gorgeous . . . and despite that frigid thing she's got going on, she really doesn't seem too crazy at all," Evan conceded thoughtfully. "Hope you were luckier than me getting her into the sack, pal."

Vic felt torn between wanting to hammer the guy's preppy, drunken face and refraining from the instinct because he needed him conscious in order to explain what he'd just said.

"What'd you mean about her *history*?" he asked, ignoring the bartender as he set his Scotch in front of him and pinning Evan Forrester with his stare.

Evan raised his black eyebrows significantly. "Guess you never got around to getting to know your pretty neighbor too well, huh?"

That flipped Vic's "pissed off" switch quicker than he cared to admit. He leaned forward a mere half inch, his eyes boring into Evan.

"I asked you a question."

Evan's eyes widened.

"Oh, right." He laughed too loud, his eyes finding the bartender to check the progress of his martini. "Nobody ever told me the story, either. Niall's got lots of loyal soldiers around her. But even Niall Chandler Sr. isn't powerful enough to hush up all the facts about his little princess.

"I read about it in the newspaper a few days ago. Seems that even Niall's daddy can't keep the press from reporting the fact that his grandson's murderer has the dubious honor of being the only man on death row for which the Illinois General Assembly lifted the moratorium on execution. And they're going to be doing it" —Evan checked his watch drolly—"oh, in about two hours or so."

"Grandson's murderer?" Vic managed with the little air he had left in his lungs. Niall had told him that she was an only child. Surely the son that Niall told him had died hadn't been *murdered*—

"Yeah, Niall's kid. Matthew Manning opened fire in front of a preschool about four years ago. Killed seven people, a good portion of them children. Seems Manning was sore about the fact that the courts had granted custody of his five-year-old exclusively to his wife. Go figure, right?" Evan muttered before he reached for the fresh martini that the bartender put down in front of him and took a drink.

Vic resisted an urge to grab the glass from the man's hand and shake the rest of the story out of him. "The papers said Manning's kid's preschool teacher gave testimony about Manning pitching a

fit and scaring the kids at school half to death a year before the
shooting occurred. She wouldn't let Manning's son leave with him
while he was so out of control. Manning paid the teacher back a
year later by making her one of the victims of the bloodbath."

"In Barrington? Is that where this happened?" Vic asked, referring to the affluent western Chicago suburb.

He vaguely recalled hearing the horrific story on the news. He'd
been living in Montana at the time but the national news had covered it not only because of the violence and the number of deaths,
but also because so many of those who died had been innocent
preschoolers. It had been one of those news stories that left you
feeling confused, raw, and bitter about the potential nature of your
fellow human beings.

No. Niall's little boy had died on that fateful day? It was too
much for Vic to wrap his mind around at that moment. He wasn't
sure that he ever would be able to—

"Yep. It was in Barrington all right. Niall was there."

Vic stared at this man who was almost a complete stranger to
him. It felt like ice water was being poured down over his head at
a trickle but was reaching the inside as well, flowing slowly but
steadily both down his skin and straight into his veins at once.

"Niall was there," he repeated flatly. "On the day that some
madman opened fire and killed her four-year-old son along with
six other people?"

Evan nodded, obviously enjoying being the one to impart such
juicy gossip. "Along with another dozen or so who were wounded.
Yeah, Niall saw the whole thing. He fired into a crowd of people—
the kids, parents dropping them off, teachers. I don't know what
happened to Niall's husband after the boy's murder, but he must
have split or—"

"You know, you really shouldn't talk about things that you

haven't got the vaguest clue about, Evan," a feminine voice accused
abruptly.

Vic's head swung around. Kendra Phillips stood behind them,
a wrathful look on her round face.

"Hi, Kendra. Don't you look nice today," Evan greeted her
smoothly, taking only a microsecond to compose himself after getting caught spreading rumors like a teenage girl.

"One of Niall's soldiers," Evan muttered under his breath to Vic.

The scowl still lingered on Kendra's usually amiable face when
she turned to Vic. "Hey, Vic. Do you mind coming with me for a
minute? There's something I want to discuss with you . . . in private," Kendra added with a pointed glance at Evan.

Evan shrugged insouciantly and took another draw on his martini. Vic stood and threw a twenty on the bar before he followed
Kendra out of the restaurant. Once they were walking down the
dimly lit corridors of the museum, she turned and smiled at him
apologetically.

"Sorry for dragging you away like that. Evan Forrester is a real
pain in the—"

"Yeah, I know," Vic interrupted impatiently. "But he was telling me more about Niall than anyone else ever has, including Niall.
Do you know where she is, by the way?"

Niall wouldn't attend Matthew Manning's execution by herself, would she?

Kendra looked startled. "I haven't talked to her for two weeks,
when she called to check in on things. Isn't she on the farm?"

"She left yesterday. I've been looking for her, but she's not at
her loft and she's not here."

"Did something happen?" Kendra asked cautiously.

"We had a misunderstanding," Vic admitted after a few seconds. He sensed Kendra studying him inquisitively. She obviously

cared about Niall, and Vic knew that Niall considered her a friend. "Listen, Kendra . . . about what Forrester was saying back there . . ."

Kendra nodded suddenly, as though she'd just made a decision. "Just a second, Vic. There are some things I want to talk to you about," she said. She went to her desk and unlocked a drawer, then pulled out a set of keys. She tilted her head for Vic to follow her.

Vic realized with vague surprise that Kendra led him back to Niall's office.

A few seconds later Vic followed her into Niall's office. The large, comfortable room was warm from lack of airing. Niall's scent lingered. A pain went through him when he inhaled that singular odor. He suddenly wanted to be gone from there. Niall wasn't here, and he was wasting his time—

"Sit down, Vic," Kendra instructed. She sat down in one of the leather chairs in front of Niall's desk and glanced significantly at the matching chair. When Vic lowered himself hesitantly, part of him wanting to be gone to search for Niall, Kendra reached for one of the frames on Niall's desk.

"Niall never told me in detail how she felt about you. As you probably know by now, that's not her style. But I've worked with her for years. There was something in her face when she used to talk about you, something in her smile . . . I think she'd forgive me for talking to you about her past, even though she is an incredibly private person," Kendra said soberly.

Vic didn't speak, but he'd gone very still when Kendra picked up the picture. He suddenly knew exactly whose photo was in the frame. It struck him as strange that he'd never noticed any mementos of Michael before, but then he recalled how Niall's residence at

Riverview Towers was a temporary one. She'd always said that she'd never unpacked the majority of her personal items.

When he held out his hand, Kendra passed him the photo without comment. Vic stared for several long seconds and abruptly set the frame back on the desk.

"Did she tell you about him?" Kendra asked, still studying his reactions closely.

"She told me that she had a child named Michael who died," Vic replied hoarsely. The vision remained glued behind his eyelids of that beautiful little boy's face with Niall's smile and her big, hazel eyes. "Forrester just told me how he died, though."

Kendra sighed and sagged back in her chair. "Well, that's something that she mentioned Michael, that she even said his name, to be honest with you. I guess from your reaction to Forrester, though, she never said anything about Matthew Manning or how her husband, Stephen, went off the deep end during Manning's trial?"

"What do you mean *went off the deep end*?"

Kendra grimaced. "I'm not saying it in the figurative sense, Vic. Stephen started drinking heavily after Michael's murder and eventually vacated the world of reality and moved to an insane one. He's been there ever since, and as far as I know, he doesn't appear to have any plans on returning," Kendra added sarcastically. "Sorry," she amended after a moment. "I don't mean to be judgmental against someone who is obviously mentally ill and can't control his actions, but if you had seen the hell that Niall's been through . . ." She shook her head.

"I remember what Niall said to me once when I was mouthing off in a particularly bitter fashion about Stephen's reaction to Michael's murder. She said, 'No one really knows how they're going to react when something awful and unexpected happens to them. Stephen has reacted in the only way that was available to him.'"

"She defended him?"

Kendra nodded. "Always. Even though Stephen became so whacked out that he was violent toward her on several occasions. Niall has never said anything to me—not that she would—but I suspect he tried to kill her, maybe more than once. He's suicidal in addition to being homicidal, so at least he's an equal opportunity lunatic," Kendra said, anger lacing her tone despite what she'd said about Niall's defense of her ex-husband.

Vic leaned forward in his chair as the ringing alarm bells in his brain notched up to a clanging clamor. The idea of Niall—*his* Niall, that warm, honey-voiced, delicate-seeming woman with a backbone made of steel—being subjected to all of this meaningless violence and horror had him feeling cornered and desperate.

"I want to know it all, Kendra. I want to know everything about Niall that you have to tell me. But before you go into it, just tell me this. Do you think there's a chance that Niall is at Joliet to attend Matthew Manning's execution today? Because there's no way in hell I'm gonna let her go through something like that on her own."

Almost an hour and a half later Vic finally turned onto I-80 West, toward Joliet. He checked the digital clock anxiously before he pressed the accelerator to the floor. He'd stayed around long enough to pluck the relevant highlights of Niall's history out of Kendra before he'd grabbed a newspaper, gotten in his truck, and left town in a hell of a hurry. Traffic had been bad only around the city, thank God, or else he'd never have had the slim chance that he wobbled on precariously at the moment.

Kendra had been shocked by his question about whether or not Niall would attend Matthew Manning's execution. She apparently didn't read the paper as meticulously as Forrester, because she hadn't even realized that it was scheduled for today. Vic had found out by reading the paper at stoplights while he was still in the city that Manning's execution by lethal injection was scheduled for three o'clock that afternoon.

Vic only had about forty-five minutes to make it to Joliet Prison. He didn't know what the hell he was going to do when he got there. He doubted they'd allow him to enter the maximum security prison, but he had to do *something*. The idea of Niall being there all by herself on such a god-awful errand was just untenable. For what felt like the thousandth time that day, he tried to call her cell phone, but for the thousandth time was thwarted by the sound of her recorded voice.

All of his doubts about how useful he was going to be once he got to Joliet Prison were immediately reinforced once he arrived. If he'd been speaking Swahili to the stony-faced guard at the single entrance gate, he'd have been just as effective in gaining admittance. Vic couldn't even get the uniformed stiff to say if Niall Chandler had recently entered or if he'd ever *heard* of Niall Chandler . . . or Matthew Manning, for that matter.

Vic found himself waiting in the small parking lot outside of the prison, wishing he could see through walls so that he might at least be able to locate Niall's car and know if she was there or not. Sitting all by himself in his truck certainly gave him time to think about what he wanted to say to Niall when he saw her. But just like a plague of writer's block, nothing came to him. The only thing that he experienced at that moment was an overwhelming need to hold her . . . to protect her.

The feeling was a familiar one. It had cropped up often enough last year, all those times when he saw the sadness in Niall's eyes, every time she awoke from her nightmares, trembling and damp with sweat. He closed his eyes briefly in remorse when he considered what she must have been dreaming about . . . seeing Michael shot down in cold blood as if they were soldiers on a battlefield instead of a young mother sending her four-year-old boy off to preschool with a cheerful good-bye.

Stuff out of nightmares all right, except that for Niall the dream never ended.

He cringed inwardly with guilt when he recalled how he'd admonished her just yesterday for being dishonest with him. *You said that you wanted to tell me back then, but you didn't, despite the fact that I wanted to be there for you. I wanted it a hell of a lot, Niall! Now you want to talk, but I'm no longer ready to listen.*

"Sanctimonious asshole," Vic muttered under his breath.

He knew all too well that there were times in the beginning of their relationship that he had consciously chosen to ignore Niall's emotional wounds, preferring to focus on the sexual aspect of their relationship.

Sure, toward the end he'd changed his mind about that. He wanted to have her trust by that point. But it had been his own distrust . . . his own scars from his relationship with Jenny . . . that had made him initially pull away from her when he witnessed her pain.

Wasn't it likely that on some level Niall had sensed his unwillingness to share her history and grief? Kendra had told him today how Niall's parents had judged her for finally choosing to divorce Stephen. Hell, there were probably loads of people who would do the same thing without understanding the circumstances, without comprehending the fact that in his own way Stephen had abandoned Niall when she needed him most—and long, long before Niall made the decision to end their marriage.

Vic had been one of those judgmental people.

The expression on Niall's face that evening in her apartment when Alexis Chandler had dropped the bomb that Niall had a husband suddenly flashed before Vic's eyes like a perfectly intact film—the sagging shoulders, the sad, deflated expression on her lovely face, as if he'd just done the inevitable . . . as if he'd just condemned her with a look.

Which he had, of course.

Vic realized with a feeling of creeping dread that that was precisely the reason why Niall hadn't told him about her history. Because she was scared, afraid that he would judge her harshly.

Then she had gambled everything and come to the farm to try to explain. He was too busy feeling sorry for himself, too involved in licking his own flesh wounds to bother to notice Niall's gaping hole.

The thought caused such a profound pain to stab through him that he jerked reflexively in the driver's seat.

He'd make it right. He *had* to. The alternative just wasn't viable.

Meg sounded glad that Vic answered his cell phone on the first ring but her joy quickly altered to anxious irritation.

"Thank God I caught you. Where've you been all day?" she demanded testily. She plowed ahead without waiting for an answer. "You've got to get over to Mercy Hospital in Bloomington right away."

"What the hell kind of 'hello' is that, Meg?" he asked sourly. He already felt helpless enough as he sat there in the outer parking lot of the enormous, depressing fortress of the prison without having Meg pull her big sister act on him, making him feel like a twelve-year-old kid caught out of bed past his bedtime. "I can't go to the hospital right now. I'm outside of Joliet Prison. Damn guards won't let me in but—"

"Yeah, right. You're trying to get *into* Joliet Prison. This ought to be good," Meg scoffed as if he'd started to tell an obviously moronic joke.

"Niall is in there."

Meg snorted. "Quit kidding around, Vic! This is serious. Damn that Errol Farrell. I knew he was going to stir up a hornet's next over there."

"What are you talking about?"

"Sheriff Madigan just called. Donny was caught in the cross fire of a shoot-out at the Farrell farm earlier today."

Vic sat up ramrod straight. "Is he okay?"

"Madigan didn't know for sure," Meg replied worriedly. "He only said that he was one of the ones they took away in an ambulance."

Vic shook his head in rising disbelief. The events of today might have been following a schedule from Hell's Daily Planner. He glanced anxiously from the one road from the prison to his fuel gauge and back to the road.

"I can't leave right now. Can you go check on Donny and call me as soon as you know anything? I've got to wait for Niall."

Several seconds of silence followed. "Were you *serious* about that Joliet Prison thing?"

"Why would I joke about something like that?" Vic thundered.

"Calm down, Vic," Meg exclaimed, half in concern and half in exasperation. "Niall isn't in *Joliet Prison*, for God's sake. Why *would* she be? She's on her way to Mercy as we speak. She just pulled into the driveway a minute before I called you, and she went ahead to the hospital when I told her what happened. I'm waiting for Tim to get back from the fields—"

Vic had already turned the ignition and was in the process of backing out.

"We really need to have a conversation about the way we communicate, Meg."

He peeled out of the parking lot, completely oblivious to the high concentration of police in the vicinity of the prison. The last thing he was thinking about at that moment was getting a ticket.

Surely this day couldn't get any worse.

TWENTY-ONE

Donny Farrell determinedly attempted to switch channels on the television set in his hospital room with a remote control, but his right hand clearly wasn't cooperating the way he wanted. His lack of coordination and the pain that shadowed his youthful features related to his heavily bandaged right arm.

"Use your left hand," Tim instructed calmly. "You're going to have to get used to using it for a while anyway, while your arm heals."

Donny grimaced in irritation more than in pain. "The doc said the bullet didn't even hit the bone. It's not serious," Donny insisted when he met the gaze of the brooding man who sat on the windowsill, the brilliant late afternoon sunlight casting his body and face in shadow. "Seriously, Vic. *Clean shot*—that's what she called it—right through the muscle," Donny explained matter-of-factly as he waved the remote control. "Doc said that they were just keeping me overnight to check on the results from some tests. I feel fine . . . maybe a little weak from losing so much blood."

Vic didn't say anything. Meg must have thought her brother's silence implied that he thought Donny should go toss a football out on the lawn right this second.

"Well, I, for one, am glad they're keeping you overnight. I don't know what's become of hospitals when a person gets shot—*shot!*—and they discharge him the following day, like he just had his tonsils out or something."

She shook her head in disgust. Niall, Tim, Vic, and she had been Donny's only visitors since he'd been admitted to the hospital. Meg had noticed how exhausted Niall appeared earlier, and both she and Donny had encouraged her to go back to the farm for a nap. Vic hadn't looked too pleased about the fact that Niall wasn't there anymore by the time he arrived, but all in all, Meg thought he was restraining himself from going after her with admirable control.

If Donny's spaced-out mother had been to the hospital at all, Meg wasn't aware of it. If she had been here, she'd likely be focusing her attention on Eric Farrell, another of Donny's brothers, who had also been shot in the fray. Eric was reportedly stable, but his condition was much more serious than Donny's.

Still, it made Meg feel heart sore that Donny had never asked where his mother was or even seemed to expect that Deloris Farrell would visit him.

Meg guessed that Donny had been riding on the natural painkillers of shock and adrenaline since the incident at the Farrell farm, which had culminated in one of his brother's being seriously wounded, another man almost being killed, and Errol being charged with the latter shooting.

As Donny's principal, Meg felt obligated to report his situation to the Department of Children and Family Services if the police already hadn't. She doubted Donny would thank her, but Meg had not only a professional but also a moral obligation. It just wasn't right that a young boy should be forced to live in such an unsavory, blatantly dangerous place as the Farrell farm.

And Meg could tell that Vic was thinking the same thing as he watched the boy fumble with the remote control.

Her heart went out to her brother in that moment. His expression and posture gave next to nothing away as he sat there, but Meg heard his suffering with the invisible sense organ that siblings often acquire in regard to each other.

"Vic, can I talk to you for a second in the hallway?" Meg asked as she stood.

Vic gave Donny a wry glance as he stood up, communicating to Donny with the speed of lightning the message, "Uh-oh, I'm in trouble with the principal."

Meg didn't mind, because Donny's sudden snort of laughter did them all a world of good, worried as they were about the boy. She sighed as she walked out to the corridor with Vic behind her. Her and Vic's invisible connection had been built over a lifetime. Vic and Donny's connection, on the other hand, had seemingly sprung up full force the first time they had met.

"Quarter?" Meg asked as she held out her hand to Vic a few seconds later when they wandered up to a coffee machine.

Vic dug in his jeans pocket and pulled out some change.

"We're going to have to do something about Donny," Meg stated as she dropped the quarter into the vending machine and made a selection.

"Yeah, I know," Vic said quietly. "I've been thinking the same thing."

Neither of them spoke as they watched the paper cup fill with steaming liquid. When Meg withdrew the cup from the dispenser, she handed it to her brother. He glanced up in surprise.

"There'll be time to talk about all that tomorrow. Why don't you go and find Niall? She looked even more exhausted than you do right now. I don't think either one of you slept last night."

The look Vic cast down the hallway told Meg loud and clear that he longed to do exactly that, despite his very real concern for Donny.

"We'll do shifts with Donny. I'll tell him that you'll be here bright and early tomorrow morning. All in all, I think Tim and I got the better deal," Meg said with a saucy grin. She gave his upper arm an encouraging shove. "Go on, Vic. I don't know for sure what happened with you and Niall, but I'm just as concerned for her right now as I am for Donny. Do me a favor though, okay?"

"What?" Vic asked as he started down the hallway.

"Just don't screw it up this time."

He gave a soft bark of laughter.

"Yes, ma'am, I'll try my damnedest," he muttered with an uncharacteristic humbleness that made Meg's smile widen.

TWENTY-TWO

Vic experienced a moment of panic when he searched the farmhouse and was unable to find Niall.

"Niall!" he bellowed into the obviously empty house one last time. Where the hell was she? He peered out the window over the kitchen sink to assure himself that he hadn't been seeing things when he pulled up the drive, but no . . . Niall's sleek sedan was still parked in the drive. His eyes narrowed when he noticed that she'd parked it close to his cottage.

His heart hammered against his breastbone fifteen seconds later when he charged into the cottage.

"Niall?" Vic shouted. Silence was his only response. A sinking feeling came over him as he crossed the kitchen to the hallway. It'd been wishful thinking on his part to think she might be here. Niall wouldn't come to his place, not after the way he'd treated her here last night, not after the way he'd insulted her time and again, not after—

His condemning thoughts dissipated to ash when he entered his bedroom and saw the small figure huddled beneath the covers on his bed and the golden hair spilled on his pillow.

"Niall?" he muttered, too softly to actually wake her. A touch of wonder flavored his tone. The realization that she was here, that she'd actually come to him after what must have been a hellacious day for her, left him stunned.

He sat on the edge of the bed and brushed her hair back from her face. It reminded him of the time in his apartment in Chicago when he'd awakened her because her parents were in the hallway. Now that he knew the context of the Chandlers' early morning visit, Vic wished he had let Niall continue to sleep peacefully on that morning.

He hadn't done it back then, but he would now, Vic vowed to himself. As much as he wanted to talk to her at that moment and ask for her forgiveness, it would have to wait until morning. He brushed his fingertip across the light sprinkling of freckles on her adorable nose.

A profound, powerful feeling surged in his chest.

Of course he loved her. He loved her like crazy. She'd had him flat on his ass in love since the first time he'd kissed her . . . maybe since the first time he'd looked into her sexy, soulful eyes.

How could he have been so dense as not to know that? he thought with genuine amazement. Dense was a pretty good descriptor, Vic recognized. He'd walked around with the equivalent of a toxic cloud of despair and distrust around his head after what had happened with Jenny. His inner vision had been so twisted, so occluded, that he was surprised he'd been able to *see* Niall clearly at all.

It was the luminosity of her spirit that had pierced his fog. Like many a male before him, he'd translated the strong feelings he possessed into something he could understand—sexual attraction and good old-fashioned lust.

He still felt that for her in spades, maybe even more powerfully now than he had in the beginning. But that was just the surface manifestation of the deep well of emotion that Vic recognized within himself as he studied the miracle of the woman who slept soundly in his bed.

His gentle, ephemeral, lovely little butterfly, Vic thought with a small smile as he lightly traced her elegant arched brow with his fingertip. He went very still when her eyelids opened and he suddenly found himself swimming in the depths of Niall's hazel eyes.

Niall stared up at Vic for one of those eternal moments that one sometimes encounters hovering between sleeping and wakefulness. She eventually smiled drowsily.

"I never knew that a man could be beautiful until I first saw you," she whispered softly.

"I never knew the meaning of beauty until I first laid eyes on you."

Niall blinked twice and raised herself on one elbow. Sleep still weighted her eyelids, but it slowly began to dawn on her that she wasn't dreaming. But surely she'd imagined Vic saying those words. The haloed quality to his deep, husky voice had certainly been the stuff of dreams.

That, along with the heavenly feeling of his long fingers delving into her hair and slowly massaging her scalp—

"What a nice surprise to find you in my bed," Vic said.

"You said it was where I belonged," Niall found herself saying while she was locked in Vic's mesmerizing stare. Her heart began to thump faster when she read what lay in the depths of his light gray eyes. God, if this was a dream, she hoped she'd never awaken.

"It *is* where you belong." The tip of his callused thumb brushed her cheek softly. "But I was wrong to tell you it was the only place you belong. I want more of you than that Niall. Much more."

Niall's lips fell open in amazement. "You do?"

Vic nodded slowly. "I'm sorry about the way I've been acting," he said gruffly. "And about what happened here last night—"

Niall shook her head quickly. She brushed her first two fingers over his warm lips, halting him. "Don't apologize for that, Vic. Making love with you is always so good . . . so right. I was just feeling vulnerable about what you'd said earlier that day," Niall tried to explain. Tears welled up in her eyes. "It wasn't the sex toys I was upset about, not really."

Vic suddenly leaned down and kissed her warmly on her forehead. Niall stared in amazement when he leaned back and she saw the profound regret that shadowed his handsome face. "You don't have to try to explain. It was callous of me to tell you I wanted you only for sex and then expect you to give yourself to me so completely." His gaze met hers. "Which you did, Niall . . . despite everything. You're so sweet."

Niall gawked at him, not sure if she could trust that Vic was staring at her with undisguised longing . . . and what looked very much to her befuddled brain like love.

"Sex toys weren't the only thing I was going to give you last Christmas," he said suddenly with a crooked grin.

"No?"

"Uh-uh," Vic muttered as he stood. He crossed the room and grabbed a black box from his dresser. Niall realized dazedly that it was what he'd placed behind his watch last night after he'd retrieved the bag from the closet.

"Go on, open it," Vic insisted when he returned to sit on the edge of the bed and held up the velvet box for her.

The sheet fell down to where she held it above her breasts when Niall reached for the box. She saw Vic go still out of the corner of her eye.

"Are you naked under there, baby?" he asked in an uneven voice.

"Yes," Niall replied, never taking her eyes off the box in her hand.

"How'd I ever get so lucky?" he asked in what sounded like genuine amazement.

Niall laughed softly, flattered by his words and tone. She opened the box and her mirth quickly faded to wonder.

"Oh, it's so *beautiful*," she whispered in awe as she lightly touched the exquisite butterfly amulet. The gold filigree had been meticulously wrought and the myriad cut gems—emerald, citrine, topaz, sapphire, and tourmaline—had definitely been cut and designed by an artist's hand.

"You had this made for me?" Niall asked with wide eyes, but she already knew the answer. She'd rarely seen such fine craftsmanship.

Vic nodded as he took the box from her and extricated the delicate gold chain. He unclasped it and signaled with a hitch of his chin that he wanted her to sit up. Niall did, clutching the bedclothes around her breasts as she did so. Vic's hands encircled her throat.

"Thank you. It's so special. How does it look?" she asked after he'd fastened it.

"Beautiful."

Niall felt happiness in its purest, most distilled form when she saw that his eyes had never strayed from her face when he spoke. Despite her increasing bliss, she couldn't help but wonder what had changed Vic's mind about her. Although she had a suspicion—

"When Meg came to the hospital, she said that when she spoke to you earlier on the phone, you told her that you were at Joliet Prison."

Vic merely nodded.

Niall swallowed thickly. "How . . . how did you find out about Matthew Manning?"

"I went to Chicago this morning. I looked for you both at your loft and at the museum. I ran into Evan Forrester at Toulouse's bar."

Niall's jaw dropped. "Evan Forrester? How does he know anything about Matthew Manning?"

Vic shrugged. "He said it was from the papers, but I wouldn't be surprised if the guy trolls for gossip about you every chance he gets. He's a real bottom-feeder."

"I know," she whispered. She toyed anxiously with the butterfly.

"Matthew Manning's execution was postponed, Vic. They sent me a letter yesterday. The state assembly's temporary lifting of the moratorium on the death sentence for the special case of Manning was ruled unconstitutional by the Illinois Supreme Court."

"My God," Vic muttered, floored by the news. "It wasn't in any of the newspapers—"

"They tried to downplay it since several political groups on both sides of the issue were threatening demonstrations today. They were informed by special delivery—just like I was—by the governor of Illinois, saying that Matthew Manning's fate now hangs in the same balance as the thousand or so other inmates on death row in Illinois."

"How . . . how do you feel about it, Niall?" Vic asked uneasily. He couldn't begin to imagine what she experienced in regard to the man who had so senselessly murdered her innocent child. Seeing Donny in the hospital this afternoon had torn him apart, and he knew what he felt about the boy was nowhere near as deep and complex as what Niall must have felt for the son she bore from her own body.

Niall stared down at the bed. "I'm not a bloodthirsty person, Vic. I'm glad I'm not the one who has to decide Manning's fate. I'll accept whatever punishment the law passes down. But I will tell you one thing. I was relieved yesterday when I got that letter."

"You were?"

Niall nodded, her head still lowered. "There's been so much violence . . . so much hatred. I'll do whatever is required to ensure that Manning never sees the light of day again for the rest of his life. But I just want all the violence to stop." She swallowed painfully. "I just want my little boy to be able to rest in peace."

She eventually broke the prolonged silence that fell between them.

"I wanted to tell you about Michael, Vic. Not just about his murder. *Everything*. He was such an amazing little boy," she said with a small, desperate laugh. "I . . . I've really hated the fact that I haven't been able to talk about him for so long. He deserves so much better than that . . ."

Vic's hand cupped her jaw, gently urging her to meet his gaze. Niall complied with his unspoken request despite the fact that tears flowed from her eyes and a choking sensation in her throat prevented her from continuing.

"Give yourself time, Niall. It'll come. It'll come because you want it to, not because it's required."

Niall nodded and waited for the painful sensation in her throat to fade. "I wanted to tell you about Stephen, too. But every time I tried, I just . . . couldn't."

"I think I know why you didn't want to tell me. You were afraid I would judge you. Evan Forrester wasn't the only person I ran into at Toulouse, Niall. I spoke with Kendra Phillips as well."

He nodded when he noticed the surprised widening of her eyes. "Unlike Forrester, Kendra would never run on at the mouth about you. But I think she saw what a mess I was and took pity on me. She told me what she knew about Michael's murder and Stephen's breakdown during Matthew Manning's trial. She explained how your parents condemned you for divorcing Stephen. You were afraid to tell me about your past because you didn't want to be judged again." He paused for a second as he caressed her. "I have a suspicion that your ex-husband laid some kind of a guilt trip on you, too, didn't he?"

Niall started. "How did you know that?"

Vic winced slightly at her question, and she realized that she'd just unintentionally confirmed his suspicion. How had he found out the truth? She'd never told anybody about how Stephen regularly ranted at her that the person killed that day should have been her. She'd never revealed how she'd discovered that Stephen projected onto Niall his own misguided guilt about not being there on the day that Michael was murdered.

"I don't know why I thought it, exactly. Maybe it was from all those nights holding you while you slept. It was like you carried the burden of the world when you dreamed, baby," he said softly.

Their gazes remained locked for several long seconds. "I'll never forget the look on your face that day when you saw how I reacted to the truth about you being married. It was like I'd just confirmed all of your fears about revealing the truth to me . . . like you accepted the judgment I passed on you. God, I'm sorry for that, Niall. You have no idea how much. I had no right to pass judgment on you."

His thumb tenderly caught the tear that skittered down her cheek.

"I'm sorry, as well," she admitted. "I shut you out after that night because of my own guilt. It's sort of hard, when you've been surrounded by so much misery and grief for so long, to think that it's possible to deserve something as wonderful as the way I felt about you . . . the way I *feel* about you," she added in a whisper.

She felt his softly caressing thumb go still.

"How *do* you feel about me?"

Niall rolled her eyes in mock exasperation, causing several more tears to course down her face. "I'm in love with you. What'd you think? That I just fall into bed with every guy who gives me a Scotch and grunts ten words at me?"

Vic grinned slowly. Heat fanned out from her lower belly to her sex. Her nipples pulled tight next to the cool sheets. God, his smile was deadly. Niall suspected he knew precisely what effect he had on her when he tugged firmly on the sheet and blanket and they fell around her waist.

"It must have been at least twenty," he said as his light gray eyes leisurely traveled down her naked torso.

"If you include your dirty talk in bed later on," Niall teased, but her voice had gone husky at the impact of his gaze. Her lower lip fell away from the upper one and a puff of air slipped from them both when Vic reached up and shaped her breast to his curving palm.

"Well, we can't forget that." Niall noticed that his voice was just as hoarse with desire as her own.

"Vic?" Niall said sharply when she saw his dark head begin to lower to her breast. She ached for him, but still . . . "Don't you want me to explain the rest of it . . . the parts that Kendra doesn't know?"

"I want to hear anything you want to tell me, but I want to make something clear to you first. We're not here like this right now because I've *forgiven* you after what I learned about you today."

Her brow crinkled in confusion.

"There's nothing to forgive. I went after you this morning because I knew I'd been wrong to judge you in the first place. I was going to apologize for the way I'd been acting before I ever talked to Forrester or Kendra. Do you understand what I'm saying?"

"Yes," she whispered.

His face tightened with emotion ever so briefly. "Thank *you*, baby. Thank you for walking into my apartment that night and giving yourself so unselfishly to me. Thank you for doing the same thing every damn time I look into your eyes." He grimaced slightly as he watched his hand caress her shoulder. "I don't deserve you, but if you'll have me, I'm yours."

"I'll have you," she said so quickly that they both smiled when their eyes met.

"Then so be it," he mumbled before he dipped his head and kissed her so sweetly and so hotly that Niall felt literally dizzy with desire.

"Now you decide, baby," Vic mumbled next to her lips half a minute later. "We can talk and then make love, or we can make love and then talk."

"Make love and then talk," Niall said decisively. "And make love in between . . . and afterward?" she finished tentatively.

Vic flashed a wicked grin. "Your wish is my command," he promised as he whipped the covers down over her lap. "Hmmm, just the way I like you—naked and ready."

"Ready for what?" Niall purred as Vic ran his hands over her hips and back.

"Ready to be loved," he replied softly. His hands found her breasts and she moaned in pleasure. "You know what I think I'd like?" he asked as he watched her face intently.

"What?"

His right hand dropped to her thigh, caressing the length of it.

"I'd like you to spread these beautiful legs wide for me, the way you do when you exercise," he stated gruffly.

Niall gave at him what she suspected was a lust-glazed stare. His slow smile when he noticed made liquid bubble from her pussy.

Vic tossed the pillows onto the floor. "Go on, baby. Sit up against the headboard and open wide for me," he instructed in that calm, confident manner that had driven her wild from the very beginning. The fact that he somehow knew she'd never refuse him made her so hot that she wondered that steam didn't rise off her skin.

Neither of them spoke as she moved to the head of the bed and spread her legs as wide as they would go comfortably. The fact that her pussy was completely exposed to Vic's penetrating gray eyes excited her immeasurably. For several long seconds he just stared between her legs as if he were trying to commit her to memory.

"Vic," she finally pleaded softly.

His eyes flashed up to her face. He came and knelt in front of her.

"Do you remember that evening I walked in on you at the farmhouse while you were like this?" he asked her.

Niall nodded quickly, recalling all too well. She moaned softly when he ran his fingertips over her right nipple and then gently pinched her.

"I came out to the cottage after that and jerked off like a mad-man while I thought about being between your legs while they were spread wide, with my cock buried in you," he admitted with-out a trace of embarrassment.

Niall instinctively shifted her hips on the bed to try and still the sharp ache of arousal that arrowed through her.

"Shhh," Vic soothed as he stilled her hips with both hands. "We're going to live that particular fantasy here in a moment. But first . . ."

Niall's head fell back on the headboard of the bed and her back arched slightly when Vic slid his finger between her labia.

"That's my Niall," he whispered as his hand moved subtly over her sex. "Always so ready, always so creamy, always so sweet . . ."

Niall whimpered as he held her still with one spread hand on her hip and strummed her clit, building a delicious, simmering friction in her. Because she sensed that it would please him, she kept her hands flat on the mattress beside her and tried her might-iest not to squirm and wiggle too much as he stroked her. After a minute of that exquisite torture she noticed his small smile. She whined plaintively when he suddenly withdrew his finger.

"Shhh, I'm going to make you come now," he promised.

Niall felt sweat bead on her upper lip as she watched him insert his middle finger into her pussy. They moaned in unison.

"I love all of you, Niall, but you've got the sweetest pussy in existence," Vic stated baldly. He withdrew and spread the bounty of juices he'd found in her depths into her already slippery cleft, doubling the amount of juices. Niall couldn't help but squirm and whimper at his touch. He used his left hand to gently pinch her spread, sensitive lips together just below her clit.

He pushed his forefinger down between the glossy lips from

the top and began playing her sensitive flesh once again. Niall groaned as he tortured and agitated her clit while he kept it in such tight confinement.

"Now that's a juicy little pocket," Vic teased lovingly when a wet, clicking sound reached both their ears as he played in her liquefied flesh.

Niall's head rolled on the headboard in ecstasy. Her hips made uncontrollable little jumping movements against Vic's finger, increasing the pressure on her clit.

"Ah, God . . . *it feels so good*," she cried out in disbelief.

"Then come for me," Vic whispered close to her lips.

When she did, he covered her mouth and kissed her fiercely, claiming her rampant cries of bliss as his own.

"You burned me back to life back then," Niall muttered hoarsely from where she'd sagged down slightly on the bed after her shattering climax. She watched Vic undress hastily at the side of the bed with a heavy-lidded gaze.

"What?" he asked with a small laugh as he rejoined her on the bed, this time completely, gloriously nude. She touched his taut abdominal muscles with a sense of awe and lust combined, fascinated at the way that they leapt beneath her touch. She met his gaze.

"I felt like I was one of the walking dead after Michael was murdered, like my heart had been put in deep freeze. But you unfroze me, Vic. Somehow, some way, when you touched me I awoke, I came back to myself . . . came back to life. I'll never forget it," she whispered emphatically.

"I won't, either. I've never lied so much in my life as when I told you that what happened between us was nearly forgettable." He leaned forward and brushed their lips together sensually, speaking to her, as always, as much with his touch as with his words. He guided his cock to her entrance and thrust his hips as he continued to pin her with his stare. Niall's face tightened with intense emotion mingled with ecstasy.

"Now burn for me again, sweet Niall," he whispered gruffly next to her parted lips.